SENTINALS
ACROSS TIME

SENTINALS ACROSS TIME

BOOK FOUR OF THE SENTINAL SERIES

HELEN GARRAWAY

Published by Jerven Publishing

Edited by Maddy Glen, SWS Publishing

Cover by Jeff Brown Graphics

Map by Fictive Designs

eBook ISBN: 978-1-7399344-3-9

Paperback ISBN: 978-1-7399344-4-6

Hardback ISBN: 978-1-7399344-5-3

Sign up to my mailing list to join my magical world and for further information about forthcoming books and latest news at:
www.helengarraway.com

First Edition

ALSO BY HELEN GARRAWAY

Sentinal Series

Sentinals Awaken

Sentinals Rising

Sentinals Justice

Sentinals Recovery

Sentinals Across Time

Soul Mist series

SoulBreather

(Coming October 4th, 2022 part of the Realm of Darkness
Anthology)

For my brother Tony and my sister-in-law Kaye
Love you both!

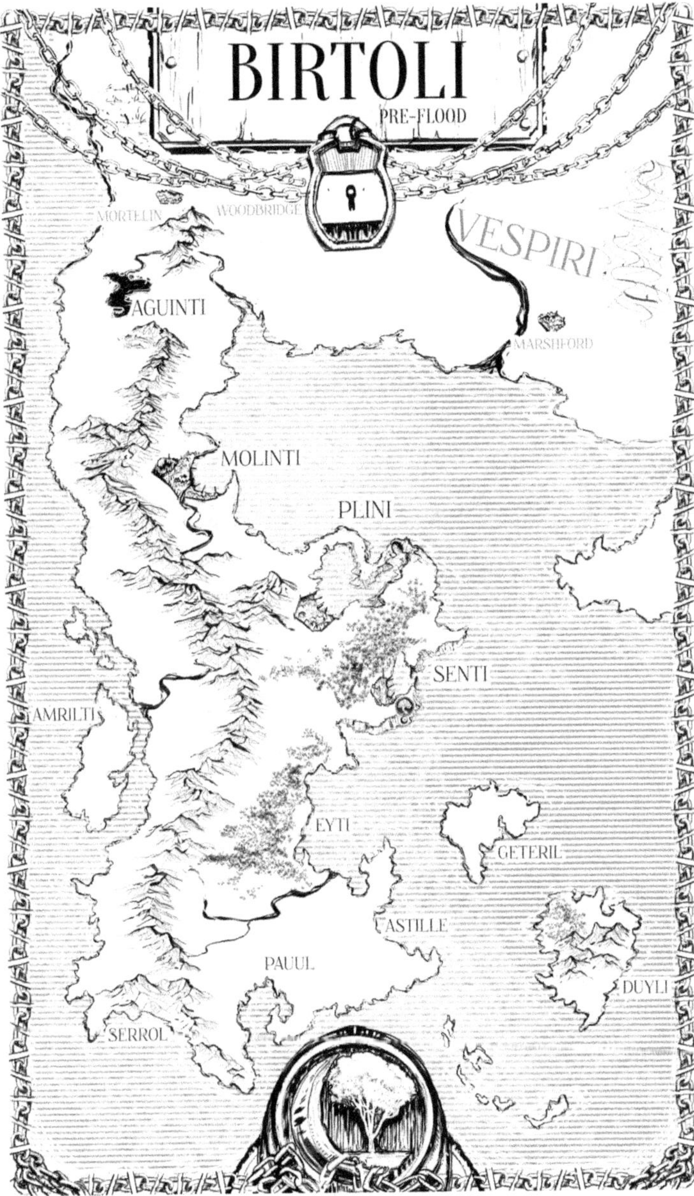

BIRTOLI
PRE-FLOOD
VESPIRI
MORTELIN
WOODBRIDGE
AGUINTI
MARSHFORD
MOLINTI
PLINI
SENTI
AMRILTI
EYTI
GETERIL
ASTILLE
PAUL
DUYLI
SERROL

BIRTOLI
POST-FLOOD
MORTELIN
WOODBRIDGE
VESPIRI
AGUINTI
NIKRI
MARSHFORD
LAKRI
HARBOUR
MOLINTI
PORLI
SENTI
POINT
DONA
STORM WALLS
AMRILTI
CHERNI
AMRI
EYTI
ASTILLE
PAUUL
DUYLI
SERROI

1

PRESENT DAY

JANU 14TH, 4128. STONEFORD WATCH, VESPIRI

A *rare moment to treasure, filled with peace and love,* Jerrol thought as he watched his son sleep. Mikke was still lost in the land of dreams, his long black lashes resting on his rosy cheeks. He looked so adorable. Jerrol wondered what trouble he would manage to get into today and how he could keep him out of it.

Taelia's waters had broken during the night, and the new addition to their family would arrive soon. His foster mother, Hannah, had pushed him out of the bedchamber and told him to look after his son.

His thoughts drifted to the past few days; the peace and contentment of his small family, a balm to his usual frantic life as the Commander of the King's Justice. A moment to stop and breathe. It was also a chance for his friend and bodyguard, the Sentinal Birlerion, one of the Lady's Guards whom Jerrol had awoken from a three thousand year sleep, to have a much needed break. Birlerion had left for Terolia the previous week with his Darian, Kin'arol, honouring his promise to return and visit the Atolea Family who had claimed him.

Jerrol admitted to himself that he missed Birlerion. After

all that they had been through, he had become even more reliant on Birlerion and his calm assurance. He seemed to cope with whatever was thrown at them. The Sentinal was one of his closest advisors, family even. Taelia treated him like a younger brother. Jerrol's lips twitched. An ancient three-thousand-year old Sentinal, who in reality was younger than both him and Taelia. He sighed. He may be younger in years, but Birlerion had experienced more horror and strife than Jerrol had, and that was saying something.

As he watched, his son's soft lashes fluttered, and then he was staring into brilliant turquoise eyes just like Taelia's. "Good morning, my love," Jerrol murmured as he reached to lift him out of bed.

"Pa," Mikke said, snuggling into his arms.

Jerrol rested his chin on Mikke's head and simply enjoyed the hug and the scent of the young child. A precious moment he stored away for a day when he might need it.

"I thought," Jerrol murmured, "we might visit Zin'talia and her colt this morning. You could help rub her down if you are good and eat all your breakfast."

Mikke beamed at him. "Yes, go see Zee an' Pip." He wriggled out of Jerrol's embrace.

"Pip?" Jerrol asked. Darians chose their riders. Had the colt already bonded with his son?

"Pip. Dress," he said, holding his arms up.

Well, Jerrol thought, *that confirmed that.* If the colt had already given Mikke his name, then there was nothing they could do to change it.

After a quick breakfast, where Jerrol had to slow Mikke down so he didn't choke, the little boy scampered in front of him as he led the way into the stable. Jerrol had no concern, allowing the child to weave under the Darian's legs and wrapping his arms around the colt's glossy black neck. The colt nickered in welcome.

"Good morning. I see the little one has found a friend," Zin'talia, his pure white Darian mare, said as contentment filled his mind, along with her voice.

"So it seems," Jerrol replied, smiling as he greeted her, their telepathic bond replacing the need to speak aloud. *"Is it usual for them to bond so young? I mean, Pip will be fully grown long before Mikke gets there."*

"Darians are long-lived, and we bond for life. This is not unusual."

Jerrol sighed with relief. *"That is good then. Mikke is calling him Pip. Is that his name?"*

"Pil'pinia is his name, but Pip will do for now. They will learn together if you allow it."

"I doubt we'll be able to stop them." Jerrol chuckled as he leaned against her neck and hugged her. He inhaled her musky scent and relaxed. *"Taelia's gone into labour. Won't be long now before my daughter arrives."*

"That is good, then. I could do with a brush if you wouldn't mind? I have an itch," she murmured, *"and I am sure Pip will enjoy one too."*

"Good idea." He reached for the brushes. "Mikke, here you brush him like this, always in the direction of his hair," he said, showing the boy.

Mikke got the hang of it straight away, happily brushing down Pip's chest and under his belly.

Jerrol grinned and started on the much larger Zin'talia.

The stable was peaceful. Zin'talia was purring in his head, and he was sure Pip was doing something similar given the expression of contentment on Mikke's face. Jerrol heard a shout from the cottage. He dropped his brush and dashed out of the stable. Hannah was beckoning him inside.

"I'll keep an eye on him; he'll be fine," Zin'talia murmured.

"Stay in the stable with Zin'talia," Jerrol said as he hurried out.

He rinsed his hands under the tap and rushed into their bedroom. Taelia was propped up against the pillows, gazing down at a bundle in her arms. As she lifted her face, he met her sparkling, brilliant blue eyes. "Our daughter," she said.

Jerrol leaned across and kissed her, then looked down at his daughter. She had a thatch of black hair, her face was bright red, and her eyes were screwed tight. Her perfect hands were bunched in tiny fists.

"Hold her," Taelia said, her voice soft as she watched his face.

He gently took his daughter in his arms and sat on the side of the bed. The tiny baby stretched, and he was surprised by the strength of her feet against his arm. She opened her silver eyes wide and stared straight at him.

"I thought we should call her Leyarille," Taelia said.

Jerrol's vision blurred as tears welled at the thought of the goddess, Leyandrii, the Lady who watched over them all, from a far distance to be true, but she watched all the same. "I couldn't think of a more fitting name," he choked.

His daughter yawned before smacking her lips, closing her eyes, and snuggling down in his arms. He watched her in amazement before gently kissing her soft forehead.

He looked across at Taelia. "She has silver eyes," he said in awe.

"Just like her father," Taelia replied.

Jerrol blinked and then smiled.

A week passed far too fast. Hannah left for Deepwater to visit her other foster son, Jennery, who was joined with Alyssa, the Guardian of Deepwater Watch and their little cottage was peaceful. Jerrol sat holding his daughter as Mikke leaned against his leg. "She won't always be this small," Jerrol reassured him, "we just need to be gentle till she grows a bit."

Mikke reached a tiny finger and stroked her face. Leyarille opened her eyes and stared at her brother, and Mikke gasped. He looked at his father and back to Leyarille. "Si'ver," he said.

"That's right, silver," Jerrol agreed, suppressing a faint stir of concern deep in his belly as he wondered why his daughter had silver eyes. Only Sentinals, Leyandrii's personal guards, had silver eyes and usually the person's eyes only turned silver when she claimed them.

Mikke climbed in the chair and squatted beside his father. He crooned gently, and Leyarille reached out and grabbed his hair. Jerrol grinned at Taelia as she entered the room and saw her family together. She sat on the side of the chair, wrapping her arm around her husband. "Bliss," she murmured.

"Indeed," he replied, tilting his head so she could kiss him.

Mikke giggled as he tried to loosen Leyarille's firm grip.

The day passed and night descended peacefully; Mikke was tucked up, Leyarille fed, and Jerrol and Taelia were sitting together on the settle. Taelia heaved a deep sigh and cuddled Jerrol.

"What's the matter?" he asked, attuned to her shift in mood.

"You won't go dashing back to Old Vespers now that Leyarille is here?"

"Promise," Jerrol said lifting her hand and kissing her fingers. "I've got at least two week's leave; I'm not going anywhere."

"Good. You owe me some of your undivided attention before Benedict calls you back."

Jerrol grinned. "I would have suggested you come to

Birtoli with us but for the fact that a state visit is no place for a new baby."

"We didn't time it very well, did we?" She snuggled into his chest and peered up at him. "Mikke always goes off so nicely when you are home; you should be home more often."

"I know. I wish I could be. Being with you is all I've ever wished for, and now," he smiled into her beautiful eyes, "well, now we are even more complete."

Taelia exhaled, and Jerrol tightened his grip on her fingers. "What is it?"

"I had a dream," she said, bending her head over his hand as she massaged his palm, running her fingers over the stumps of the missing fingers on his right hand, a legacy of the Ascendant threat they had defeated two years previously at great cost.

"About what?" he prompted.

Her cold fingers convulsed around his. "I dreamt you disappeared. No one knew where you had gone; no-one could find you and you couldn't come home."

"I will always come back to you, you know that," he reassured her.

"What if you couldn't?" she asked, her eyes wide with fear.

"Taelia, wherever I go in this world, you know I will always return to you, and I would never stop trying."

"Yes, but …"

"Taelia, I would find a way, I promise," he said, more to reassure her than out of any belief that it would ever happen. "I would invade your dreams, write you clues in terrible songs, write a memoir for you to read, surprise you with unexpected gifts, kiss you every night under the Lady's moon," he finished, running out of ideas.

"Promise?"

"I promise," he said, kissing her, and she leaned into him.

The fine tremor running through her made the hair on his arms prickle in fear. Taelia had once been a seer of note, but the premonitions had faded after she had joined with him and the Lady had restored her sight, but that didn't mean her dreams should be ignored. But how does one prepare for the unknown?

That night, Taelia had her husband all to herself, and she was determined to make the most of it. She slid her hands over the smooth skin of his chest and sighed into his embrace.

Jerrol smiled. "Are you sure you're ok? It's not too soon?" he asked.

"I've been dreaming of this for months. Of course I'm ready," she replied, trailing kisses across his chest. The feel of his body against hers was sheer bliss as she slid against his length, her skin sensitised to his touch. She pressed close, wanting more, basking in the heat of his skin. She shivered as his hands caressed her back and then circled around her ribs and up to her breasts.

He shifted her under him as he kissed the pulse at the base of her throat, working his way down across her breasts, currently swollen with milk. He teased them gently, but not wanting to waste his daughter's breakfast, he moved on and worked his way down to her much reduced stomach, his hands smoothing her skin, his lips treasuring every taste, every sensation.

Taelia arched under him as her body shuddered in response, pressing close, his touch an exquisite agony. Her need for him grew as he hovered over her, and he caught his breath as her questing fingers found him and he kissed her long and deep, exploring her mouth as he pressed against her.

She kissed him back, trailing kisses along his jawline and nibbling his shoulder, pressing herself against whichever piece of him she could touch. His arousal was hot in her hands; he was as ready as she was. She gently guided him in, his soft intake of breath all she needed to hear as she pushed herself against him, feeling him slide deeper. He groaned deep in his chest as she clenched tighter. In unison they moved, melding together as one until they climaxed and shuddered together in harmony.

She sighed in sheer contentment. His weight on top of her was where he belonged. The feel of him inside her was something she never wanted to end. She clenched tighter, trying to keep him inside her, but she knew it wouldn't last. He was slipping out and it was over. Unless of course … she nibbled his salty shoulder.

Jerrol choked. "What are you trying to do to me, woman?" he breathed as he rolled over.

"Making up for lost time?" she murmured against his skin as she worked her way down his sweaty body. She inhaled the exquisite scent of him, wanting more, lips questing, her fingers gently stroking his skin. Jerrol shivered beneath her fingers, his body responding to her touch, and he surrendered completely, leaving Taelia in no doubt of his love for her.

The next morning, Jerrol stretched lazily, feeling content. He opened his eyes. Taelia was snuggled against him, and he smiled as he wrapped a soft curl around his finger and kissed her. Then he opened his eyes wide. The sun was up, yet the children had not stirred? He frowned as he eased out of bed and slipped on shirt and trousers before heading out to check. Mikke was cooing at Leyarille in her cot, and Leyarille seemed quite content, even though it was hours past her feeding time.

"Morning, my children," Jerrol grinned as he scooped Leyarille up in one arm and gathered Mikke in his other. "Mikke, my love, have you been keeping Leyarille company?"

"Pa, 'ily hungry."

"I'm sure she is," Jerrol murmured as he carried them back into his bedroom.

"Mama, your daughter needs her breakfast," Jerrol said as he sat on the bed.

Taelia stretched luxuriously and then opened her eyes. "My goodness," she murmured, "how did we get such a lay in?"

"Seems Mikke delayed the inevitable." Jerrol grinned as he watched his daughter's lower lip tremble.

"Well, give her here; you'd better feed Mikke," she said, reaching for the baby.

Jerrol chuckled, leaning over to kiss her before rising with Mikke in his arms. Taelia shivered as his loving gaze caressed her, reminding her of the previous night. "Later," she whispered.

Jerrol and Mikke had finished breakfast and washed up by the time Taelia came out of the bedroom, Leyarille dozing in her arms. A plate of pancakes awaited her. "My, a treat," she said as she popped Leyarille in her basket and sat at the table.

"You've got to keep your strength up," Jerrol replied, a mischievous glint in his eyes.

Taelia flashed him an appreciative smile. His dark hair was threaded with silver glints even though he had not yet reached twenty-six years, a result of the pressures of his many jobs; Commander, Captain, and Oath Keeper. His hair flopped over his forehead and she smoothed it back. "You need to get your hair cut again," she said.

His silver eyes gleamed in the morning sunlight. "It'll have to wait till I return to Old Vespers."

She nodded, satisfied, and then flicked a glance at him. "What is the plan for today?" she asked around a mouthful of pancake. Mikke eyed her pancakes, and she offered him a forkful. He sat next to her, munching happily.

"I think we ought to weed the vegetable patch," Jerrol suggested. "It's getting somewhat overgrown. Or maybe a visit to Stoneford? I'm sure Jason would love to see Leyarille."

Taelia tilted her head. "If we go to Stoneford, won't that be the end of your leave?"

"I promised you two weeks minimum; we still have a few days to go, and Jason would be pleased, I think," Jerrol replied, thinking of the elderly man responsible for Stoneford Watch.

"I suppose so, then."

Jerrol harnessed Zin'talia up to the buggy, ignoring her protests, and helped Taelia up before handing her Leyarille. He swung Mikke up beside her before climbing up himself. He clucked, and Zin'talia started off down the road, muttering darkly under her breath at being used to pull a cart.

Within a chime they were pulling up at the keep, stable boys scattering before them, vying to care for Zin'talia. Jerrol jumped down, helped Mikke, and then took Leyarille so that Taelia could jump down, and by then, Jason was in the courtyard, beaming at them.

"Jerrol, Taelia, come in, come in, it's so good to see you. Mikke, you scamp, what have you been up to?" he asked as he swung the small boy up into his arms.

Mikke hugged him. "Playing wiv' Pip, Ganda," he said.

"Pip?" Jason asked, raising an eyebrow.

"Zin'talia's colt," Jerrol supplied.

"Ah," Jason said. "And he likes playing with you?"

"Yep," Mikke said, a huge smile on his chubby face.

"I see," Jason said with a laugh as he led them into the keep.

"And this," Taelia said with a proud smile, "is our new addition, Leyarille."

Jason peered at the bundle in her arms, hesitantly accepting it as he sat in his chair. "You forget how tiny they are, don't you?" he said in a hushed voice. His lined face softened as he gazed at the baby.

Jerrol's face tightened as he watched Jason. He was, in truth, the only father figure Jerrol had known since he had been orphaned at a young age. Fostered to Hannah, the Keep's seamstress, he had grown up scampering around the Keep's corridors, under the feet of both the arms master and the horse master. Jason had guided his steps to the Chapterhouse and then onto the King's Rangers. He wouldn't be where he was today without Jason. To Jerrol, Jason was the grandfather of his children.

The stress and uncertainty of the last few years had taken its toll. Jason had never really gotten over the loss of his two Watch Sentinals, Chryllion and Saerille, in the final confrontation with the Ascendants nearly two years ago. Although another Sentinal, Darllion, had relocated with his sentinal tree to Stoneford, it wasn't the same.

It really was time Jason retired, but with no children of his own, he was reluctant to step down until the king was ready. Stoneford had played a large part in the defeat of the Ascendants, protecting both the Watchers in the Watch Towers and providing troops to defend the Vespirian border against a neighbouring Elothian attack. That Elothia and Vespiri were now in peaceful accord was as much due to the men and women of this Watch as anyone else.

They passed a pleasant chime reminiscing before the cook tempted Mikke into the kitchen with fresh bread twists and jam and a glass of milk for lunch before Jerrol scooped up his family for the return journey home. They were all pleasantly weary when their cottage finally came into sight, and Mikke whooped as he heard a lonely Pip calling him.

Mikke patted Pip as Jerrol stabled and brushed down Zin'talia, and it was back in the bathtub, then supper and bed for the tired little boy.

Jerrol and Taelia relaxed on the sofa for a moment in peace, Taelia snuggling in his arms as he stretched out his legs. "Home," Jerrol murmured, inhaling the scent of her hair before his stomach grumbled, and Taelia levered herself up with a laugh as she went to prepare their supper. She was contentedly clattering around the kitchen when she heard Jerrol cry out. The pans slipped from her nerveless fingers as she dashed back into the parlour.

"My Lady, noooo …" Jerrol's voice cracked in anguish, his arms reaching for Taelia as he was pulled away, elsewhere.

Taelia shrieked as she rushed towards him, but he faded out of sight before her eyes. "No," Taelia wailed in despair, collapsing to the floor sobbing. Suddenly, the air was full of a distressed Arifel, his claws pulling at her cloudy hair as he tried to land on her shoulder. Taelia took a deep breath, trying to control her shudders as she attempted to soothe Ari.

She stroked the small, fluffy cat-like creature, rubbing him behind his ears as he flipped his scaly reptilian wings back and wrapped his smooth tail around her wrist. Arifels had once been regarded as mythical creatures, but when the Lady had made Jerrol her Captain, so was born the first Arifel in centuries, a somewhat unreliable messenger who could travel from one place to another instantly, only visible to Guardians and Sentinals unless the Arifel chose to reveal himself.

She pulled herself together. *Check the house first.* She dashed from room to room, followed by Ari. No Jerrol. The children were thankfully sleeping undisturbed. Leaving the house, she ran through their small garden and round to the stables.

"Zin'talia, can you hear Jerrol? Do you know where he went?"

Zin'talia stared at her with liquid brown eyes before shaking her head.

"Not at all? The Lady took him, I think." She stared around frantically. She had never traversed to their sentinal tree in Vespers without Jerrol. Could she go on her own? Should she risk the children? She bit her lip, uncertain. Maybe she should go to Jason.

Zin'talia nudged her saddle and stared at Taelia, and Taelia brightened. "Zin'talia, you'll have to help me," she whispered as she rubbed the Darian's nose. Pip whickered beside her.

Taelia looked at Ari. "We have to find him," she said as the little Arifel hovered, staring at her with his big emerald green eyes. He meeped before landing on her shoulder. He rubbed his soft head against her cheek and then he popped out of view, leaving Taelia feeling oddly comforted.

2

PRESENT DAY

JANU 22ND, 4128. MISTRA, TEROLIA

Birlerion spun to a halt in the middle of the sparring ring in the garrison of the King's Terolian Guards, his tanned skin gleaming with sweat as he finished the move. His muscles rippled as he drew the curved sword up in front of his face in salute to the Terolian he had been sparring with, and then he carefully sheathed it. Fer'ilan, one of the Terolian guards, mirrored his move, his black eyes sparkling at the exhilaration of completing a challenging sparring session.

Retrieving his waterskin, Birlerion drank deeply, his throat dry in the baking heat.

"Now you've shown us all how the experts do it, do you think you can stoop to teaching the rest of us?" Oscar Landis, the Commander of the King's Terolian Guards, said from behind him.

Birlerion laughed as he turned, saluting Fer'ilan with his water skin and wiping his face with a towel that one of the men passed him. He observed the slender commander, who had joined with one of Birlerion's best friends and represented the king in Terolia. "Oscar, you have excellent teachers already. You don't need me. And anyway, I am visiting, not working."

"Coulda fooled me," Oscar muttered as they walked into the cool interior of the garrison.

Birlerion dragged a thin shirt over his head and began to roll up the sleeves.

"Kayerille is expecting you for dinner tonight, no excuses. You were such a big hit with Kayen that I expect you'll get a standing invitation." Oscar's thin face softened as he thought about his wife and young son.

"Thank you, I'd love to. Maraine said the Atolea were moving on, and I must go home next week, so make the most of me while you can. Leyarille will be a week old by now. Our leave is up and the king will be expecting us back."

"I bet Taelia will be pleased about that."

"Especially as we are off to Birtoli. The king has a state visit lined up."

Oscar quirked an eyebrow at him. "When are you going to settle down, Birlerion? Isn't it about time you found yourself a nice girl?"

"Why is it that, as soon as someone gets joined or has a baby, they expect everyone else to as well?" Birlerion demanded.

Oscar laughed. "We want you to be happy."

"What makes you think I'm not happy now?"

Oscar was prevented from answering as Ari appeared in the air between them, screeching. Birlerion was buffeted by a series of images, of Taelia in distress, of Jerrol disappearing. He didn't try to soothe the Arifel; he called his Darian stallion, Kin'arol, and rushed out the door.

"What's the matter?" Oscar asked as he hurried after Birlerion.

"Something's happened to Jerrol," Birlerion replied, meeting Kin'arol as he let himself out of his stall. He slung the nearest saddle over Kin'arol's honey-gold back and buckled the girth strap. "I have to go; Taelia needs me. I'll send word when I know more."

"Birlerion, you're not even dressed properly."

"I'll change in Vespers. Oscar, give my apologies to Kayerille."

"Of course, she'll understand. Make sure you do send word, Birlerion."

Birlerion urged Kin'arol into a trot and men parted as they left the garrison at a canter, headed for the waystone.

Oscar exhaled in concern. Birlerion hadn't even stopped to put on his boots, and in his thin shirt and trousers, he would freeze in Vespiri. After all, it was still Janu.

Niallerion was on guard duty in King Benedict's throne room. The Lady's Captain always insisted that one Sentinal be on duty in the palace at all times. Not just for show, Niallerion thought idly; the Oath was magical, in a world without magic and, in theory, a Sentinal was just as magical, having survived for three thousand years encased in a tree. It seemed right that they should keep each other company. He gazed at the words of the King's Oath, carved into the smooth marble wall behind the throne and emanating a soft golden glow.

"Do your Duty, Never Falter, Never Fail,
Lady, Land, and Liege obey.
All are one, Entwined ascending,
Keeper's Oath Never Ending."

The Oath had never been invoked in the history of Remargaren until four years ago, when the king, in desperate fear for his life, had said the words to Captain Haven, the current Commander of the King's Justice. The Captain was now bound to the Oath, responsible for ensuring the king kept his oath to his people and the Watches of Vespiri. The Oath covered all of Remargaren, from the desert lands of Terolia to the icy wastes of Elothia. The Captain was supposed to solve their problems, and amazingly enough, he had. Niallerion wasn't sure if the island empire of Birtoli was included, but he guessed it must be, as in his day, it had been joined to the mainland.

Niallerion mused on the last three years or so that he had been awake. He was one of a heartbreaking few, even though the Captain had systematically awoken every Sentinal he could find. Many Sentinals were struggling to cope with the loss of all that they knew now that peace had descended and their skills were no longer required. He was glad he could retreat to his sentinal tree, which had relocated to a secluded spot in the palace grounds, fortunately not in the central palace courtyard as the Captain's had. The sentinal trees had protected the Lady's Guard, who had slept for three thousand years until they had been awoken in Remargaren's time of need; a result of the goddess Leyandrii banishing all magic from the land when she brought down the Veil to protect her people against the Ascendants' threat of wild magic.

Marianille, another Sentinal rescued with Niallerion in Terolia, had relocated to Old Vespers at the same time as him, and her tree stood in the palace gardens next to his. His mind drifted onto more pleasant plans of how to persuade her to join him for a meal when they were next off duty at the same time. His brow wrinkled as he considered how to convince her brothers, Tagerill and Birlerion, that he had honourable intentions towards their beautiful sister.

His pleasant interlude was interrupted as he was blinded by the Oath flaring white, the brilliant light dancing before his eyes before it settled into a pulsing blue glare tinged with red and purple glints.

Niallerion watched the Oath for any further light shows before, step by step, he backed up to the door. He fumbled for the door handle, and keeping an eye on the Oath, he called over the King's Guard on duty outside in the corridor. "Corporal, would you be so kind as to advise the king that he needs to come to the throne room, now? The Oath is behaving strangely."

The corporal's protest died on his lips as he saw the brilliant light emanating from the wall. He saluted the silver-eyed Sentinal, stammered "Yes, sir," and scuttled off. Niallerion shut the door and returned to his position, staring to the right of the Oath, its blinding light too painful to look at.

In a surprisingly short space of time, King Benedict arrived, closely followed by Fonorion, an older, stockier Sentinal, and with them the second in command of the King's Justice, Lieutenant Commander Bryce.

King Benedict stopped in shock in front of the Oath. The King of Vespiri and Terolia was a large man. His girth had thickened with age, but his clear blue eyes were still sharp. He was dwarfed by the tall Sentinals, each dressed in the archaic silvery-green uniform the Lady had bestowed on them. They were distinctive, different, and drew the eye. Lieutenant Commander Bryce, a trim, brown-haired soldier, shut the door behind him and waited in the shadows.

The king turned to the slender young Sentinal on duty. "What happened?"

Niallerion bowed. "Your Majesty, the Oath flared a brilliant white. It was blinding, and now, as you see, it seems unsettled."

The king pursed his lips. "White? The colour Commander Haven is greeted by?"

"Yes, Your Majesty."

The king turned to Bryce. "Any word from Jerrol?"

"Not since his visit to Stoneford. Lord Jason sent word that they had dropped by, but nothing more. Jerrol intended on staying with Taelia for a few more days." Bryce caught Fonorion's eye. "I thought Jerrol wasn't due to return for another week?"

The dark-haired Sentinal nodded. "Jerrol promised Taelia two weeks." He smiled. "I believe she was holding him to it. Birlerion is still in Terolia; he's not due back until then, either."

"Niallerion, go check on them. Make sure they are all right. You can still feel him, can't you?" the king asked.

Niallerion's face stilled as he checked. "Yes. It is a little muted, but that happens on occasion, so not usually a concern. By your leave, Your Majesty." He bowed and was out the door.

The king watched him go. "Not a concern?" he asked, turning to Fonorion.

"It's difficult to explain. It's more of a sensation. We know there is a Lady's Captain, though not where he is or what he's doing." Fonorion struggled to find the words. "Just the fact that the position is filled. Birlerion would have a clearer view."

The king nodded. "Bryce, get one of your men to keep an eye on the Oath. Note any changes, anything at all, and get a message to Scholar-Deane Lillian. See if she can find any mention of the Oath in the archives, though it's highly unlikely, I suppose. Send a message to Birlerion; ask if he's heard anything."

Bryce left. The king watched the Oath for a few minutes before leading Fonorion back to his office. He had been in the depths of planning the logistics of his state visit to the island empire of Birtoli. His daughter, the Empress Melahney, was due to give birth to his first grandchild, and he was eager to arrive in time. He was leaving his son, Anders, to look after things whilst he was away. This would be his first state visit to the islands, and by its very nature, they would have to travel by ship.

It was a logistical nightmare trying to manage who would go and who would stay, and he had almost reached the stage of calling it off, except his daughter would never forgive him. He sighed as he returned to his lists.

The return of Bryce was a welcome interruption, and he leaned back in his chair as the Lieutenant Commander entered. Bryce was an extremely competent officer. He had been fortunate to have both Jerrol Haven and Bryce at hand during the crisis of four years ago. With Jerrol being dragged all over the place to solve outlandish problems for the Lady, Bryce had provided stable leadership in his place. They had thought the Ascendants had been dealt with for good, but what if they hadn't been? Would the Lady still expect Jerrol to respond? She had never given him warning previously, so why would she start now?

"Well?" he asked.

Bryce shrugged. "She's set some scholars onto it, but she said up to now, they've uncovered little regarding the Oath or its keeper. And even then, it was Jerrol and Taelia who discovered what little they have found."

King Benedict nodded. The engraving explicitly said that the Oath Keeper was thrice bound for life, by Lady, Land, and Liege. But with the Veil protected, the Bloodstone healed, and the Ascendants routed, there was little left to cause them problems. "I suppose we'll have to wait and see what my Oath Keeper has to say about it," he said.

Bryce grimaced. He knew Jerrol would not be pleased to be called back to Old Vespers early. Jerrol had earned his time with his family many times over. Being happily joined with Lady Olivia these last two years, Bryce knew the importance of a supportive spouse and the struggle Jerrol had of balancing his commitments with his young family. The deities pushing him from pillar to post had taken their toll, and it had only been in recent months that Bryce thought Jerrol had finally readjusted to life in Vespiri and laid his ghosts to rest.

"Roberion is due back in port by the 25th. He'll need at least two days to re-provision, so, weather willing, we could possibly set sail by the 28th of this month," Bryce said.

"We have to arrive by Febu 16th. Melahney is expecting to be confined by the seventh ; we can't leave it any later than that."

"The port master is on the lookout for Roberion; as soon as the *Lady's Miracle* hoves into sight, we'll know, Your Majesty."

"Good. Well that's it then. Give these lists to Darris; he knows what to do. And make sure the number of courtiers is halved; they are not necessary. I am not dragging the whole court to Birtoli."

"As you wish, Your Majesty."

"Do you think it's something to do with Jerrol?" the king asked, betraying where his thoughts really were.

"I'm very much afraid that it might be," Bryce admitted. "The Oath only flares white for Jerrol. A response to the Bloodstone, I would imagine."

"That's what I was thinking. Tell Darris to prepare his rooms just in case."

3

___

AN OCEAN SOMEWHERE IN
REMARGAREN

Jerrol gasped and staggered as the wooden deck rolled in the swell. Lurching for the handrail, he gripped it securely as he gazed around his surroundings. He was on a small vessel, in the middle of the ocean. His gaze swept the horizon, but there was nothing but blue sky, blinding sun, and empty seas. The deck rolled again, and his stomach heaved. He leaned over the rail and emptied his guts, and then thanked the Lady that the wind was behind him. He stiffened as a hand slapped his shoulder.

"Jerven, I told you not to drink so much last night; you shouldn't have gone down to the Taverna. You know we have a long trip through the outer islands. The sea doesn't care how much you drank!"

Jerrol staggered upright and wiped his mouth. "It seemed a good idea at the time," he said, staring blearily at the unfamiliar boy.

The youth laughed. His olive skin was well-tanned, and his black hair curled at his neck. He had black eyes which sparkled with mischief, and Jerrol had no idea who he was. A youth shining with vitality and life. "Go man the tiller; you know it's more stable there. I'll sort out the nets, but remember, you owe me."

Jerrol waved a vague hand and, staggering back to the stern, grabbed the wandering pole. He collapsed onto the bench and hugged the tiller to his chest. Where in the Lady's realm was he? And how had he gotten here?

Shielding his eyes against the glare of the sun, he watched the youth nimbly fling the nets out into the sea, drop the floats, and begin coiling the ropes. The boy was barefoot, dressed in linen cut-offs and a thin shirt, just as he was, he realised as he looked down. His skin was burnt brown; the hairs on his arms bleached white. He was still missing his fingers on his right hand, he saw, so at least he was still in his own body, which eased one frightening fear. His stomach roiled, not just due to the rolling deck. Where was Taelia? Was she still at home, frantically trying to find him? He whispered a fervent prayer to the Lady that she was safe with the children.

Rubbing his green stone pendant, which he still wore around his neck, Jerrol watched the young boy scampering about the deck as if it was his home. The boat was constructed of a single hull, with a tall wooden mast in the centre. The mainsail was fully raised, the canvas a brilliant red. A smaller jib caught the wind, and its rigging clattered against the mast. It seemed that below decks was a space for storing their trade goods. A box on the deck led to a chute that also fed into the lower hold to store their catch. Faded yellow rails edged the deck, and he somehow knew the hull was painted blue. Bright and colourful like the islands of the Birtolian Archipelago.

Looking around, the sky was a cerulean blue; he had never seen such a clear and vibrant blue. The sea was a sparkling silver under the brilliant sunlight deepening to dark blue on the horizon. The air was warm and moist, the tang of salt rife. He inhaled the warm air, and his stomach settled.

The canvas sail flapped in the breeze, a soothing accompaniment to the unfamiliar view. A fine spray of water splashed his face, and he licked the salt off his lips. Accepting the water skin the the youth handed him, he unstoppered it and drank, even though the water was tepid.

The boy squatted beside him and spoke to his feet. "Are you going to ask Surita to join with you?" he asked, kneading a faded blue cap in his hands.

"No," the word exploded out of Jerrol before he could stop it.

The youth jerked his head up, his inky black eyes startled at the vehemence of Jerrol's response, uncertainty clouding his expression.

Jerrol gripped the boy's shoulder. "No," he said more softly.

The youth breathed a sigh of relief. "I'm glad," he admitted, before raising horrified eyes. "Not that I don't think you're good enough for her. It's just she's not right for you," he blurted. "I know I'm only your brother, but even I can see she would not make you happy."

"Don't worry, I would never bring a woman into our home that you did not approve of."

His brother grinned sheepishly. "It's not my choice."

"No, but you are my family, and we are in this together," Jerrol said, the truth of his words burning through his soul. He took a breath as the boy's name filtered into his mind, along with the image of a beautiful, black-haired young woman. A memory he knew was not his own. "Gael, I'm sorry if I led you to believe I would leave you out of my life."

Gael looked up, eyes wide. "Jerven, I never thought that, honest, but Granfer said I had to let you make your own choices."

"And I will, but never without you," Jerrol promised, wondering whose life he had inherited. "I think we'd better check our nets else we won't make much of a trade in Molinti, will we?"

Gael grinned, his face lightening. "Your turn. I set them. You collect them." He handed Jerven his cap.

"Fair enough," Jerrol agreed, relinquishing the tiller and tugging the cap on his head as he made his way down the deck. The rhythm of hauling in the nets felt familiar. He had done this hundreds of times before. The silver fish flapped in the mesh, the bug-eyed shellfish balefully glaring at him. The large mullet found in the deeper waters and much-prized gleamed pink on the deck.

He grinned as he pulled in the haul and tossed them into the waiting chute; a good haul, bless the Lady. He efficiently gathered the nets and reset them, marking their position with the floats. He rested his arms on the wooden rail and stared out to sea as they dragged the nets behind them.

Eyti lay off over the horizon on the starboard bow, the curve of smaller, unnamed and deserted islands blocking the entrance to the bay. They would travel on to Astille before swinging back around the larger island of Duyli, where they occasionally stopped to gather some of the emerald green samphire growing in the rockpools and marshy margins of the islands.

Then on to Geteril before working their way back to Molinti, the largest port on the mainland, with the most demand and best prices for their haul; the seat of the emperor. He knew they hailed from the smaller sister port of Plini, where their Granfer still lived, and that's where they would return to resupply and where he would have to deal with Surita, whoever she was.

How he knew all this, he wasn't sure, but he did. He was in a boat amidst what he knew as the island Empire of

Birtoli, though the grey smudge of mainland approaching off his starboard bow did not match any of the maps he knew.

He reached for Zin'talia, but there was nothing; a hollow silence. The low murmur of his sentinal that usually filled his head was missing as well; the gentle backdrop that comforted him was gone, and his stomach stirred uneasily at the realisation that he was on his own and he didn't know where he was.

Sighing, he went to duck below the deck, where he opened the salt barrel and began gutting the mullet. Rinsing out the cavity, he rolled each fish in the salt and laid them out in flat crates, liberally covering them in more salt and then a damp cloth to preserve them.

A second haul and the hold was full of tiny silvery fish, a local delicacy called phrist and popular with the islanders. Jerrol set Gael to sacking them up, ready to trade, and took the tiller to steer around the tiny islets that guarded the eastern coastline of the district of Eyti.

He threaded the boat through the rocks, clearly visible in the blue waters, and they sailed up to the rickety jetty. The harbour wasn't really a harbour; it was more of a curved beach, shelving down into the sheltered bay. The sound of hammers and the smell of heated oil filled the air. Skeletal ribs of wood rose up from the sand, the beginnings of a new hull; two further half-made boats lay in brackets on the beach.

Eyti was famous for its wooden boats, the sheltered bay providing the ideal open-air workshop. The district of Eyti was fortunate enough to have a seemingly unending supply of hardwood trees. Trees covered every possible square inch of the rising lowlands edging up over the bay, and the regimented ranks of trees reminded Jerrol of the forests of Greenswatch.

Gael jumped down to the jetty and tied them up both bow and stern. They wouldn't bother selling their catch here. The people caught enough fish of their own using floating rafts to cast their nets from, though they would trade some of the sacks of flour and casks of oil they also had stashed in the hold.

Jerrol offloaded the sacks and casks to Gael before jumping down onto the unstable jetty himself. He hefted two of the sacks over his shoulder and staggered down the jetty, cursing the swells that tried to tip him in the water. Gael rolled the casks ahead of him, expertly keeping them straight, though they were sealed with wax, so they should survive a dunking in the sea. His sacks though … he sighed out a breath of relief as he reached the beach.

A tall, white-haired man left the treeline and met them on the sands. He gave a low grunt and held out a cloth of creamy white pearls and round black beads.

Trade went swiftly, Jerrol suggesting an investment in one of the half-built hulls instead of the gems in exchange for payment. The man was willing, and they agreed for Jerrol to return in two months to collect his new boat and pay the balance. The villagers returned to work and Jerrol returned to his boat and Gael, aware of his brother's concern. Another boat was a serious investment; Jerrol hoped he would have found a way home by the time the boat was ready and it wouldn't be him collecting it.

Jerrol threaded his way back out through the rocks, and they were soon skimming across the waves and out to sea, the bright red sail billowing before them. Gael set the jib, and the added push had them scudding across the waves. Even at this speed, they would have to sail all night to reach Astille, but the skies were clear, and as the sun set, Jerrol watched the stars brighten and began readjusting his internal compass to their new positions. Gael offered him some dried strips of fish, and they sat chewing in companionable silence, washing it down with fresh coconut milk and watching the waxing moon rise.

"Lady guide me on your quest," he prayed silently, as he watched the gleaming orb traverse the sky. If only he could find out why he was here, then he might be able to return home to Taelia and his family. He felt a wrench in his gut as he thought of Taelia's distress at his abrupt disappearance. He should have heeded her dream more closely. At least put some contingencies in place just in case. He had left her distraught and alone with no idea what had happened. His gut roiled with guilt and uncertainty.

Jerrol sat the night watch. Imagining Taelia was in his arms and staring at the moon, he planted a kiss firmly on her lips, trying to reassure her all would be well. He grimaced. He had no idea how he would get back to her, but he had made a promise, and he would get back somehow, he swore.

At dawn, he handed the tiller over to Gael, and as the sun began to rise, he snuggled under the canvas to get some much-needed sleep before they reached their next port of call.

Later that day, Jerrol stared out across the blue ocean, casually leaning against the tiller, and grinned at Gael. "What date is it, Gael? I've sorta lost track," he said, shifting his gaze out to sea.

Gael burst out laughing. "As if! You always say you can tell the time by the sun and the stars. You don't lose track."

"Humour me."

Gael snorted. "It's the twenty-second day of Novu, the year of our Lady 1123."

"1123!" Jerrol couldn't help the gasp that escaped his mouth. He felt breathless, like he had been kicked in the stomach. *He had gone back in time? Three thousand years? How was that even possible?* Jerrol's thoughts skittered off in all directions.

"Jerven, stop it, it's been 1123 all year, as you well know."

"Just checking," he said slowly, trying to ignore the voice shrieking 1123 in his head. He blindly looked back out to sea, trying to control the growing sense of panic that threatened to overwhelm him.

Gael cast him a suspicious glance before shaking his head as he climbed down into the hold to rebalance the crates; the *Scout* was leaning heavily to starboard.

Jerrol gripped the tiller, grappling to achieve a sense of calm but failing as the voice chanted in his head. *'What are you going to do now? How will you get home from here?'* His knuckles gleamed ivory and his grip tightened on the tiller as he desperately tried to find something real to hold onto. His sight blurred as he realised he had no way of getting a message to Taelia; he had no way of even telling her he was still alive.

It took them a month to complete the round trip. Every night under the Lady's moon, Jerrol kissed his wife goodnight. During the long nights he watched the constellations with growing concern; they weren't quite in the positions he remembered. By day he mapped the islands; their resources, the communities, and their leaders; instinctively collecting information, trading fish, and carrying messages or goods and occasionally passengers on his little boat. A rare lifeline between remote and isolated islands and highly valued. He was still unsure why he was here, but he was relaxing into the rhythm of the simple life, getting his bearings and watching closely.

They were finally on the last leg of their trip, heading

home, when they sailed into the small sheltered cove of Geteril, part of a tiny group of islands that Jerrol thought didn't exist. In fact, half the tropical islands he had mapped the last few weeks either didn't exist or the maps that King Benedict had were sorely out of date. The horseshoe cove was rimmed with white sands and tall palm trees, reminding him of the sentinal trees.

Swallowing against the tightening of his throat, Jerrol admitted that he missed the comforting hum of his sentinal and the snippy comments Zin'talia often brightened his day with, but he missed his family even more. Leyarille would be growing and Mikke learning new things without him. He sighed and stared out at the turquoise blue waters of the cove, a turquoise that defied belief. He had never seen such amazing colours, and he promised himself that one day, he would bring his family to see them.

An innocuous wooden jetty stretched out into the bay, out of place, and yet a sign the island was occupied. So many islands were not, being too small to sustain people or worse: without a source of fresh water.

As Jerrol's boat eased up to the jetty, the islander's children came rushing out of the tree line, whooping in welcome. The island was a low mound of vegetation in the wide blue sea; a speck of life in the middle of the ocean.

Jerrol leapt over the side of the boat onto the rickety jetty and tied the trailing rope to the post. He bowed, hands clasped against his chest as an ancient man, desiccated and wrinkled by many years of exposure to the sun, came to greet him. Elder Tuan, so Gael said. He was dressed only in a loincloth and shell necklaces, which clinked around his neck.

The man gave him a gap-toothed grin and expansively welcomed them to his island. He led the way into the trees and the welcome shade, his sons carrying the goods easily.

The small village nestled in the centre of the palm trees, beside a tiny spring that burbled merrily to itself. The spring was no doubt the reason the settlement was here.

The women of the village peeked from behind woven screens and watched as the men bartered for the goods. The Elder finally grinned, Jerrol bowed in acceptance, his hands clasped before his chest, and he discreetly tucked the small bundle of pearls into his belt. The Elder invited Jerrol to sit. "Please tell us the news. We rarely have visitors. What is going on in the world outside?"

Jerrol shrugged as he sat on the proffered log and smiled his thanks as he accepted a gourd of water. He took a swallow and passed it on. Water was a treasured commodity in these islands, and he didn't want to take too much, yet there was a delicate balance between accepting and offending. He was honoured to be offered such a gift.

"Elder Tuan, my thanks for the honour you bestow upon us. It is our pleasure to bring you news of the outer world. Time slides by, unseen by the ocean's tides, and pushes us from one place to another." Jerrol paused as he gathered his thoughts. "The empress grows heavy with child. The emperor looks to celebrate in the next three months or so. I will bring news when the celebrations are announced.

"Building continues apace in Molinti. The quarry releases more white stone than ever before, though I fear the cost in both lives and coin may be more than the emperor can pay. His palace will be a vision, visible as far as the eye can see; even the nomads of Terolia will see it from their redstone cliffs and be in awe." Jerrol faltered as he realised what his tongue was saying. The emperor was building his palace? But that was built centuries ago. He swallowed, his throat dry, as his stomach fluttered.

The Elder snorted. "I doubt they will even look."

Jerrol smiled in agreement, trying to ignore the growing

queasiness in his stomach. The Elder gave him a keen look but allowed himself to be distracted as Jerrol numbly replied. "I am but repeating the scribe's report. I agree, they won't care, but the emperor's pride needs bolstering now and then."

"His pride will be his downfall. There are more important things needed than a new palace," the Elder said. "He should be protecting our heritage, providing for future generations, ensuring our names continue."

Jerrol stared at him. "Have you seen something, Father?"

"I see many things. Not all are good, not all are bad, but dark times approach, and the emperor needs clear eyes."

"I'm sure the Lady will guide his steps and ensure that he sees what he needs to," Jerrol replied.

The Elder stared at him and nodded. "The line protects," he murmured.

"As the Lady watches," Jerrol completed.

The Elder's eyes widened and he looked at Jerrol anew. "As you say, Captain," he said, his voice slow. "I look forward to your return, my son."

"We'll be back in about a month." Jerrol smiled as he rose. It was time to leave for Molinti.

4

PRESENT DAY

JANU 22ND, 4128, STONEFORD KEEP

Stepping through the waystone to Jerrol's cottage, Birlerion's heart thrummed in his chest. He shivered in the chill air and sheltered against Kin'arol. Ari had harried Birlerion and Kin'arol all the way to the nearest waystone before popping out of sight.

Taelia appeared in the cottage door, her baby strapped to her chest and a sleepy Mikke by her side. Mikke was dressed in a mishmash of clothes, evidence of Taelia's distress. Her face screwed up as she saw Birlerion, and she tried not to cry.

Birlerion gently wrapped her in his arms as the tears trailed down her cheeks. "We'll find him," he murmured, hugging her close.

"I'm so glad you're here. I didn't know what to do. Birlerion, he disappeared right in front of me. The Lady took him."

"We'll find him," Birlerion repeated.

"I was going to go to Jason."

Birlerion glanced around him. "Where are your guards? That was the deal; you would have one within call at all times."

"Don't. They are searching, but I know they won't find

him. We had settled for the night. They couldn't have done anything."

"I should have been here. I knew it."

"It was the Lady, Birlerion, you couldn't have stopped her."

"I could have gone with him."

"If you were supposed to be with him, you would be. So don't start castigating yourself for actually taking a break. You deserve a life too, Birlerion. It's not your fault."

Birlerion stared at her, his face tense. He should be at Jerrol's shoulder; that was where he belonged.

"You're here because I need you. You keep me together. Please, Birlerion, stay with me. *I* need you."

Birlerion stilled and then heaved a deep sigh. He smiled down at Mikke, who was leaning against his leg. "Hi Mikke, look, Kino's here. He wanted to see you," he said as he lifted the little boy into his arms and then onto Kin'arol's back. Birlerion rubbed Zin'talia's white nose. "I think we should go straight to Vespers."

Taelia sagged against him in relief, and Birlerion peeked at the baby swaddled against her chest. He smiled and then shivered as a gust of wind whipped around them. He helped Taelia mount.

"Kino, tell Pip to follow."

"I have," the deep voice of his Darian replied.

Mikke clung onto Kino's saddle as Birlerion led them through the waystone and stepped out by the palace entrance. Mikke began retching, and Birlerion lifted him off and hugged him tightly, murmuring in his ear until the little boy relaxed.

Jerrol had created a waystone that all could use. It was a bit difficult leading a horse out of his sentinal tree in the king's inner courtyard. But even so, non-Sentinals tended to suffer, as Mikke was. Birlerion's friend Kayerille had a theory that Darians muted the effect, which might be true as Taelia swallowed fiercely as her face paled but managed not to retch, and Leyarille seemed fine.

Birlerion helped Taelia dismount and then shifted Mikke so he rested against his shoulder. The little boy drooped and snuggled his face against Birlerion's neck, exhaling as he closed his eyes. A stable lad came running and led the Darians off to the stables.

"Come, let us find the king," Birlerion suggested. "Then we can get the little ones to bed. I am sure your rooms will have been made ready." Birlerion wrapped his free arm around Taelia's shoulders and gently steered her towards the entrance.

Niallerion came rushing out of the palace as they climbed the steps. "Birlerion, how did you know? Taelia, what happened? The Oath, it's acting strange; it's a brilliant blue."

Birlerion fended him off, shielding Taelia from the explosive questions. "Let's get the children inside first. It's freezing out here," he said as he led her to the king's chambers, Niallerion hovering behind them. Darris opened the door as they approached, his concerned gaze embracing them both as he waved them in.

King Benedict stood as Birlerion and Taelia were ushered in. He knew he wasn't going to like what she had to say when he saw her pale face and huge eyes and the fact that Birlerion was barefoot and ill dressed for the season. "Taelia my dear, please come in, sit. Darris, some tea please." He led Taelia to a chair. "Birlerion, lay the boy on the settee; we'll get him to bed shortly, and is this young Leyarille? Congratulations, my dear, well done." Benedict would never admit that he prattled, but he did prattle to fill the void. Taelia unwrapped

Leyarille and wedged her in the opposite corner to Mikke. The king continued talking until Darris returned with tea and cake and then left to find Birlerion some warmer clothes. Benedict made sure that Taelia had a cup before he looked at her gravely. "What happened?" he asked.

"I had a dream," Taelia said, staring down at her tea. "Just after Leyarille was born. I dreamt that Jerrol disappeared right before my eyes, but when I awoke the next morning, he was there next to me. When I told him, he promised he would always come back to me wherever he went. He said there was nowhere in this world he could not return from. He reassured me that he wouldn't stop trying, and I thought nothing of it.

"But this evening, I was in the kitchen when I heard him cry out. He said, "My Lady, no," and then he faded away. I searched the house and the stable, but he wasn't there; he was gone. I was going to go to Jason's when Birlerion arrived."

Birlerion nodded. "Ari came for me."

King Benedict gave the lean Sentinal a searching glance. He was shivering in his thin clothes; he must have been worried enough to drop everything.

"Niallerion said the Oath is acting strange," Taelia said, taking a deep breath. "Do you think the Lady has a job for Jerrol?"

"We'll send Sentinals to Terolia and Elothia," the king said slowly, "but I have an awful feeling this is going to be connected to our visit to Birtoli. Don't ask me why, but with the other regions settled, there is no reason for the Oath Keeper to be called."

"Why would the Oath pulse blue, though? Is there any record of it changing colour?"

"We've got Liliian searching the archives, but the Oath is not chronicled much; they won't find anything," the king said. "Come look at the Oath; see what you think. Darris will keep an eye on the children."

Benedict led the way to the throne room, and the guard on duty pushed open the doors. They stood before the Oath and stared. Red highlights roiled in the blue glare, flaring gently at the edges. The blue light pulsed, and it was clearly unsettled. It was impossible to read the words engraved in the wall, the glare was so bright.

Taelia rubbed her face. "How are we supposed to know what to do? We are just guessing. How do we find him? How do we help him?"

"I think we will only find that out if you come with me to Birtoli. A scholar of your calibre should be able to find the clues to his whereabouts," the king suggested.

"Clues," Taelia frowned. "That's what Jerrol said when he was trying to reassure me. He said he would leave me clues, write memoirs, terrible songs, find things that would stand the test of time." She looked at the king. "Why would he say such things unless the Lady was guiding him?" She flinched as the Oath flared a brilliant gold before returning to its unsettled glare.

"That's confirmed, then. You need to come with us. Darris will arrange it all."

"But the children; I can't leave them here."

"Then bring them with you."

Taelia laughed for the first time since she had arrived. "A two-year old and a baby on a ship with you? Are you sure, Your Majesty?"

The king smiled. "I am about to become a grandfather; I could use the practice."

Within a week of Roberion's ship, the *Lady's Miracle*, arriving in port, they were all loaded onboard and headed for the island Empire of Birtoli. Taelia had sent a message to Deepwater, begging Hannah to accompany her, and Hannah had deserted Jennery and Alyssa immediately. With Hannah looking after the children, Taelia had dived into the Chapterhouse archives, researching the history of Birtoli, finding out as much as she could before they left.

Roberion leaned on the railing of the upper deck and watched Taelia stare out to sea. It only seemed like yesterday that he had officiated at her joining to Jerrol, here on the *Miracle*, becalmed on the silver ocean under the Lady's moon. A magical few days before their arrival in Elothia nearly three years ago.

Jerrol had been sent as the king's emissary to the Grand Duke of Elothia, trying to sue for peace and avoid all-out war with Vespiri. Unfortunately, the grand duke had not been the elderly man they had expected to meet but his son, new to the throne and influenced by the warmongers among his advisors. Things had not gone to plan, and Jerrol had been lost, thought dead. Roberion's mouth twisted at the memory of the months of anxious waiting for Jerrol's return. It had been a fraught time for all. He had thought Jerrol and Taelia had settled down now that they'd had Mikke and Leyarille, and the world was at peace.

Taelia suddenly turned and looked up, their eyes connected, and Roberion raised a hand in greeting. Taelia made her way along the deck to the steps, and Roberion held out a hand to help her up to the upper deck.

"Thank you," she breathed as she shielded her eyes. She had to look up at him as Roberion was a typical Sentinal, tall and broad-chested, with bright silver eyes that stood out against his deep brown face.

He smiled. "I was remembering the last time you were aboard with Jerrol."

"It seems so long ago, yet I keep thinking I could turn

around at any moment and he will be standing right behind me."

"We'll find him," Roberion promised.

"I know, it's just ..." Taelia's breath caught. "Why is it always him? I mean, I only just got him back, truly. He's only just begun to forgive himself for everything, and now this."

Roberion's lips twisted. "Who else would you trust the fate of our world with? I don't think anyone else could untangle the mess we seem to be able to create."

"There are other Sentinals; one of you could be promoted."

"Lady forbid," Roberion breathed.

Taelia glared at him, and Roberion laughed as he held up his hands as if to fend her off. "Don't look at me like that! I mean it; we're just soldiers. We couldn't negotiate our way out of a paper bag; we pile straight in." He paused. "Well, maybe not Birlerion, but I think he's been through enough, too. I wouldn't wish it on him, either."

Taelia huffed. "It's not fair!"

"I know, but there is only one Captain."

"No, there isn't, there's two. If there can be two, why not three or four?"

"I don't think it works like that, and anyway, Guerlaire isn't actually here, as you know, so there's only one really. At least the Captain is still with us on Remargaren."

"How do you know that? Where is he?"

Roberion shrugged. "I just know. He's here somewhere, waiting for us to find him."

Taelia staggered against him as the deck canted in a sudden swell, and Roberion wrapped an arm around her to steady her. He squeezed her shoulders. "We'll find him," he repeated.

Taelia nodded. "We have to," she murmured as she

looked back out to sea, sheltered by the strong arms of the Sentinal.

Later that afternoon, Taelia sat with the king at the dining table in Roberion's large day cabin, which the king had taken over, briefing him on the Island Empire's history. She was utterly fixated on researching the subject. She was a bit annoyed that Birlerion and Hannah had ganged up on her and resorted to asking the king to demand her presence at every meal, but it was the only way they could get her head out of the manuscripts.

"Birtoli used to be joined to the Vespirian mainland," she said, "a solid stretch of land down past where the island of Senti now lies. They say it took four days to sail around the horn. It also says that much of Birtoli was drowned when the Lady sundered the bloodstone. Many low-lying islands and their people were lost forever; the census taken the following year shows a reduction of over half the population. It must have been awful."

"Eat," the king said, tapping her plate with his knife.

Taelia took a mouthful and chewed. "The emperor's palace at Molinti was actually built in 1136; well, it was finished in 1136, it took over fifteen years to build. That was fast considering the tools of the time; they must have had some clever stonemasons." She jotted a note on her pad.

"Eat," the king repeated, a smile in his eyes as he watched her.

Taelia gave a martyred sigh and addressed her plate. She suddenly realised she was starving. "When is the empress due to give birth?" she asked politely as their plates were cleared away.

"Well, the best guess is the week of the seventh, but I promised I would be there a few weeks before for the state visit, just in case. She seemed quite distressed, so I said we'd stay until the baby arrived. Just seeing you with Leyarille and Mikke warms my heart. I am looking forward to having a grandchild."

"Even when you know you will be ordering him down from the rigging with your heart in your mouth?" Taelia asked, remembering the heart-stopping moment when she had seen Mikke halfway up the ship's rigging, determined to see the crow in its nest. Hannah swore she had only taken her eyes off him for a moment. He had won over every single sailor with that escapade; the child had no fear.

The king laughed. "Well, I doubt my grandchild will have the same opportunities that Mikke has to get into trouble, but I think your boy will be an excellent friend for my grandchild to have. Has Hannah recovered yet?" he asked, his clear blue eyes glinting with amusement.

"Birlerion took Mikke up to steer the ship so she could have a rest. So, if we are suddenly heading in the wrong direction, you'll know why."

The king smiled and raised his cup in salute. "To our children. May their sense of adventure never fail."

Taelia raised her cup in return. "And their fathers who are surely to blame."

5

DECU 24TH, 1123

MOLINTI, BIRTOLI

J errol marvelled at the speed of the little fishing vessel, even with a hefty catch in the hold. The *Island Scout's* red sails were bulging as the wind drove them forward. He was thankful that the straits had such strong winds; he would hate to be becalmed in such a treacherous stretch of water.

A veritable army of barriers and reefs protected the unoccupied island of Allerith. He paid them the respect they were due and carefully skirted the foaming eddies, heading through the Plini straits before turning to run parallel with the mainland after they rounded Plini point. They sailed into the wide-mouthed harbour of Molinti later that afternoon.

The emperor's palace dominated the landscape; a collection of golden stone towers facing all directions, perched on a promontory above the harbour. Small, golden-bricked dwellings jostled for space as they lined the base of the headland rising up from the beach in ranks, the warm stone glowing in the sun. The harbour nestled at the mouth of the little river, emptying into the bay, and Jerrol knew there was a marketplace tucked in behind.

Jerrol observed the harbour as he approached the dock.

A triangular blue flag flapped in the stiff breeze, marking where the loading berths began. He slid the *Scout* into an empty berth and Gael jumped down with the mooring rope.

They unloaded the crates of mullet and sacks of silver phrist onto the dock; the hold emptied quickly as Jerrol swung the crates up into Gael's arms. The growing stack brought interested spectators, and the harbour master hurried up to their berth, a slate and chalk in his hand. He swiftly began a tally. Jerrol finally handed a small leather wallet of papers to him as he followed the last crate over the side.

The harbour master tucked the wallet under his arm and showed Jerrol the slate. Jerrol pursed his lips. Twenty crates and eight sacks; a tidy sum they would make at the market, after tax of course. He nodded. One molin and 16 coppers' tax; five aguin more for the berth, another aguin for a carter to take the goods up to the market, add back in the two aguins he was paid for taking the letters to the islands. The fees were nearly two molins, a fifth of his haul; the emperor had increased the fees again.

Jerrol initialled the slate. "Any news we should be aware of?" he asked as he handed the slate back.

The harbour master shrugged. "Building continues. The emperor's started a new quarry out by the road to Aguinti. Offenders are chain-ganged with the slaves he's brought in from Terolia to cut the stone. So make sure young Gael behaves himself," he warned. "Move your boat to the east bay; plenty of space there. Oh, and there'll be a speaker in the market later; some man from Terolia preaching about something."

Jerrol grinned. "Not your idea of entertainment, then?"

The harbour master snorted. "Got better things to do with my time."

"Gael, get a carrier and load up whilst I take the *Scout*

around the bay. We'll stay here tonight."

Gael nodded and scampered up the jetty.

Jerrol untied the *Scout* and then sculled backwards with the steering oar, manoeuvring over to the east bay. The small, golden, sandy beach curved around to the low head-land that separated Molinti from the town of Aguinti further up the coast to the north. He tied off to a mooring post and, holding his sandals, jumped down into the warm, clear water and waded up to the beach; the ends of his trousers were plastered to his legs, but they would dry soon enough.

He brushed off as much sand as he could and slipped his gritty feet into his sandals, then headed for the market to meet Gael. He tugged his faded cap lower on his brow against the sun's glare as heat rose from the baked dirt path, a warm, musky scent drifting on the stifling air.

The road from the harbour to the town curved up an incline that led into a central marketplace, where tavernas and stalls lined the walls. The road followed the shallow river and continued up to the palace, which was perched at the top of the rise, overlooking the town.

A new palace was being built further inland. The emperor wanted a more prominent building, one that made a statement, and Jerrol thought he had achieved it, for the palace he had once visited on behalf of King Benedict was magnificent. It had been sheathed in white marble and glis-tened in the sun. The old palace had become the minister's offices, nearer the market and port. His stomach fluttered at the idea that he was going to see the palace of Molinti being built; it felt unreal.

The market square opened before him, a mass of moving people and fragrant aromas; of roasting meat and sweet pastries. His stomach grumbled, a reminder that they hadn't eaten today. Business first, though, and he weaved his way through milling people dressed in light linen robes. There were few women in the market. Usually, only men came to barter. The women remained hidden away indoors, only venturing out in the evening dusk.

Robed men went about their business or collected in the doorways of tavernas to exchange news, smoking sweet-smelling tobacco that blended with the drifting aroma of coffee. Jerrol spotted Gael by the trading counter, fending off eager buyers. It wouldn't take long to clear their catch.

Gael heaved a sigh of relief as he saw Jerrol approach. "Jerven, the palace cook has asked for half the crates, only I didn't know what to charge him. He took them and two sacks of phrist. I said I'd send you up to collect the payment, is that alright?"

Jerrol grinned and slapped him on the shoulder. "Of course it is. I'll see him later. Now, how can I help you, gentles?" he asked genially, looking around the jostling crowd. His catch was soon divided up, either singly or by the crate. If he had to split a sack or crate, he charged higher, preferring to sell in bulk.

Hefting his purse in pleasure, he felt the reassuring weight. According to the running tally in Jerven's logbook, he would soon have enough to clear his debt for a plot of land that he had his eye on to the south of Plini harbour. Jerven had paid the deposit to hold the preference, but he needed to clear the balance soon. Jerven's plans scrolled through his mind. He would build a harbour, a warehouse, and a small home for him and Gael beside it. One day, he might even add a boatyard next to it. Jerven Shipping. He smiled in anticipation.

Gael was hopping from one foot to the other in impatience. "Can I go now?" he pleaded.

Jerrol laughed. "Alright, just keep out of trouble. I don't want to hear that you've been press-ganged into the quarries," he warned, handing Gael a handful of coppers. "Be back to the boat by eleventh chime, agreed?"

"Agreed." Gael nodded happily before flitting off.

Jerrol sighed and stacked his empty crates. He folded the sacks and piled them on top before carrying them back out of the market and down the incline to the harbour. He left them stacked on the beach opposite the *Scout*. He'd take them over later.

He looked out over the empty bay. The turquoise waters extended into a deeper blue towards the distant horizon, the grey smudge of the Terolian mainland creeping out across the water. The gentle lapping of water on the wooden hulls moored in the bay soothed his nerves; he felt all a jangle, uncertain what he was doing here, far from home and all alone, living someone else's life.

He remembered one of Hannah's favourite sayings. *'Do what you know best and the rest will follow.'* Well, it seemed like good advice. Fishing was what he seemed to know best, so he supposed he'd better continue doing that.

He turned away from the calm waters of the bay and looked up at the sprawling city of Molinti. He would go get his money from the palace cook, sound out a couple of taverns for orders and then he could relax and eat. Decision made, he strode off into the city.

Later that evening, Jerrol sat nursing his glass of wine in a small taverna off the marketplace. Lamps were being lit around the square, softening the edges of the buildings into shadows as the sun set. The air swirled with drifting smoke and appetising odours. He liked the smell of the tobacco but had never smoked it himself. Men of all ages were sitting around small tables with small glasses of liqueur or brandy or clay mugs keeping the ale cool. They sat on steps and walls, collecting in the cooling evening air.

The group next to Jerrol were teasing a young lad, encouraging him to try a long pipe of what Jerrol thought might be applewood. The boy inhaled cautiously and then choked the smoke out, coughing and spluttering as his eyes watered and he tried to draw breath. The bronzed men laughed and teased, their black eyes sparkling in the candle-light, slapping his back and encouraging him to try again. Jerrol smiled as the youth handed the pipe back, refusing to try more.

Staring down at the creased and dog-eared piece of parchment before him, he scowled at the poem he was trying to write. He had wasted so much time staring out to sea over the last month, trying to come up with ideas for how to embed a message for Taelia and his friends to find.

He had decided to try and write a poem, something that would have some longevity, something that might last through the ages and although he had a few verses down, he couldn't find the right words to capture what he wanted to say to Taelia. He had no idea how he would get it to her, but if he didn't write something to begin with, there would be nothing for her to read.

Giving up, he leaned back in his chair and watched the square fill. People were collecting around one corner – ah, yes, there *was* a speaker tonight, from Terolia. He looked up as someone paused by his table and smiled in welcome as he recognised the captain of the *Mari Rose*, a long-time friend and neighbour from Plini. Folding the paper, he slid it in his pocket as he gestured at an empty seat. He would try again later.

"Marin, please sit. I didn't see the *Mari Rose* in the harbour when we came in."

"Just got in," Marin said as he dropped into the chair next to him. "Saw the *Scout* and decided to stay and find you instead of going home. Myriam can blame you for me being late returning."

"Oh no, you're not using me as a scapegoat again. I remember last time. I barely made it out of her arms alive."

Marin cocked a knowing eyebrow at him. "And why were you in my wife's arms in the first place?" he asked with a grin, placing his cap on the table and running his tanned hands through his bleach-blonde hair. His sparkling blue eyes glared mockingly at Jerrol. Marin ran counter to the typical Birtolian olive skin and dark hair, a result of some Elothian ancestor, or so he reckoned. He was a stocky young man, muscular in build, and a competent seaman.

Jerrol laughed, pleased to see his friend. His smile faltered for a moment. Marin was Jerven's friend but Jerven's memories were his and he was glad to see someone he recognised. "I haven't seen you for months; where have you been?"

"About two weeks behind you, by the sounds of it. Every time I get in port you've been and gone; you don't stay long do you? I was surprised to see the *Scout* berthed in the bay, so I thought I'd catch you while I could and run into Plini with you tomorrow. Aiden will be along soon, he docked just behind me. He wanted to speak to you as well, he's interested in joining your venture."

Jerrol nodded. "In that case ..." He signalled a waiter and indicated another round. "That would be good as I need to speak to him. Everyone I've spoken to would take more of our haul if we can deliver it. It seems there is a lot of demand for the deep sea fish. I am going to need more boats just to keep up. I didn't realise so few of the local boats fished deep."

Marin frowned at the server as he decanted another jug of wine and mug of ale on the table. "Since when did you drink wine? I thought you stuck to the beer."

"I don't know," Jerrol said, holding up the glass of ruby red liquid to the light, the rich colour gleaming like blood. He took a sip. "I seem to have acquired a taste for it."

"Well, I'll stick to ales, thank you."

"Be my guest," Jerrol said agreeably. "Did you see Gael in the market? He's around somewhere."

"No, I spotted you and came straight over. I heard you had quite a haul; had the market buzzing, you did."

"The Lady was watching. I was fortunate, brought in what people wanted." Jerrol eased his shoulders. "How about you?"

"I offloaded sardines and phrist, nothing like your mullet, though. I don't know how you find it."

"Just lucky, I guess."

"It's nothing to do with luck; you read the waters really well. I wish you'd tell me how you do it. I heard you sailed overnight to Astille. Taking a risk, weren't you?"

"There's nothing to hit out there. Deep waters are safe enough."

"Hit a wave wrong and that could be the end of you. Flip you over, it would." Marin took a deep swallow of his ale. "Risky, and on top of that, how do you know which direction you're going?"

Jerrol looked up at the sky above. "I watch the moon and the stars," he said, pointing up at the tiny pinpoints of light sprayed across the night sky, the Lady's moon hidden behind the buildings rising around them.

Marin choked on his drink. "Are you mad?"

Jerrol looked at him in surprise. "Not at all. The stars

follow a set pattern; if you know where they are supposed to be, you can use them to navigate. Terolians use them all the time."

"That I'd like to see," Marin said in disbelief.

"Very well. Tomorrow night in Plini, I'll show you."

Marin cocked his head at Jerrol. "You're not trying to trick me, are you?"

"I'll show you tomorrow night," Jerrol promised, raising his glass and taking a sip. He waved at a tall dark-haired man who entered the square and hesitated searching the crowds. The man raised his hand in response and made his way towards them through the milling people. Marin tugged another chair over as Aiden arrived.

"Thanks," Aiden said as he dropped onto it. His sun-burnished face was lined and weathered, and deep creases flared around his brown eyes. Broad-shouldered, his shirt strained at the seams as he twisted around to flag down a server. "I've never seen it so busy, gives me the shivers being around so many people."

Jerrol grinned. "I thought it was just me. You do get used to being alone out on the sea. Much more peaceful," he said with a grimace at the chattering crowd.

"Never a truer word said. I wouldn't have stopped, but I saw your boat and wanted to catch you. Marin mentioned your plans to start a fishing line, and I'm interested if you need another skipper."

"Are you prepared to fish deep? That is where the market is."

"I'll fish wherever you need me to. I've fished these waters for years, so I know the good spots. I struggle with getting the private customers, relying on the open market is becoming a mug's game."

Jerrol nodded, pursing his lips in thought as Aiden reinforced Jerven's decision to build his own harbour. "I intend to build a harbour further south. Plini is too crowded; we'll need more space and it will save us on berthing fees."

Aiden gave a sharp nod. "Whatever you're planning, count me in."

"Let's drink to it," Marin said raising his mug. "Here's to … what are you calling it, Jerven?"

"To the Jerven Shipping line, may it be blessed by the Lady," Jerrol chanted and Marin and Aiden repeated it as they tapped his glass.

"What have you heard about this speaker tonight?" Aiden asked as he wiped his mouth.

Marin relaxed back into his seat. "Terolian, apparently. What he's doing here I have no idea. Everywhere I go though, people keep telling me I have to come and listen; they've managed to get the word out effectively."

"Well, if they try and convince you that they are the better people and you should follow them, take it with a pinch of salt; there won't be any benefit for you, I'm sure," Jerrol said.

"Aren't you going to listen?" Aiden asked.

"I hadn't intended to; got to get back to the *Scout*."

"Take a break, Jerven. Give us other fishermen a chance for once," Marin laughed. "One night won't hurt."

"Maybe, depends when they intend to start."

"Any time now, by the looks of it. Come on, let's go hear what the speaker has to say. Isn't that Gael over there?"

"Where?" Jerrol frowned at the gathering people.

"I thought I saw him in the crowd," Marin said.

Jerrol finished his drink. "Let's go get him then." He stood as Marin finished his ale. Dropping a coin on the table, he led the way towards the crowd. They pushed their way in, searching for Gael, but they couldn't see him in the crush. They wriggled their way out the other side and stood at the edge.

Jerrol's heart dropped as a tall, dark-haired man stood at the front and raised his hands. He had seen the like before and no good had come of it. He searched the crowd more urgently.

He knew there were few Sentinals in Birtoli; the Lady's influence here was minimal. The families believed in their ancestors guiding them through life and into death, not a mysterious lady they had never seen.

Pockets of belief in the Lady could be found in the outer islands, where time seemed to stand still. The mainlanders shrugged their shoulders and said they were too busy to worry about worshipping anyone, and apart from nodding their heads at the emperor, left it to the individual to believe in what they wanted.

The black-haired man began to speak. "Welcome, my dear people, welcome. I am so happy to see many of you gathered here today. Listen to the words that will change your lives forever; no more the humdrum of life being parched by the sun, but an opportunity to build a new life in support of those who will lead you to everlasting prosperity and peace."

"Try not to listen to him," Jerrol murmured, breaking the start of the spell.

Marin shook his head muzzily. "What?"

"Don't listen to him. believe in the Lady and you will be protected."

"The Lady?" Aiden repeated in confusion.

"The Lady guards us all and will protect you if you bespeak her," Jerrol said a little louder. A murmur of voices followed as the men beside him looked at each other and frowned.

"A world of possibilities, peace, and prosperity for all," the sonorous voice continued, "offered for free to those who step forward now and choose a new life. Join us in peace, join us in prosperity, serve those who are best positioned to lead, and you will be rewarded."

The listening men took an involuntary step forward.

"With what?" Jerrol asked loudly, breaking the effect of the words on those next to him. The men shook their heads in confusion.

"Do as I say and you will be saved," the man intoned. "Join us in peace. Join us in prosperity. Serve those who are best positioned to lead, and you will be rewarded."

There was a slight scuffle in the front, quickly suppressed as the man continued speaking his spell. Jerrol moved towards the front, catching a glimpse of Gael being dragged forward.

"Take your hands off my brother," Jerrol shouted as he approached the group of men around Gael. His brother's face was pale, his black eyes wide with fear. Marin stepped up to Jerrol's shoulder as the spectators jostled beside them, giving them some space, sensing a fight.

The men around Gael laughed as another tall, dark-haired man stepped forward. "Go back to your toy boats. This is our business," the stranger snarled. "These men have decided to join our brotherhood; take them to the ship," he instructed.

Aiden stepped forward ready to take issue and Jerrol grabbed his arm, his stomach twisting at the words. "I believe you said that only the pure-blooded will rule. What is the point of tainted Birtolian blood going with you? when all you are going to do is plunder their souls and cast out free will?"

The man stared at Jerrol before stepping back and gesturing his men forward. "I believe we have some more volunteers," he said, curling his lip, his black eyes glinting in expectation.

Jerrol moved with precision, thankful Birlerion had

insisted he still train every day. His body flowed into the familiar routine and he snapped his hand up into the face of the oncoming Ascendant, followed by a jab to his throat. The man staggered back, gasping, as Jerrol swept the feet out from under the second man, and following the man down to the ground, Jerrol slammed his head on the rock, ensuring he would stay there. The lead Ascendant stood frozen, mouth open in shock as in one smooth move, Jerrol rolled over the slumped body and kicked the back of the Ascendant's knee; the man collapsed to the ground. Jerrol grabbed his arm, and wrenched it behind him as he pressed his knee into the man's back, forcing him face down into the gritty sand.

"I said," Jerrol hissed, "to unhand my brother." He twisted the dark-haired man's arm higher, and the man's joints cracked in the sudden silence.

"Jerven, for Lady's sake," Marin said, horrified. "You'll break his arm."

"Then he won't be able to attack harmless children, will he?" Jerrol said, his voice biting. His eyes gleamed silver in the torchlight. "I suggest you go back to where you came from and leave these people in peace," he said into the man's ear.

"You'll regret this," the man threatened, his eyes rolling in pain.

"No, you will regret it if you don't leave now," Jerrol said, twisting the man's arm further, and the man groaned. Jerrol looked across at Gael, now standing beside Aiden. "Are you alright?"

Gael nodded, his eyes wide and fearful.

Jerrol released his hold and wrapped his arm around his brother's shoulder, then turned away from the men on the ground. "Show's over, folks," he said as the people parted for them to leave; whispers followed them as they left. The emperor's guards hurried into the square and began to disperse the crowd, restoring order, ignoring the speaker's complaints.

"Jerven, what did you do back there?" Marin gasped as he and Aiden followed close behind.

"Stopped a travesty," Jerrol murmured, hugging his brother.

"What?"

"Got my brother out of a scrape," Jerrol said, raising his voice. "What did I say about not getting into trouble?" Jerrol glared at Gael.

"How did you knock down those men, Jerven? You moved so fast! Could you show me?" Gael asked.

"Not now, let's get back to the *Scout*. Marin, Aiden, thanks for watching my back; you didn't have to."

"You're our friend, of course we've got your back. But Jerven, who were they and what did they want?" Marin asked, still a little breathless.

"Stopped an illegal press gang, by the looks of it," Aiden said, casting a glance behind them. "I'll report it to the harbour master and meet you back at the boats." Aiden strode off into the darkness.

Jerrol shrugged. "It looked like they were trying to recruit people to their cause, only their cause is detrimental to the health of the people. As I said, believe in the Lady and you will be safe."

Marin fell silent as he followed them down to the harbour, through dark and quiet streets. They parted at the waterfront, with promises to leave together in the morning. Jerrol stooped to pick up the crates he'd left on the beach and waded out to his boat. Passing them up to Gael, he hauled himself out of the water.

They stowed the crates and settled themselves on the deck in their blankets.

Jerrol waited.

"Jerven, there were three of them. How did you knock them over so fast? When did you learn to do that?"

Jerrol exhaled slowly. "In another life."

"What?"

"Oh, here and there. I meet many people around the islands. You're not on every trip, you know."

"Could you teach me?" Gael asked, his voice hesitant.

"Well, it seems you need to know how to defend yourself. What happened? How come you were going to go and bind yourself into slavery without saying goodbye?"

"I wasn't!" Gael protested. "Well, I didn't intend on doing that. I don't remember how it came about."

"Do you not hold the Lady in your heart?" Jerrol asked, staring up at the moon.

"Granfer said it was all nonsense. There is no such lady and not to waste my time bothering with it." Gael looked at him shyly. "Do you believe differently?"

"Oh yes," Jerrol breathed. "Look up there," he said, pointing at the brilliant sliver of the new moon. "What do you see?"

"The moon."

"And where does the moon come from?"

"Nowhere. I mean, it's always been there."

"Well, someone had to put it up there to watch over us through the day and night."

"It's not out in the day," Gael protested.

"Not here, but it is elsewhere. The Lady created the moon as She did the world we live in. Just because you can't see the moon doesn't mean She isn't there. She watches over us and protects us as best She can, if we believe in Her. She is busy right now, trying to prevent people like those in the square tonight from destroying the world we live in."

"But how do you know that?" Gael frowned.

"Because I believe." Jerrol smiled. "I always have, and I

always will. I look up at Her moon every night, and I tell Her so."

"Could you help me believe?" Gael asked, wonder in his voice.

Jerrol laughed. "It has to come from inside you, not from me; I can't tell you to believe. But I will tell you what I know. Let me tell you about a Lady I once met." His voice softened, and he began to tell Gael about the first time he met the Lady. He described how he fell into the water fully-clothed and found himself swept up on a gritty beach. Looking up, he had seen the most beautiful woman with tumbling golden curls, brilliant green eyes and a smile that melted his heart. "She asked me to help protect her guardians; those who protected her people and the world they lived in."

"Like the clan elders? Aren't they the guardians of their people?" Gael interrupted, eyes alight.

"Yes, exactly like them; they protect their people."

"It all makes sense now," Gael said, staring at the moon in awe. "No wonder you love the islands so much. I'll help to protect the guardians, I promise."

"The Lady will thank you when she can. Only, be warned, meeting the Lady can be a double-edged sword. She may bless you, but she often returns you to your turbulent life with a kick in the pants," he said with a chuckle, describing how she had dumped him back in the water where he had almost drowned again. He omitted the fact that it had not occurred in Birtoli, for Gael would never have believed him, and anyway, the boy naturally assumed Jerven had meant he had been washed up on one of the island beaches.

Gael laughed with him at the end of his story, and he hugged Jerven's description of the Lady close to his heart. He had a smile on his face as he closed his eyes and fell asleep.

Jerrol watched Gael for a moment and then he looked up at the Lady's moon. He imagined Taelia in his arms and kissed her gently before taking a deep breath and asking the Lady for guidance. The moon stared down at him silently. Jerrol gave up and settled down beside Gael.

6

PRESENT DAY

JAN 31ST, 4128, MOLINTI, BIRTOLI

Three days after leaving Old Vespers, King Benedict and his entourage arrived in Molinti, still with one two-year-old and a baby on board, much to their mother's relief, though Taelia feared even the king had been tempted by the idea of tossing Mikke overboard.

Roberion brought his ship neatly into the open-mouthed harbour and drew up against the stone quay. The towers of the old palace, now used for administration, gleamed golden in the sunlight as it overlooked the harbour. A small sandy beach extended in a gentle curve away from the boats moored along the jetties. The emperor's glistening palace on the headland, which was visible from the sea, was hidden by the rising landscape once they were docked in the harbour.

Everyone breathed a sigh of relief as the king disembarked into the full paraphernalia of an official state welcome. Birlerion held onto an excited Mikke as they watched the guard's parade and the trumpets sound.

Emperor Geraine stood at the end of the dock, resplendent in formal robes of gold brocade and glittering with jewels. He was a short man, with a pointed nose, and sharp brown eyes which inspected Roberion's ship with a glint of envy. At his side, a tall aide, dressed in a fitted black suit with a white shirt peeping out at the collar, clasped a book to his chest as if he needed to defend himself against the arriving Vespirians.

Once the fanfare died away, Geraine walked down the dock, meeting Benedict in the middle.

"King Benedict. Welcome to Birtoli. Melahney waits for us at the palace. It was far too hot for her to come and greet you. She was sure you would understand."

Benedict gripped the offered hand of his son by joining. "Emperor Geraine. I am so glad to see you. Thank you for your kind welcome. I am sure my daughter, the empress, made the right decision. Although it is a beautiful day, she would have suffered in this heat."

"We're all suffering in this heat," Geraine replied with a slight grimace. "Please, we have refreshments awaiting you at the palace. If you would join me, we will be with Melahney in no time. How was your trip? Your ship is impressive."

Benedict laughed as he followed the emperor to the waiting carriage. "Sentinal Roberion will be honoured to give you a tour. It is his pride and joy." He waved his hand acknowledging the crowds who peered down at them from the terraces above the harbour. A few waved back as he climbed in the ornate, gilt edged carriage and relaxed against the plump cushions.

Fonorion and the aide climbed in with them, and Geraine waved out the window as the carriage smoothly pulled away from the dock. The honour guards lining the harbour walls marched after them.

Once the king had left with the dapper emperor and the crowds began dispersing, Taelia and Birlerion disembarked with Hannah and the children, leaving Roberion to restock and move his ship further out into the bay, his crew looking forward to some shore leave. Taelia breathed in the warm, scented air and felt comforted, her heart eased. Jerrol was here somewhere, she was sure of it.

A much plainer carriage awaited them, and Birlerion lifted Mikke onto the seat next to the driver. "I'll keep hold of him," he promised as he climbed up next to him.

Taelia leaned back against the cushion and smiled at Hannah. "Well, we made it," she said with a grin.

"Only just," Hannah laughed. "But this heat already, and it's not even Febu. You must watch your skin; it will burn in this strong sun."

"I know, I'll try to keep covered. I'm going to be in the archives most of the time anyway. It's Mikke you'll have to keep an eye on."

Hannah snorted. "He'll tan like a berry, I'm sure," she said comfortably. "Jerrol always did at that age."

Taelia smiled. "I can't wait to see him. Let's hope we find him soon."

Hannah nodded, though her smile faded as if she wasn't so sure Jerrol was just going to pop up conveniently.

Taelia gazed out at the passing countryside. Stunted olive bushes and dry-stone walls lined the rolling slopes, fat succulent bushes sprouting in odd places, interspersed with brightly-coloured foliage covered in red and pink flowers. The sweet scent of blossom perfumed the air, and plumes of dust rose as the carriage passed by.

By the time they arrived at the palace, all the ceremony had dispersed, and Taelia thankfully stepped down into an empty courtyard. The glistening white walls of the palace rose around them, cylindrical towers with cone-shaped roofs reaching for the deep blue sky. Taelia gasped as she saw the ornate frescos leading the way into the palace.

As they were led through the marble-lined corridors, a small oasis of greenery and running water would appear in the intersections. The tiny gardens held a collection of elegant plants, scenting the air with their sweet perfume; a welcome relief from the sheer marble walls. They were led down another passage and shown into a large, airy chamber, where maids awaited them with offers of perfumed baths and soft towels to rid them of the grime.

Eager to accept the offer, Taelia was soon relaxing in the warm water, smiling as she heard Mikke squeal excitedly as Hannah gave him his bath. She floated in the water before making an effort to wash the salt and dust out of her hair. Dressing, she went to retrieve her daughter. She was determined to give Leyarille her bath. The children would be in bed and asleep in no time; the long journey must take its toll eventually.

Even Birlerion had found time to bathe. When he arrived to escort her to the king's chamber, his dark hair was slicked back, and he smelt of soap. His silvery-green uniform was clean and smart, reminding her of Jerrol's; or, she supposed, Jerrol's was reminiscent of his. It was difficult to believe Birlerion was from a past age. He fitted into their life so seamlessly, and she knew she would not be able to cope without him. Both Mikke and Leyarille responded to him without a peep of complaint.

His silver eyes were bright and alert in his intelligent face. High cheekbones and sharp angles were softened by a dimple in his chin. Such a striking young man, and yet he often managed to blend into the crowd. Taelia wasn't sure how he did it. She knew exactly where he was at all times. A sense of his presence remained with her, and she knew if she turned just so, he would be standing there. Similar to how she knew where Jerrol was. She caught her breath as she realised that was no longer true.

King Benedict looked immaculate. He wore a blue sash

across his chest, adorned with sparkling jewels and awards. He looked up from his desk as she approached. "Ah, Taelia, the children all settled?"

"Yes, thank you, Your Majesty."

"Good, good," he said, his mind obviously elsewhere.

"Is everything alright, Your Majesty?"

The king smiled. "We'll know after we've spoken to my daughter. She should be here soon. She insisted on speaking to me tonight, and I think you should hear what she has to say."

"Do you think your daughter's concern has something to do with Jerrol?"

"I am afraid my daughter *is* the cause of your husband's disappearance."

Taelia couldn't see how, but she obediently sat as directed and folded her hands in her lap. Birlerion stood by the wall with Fonorion, silently watching.

The Empress Melahney waddled into the king's chamber. She was heavily pregnant, and her lack of height meant that her girth was even more accentuated. Her face was red and perspiring, her blond hair hung limp around her face as she leant against the back of a gold brocade winged chair. She smiled drearily at her father. "Remind me not to get pregnant again," she said. "It really doesn't suit me."

The king hugged her and escorted her to a seat on the sofa. "Your mother struggled as well. I'm afraid you get it from her," he said with a sympathetic grin.

She mopped her face. "It's the heat. I seem to be hot all the time; I can't get cool."

"Be thankful it's not the height of the summer. It could be worse, you know."

"Don't!" The empress threw her hands up in horror. "This is bad enough." She mopped her face again and thankfully accepted a beaded glass of water, which she held against her cheek.

Taelia watched her sympathetically. She knew how hot her body had run towards the end of her pregnancy; add the Birtolian humidity and it would be twice as bad.

"Let me introduce Scholar Taelia Haven, Commander Haven's wife. She recently had a little girl."

Melahney smiled. "Yes, I saw you arrive. Such a beautiful baby, and you have a young boy as well?"

"Yes, Mikke is just over two now. I wanted to thank you for the lovely cradle you sent to my room; it was very thoughtful of you."

The empress waved her hand. "It was my pleasure. I hope you and your children will come and visit me. I don't get out much now, as you can see."

Taelia nodded. "The last few weeks are the most awkward."

"Especially when you are the size of a beached whale, like I am." She sighed, toying with her handkerchief before looking up at her father. "I was hoping Commander Haven would accompany you, but I didn't see him arrive."

"Ah, no, I have a feeling he came on ahead of us," Benedict replied.

The empress stared at him. "I can assure you he isn't here; we'd know if he'd arrived in the islands."

"Why did you want to see him?"

She twisted her handkerchief in her hands. "We have a problem. Geraine is acting strangely. I don't know why, and it's not always obvious, but he keeps coming out with odd requests and behaving as though someone is trying to restrain him. He is becoming crafty, keeping things hidden, from the ministers as well as his guards." She gestured towards the window. "We found him trying to sneak down to the harbour yesterday; he was searching for some fishing boat captain."

Benedict leaned forward and grasped her hands. "Take a deep breath and start from the beginning. When did you start noticing his behaviour? Did anything trigger it, do you think?"

Melahney frowned. "Not that I know of. We had the celebration of Continuance at the turn of the year. It's a celebration of the lives saved in the great floods; we honour the Lady and the fishermen who saved so many. The celebrations run for three days, starting in Molinti then on to Aguinti and ending in Senti, with the festival of life. I couldn't go this year, I wasn't well, but Geraine led the celebrations. It started after that, but I couldn't say whether it was connected." She looked at her father. "If it becomes known, it will cause civil unrest. If the ministers deem he is unfit to rule, then it will throw the succession into chaos."

"Who would benefit from putting the succession in turmoil?

"But that's just it. I don't know. Geraine is popular with the people. He has always put their needs first. He doesn't overly interfere in the policymaking; only if the ministers get a bit ahead of themselves. No one would want to see him deposed."

The king frowned in thought. "He hasn't met with any delegations recently from other kingdoms?"

"I don't think so. You'd have to speak with his secretary to be sure as I haven't been with him so much lately. I've not been sleeping well; I can't get comfortable, bad dreams."

"Dreams?" Taelia asked. "What were they about?"

"A terrible storm. I keep dreaming that we can't get high enough; you know, one of those dreams where no matter what you do, you can't escape it."

"And do you have the same dream each time?"

"Yes, or a variation of it. Sometimes I'm on a boat and we can't sail fast enough, or I've lost something and I can't find it, and there is always this approaching storm that I can't escape."

"Did something happen about two weeks ago? Did you call for help at all?"

Melahney looked at her in surprise. "How did you know?"

"What did you do?" Taelia kept her voice soft, even though she wanted to shake the information out of the empress.

"I wasn't sure if it was real or a dream. Geraine had been talking about the islands south of Duyli. They've had a shortage of water, and there is talk of relocating the people because the islands can't sustain them anymore, but the clan won't leave. Geraine wanted to send a representative, but none of the ministers wanted to go as it is quite remote.

"I dreamt of a fisherman. He held out his hand and said 'I'll go'. I was so relieved I accepted his offer, but the storm was approaching and his boat was engulfed in waves, and I called out to the Lady to help him, to help us. It seemed so real, but it was just a dream."

"I think it was more than a dream, my dear. I think you invoked the Oath and called the Oath Keeper to your side," Benedict said.

"But how? I didn't say the Oath, I'm sure I didn't. I only accepted the help that was offered. I didn't call anyone."

Benedict patted her hands. "The Oath has already been invoked by me. It is active. The words are lit by a golden glow above my throne, and they are currently pulsing an unbearable blue. You are my daughter. If you were in need and the Lady or even Lady Marguerite heard, she would send the Oath Keeper to help. Only we don't know where he is. Commander Haven vanished two weeks ago and hasn't been seen since."

Melahney gasped, her eyes widening in shock as she realised what he was saying. She looked at Taelia, "Taelia, honestly, I never meant to call anyone … but if you don't know where he is, why do you think I called him?"

"Because all the other kingdoms are at peace and you are worried," the king said gently. "Worried about your husband, your impending child, and the possible upheaval of your people. Something is happening here, and we need to discover what."

"Commander Haven isn't in Birtoli. We would know. The islanders would say if a stranger landed on their beach."

The king shrugged. "Maybe they don't realise who he is."

"But he would speak up, wouldn't he?"

"Not necessarily. We don't know his circumstances or what he has been sent to do."

"We'd know if he was here. The clans talk, share news. There is a network that runs between the islands; it's an early warning system. A shipping company provides it for free; they've been doing it for centuries. If anyone arrived within the last two weeks, we'd know about it by now," Melahney said, mopping her face.

"Well, wherever he is, we need to find him. Taelia is a Scholar of the Remargaren Chapterhouse. If you could get her into the archives, she'll start searching the reports to see if she can find anything."

"Of course, I'll see to it that you have access. The archives are in the old palace buildings down by the harbour. The ministers are located there as well, so they could probably assist with the latest reports that have come in from the islands." Melahney stood. "I'm so glad you are here; I feel much better already. I'd better return to my rooms; Geraine will be searching for me."

The king smiled at his daughter. "I'll spend some time with him tomorrow, maybe get him to show me the island, see if I can find out what is worrying him. Don't overexert yourself, my dear. Make sure you rest in this heat."

The king's smile descended into a frown as he watched her leave. "Melahney knows these people. If she says Jerrol isn't here, then he isn't here."

"But then, where is he?" Taelia exclaimed.

"Let's hope he's been wherever he is long enough to leave us some clues. Tomorrow, Roberion starts searching the islands. You and Birlerion search here in Molinti and I'll speak with the emperor. We reconvene tomorrow evening before dinner. I expect you all to accompany me." The king nodded his dismissal, and Taelia rose and curtsied before leaving the room to find her children.

7

DECU 25TH, 1123
MOLINTI, BIRTOLI

Jerrol awoke with the rising sun, stretched luxuriously, and then sat up as he remembered the night before. Gael was lost in his dreams, a gentle smile of wonder still on his face. Jerrol unravelled himself from his blankets; it was time to go home. He looked across at the *Mari Rose* and saw Marin and the lad that worked for him, Dion, moving about the deck. Marin acknowledged his wave, and Jerrol gently woke Gael. Movement could also be seen on Aiden's boat, where he was already casting off, a brief wave and they were gliding out of the harbour.

"Time to go home, lad," he said as he watched Gael awake.

Gael looked up at him before suddenly sitting up. He looked around with newly opened eyes. "Yes, time to go home," he agreed, getting ready to set the mainsail as they left the harbour, the *Mari Rose* close behind.

By midday, they were approaching the narrow entrance to Plini harbour, running under the large natural stone arch and into the narrow channel that led through the cliffs. Plini harbour was in a deep inlet that was gradually being eroded wider and wider by the relentless inrushing of water at each high tide. A natural arch marked the entrance, allowing egress through the towering cliff walls that made the approach intimidating. Still, the waters were so deep it was simple enough to navigate as long as you avoided the walls. Gael and Dion whistled and shouted, listening to the echoes bounce back off the sheer stone until the sheltered bay opened in front of them as they exited the channel.

The two boats sailed demurely up to the jetty, and Gael and Dion jumped down to tie them off. Jerrol hauled in the mainsail, folding the canvas deftly and tying it to the boom. He cast one last look around the deck, but Gael had tidied everything away and it all looked neat and tidy. He was obviously eager to rush into town and meet his friends.

"Granfer may have dinner ready for us when we get in," Jerrol pointed out.

Gael snorted. "As if. He doesn't know we're coming in tonight, and anyway, you know he's always out every evening on Lady's day and the week of moonset. He won't be at home."

Moonset was the last day of the month, when the Lady's Moon was in her final phase. It was the night when all fishermen relaxed and partied if they were in harbour, so most of them made sure they made port before then, as only madmen sailed without a moon.

"I don't know why you're in such a rush. You've got at least four or five days to catch up with your friends while I sail up to Vespers."

Gael hesitated. "You sure you don't need me to help? It's a long trip to Vespiri."

Jerrol ruffled his hair. "You'd only get bored. This trip is all paperwork. You can come with me on the next one."

"You promise?" Gael asked eagerly.

Jerrol rolled his eyes, but nodded and allowed the excited Gael to dash off as soon as they were berthed. He sluiced down the deck with buckets of seawater, rinsing out the chute and the holds below, the water draining out of the scuppers. Checking the salt tub, he made a note to purchase some more. Catching his skin on a rough edge, he gently rubbed the new calluses that had formed on the surface of his palms and fingers. The ropes and nets had taken their toll and hardened his skin. He flexed his right hand thoughtfully; his remaining fingers felt stronger and he no longer had to compensate.

The sky was clear and bright, the sun beating down on his back a constant companion. He squinted across the harbour. It looked like most boats were in for Moonset. Few vessels sailed on the seas at night, and none did without the moon. Marin had already disembarked, eager to return home to his wife. Jerrol unwrapped his logbook from the oilskin cloth and wrote the date. He sat staring at the numbers he'd written until his sight blurred. Sighing, he wrote a brief entry and put it away again.

He hauled his buckets across to the well at the end of the dock and ratcheted the buckets down and back up in the echoey darkness. Carrying them back, he carefully topped up their water barrel and resealed the lid tight to prevent it from being contaminated by salt spray. Stowing the buckets, he couldn't see any other reason to delay going into town.

The air was warm and balmy, and a soft scent of herbs drifted across the harbour, thyme and mint warmed in the sun. He sat on the bench and stared up at the town. A town at peace. He knew this town wouldn't exist in the future. The arch and the headland were lost to the sea; the harbour flooded by the sheer force of water, which would have been funnelled through the narrow entrance, the water level rising unchecked.

He shivered at the thought of all these people lost. Blamelessly leading their lives, oblivious to the powerful forces being recklessly thrown around them. He knew he wouldn't be able to get them to move; this was their home and had been for generations. He also knew there was no way he could save everyone from the impending disaster, but he didn't think that was why he was here. The Lady would destroy the bloodstone; the upheaval would follow. Not that there was any sign of it today.

Jerrol slowly walked up the track leading out of Plini harbour and into the town. Small houses were scattered along the valley floor and dotted along the gently rising valley sides. The village square was centrally positioned, taverns, eateries, and stalls jostling around the edges. The village was buzzing; the inns would be full tonight. A large roasting pit had been set up to one side of the square, where a whole sheep was being rotated over the flames, and the smell of roasting meat and garlic made his mouth water.

A tall broad-leafed tree spread its branches over much of the square. The massive trunk was twisted and knotted, the canopy thick and providing much-needed shade during the day and a sense of shelter in the evening. Youthful voices drifted down from above as youngsters scampered around in its branches.

A young man was serenading a group of couples seated around the fountain, and women called out requests, keeping him occupied. He was joined by an older man playing a wooden pipe, and as the couples started to dance, laughter drifted on the air.

Marin crossed the square towards him. "Jerven, come join us, we have a table under the tree."

Jerrol veered towards them and bowed in greeting at the petite, black-haired woman already seated. He sat on the wooden seat next to her as her face lit up in a smile of welcome. She wore colourful robes, which she draped around her, hiding her condition. Smiling genially at

Myriam, he accepted the glass of wine Marin offered him and relaxed in the peaceful atmosphere, trying to ignore his sense of unease.

"Marin was telling me about the trouble in Molinti; it was fortunate you were there," Myriam said as her dark eyes flashed in the candlelight.

"I had to stop them from taking Gael. I'm sure another brother or father would have stepped in if it was their family," Jerrol said.

Marin shook his head. "I'm not so sure. They were following like sheep, and if you hadn't spoken out, I'm half afraid I was going to be next."

"Do you think they will come here?" Myriam asked as she tapped her finger on the table.

"It's possible," Jerrol said. "Depends what they are after. Keep the Lady in your heart and stay away from them if they do. Encourage your neighbours to do the same."

Myriam shrank back against her husband, her eyes widening. "Do you think they mean harm?"

"Well, they didn't mean any good from what I saw," Jerrol said. "I'll mention it to the controller before I leave tomorrow. Marin, you do the same; at least he'll be warned."

They were interrupted as the serenading duo reached their table, and Myriam's concern eased as she listened to the music. "Oh, Marin, ask them to play our song," she whispered.

"Only if you'll dance with me," he replied, a smile in his eyes just for her. He turned and made the request, and theatrically, he extended his hand to his wife. She rose, laughing, and Jerrol watched them twirl around the small area. His attention was drawn back as an elegant young woman draped in bright yellow robes stopped by his side.

"When were you going to ask me to dance?" she asked as she glared down at him, her black eyes glittering with annoyance. Jerrol sighed internally as he rose. Surita. She wasn't mollified.

"I didn't see you," he said, keeping his voice soft. "Are you with your parents?"

"I'm with Giron. I can't sit around and wait for you forever."

"I never expected you to, but a life on the boats means extended trips away from home. It won't change any time soon."

"Excuses," she sniffed. "Marin manages it, and he is the same age as you. He's already joined and has family on the way."

Jerrol spread his hands as he tried to soothe the young woman. "I am sorry, Surita. I never said I intended to join with anyone right now. I have my brother to look out for and my Grandfather. I need to work to support them first."

Surita stilled as her pretty face paled in anger, her glossy, black hair coiling around her neck. "You had no intention of offering. I knew it, no matter what Gramma said. I knew you were a waste of time."

A stern-looking young man came up and grasped her arm. He shot Jerrol a warning glance. "Surita, come, this is our dance." Surita allowed herself to be dragged away, and Jerrol sat back down in relief. He ignored the daggered looks she threw at him as she twirled around in the arms of another man. He was relieved when the dance came to an end and the couples returned to their seats.

Marin shot him an amused glance. "Why is Surita throwing you nasty looks?"

Jerrol heaved a dejected sigh. "It seems I am not meeting her expectations and she has thrown me over for another."

"Don't look too sad or she'll be back." Marin muffled a snort of laughter.

Myriam hit him on the arm. "Don't, it's not funny. The poor girl has been pining for Jerven for months."

"Well, trying to make me jealous looks like it's going to backfire. I hope she likes Giron as he looks serious to me. He's unlikely to let go again; he's already warned me off."

"As if that would make any difference if you really wanted her," Myriam said. "If Marin ever looks at another woman, I'll scratch his eyes out."

Marin looked at her a little apprehensively. "Now, sweetheart, just because I look it doesn't mean anything, you know."

Myriam laughed. "It better not! If you know what's good for you."

"Oh, I know what's good for me, and she's sitting right here in front of me."

"Please, Marin, go canoodle somewhere private. We don't need to see it," Jerrol protested.

"You need to find yourself a good woman, Jerven, you don't know what you're missing." Myriam's smile faded at the expression on his face, and she changed the subject. "It must be time for food. That lamb has been making my mouth water all night. Marin, go see if it's ready."

Myriam glanced at Jerrol as Marin dutifully left. "I'm sorry, Jerven, that was insensitive of me. Of course you have someone. Surita never had a chance, even I knew that. I hope it all works out for you. It would be lovely to meet her one day."

"I'm afraid that won't be possible," Jerrol said, his gut churning.

Marin returned loaded with platters before Myriam could ask further, and the sight of roasted meat, flatbreads, and garlicky vegetable skewers took up all their attention.

Jerrol groaned in appreciation. "So much nicer than fish, even if I do say so myself."

"Blasphemy!" Marin grinned, wiping his greasy fingers on his bread.

"I know, but a nice change all the same." Jerrol looked around the square and smiled at the lazily replete folks relaxing in their chairs. "I doubt anyone is going to be able to move after that."

"You'd be surprised. The right song and they'll soon be up," Myriam murmured, rubbing her tummy.

"The right song," Jerrol repeated, an idea stirring as he watched the musicians reassemble. He rose and ambled over to them. Offering the men a drink while they settled down, he asked them where they got their songs from. "Do many songs get handed down over the years?"

"Most of the popular ones get passed from father to son. My granfer taught me most of the ones I know."

"How do you know which are the most popular? The ones that will last over centuries."

"Take this one fer'instance." The young man strummed a chord, which caught the attention of the people sitting near them. "See that reaction? They recognised it." He played a short burst of music and stopped. "A good story, an event, strong emotions linked to music that anyone can sing along to; that's what is memorable."

"I have some words. I've been writing a poem to a loved one. A song would be much better only I don't play any musical instrument. Do any of you write your own music? I want a song that will evoke emotion and that will last forever."

"Giorgi here writes his own stuff; play him something," the older man suggested.

The young man grinned and trilled off a cascade of notes. He began to sing a ballad about a man going off to find his fortune so he could win the hand of a pretty lady—a ripple of clapping encouraged him to continue with a flourish. "Come see me after, I'll take a look at your words," he offered as the group swung into one of the more popular square dances.

Returning to his seat, Jerrol made sure he kept his distance from the glowering Giron and the increasingly sulky Surita. He danced with Myriam and reluctantly declined the offer of a bed at their house at the end of the night. "I've got an early start, and anyway," he said with a twinkle, "I thought you two had some catching up to do."

"You were going to teach me the stars," Marin protested.

"When I return. I'm only away for a few days. I'll stop with you when I get back."

"Don't forget."

"I won't," Jerrol promised as he wandered over to the musicians. He handed the young man a piece of paper. "Giorgi, this is as far as I've got. Do you think you could set this to some music, something haunting but hopeful?"

Giorgi read the words slowly, frowning in thought. He pondered as he gazed at Jerrol. "Something to last for years? Can you leave it with me for a few days? I'll play around with some ideas. The lyrics are haunting enough, but it needs to be memorable so people will want to hear it often. It needs to become an anthem or a hymn." Giorgi's voice trailed off as he stared into the distance. He shook himself. "Leave it with me."

Jerrol nodded. "I'm away for a few days, but I'll find you when I return. You'll still be in Plini?"

"Yes, we're here until Lady's Day, the fourteenth, then we move on to Serrol on the west coast."

"I'll see you before then." They shook hands and Jerrol went back to his boat. He intended on being in Vespers within the week.

8

PRESENT DAY

JANU 31ST, 4128, MOLINTI, BIRTOLI

As the day drew to a close, Taelia sat alone, on the stone bench on the open rooftop terrace gazing sightlessly at the spectacular view. The sun was setting across the island, the water a continuously rippling molten orange. Small fishing boats bobbed at their moorings, dark silhouettes in the harbour.

She gently rocked Leyarille in the cradle that the empress had loaned her and crooned softly, breathing in the scent-filled air. Swathes of bright pink bougainvillaea and purple mint were draped down the walls, softening the building's edges and the glare of the sun. Her gaze focused on the single red sail of a boat, tacking around the tiny island in the harbour, one of the many small fishing boats heading for the network of rickety jetties that crawled out over the water and hung together precariously as tides swept them to and fro. A temporary structure made of slats of bleached wood which were swept away by the occasional squalls and storms and diligently replaced afterwards.

The sound of a guitar drifted in the evening air. A man's soft baritone from down below in the street, started to sing a jaunty sea shanty, encouraging his listeners to sing with him.

He strummed a merry tune as his audience laughed, and then he dropped a key and began a haunting love song. The hairs on her arms stood up as the words filtered into her mind. She stiffened. It couldn't be. She rushed to the balcony and teetered over the thick wall, trying to see who was singing, but she couldn't see him.

"Birlerion," she screamed.

Birlerion rushed out onto the balcony, his sword in his hand.

"That man, that man who's singing. Go and get him, now, don't let him escape. We must know who he is," she babbled, hysterically.

"Taelia, what's happened? What's the matter?"

"Now! Go and find out who he is, and bring him here," she insisted, pushing him towards the stairs.

"Who?" Birlerion stared at her bewildered as he slowly sheathed his sword.

Taelia huffed in exasperation and took a deep breath. "A man is serenading down below the balcony, probably to the customers in the café on the corner. Go and find out who he is. I want to speak to him, now. He was playing the guitar, and he just sang a - a lovely song. Now, Birlerion." She pushed him towards the archway that led to the lower floors.

"Alright, alright I'm going, just don't scare me like that. I thought you were being attacked or something."

"Sorry," she said. "Hurry before he leaves." She picked up the murmuring Leyarille, who was protesting at the cessation of movement. Her silver eyes stared up at Taelia in reproach. "Sorry lovey, I didn't mean to wake you up."

Birlerion soon returned, dragging an apprehensive young man and his guitar. His vivid blue eyes stood out in his tanned face, wide with concern. His blonde hair was tied back in a queue with a blue ribbon, which matched his eyes, and his short-waisted jacket and cut off trousers set off his slender figure, but Taelia wasn't interested in how he looked.

Birlerion introduced him. "This is Guidien. His father runs the taverna in the harbour. He sings his way around the bars and eateries each evening."

"Guidien. I apologise for the inconvenience, my name is Taelia Haven," Taelia began. "That song you just sang, about lost love. Where does it come from?"

Guidien frowned at her. "The Lost Traveller?"

"Is that what it's called? Do you know who wrote it?"

Guidien shrugged. "It is a famous love song, been around for centuries. Usually sung at joinings and celebrations. Gets the ladies emotional, y'know, always requested," he said with a grin.

"I can imagine," Taelia agreed. "Would you sing it again for me? Please?" Taelia pleaded as Birlerion frowned at her in concern.

"Well, I suppose so." The man leant over his guitar and tuned a couple of strings before beginning to sing. Taelia's lips parted in wonder, and Birlerion stiffened in shock.

"I made my love a promise that I would never leave,
But fate and oaths befell us and I left her there to grieve.
My heart she holds no matter where I've been
Every day I write a note and find ways to be seen.
I've travelled far from home, 'cross land and time and seas.
I promised her this song, so she'd believe in me.
I will always come back to you.

A desperate cry in the night, reft life away from me,
I never meant to leave her, nor my family.

I dream of her in my arms 'neath every rising moon
And plant a kiss upon her lips and vow I'll be home soon.
I've travelled far from home, 'cross land and time and seas.
I promised her this song, so she'd believe in me.
I will always come back to you.

I fill my days amongst the islands, learning where I am.
Sailing, fishing, diving, scouting out the land.
Pearls and gems, the waters gifts, glisten like your eyes,
Treasures hidden beyond my reach, horded, veiled, and wise.
I've travelled far from home, 'cross land and time and seas.
I promised her this song, so she'd believe in me.
I will always come back to you.

Troubles rise, storm clouds build, a blinding light, the
Captain shields
Waters boil and fire threatens, the Miracle's here, a promise
filled.
Far from home trials are suffered, yet honour and strength
prevail,
From icy shrouds to balmy waters, again the scout will sail.
I've travelled far from home, 'cross land and time and seas.
I promised her this song, so she'd believe in me.
I will always come back to you.

Find my heart, my home, my clan, standing tall and proud,
A lasting sign as firm we stood, 'gainst rising fury, storms,
and cloud.

> *My heart is hers, where'er I be*
> *Here or there or lost at sea.*
> *I've travelled far from home, 'cross land and time and seas.*
> *I promised her this song, so she'd believe in me.*
> *I will always come back to you.*

There was a long, drawn out silence after he finished, broken by Leyarille's wail of protest at her mother's grip. Taelia's eyes brimmed with tears as Birlerion came to stand beside her. Lifting Leyarille out of her arms, he hushed her gently.

Taelia turned towards him. "It's him, isn't it? He once said …" her voice choked, "he once said he would write terrible songs to leave me clues if ever he couldn't come home. H-he said he would kiss me under the Lady's moon every night until he came home." She burst into tears against Birlerion's chest.

Birlerion eased her onto the bench and wrapped an arm around her shoulders as he hugged her gently. "That is not a terrible song."

"No, it's the most beautiful song I've ever heard," Taelia sniffed, "and Jerrol wrote it. I know he did." She looked up at Guidien. "How do I find out more about that song? Is there an archive? A scholar's library anywhere?"

The young man gripped his guitar to his chest and took a step back at the desperate edge to her voice. "The songs are passed down from family to family around the fires. An elder may know more. I have heard that there are different versions of it out in the islands. I expect some verses meant more to some folks than others. I'm afraid I don't know if there is a record of the original song anywhere. As I said, it's ancient, written before the islands were overwhelmed by the great waves. When Birtoli was a young and upcoming empire."

"Before the great waves? When was that?" Taelia asked slowly, dread in her heart.

"The waves submerged most of the low islands when the Lady sundered the Bloodstone, over three thousand years ago. What's left is the archipelago you see today."

Taelia swayed, her face a sickly grey. Birlerion held her tight. "Don't assume the worst," he murmured in her ear. "You know how Jerrol always wins through." He gave her a reassuring hug. "I think we need to speak to the king." He looked at Guidien. "Could you write down the words that you know? All the verses you've heard of and can remember? And any detail you can remember about the song and its origins? We'll make it worth your while. Maybe even a performance for the King of Vespiri?"

The young man swallowed, visibly shocked. "It would be my honour to play for the king," he said and then shrugged. "It would be my pleasure."

"If you would wait here for a moment, I will return." He escorted Taelia inside and sent a servant to request an audience with the king. Taelia allowed herself to be led to her room so she could gather her composure and soothe Leyarille while Birlerion dealt with Guidien. She sat in the chair and gazed down at her feeding daughter. Her heart melted as she watched her daughter's content face. She rocked her gently and allowed herself to hope.

Tucking Leyarille in the cradle that was now returned to her rooms, she stood, gently rocking her until Birlerion came to find her. Silently, he handed her the papers. She read the words, tears spilling over, and she gasped as she reached the penultimate verse.

The rising words an emperor's burden, words by which he's
bound
Warn the people, prepare the defences, climb to higher
ground.
I hope the ones who search will gaze upon my trail
For Sentinals blazing can traverse the veil.
I've travelled far from home, 'cross land and time and seas.
I promised her this song, so she'd believe in me.
I will always come back to you.

She looked up in shock. "What does it mean?" she gasped.

Birlerion shrugged. "I'm not sure. At a guess, I would suggest the Ascendants found Birtoli all those years ago. They would have searched here as they did elsewhere. Guidien said that verse is rarely sung as people don't understand its meaning, but it's been passed down anyway.

"Maybe Jerrol was sent here to stop them. It's possible there are other verses out in the islands as Guidien suggests. That will help us understand more. It certainly sounds as if Jerrol left us a trail of clues to follow and the Sentinals are the ones to follow them.

"I suggest we speak to the king in the morning. There's nothing he can do tonight, and it's getting late. He's expecting us for breakfast. We can tell him then. I have Guidien's details if we need to call him back."

Taelia reluctantly nodded in agreement.

9

―――――

PRESENT DAY

FEBU 1ST, 4128, MOLINTI, BIRTOLI

Taelia and Birlerion arrived outside the king's rooms early the next morning. Darris raised an eyebrow at their prompt appearance but let them in. Benedict was standing on the balcony, looking over the rolling countryside and out towards the sea. He was dressed in a loose-fitting blue robe, his dark-hair tied back in a queue. Taelia was struck by how handsome he was. She had never really seen him as a person before. He was usually hidden behind the facade of the king. Seeing him display his concern for his daughter and her children had broken a barrier that she wasn't sure they would be able to build again.

Fonorion stood beside him, his silent shadow. Never far away.

Taelia bobbed a quick curtsey as the king turned away from the view. "Apologies, sire, for disturbing you so early, but we have news."

The king indicated the chairs and joined them at the table. "So soon?"

"Last night I overheard a minstrel singing a song, this song," she said, passing the paper over to the king. "I think Jerrol wrote it."

"What makes you think that?"

"He said he would never stop trying to find ways to get back to me. He said that he would write me a song. I think this is him trying to send a message."

The king read the lyrics, his eyes slowing as he reached the bottom of the page. He reread them more slowly.

"It describes his situation. He's trying to get home. It mentions the Sentinals following his trail," Taelia persisted.

"Are you sure this is Jerrol?"

"Yes, I'm sure," Taelia replied, holding his gaze. "The only problem is that this song was written before the Lady sundered the Bloodstone, which suggests that the reason we can't find him here,' she swallowed, "is because he isn't here *now*. He's gone back in time, and he's sending us clues and messages in the words. We have to figure out what they mean."

The king's jaw dropped, though he snapped it shut quickly enough.

"I can research the final days before the great waves for any mention of the Ascendants in the archives. Roberion can search the islands for news of him and the song. Birlerion can go down to the harbour and find out who the families are that run the fishing boats. Jerrol says those who search should follow his trail, so there has got to be evidence of him somewhere, even if it's just in the census."

"I'm not going to say you're crazy, because we have living proof of people moving between time before us, but …" Words failed the king. "It sounds like you have a plan, but I'm not going to believe he has gone back in time as a Birtolian fisherman until you find me some proof."

"I'll find it, Your Majesty," Taelia promised. Even though the king smiled, she knew he didn't believe her. Her smile faded as she thought of the dangers Jerrol could find himself in, alone and unprotected. She saw by the serious faces of the Sentinals that they had already reached the same conclusion.

Later that morning, Birlerion stared out across the harbour at the colourful boats bobbing at the moorings. He breathed in the warm salty air and sighed. The only reassuring thing in this whole situation was that both he and Fonorion had agreed that the Captain was alive, a fact that he knew Taelia clung to.

He had escorted Taelia to the archives earlier, and he was sure she wouldn't be weaseled out of there until she found something. He was glad the king had demanded her presence at dinner; otherwise, she would work all night. Though, to be fair, she would not neglect Leyarille or Mikke.

He strolled down to the quay, where the *Lady's Miracle* was moored. Taelia had been strict in her instructions. He smiled to himself. Roberion was about to go off on an impromptu trip around the islands. He hoped he hadn't given all of his sailors shore leave. He strolled up the gang-plank and onto the deck, acknowledging the sailor on duty.

"The captain's in his cabin, sir," the man said.

"Thank you," Birlerion replied as he crossed the deck and tapped on the door.

Roberion's deep voice bid him come, so he entered the shadowy cabin, a relief after the glaring sun.

"Birlerion, what news?"

"Nothing if it's the Captain you're after, though we believe we might have found his trail. Taelia's up at the archives searching now."

"Well, that's a start at least."

"Well, a small one; all we have are the words of a three-thousand-year-old song."

"Oh, yes? Which one?"

"The Lost Traveller."

Roberion frowned. "I think I may have heard that one; isn't it about a man parted from his family or something?"

"We think Jerrol wrote it for Taelia."

Roberion froze. "No. You can't mean you think he's gone back …"

"Yes, we do think that. We think Jerrol's gone back in time to before the Lady sundered the Bloodstone."

"But, how? Why now?"

Birlerion ran his hands through his hair. "Who knows how the Lady works. All we know is that the song was written before the islands were flooded."

"Oh my, it does rather fit, now you mention it. But Birlerion, it has a tragic ending. The man dies."

"What? The song we heard didn't say that."

"Let me call Jacob, he'll know all the words. Many songs have different versions, you know. People add or remove verses, depending on the occasion." Roberion rose and yelled for Jacob.

A rangy, disreputable-looking sailor responded to the summons. A silver scar ran down the side of his face and puckered the skin, but his blue eyes looked alert enough in the dim cabin. "Cap'n?"

"You know the song The Lost Traveller, don't you?"

"Yes, Cap'n"

"Sing it for us."

"Now?" Jacob gave his captain a searching glance, probably wondering if he'd been out in the sun too long.

"Yes, now, I need to hear all the verses you know."

Jacob shrugged and opened his mouth. A surprisingly smooth tenor emerged as he sang the verses that Birlerion had already heard before his voice deepened and he sang the final verse. Goosebumps rose on Birlerion's skin as he listened.

"He sailed the seas searching for what he could not find
He called upon the Lady, though he was before his time.
The storms they did descend on us, his brother he left
waiting,
The *Island Scout* saved many lives, but not that of the Captain.
He travelled far from home, 'cross land and time and seas.
He promised her this song, so she'd have her memories."

There was silence in the cabin after he finished, and Birlerion stared at Roberion, aghast. Roberion nodded at Jacob. "Thank you. Could you write that final verse out for me as soon as possible?"

"Yes, Cap'n," Jacob said and left.

"It doesn't mean it happened that way, it's just a song," Roberion said.

"But it's possible it does. We can't let Taelia see this."

"She may find it for herself; you can't let her stumble across it."

"We can't put her through that again. The uncertainty about whether or not Jerrol survived almost destroyed her last time."

"She has her children now, she has us. You know perfectly well that he is still alive. We have to figure out how to get him back, before anything does happen to him." Roberion tapped a finger on his desk. "*Island Scout*, that name rings a bell." He twisted and reached for a leather-bound book sitting on the shelf behind him. He flipped through the pages. "Ah, here we are. *Island Scout*, a fifty-foot, single hull fishing boat, trades for the Jerven Fishing fleet out of Senti. I've been trading with them out of Selir for years. They trade goods, fish, carry the mail. The Jerven line is a big company; Taelia should be able to find them easily."

"There was another verse that we heard that's not in your version, look." Birlerion handed the song sheet over, tapping the verse that mentioned Sentinals searching. "Apparently it's not sung often as it doesn't make much sense."

"I hope the ones who search will gaze upon my trail, For Sentinals blazing can traverse the veil." Roberion read aloud. "He believes we can reach him? Using the veil? But how?"

Birlerion shrugged. "That's what we need to find out. There may be other verses like that one out in the islands; maybe in Senti if that's where he is. Taelia wants you to go and find out."

"Me?"

"You're the one with the boat."

"Ship," Roberion corrected absently.

"Ship, then; you're the only one who can go and search the islands for us. Find us the missing verses, we need to know what they say."

"I'll need better maps of the outer islands. I don't want to run aground on the reefs."

"Get them then, find word of the Captain. He's out there somewhere on his own, and we need to find him."

Roberion nodded slowly. "I'll recall the crew, but we should be able to sail for Senti before nightfall and start there."

"I'll leave you to it. Send word via Ari if you find anything."

"I'll try. He's been in a bit of a panic ever since the

Captain disappeared. All he ever does is scold when I see him, as if I know where the Captain went."

"Much like the rest of us, then," Birlerion laughed grimly as he left.

Taelia leaned back in her chair and eased her aching back. It had been quite easy to find a prominent family in the fishing industry; the most probable candidate was the owners of a fleet of fishing boats owned by the Jerven family of Senti. A fisherman called Jerven had begun building a homeport for his fleet in 1123 in a place he called Senti. He bought the land and built the harbour from scratch. He'd gradually added to his fleet the *Island Scout, Moonlight Kiss,* and the *Mari Rose*. Taelia had caught her breath when reading the other boats listed: *Mikke's Ride* and *Lady Leya*. It was obvious it was Jerrol. The fleet always had boats that held those names. If one was lost at sea, although rare, it did happen, or if one retired due to old age, the next replacement would take the name.

The Jerven family still lived in Senti, running their fishing fleet and boatyard, managing the harbour. The family had an office in the harbour in Molinti. When Birlerion arrived, they would go down and speak to them. On that thought, she closed the books, leaving her marker in the page for the next day, and stacked them ready to return to the shelves. She let herself out and walked out of the building and down towards the harbour.

Taelia sat on the harbour wall and watched the small fishing boat with the red sail leave the harbour. She looked up as a shadow paused beside her and realised it was the little Transport Minister from the archives. He was a dapper little man with thinning hair and sharp brown eyes. He peered at her through small round spectacles perched on his nose. He kept rubbing his hands through his jacket collar as if he had some nervous twitch.

"Was everything as you needed, madam?" he asked.

"Oh yes, thank you, I will continue tomorrow. I needed to take a break."

"Yes, some of those old scripts can be difficult to read. We have some that are worse, faded with age. Not much we can do about that. If there is anything further I can help you with, please do let me know."

"Whose boat is that? With the red sail. It is very industrious, back and forth between the islands," Taelia asked.

The little man peered out to sea. "That is the *Island Scout.*"

Taelia jerked in shock. "The *Island Scout?*"

"Yes, one of the fishing vessels belonging to an old Senti family, been running between the islands for years. They always have one vessel named *Island Scout* in memory of the founder's first boat, the fishing boat captain who started the business, oh, centuries ago. They trade between the islands, provide a much-needed lifeline for many isolated communities."

Taelia breathed out frustration. She should have just asked instead of wasting all that time buried in musty manuscripts, but then corroboration was always a good thing. "Which family is it?" Taelia asked, idly rubbing her neck.

"The Jervens. As I say, the family dates back centuries; a respected family. Their elder will travel here for the state dinner next week. Their business is key to our trading agreement with both Vespiri and Terolia. They give us a much-needed route into those markets through the agreement that the first captain put in place. The taxes and duties they pay keep the economy running. As I said, extremely important, extremely important." The little man repeated to himself.

"Dear Minister, could I ask that you introduce me to Elder Jerven next week? I would be honoured to meet him."

"Certainly, my dear, certainly." The little man puffed out his chest importantly before clucking to himself, nodding benevolently at Taelia, and taking himself off.

"Jerven," Taelia repeated softly. Could it really be that simple?

10

DECU 26TH, 1123
WEST COAST OF BIRTOLI

The coastline passed off his starboard bow as Jerrol skirted the island of Amrilti. The makers of Amri crafted the most exquisite jewellery out of the pearls, shells, and gems that they dived for in the depths of the surrounding seas. Amrians were expert deep-sea divers, able to hold their breath much longer and swim much deeper than the average person. They benefited from a rich coral reef that curved up and round, parallel to the coast; the reef shelved off into the deepest, darkest waters a mile or so offshore. The area was dotted with small skiffs, shining brown bodies diving into the water, and a short while later slick, black heads bobbed back up like basking seals and climbed back out with their drawstring nets full. Jerrol kept his distance.

He would love to get Taelia a necklace of turquoise gems the colour of her eyes, which was the the colour of the sea around all the islands. The clear blue waters reminded him of her and Mikke every day, such a vibrant colour that matched their eyes, but he sailed on; he didn't have time for side trips if he wanted to return to her arms. Shivering, he pulled on a canvas jacket over his thin shirt; not much help as the temperature cooled as he travelled north. It hadn't taken long to acclimatise to the light and warmth of the south.

Jerrol sailed into the port of Vespers on a cold and misty morning, two days later. He frowned at the lack of vessels in the harbour. There was only one other boat leaning against the wharf, which was being unloaded. He tied his boat to the sturdy jetty, leading up to the single storey warehouse fronting the water, and gaped at how small and unassuming the port had become.

He had not thought it through. If he was in a Remargaren of three thousand years ago, of course everything would be simpler; less advanced than he expected, less populated. He swallowed, his throat tight. What if he couldn't find the Sentinals? Would they even speak to him? The sheer contradiction of what he was trying to do suddenly overwhelmed him. How much should he tell them? Would they even believe him? Would he come face to face with the Lady or her Captain? And if so, what should he say? His stomach roiled as panic clutched him.

Take it one step at a time, he told himself. *Pay the docking fee and get to a temple.* He should take some time to compose himself before searching for the Sentinals. He had no idea who would be in Vespers; they could be anywhere. He suddenly stopped dead. What if he came face to face with Serillion or any of the others lost at Oprimere? He was torn between wanting to see them, to embrace them again, and trying not to burst into tears.

Forcing himself to take a step, and another, he concentrated on getting off the jetty and up to the port master's hut. Offering the man seated behind the desk the docking fee, Jerrol sighed out his relief as the man took the coins, aguins were the only currency he had. In the islands, trade was mainly made by barter; there was little need for coins. He hoped he had enough for one day and that he would be able to sell some of his pearls.

Jerrol followed the muddy track up the hill and out of the port. The air was moist and fresh after recent rainfall, and after weeks of balmy, salt laden air, he breathed in the musky-sweet smell of rotting vegetation as winter set in. He walked along the edge of the track as sturdy mules nodded their way past him, dragging woven mats loaded with goods across the ground. The track curved around a copse of trees and Jerrol stopped dead. He had nodded and smiled when his friends, Birlerion and Tagerill, reminisced on the beauty of the Lady's city, but he had never truly understood what they meant until now.

The city of Vespers, spread out before him, was beyond anything he had imagined, from the crude port to this sophisticated arrangement of golden buildings and domed temples. The most beautiful and delicate structure, sparkling in the weak sunlight, spanned the air between the sturdy golden towers of what he knew to be the original Chapter-house of the Lady's Order of Remargaren to the silver spires of the palace of the Lady, standing ethereal and magical atop the headland above. His eye was drawn back to the Captain's bridge. Words did not capture the beautiful delicacy of the gossamer threads that framed the structure and curled and swirled towards the Lady's palace in sheer joy. A soft smile spread over his face as he stared.

The air was perfumed with the scent of roses, even though it was the depths of winter, and Jerrol was reminded of Tagerill's love of roses, now he understood why. The scent soothed and uplifted the spirit. Tagerill often mourned the loss of the Lady's roses in Old Vespers. As Jerrol gawped, the soft tone of the quarter bell chimed across the city, it's deep note resonating through his bones and reminding him that time was passing. History stood before him, and he was overwhelmed until he was jostled from behind by a flock of sheep being herded by a shepherd down the track. The animals milled around him, bleating forlornly.

He extricated himself from the flock and entered the city through a tall, welcoming arch of golden stone so tightly packed that the surface was completely smooth. It was connected to a thick defensive wall, which circled the whole city. He made his way to the Lady's temple; the same temple that stood in Old Vespers in his time.

The simple structure gleamed in the weak sunlight. The white marble reflected the light, topped by an impossible dome and surrounded by well-tended formal gardens, planted with delicately scented rose bushes. A large oak tree guarded the entrance, but there was no graceful sentinal tree hovering over the temple; it didn't look right without it. He hesitantly entered through the arched porch and made his way up to the white marble altar, where he prostrated himself on the stone-paved floor and prayed fervently for help and guidance.

The reply was silence, and he suddenly wondered if he was praying to the wrong Lady. Maybe he should be pleading with Marguerite? But her voice was worryingly absent. He frantically tried to remember his history. He wasn't sure where Marguerite was in 1123; maybe she hadn't bonded with the land yet. After all, there didn't seem to be any air of concern in the city, considering impending doom was on the horizon.

And there was another conundrum; should he warn them? What could he say without causing absolute mayhem in his own time? Was he supposed to try and avert disaster now? Was that even possible? He somehow doubted it, but if not, then what was he here for? How was he supposed to know?

He breathed out doubt and breathed in strength, focusing on the discipline of the air, and brought his ragged breathing under control. The cold stone beneath him finally made him lever himself up onto his knees, and he exhaled. Find the Sentinals, and what would be, would be.

Jerrol froze as he heard Birlerion's voice behind him. Slowly, he turned his head, and there he was, dark-haired and lean, exactly as he knew him. He felt absurdly reassured at the familiar sight, and he caught his breath, Birlerion's brother, Tagerill, stood beside him, his red hair glinting in the candlelight, an irrepressible grin on his face. Both were tall and straight, dressed in the Lady's uniform and wrapped in nice warm cloaks, silver eyes gleaming and somehow looking younger and more carefree.

They both genuflected in front of the altar and then knelt in sober prayer before rising and moving over to light a candle on the bench by the wall. Jerrol followed as they left. He dithered. How to approach them? He didn't know what to say.

The difficulty was taken out of his hands as Tagerill suddenly wheeled and blocked his way. "Kind sir, is there something we may do for you?" he asked, an edge to his voice.

"I'm not sure, Sentinal Tagerillion." Jerrol nodded at Tagerill and then Birlerion. "Sentinal Birlerion. I have a story for you, but I'm not sure whether you will believe it." His stomach fluttered at the sight of Birlerion's unmarred face; he had yet to suffer the agonies of Adeeron.

Tagerill's eyes narrowed, and then he suddenly grinned and clapped Jerrol's shoulder. "Then you'd better tell us and let us decide." He turned to Birlerion. "It's time for lunch, anyway."

Birlerion rolled his eyes. "And I suppose you have an inn selected already?"

"Let me lead you to the most succulent lunch you will experience today," Tagerillion said, gesturing grandly.

"You mean the only lunch I will experience today." Birlerion sighed. "Lead on."

"Um, I'm not sure I have the coin for a succulent lunch," Jerrol murmured, thinking of his empty purse.

"Then your payment will be the story and we will provide the lunch," Tagerill said as he tucked his arm in Jerrol's and almost dragged him down the path.

Jerrol allowed himself to be dragged. Maybe the Lady was watching him, after all? Tagerill led them to a small inn behind the Chapterhouse. It looked a little forlorn, but a jaunty sign depicting a smiling dog with its tongue hanging out creaked on a pole in front.

"The Laughing Dog, famous for its lamb stew." Tagerill grinned.

"Famous for what they put in it? Or the fact that it's edible?" Birlerion asked, his lips twitching.

Tagerill looked affronted but led the way into the taproom.

The room was filled with crude wooden tables and benches, a few occupied, but most were empty. Birlerion slid into the rear seat, leaning back against the wall while his gaze darted over the exits and the other patrons. Tagerill smiled easily, his alert eyes betraying the fact that he was not wholly playing the fool. He indicated the bench. "Please sit. You have our names; would you be so kind as to share yours?" he asked as he slid in beside Jerrol, neatly trapping him.

"My name is Jerven, I'm a fisherman from the island of Senti in Birtoli. I'm afraid my name will mean little to you now, but I ask that you remember it and my story for the day when it will mean something."

Birlerion frowned. "The island of Senti? You lie; there is no such island."

Jerrol nodded his head. "You are right, of course, but in my time, it is an island on its own. The Empire of Birtoli is drowned by rising floods and Plini is lost; only the higher ground remains, peering above the greedy waters."

Tagerill flicked a sharp glance at Birlerion. "Maybe you ought to start at the beginning," he suggested. "You are far from home and maybe a little confused." He raised his hand and ordered their food when a young woman responded to his signal.

"Far from home, indeed, across land and time and seas." Jerrol heaved a heartfelt sigh as he bore Birlerion's intent inspection. He flexed his damaged hand, drawing Birlerion's eye, and Birlerion winced in sympathy.

"Far from home?" Birlerion asked.

"And family. I miss them dearly and need to get back to them."

"Them?"

"My wife, Taelia, son, Mikke, and a new daughter, Leyarille."

"What's stopping you?"

"Time," Jerrol said bluntly.

Tagerill stilled next to him. "Time?" he asked.

Jerrol shrugged and then dropped his face in his hands. "I'm in the wrong time. I'm supposed to do something for the Lady, or maybe Marguerite, I'm not sure, only I don't know what and I can't find my way home."

There was a stunned silence. "Marguerite?" Birlerion asked.

"Yes, the Lady of the Land; is she still here or has she bonded?"

"She is at the palace with her sister, Leyandrii. What do you mean by bonded?"

Jerrol looked up, gripping his hands together as he tried to organise his scattered thoughts. Seeing his Sentinals looking so well had jarred him. "It doesn't matter. What *does* matter is that I need your help. In my time, when you wake up, and you will wake up, you need to go to Birtoli after my daughter is born and follow the trail. I will leave you clues in anything I can think of that will stand the test of time. Keep an open mind; nothing is impossible. I can't come home without you, please believe me and remember," he pleaded. "The Ascendants are driven, they will stop at nothing; they will destroy all before they are satisfied. Don't believe their platitudes. They lie, they destroy, and they kill," he said. "I need your help; you are my best friends. My family and I need you."

Tagerill stared at him. "I think you are mistaking us for some other acquaintance; we have never met," he said, his voice gentle.

"But we will. All I ask is that you remember, nothing more."

"We will never forget this conversation, I can assure you." Birlerion smiled. "Worth a lamb stew, that's for sure. So, tell us more about life in Birtoli. I've never had the chance to visit." He gestured to the serving girl to pass the bowls of steaming stew.

Jerrol described his boat, the *Island Scout,* his brother Gael, and the circuit, hoping the more detail he gave, the more likely they would remember. After all the destruction and despair they would go through, he needed to stand out as much as possible. He went on to wax lyrical about the beauty of the sea and the exotic island reefs and blue lagoons, painting a picture as strange and unreal as possible to two city-bred soldiers; vivid images he hoped would stick in their minds. He even mentioned the Tu'ani and their belief that strife was on the horizon, an oblique reference to the troubles looming for all.

"Well," Tagerill said with a lazy grin as he leaned back from the table, his bowl empty. "I'll say that was worth the price of a meal."

"I thank you for the meal, and I would ask one last boon if I may?"

"You can ask," Birlerion said, watching him.

Jerrol grinned, and Birlerion instinctively smiled back.

"I wanted to find out about setting up some trade agreements. I have goods to trade here in Vespiri, only I don't know how to go about it, who to talk to."

"What type of goods?" Tagerill asked with interest.

"Fish, shells, samphire, pearls, and some gems. I have a boat, the *Island Scout*. I need an outlet for the goods."

"I would suggest you speak to the trade office. The administrators there would be able to set up a trade agreement for you. You will find their office in the Chapterhouse," Tagerill replied.

"And Sentinals Serillion and Roberion, where would I find them?"

"Serillion? Definitely in the Chapterhouse. He will be knee-deep in manuscripts, I expect. Roberion now, that's a little more difficult. He's likely to be off the coast of Terolia somewhere, but where?" Tagerill shrugged. "You probably know the winds better than we do."

Jerrol grinned in appreciation. "I thank you for the meal and the information; I look forward to meeting you again."

"Somehow, I am sure we will. I wish you luck on your ventures, and I sincerely hope you find your family soon," Birlerion said.

Jerrol nodded his thanks, his throat thick with emotion and reluctant to leave them. He endured Tagerill's scrutiny and exhaled when Tagerill finally rose and let him slide along the bench and leave.

Jerrol made his way back to the Chapterhouse, comforted by the fact that the Sentinals had followed at a distance. Even though they were probably suspicious of him, their presence eased the tension building within him.

Approaching the administrator on duty and explaining what he needed, Jerrol took the proffered papers over to a bench where he began filling them out. Once he had completed the forms, he returned to the administrator's desk.

"That's 40 orbols," the administrator said as he shuffled the papers into a pile.

Jerrol's heart sank. Rummaging in the pouch at his belt, he offered a handful of creamy pearls in payment for the fee, but the administrator shook his head.

Birlerion drifted closer. "Is there a problem?"

Jerrol looked over at him. "I don't have the right coin."

"What do you need?"

"40 orbols or four talents."

"Well, I can loan you four talents for two of those pearls, held against you paying me back the next time we meet," Birlerion suggested.

Jerrol jerked his eyes up to meet Birlerion's. "You'd do that for me?"

Birlerion grinned. "Two pearls are worth more than four talents, which I am sure the administrator knows if he has any sense."

"Four pearls against me paying you back the next time we meet," Jerrol said firmly, hoping the pearls would be another reminder of their meeting.

Birlerion ducked his head. "You drive a hard bargain,"

he said, dropping four talents on the table in front of the administrator.

The administrator melted a stick of wax in the candle flame, dripped it on the paper, and pressed a seal into the resultant pool. He scribbled his signature and handed a copy back to Jerrol, who dropped four gleaming pearls into Birlerion's hand and turned away from the desk, tucking the paper in his shirt.

He froze as he came face to face with Serillion; his heart stuttered and he struggled to breathe. Birlerion placed a hand under his arm to steady him as he swayed, then leaned his head closer as Jerrol muttered a desperate plea under his breath. "Lady help me." His shaking hand strayed to the stone pendant at his throat. An unconscious gesture, one he had made many times over the years since he had found it, of drawing support from the Lady.

Birlerion gripped Jerven's arm and stared at Serillion, whose complexion had similarly paled.

Tagerill looked from Jerven to Birlerion and back to Serillion in some bewilderment. "What? You asked to meet Serillion. Well, here he is. Serillion, do you know Jerven of Birtoli?"

"I didn't necessarily ask to meet you, I just enquired where you were," Jerrol said, his voice faint as he stared at the slight blond-haired young man in front him, clever and bookish, a quiet historian. The man he had let die.

Serillion frowned. "Why?"

"I wondered if you were here in Vespers, and if you were, if I could build up the courage to come and see you," Jerrol said, running his hand through his salt-encrusted hair.

"Why?" Serillion asked again, more intense; his silver eyes bright.

Jerrol scrunched up his face as he struggled to put his thoughts into words. "I-I just wanted to say how sorry I am. I can't explain why. Birlerion and Tagerill can tell you what I've already told them. We will meet again, in another time …" he faltered. "I never meant for it to end like it did. I wish it could have been otherwise."

Serillion considered him for a moment and then shrugged as a slow smile spread over his face. "So Tagerill's tales are true for once?" Tagerill snorted, and Serillion chuckled. "He is known for his tall tales. I wasn't sure whether to believe him or not. What I do know is that what will be, will be. The Lady guides our steps for a reason, and if she needs me to do whatever it is that I do, then I am prepared to do it," he said, his voice determined. "There is no blame to lay, and you should have no need to apologise for whatever I choose to do. We are all here for a reason, and we are uniquely placed to fulfil whatever task is demanded of us, some more than others, but no less honoured for it," he said, gripping Jerrol's shoulder. "Do not take blame where it is not owed," he said softly, for Jerrol's ears only.

"I c-can't help it," Jerrol stuttered, and he rubbed his face with a shaky hand. He was speaking to Serillion. One of the first Sentinals he had awoken and who he had never truly had a chance to get to know. All he really knew was that he was one of Birlerion's best friends. He was suddenly thankful that he had seen the three of them together, relaxed and unconcerned, subtly different and yet in full accord. "I need to return to Birtoli, but I need to sell my fish first. I wondered if the cook here would be interested."

Serillion's eyes brightened. "I'll make sure of it," he said with a grin. He linked his arm in Jerrol's and hauled him off to the kitchens. Tagerill and Birlerion followed, bemused.

"Saul," Serillion hailed the large man in charge of the kitchen. "It's time you updated your menu; you have the option of some fine fish for our table."

The red-faced cook looked up from the cauldron he was

stirring. He frowned at Serillion. "And what would you know of fish?"

"My friend Jerven supplies the best fish in Vespiri, and he has come to you first, even before the palace. He shows great initiative. Fish is good for the brain cells; our scholars need the stimulus."

Saul laughed. "You mean, you do?"

"Oh, come on, Saul, take a look," Serillion wheedled. "A chance of fresh fish. What harm would it do?"

Saul rolled his eyes, but he pulled the cauldron off the heat and turned to Jerrol. "What do you have?"

"Caught and salted yesterday; eleven crates of mullet, two of brannock, two sacks of shellfish. I can get phrist, sardines, even samphire if you place a regular order."

The cook's eyes brightened. "Which boat?"

"*Island Scout*, Jerven shipping. I have a regular route, once every two weeks, but we could do weekly if there is demand."

The cook nodded thoughtfully. "Show me your fish and then I'll decide. I have half a chime now; let's go take a look."

Serillion grinned at Jerven and slapped him on the shoulder. "Come on, we'll help you unload, and these two strapping lads will help," he said with a grin at the Sentinals watching them from the door. "He'll take it once he sees it. We don't get fresh fish often; it all goes up to the palace. We'll walk you back to the harbour." He linked his arm in Jerrol's and led him out of the kitchens. Tagerill and Birlerion exchanged exasperated glances and followed.

"Don't worry that we might have other things to do," Birlerion said as the deep-toned bell chimed four, and there was a clatter of doors and footsteps as scholars made their way through the corridors.

"You wouldn't be standing there if you did," Serillion replied.

"Well, now you have a line on your fish supply, please don't let us stop you."

Flashing a grin at his friend, Serillion dragged Jerrol through the corridors. "Ignore him. Birlerion can be stuffy sometimes. Once you get to know him, he's a really good guy."

"Stuffy!" Birlerion's outraged voice followed them, and Jerrol grinned as they continued to bait each other as they left the Chapterhouse.

"Tell me," Jerrol said, glancing at his friends as they walked back to the harbour, "the Captain's bridge; what is its purpose?"

Serillion burst out laughing.

A little later, Jerrol grinned to himself as he steered his boat out of Vespers harbour. He had revelled in the unexpected companionship of his friends; even though they didn't know him, they had been generous and kind. The cook had taken all his fish and placed a regular order every two weeks to begin with and paid good coin for it as well.

He hugged the knowledge that the Captain's bridge had no other purpose than to prove that the Captain could build it, and he chuckled as he remembered Serillion's laughter, at peace at last with the loss of his friend.

The Sentinals had admired his boat but been somewhat concerned with him sailing it out on the open sea and at night, even to the extent of offering to pay for another day's mooring, but he knew he couldn't stay; he felt that he was on borrowed time and he needed to get back. The Sentinals were vocal in their preference for the somewhat larger vessels that the administrators commissioned.

He headed out to sea, making sure he skirted the Vespiri

shoals that caught many sailors unawares, and set sail for his home in Plini. He was sure Gael was going to be annoyed at being left behind when he heard he had met the Sentinals, but Gael could come on the next visit now that he had permission to trade. Once he got back, they would have to go on another circuit of the islands before he would have a chance to search for Roberion. He wondered what he should say to him; maybe by then he might have found out more about why he was here.

11

PRESENT DAY

Birlerion lurched out of bed, his heart racing as he tried to untangle himself from his sheets. He sat on the edge of the bed and tried to control his breathing, recalling his meeting with an intense Birtolian fisherman called Jerven as if it had just happened. Jerven had *sailed*, on his *own*, around the Birtolian mainland and up to Vespers, in a tiny fishing boat! Looking for him and Tagerill, Serillion, and Roberion.

His heart stuttered as he remembered the look on Jerven's, no, it was Jerrol's face, when he saw Serillion. Birlerion held his head in his hands. Jerrol must have been distraught; it explained much about that encounter that had perplexed them.

He stood and walked over to the dresser where he had left his belt the previous night. He rummaged in the pouch, and there in his hand lay four perfect gleaming pearls. His hand convulsed around them, and he breathed in deeply. Replacing them in his pouch, he dressed and went to find Taelia and the king.

.   .   .

King Benedict sat in his outer chamber dressed in an ornately embroidered dressing gown and scowled at the Sentinal before him. "This had better be good, Birlerion, it's the middle of the night!" Even Fonorion was eyeing him dubiously. A soft tap on the door, which was opened by Darris, revealed Taelia, obviously dressed in haste.

"Your Majesty." She dipped a brief curtsey. "What's happened? Is it Jerrol?" she asked.

"Birlerion is about to tell us, but he wanted to wait for you." The king gestured for her to take a seat. She sat and looked expectantly at Birlerion.

Birlerion cleared his throat. "I just woke up and remembered that I once met a Birtolian fisherman named Jerven, in Vespers, about three months before the Bloodstone was sundered. He had sailed from Plini in the Birtolian empire to Vespers to find me, Tagerill, Serillion, and Roberion. The year was 1123."

Taelia gasped, heart fluttering in her chest. "You think it was Jerrol?"

"I know it was Jerrol, now. I recognised him. I didn't at the time. This isn't going to make sense, but I think it *just* happened. It's a new memory that has just occurred in 1123, and now I remember it happening."

The king frowned. "Are you trying to tell us that Jerrol was in Vespers in 1123?"

Birlerion nodded. "He is a fisherman called Jerven from Plini in Birtoli, and he said he was far from home. He said he had crossed land and time and seas and didn't know how to get home to his family."

Taelia gasped again. "The song."

"Yes, he said he would leave clues in anything he could find that would stand the test of time. He didn't know why he was there or what he had to do, and he asked for our help to follow his trail and find him."

"How was he?" Taelia asked, leaning forward. She gripped Birlerion's arm as her face flushed.

Birlerion covered her hand with his and squeezed it gently. "He looked well. Lean and fit, sunburnt, dressed in the loose shirt and cut off trousers of the islands; he's been there a while, I think; he wore his pendant," Birlerion said. "He was still missing his fingers on his right hand, but otherwise he looked well. A little desperate as you can imagine; he is lost in time and doesn't know how to get home."

"Start at the beginning and tell us everything you can remember, even the smallest detail," the king instructed. "Darris, make notes."

Birlerion thought back. "It was Decu, the weather was chilly. Tagerill and I were in Vespers. We went to the Lady's temple to pay our respects, and this man was lying prostrate on the temple floor; some supplicant, we thought, with a knotty problem. Anyway, we prayed, lit a candle, and left, but he followed us. When Tagerill accosted him, he said he had been searching for us; he had a story to tell us, but he wasn't sure we would believe him." Birlerion grinned briefly. "Tagerill being Tagerill invited him for lunch and said we would be the judge of that. Jerven said he didn't have any coin to pay for lunch so Tagerill said the story would be payment enough. Tagerill found one of his grotty inns, and we sat and talked.

"Jerven, no, I mean Jerrol, had sailed his fishing boat from Birtoli. He showed it to us in the harbour, blue hull with red sails, called the *Island Scout*, tiny little boat, but he sailed it on his own from Plini. He confused it with the island of Senti; of course back then there was no such island. He introduced himself as Jerven, explained he was away from his family and he was trying to get home.

"The Lady had a task for him, only he wasn't sure whether it was Leyandrii or Marguerite, nor what the task was. He had been fishing amongst the islands of Birtoli with his brother, Gael. He said the islands were different, not yet drowned. He described them in explicit detail, turquoise blue waters, white sands, island communities, and he mentioned the Tu'ani specifically. He was insistent that, even if we didn't believe him, we should remember him. He was emphatic about that. Makes sense now, of course.

"He said a lot of stuff that didn't make sense at the time, about Marguerite bonding with the Land, that the ascendants were evil and not to be trusted, that we would wake up in his time and when we did we were to come to Birtoli after his daughter was born and follow the trail he would leave for us. He said we were his best friends, his family, and he needed us." Birlerion looked up as the silence in the room intruded on his reflections. They were all staring at him in shock.

The king cleared his throat. "And, ah, did he say anything else?"

"He thanked us for lunch, and I remember he seemed quite reluctant to leave; I can see why, now. He wanted to set up a trade agreement so we directed him to the Chapterhouse, so he could fill out the forms. He also asked if we knew where Serillion and Roberion were. We said Serillion was probably knee-deep in manuscripts at the Chapterhouse and Roberion somewhere on the seas around Terolia. I don't think he intended to see Serillion; he seemed rather torn, and then he left.

"We followed him. It didn't feel right to leave him on his own. He went to the Chapterhouse and completed the forms and then hit a snag as he didn't have any coin. He tried to pay with pearls, but the administrator wouldn't take them. He was getting a little desperate, so I offered to loan him the money; four talents he needed. I told him to give me two of his pearls as security and he could pay me back when we next met. He gave me four." Birlerion silently held out his hand.

Taelia carefully picked up one of the smooth, creamy pearls, tears filling her eyes. "It's all true, then. Jerrol is stuck in the past, and we don't know how to help him." She sniffed and then wiped her eyes, blinking back the tears.

"Was there anything else?" the king asked, offering her a handkerchief.

"He completed his transaction, got his papers so he could trade with Vespiri, and then Tagerill introduced him to Serillion." Birlerion paused briefly, his face bleak. "I thought Jerven was going to faint when he turned around and saw him. I couldn't understand why he was so distraught. He was trying to apologise to Serillion for something, but Serillion wouldn't have it, said he was here to do the Lady's bidding and that Jerven should not take the blame for something he would choose to do. None of it made sense. Serillion said he'd never met Jerven, yet they acted like they knew each other. And then Serillion hugged him, I thought Jerven was going to collapse, but something Serillion said seemed to ease his distress. Serillion wouldn't let go of him after that, and he helped sell his fish to the chapterhouse cook and insisted we escort Jerven back to his boat in the harbour.

"When we saw how small his boat was and that he intended sailing at night, we tried to persuade him to stay another day, but he wouldn't; he had to get back, he said. And so we let him sail off into the sunset, as it were." Birlerion drew to halt and looked around at his stunned audience.

"I suppose we ought to expect Tagerill and Roberion to arrive shortly, then, with their version of the meeting," the king said wryly into the silence.

"Tagerill for sure; he'll be frantic." Birlerion grinned at the thought. "Jerrol was clear we had to go to Birtoli after his daughter was born. Tagerill will be on his way. Roberion can't have met him yet if I only met him last night, as Jerrol still has to return to Plini and then travel on up to Terolia and find him. He'd have to sail all the way around the mainland; the islands have not been drowned yet. He won't have had time to meet Roberion yet, assuming his time is paralleling ours."

"See if you can get hold of that Arifel. We need to warn Roberion that he will soon recall meeting Jerrol, or Jerven, back in 1123 and to make sure he tells us as soon as he remembers it happening," the king said firmly. "We can't do anything now. All of you go back to bed. I think you should focus on finding out all you can about the Jerven shipping family and the trade agreement, if it still exists. It's an obvious starting point, as well as the Tu'ani clan. The commander knows how to leave a trail; it's beginning to seem like it would be hard to miss."

"He really is stuck in the past," Taelia said, her fingers twisting her ring round and round. "How do we get him back?"

"I have no idea. Maybe we'll find that out as we discover what he's been up to?" the king replied. "Very well, I'm spending some time with the emperor later today. Let's reconvene and compare notes tonight before dinner. I expect you all to join me tonight, so be ready." He nodded dismissal, thoughtfully watching them leave.

Benedict leaned back in his chair as Darris approached. "I am spending time with Geraine this morning, aren't I?"

"Yes, sire, he is expecting you in his study by eighth chime."

"What's the mood in the palace?"

"Supportive of the emperor, excited at the arrival of the next in line. He is well-liked by his people, as is the empress; they understand the needs of the islands, they don't overlook those who are more remote, they honour their history and support the clans. Though I did hear a rumour that the Ministers are looking to disband the clans. From what I've heard, I believe that would be a grave mistake."

Benedict nodded. "See if you can find out where that rumour came from."

"Yes, sire."

Benedict rose, debating whether to go back to bed or not. Maybe he should get ready for his meeting. He was drawn back to the open balcony, and he looked out at the expanse of silvery sea and deep blue sky that filled the horizon. The waxing moon was fading and low in the sky as the sun began to rise. "Jerrol, where are you?" he murmured under his breath.

12

JANU 3RD, 1124

MOLINTI, BIRTOLI

Jerrol gazed across Moliniti harbour as Gael loaded the supplies in the hold; casks of oil, sacks of flour and grain, barrels of fresh water. He had a thick wallet of correspondence from the Administrator's office, which meant they would have to call in at every major island and port on this trip; they would be out for at least a month.

Gael was annoyed with him. He kept throwing dirty looks at him as he worked. Jerrol had to promise he would take Gael with him next time he visited Vespers or his brother would not give him any peace. He sat planning his route as Gael huffed up and down the jetty. They would call into the Senti site on the way home and make sure the workers he had hired had begun building the warehouse and the harbour. He would only pay them on the completion of each phase, so he knew they would be working furiously, some hoping to be taken on in his boatyard.

He looked at his map. Due east round Senti point, then on to Geteril and the outer islands. Then south to Duyli, visit the unnamed islands, and hopefully catch the mullet on the way to Pauul. Back up to Astille, drop into his new holding and get the workers started and then return to Molinti. He sighed. He needed to get his second boat launched, and then he would get Aiden to take over the long trip. Whatever he was here to do, he was sure it wasn't spending months at a time island hopping.

"That's all of it." Gael dropped to the deck, his face red and sweaty. "'preciate your help."

"You're welcome," Jerrol said with a grin. "Geteril first, then Duyli. Let's get moving. Cast off the bow and let's get out of here."

Gael hauled himself up and went to untie the bow rope. Jerrol gently sculled them out into the main harbour, threading their way through the other boats, and at his signal, Gael scurried about hauling up the mainsail and tying it off. The wind caught, the sail billowed, and they headed out to sea.

Their first stop was Geteril. Jerrol completed his trade, accepting a small package of gems in exchange for the sacks and casks before he rummaged in the leather wallet where he kept all his papers and return mail. Selecting a folded piece of parchment, he offered it to the Elder. The Chief looked at him and spread his hands. His eyes gleamed, pale as the sky overhead on a face wrinkled by time and the sun. "You read."

Jerrol dipped his head and unfolded the paper in his hand. "For the eyes of Elder Tuan, Chief of the Geteril people, esteemed leader of the Tu'ani clan," Jerrol read aloud. "His Imperial Highness, the Emperor of all Birtoli, the beloved husband of Empress Olini, expects you to attend a formal oration by enlightened speakers at the Palace of Light in Molinti. Celebrations commence at the welcome light of day on the twenty-second day of Febu in the year of our Lady 1124 and continue until darkness descends. By the hand of the palace scribe dated, this first day of Novu, in the year of our Lady 1123."

Jerrol stared at the words. It still seemed unreal that he had travelled back in time over three thousand years. 1123! He felt faint. A faint buzzing noise grew in his ears as he swallowed the rising bile. His stomach ached.

1123 was just before the Lady sundered the Bloodstone. She was still walking the land; should he reach out to her? But in 1123 he didn't exist. He wasn't the Lady's Captain and she wouldn't know who he was. The conundrums swirled around in his head, confusing him.

The Elder was looking at him in concern.

"Captain Jerven?"

"I apologise, Elder Tuan, I was surprised at the date. I hadn't realised we'd been so long at sea." Jerrol forced the words out of a tight throat, the rising panic threatening to suffocate him.

The Elder studied him for a moment and then snapped his fingers. "Captain Jerven, please be seated." A young woman approached with a bright yellow gourd, her gleaming black eyes flicking over him before dropping to the sand. The Elder took the gourd from her with a smile. "Please, it would honour me if you would drink." He offered it to Jerrol, who numbly took it, blinking as the small clearing blurred.

"Drink," the Elder repeated, his voice a soft command.

Jerrol took a deep breath and tried to rein in his riotous thoughts. He raised the gourd, swallowed, and choked as the liquor hit the back of his throat. He inhaled sharply, the shock calming his breathing, and he exhaled on a huff.

"Again," the Elder said.

Jerrol gripped the rough gourd as his fingers trembled, and he shook his head as he offered it back to the Elder. "I thank you, but I have to sail my boat onwards; this is potent stuff."

The Elder insisted. "You will be fine. Again."

Jerrol stared at him before raising the gourd to take another more careful mouthful. The liquor burned its way down his throat and set fire to his belly, burning away the fear and distress, leaving him calm and centred.

"Welcome, my son," the Elder intoned, his voice vibrating in the salty air. "Welcome to the Tu'ani. Blessed be the day the Lady delivers a son to the clan. Take our blessing with you on your travels and know that you are never alone; you have but to ask and help shall be granted." The Elder signed the moon and tree in front of his chest and smiled.

"Father, your desire is my command," Jerrol whispered as an unnatural stillness embraced him. He waited, his distress soothed. The welcome of the Tu'ani swirled around him, claiming him.

"There is a task that the son of the family must fulfil. It is time to pass our burden into safer keeping. I wasn't sure if it was you or another, but I see you are a builder. As you build you need to conceal what I give you within the foundations; the foundations of a new clan, which will help protect the safety and prosperity of Birtoli.

"Tell no one. It is time it is lost, as must we be. Others crave what we protect and will hound us soon. As the Lady wills, so we will continue." He placed his palm against Jerrol's forehead, and Jerrol shuddered as a weight descended upon his shoulders. He bowed under the pressure before straightening up, the familiar hum of the Oath vibrating though his bones. He breathed in deeply as the Elder's instruction percolated his body, and he knew what he had to do.

"Now," the Elder said in a more normal tone of voice, straightening his bony shoulders as if he had shed a load. "I would request that a son of the clan takes our message to the emperor. I fear my days of travelling are over, and I would not be comfortable away from my home and family." He paused as Jerrol stiffened before him. "I see," he said, gentling his voice. "You have a long way to travel, may my blessings speed you on your way. You will return on your next trip and collect our gift and hand it to the empress in the name of our clan and wish her a safe and happy birthing." The Elder paused and rummaged in a concealed pocket. "You will know what to do with these when the time comes," he said, dropping a silver pearl and a turquoise gem in his right hand and folding Jerrol's remaining fingers over them.

"Of course, my father," Jerrol murmured, his mind grappling with the Elder's words.

The Elder nodded. "Son, the day progresses; you must be on your way."

Jerrol started, his eyes refocused and darted around the clearing. The shadows had shifted significantly; he had been sitting here much longer than it seemed. "Father, I thank you for the welcome. I will do as you bid; we will return to collect your gift and deliver it to the empress, I promise."

"Good, then be on your way. We will look for your return."

Jerrol slowly walked back to the jetty, still trying to come to terms with what had just happened. He had never considered where the Oath had come from. It had just been thrust on him by the king in a moment of desperation. He had thought of it as a binding between him and the king but realised now it was much more. He climbed aboard the *Scout* and found Gael asleep under the canvas. He carefully pocketed the gems and his barter in the belt around his waist, and stashed his wallet in one of the cubby holes before waking Gael.

"Hey, sleepyhead, we need to catch the tide before we're becalmed here in this paradise."

Gael snorted sleepily. "I thought you were never gonna stop chatting. Anyway, when did you learn to speak Tuani?"

"Tuani?"

"Yeah, I heard you talking to that old man. Couldn't understand a word either of you were saying, so I came back here. You were dickering like mad, so I left you to it."

"I don't know, I must have picked it up over the years, as you would if you stayed awake long enough and listened. C'mon, get the sails up it's time for us to head for Duyli. I have a buyer for the mullet back in Molinti. We'll be on the return leg once we've stopped at Pauul, then we can head home."

Gael's eyes brightened at the thought. "You think we will get in for moonset, then?"

Jerrol nodded. "Definitely."

They stopped at each of the smaller islands, delivering the palace notices, collecting messages, and filling their hold with gleaming mullet off the coast of Pauul, the furthest South they travelled, before heading back up the coast towards his holding, which he had named Senti.

A broad smile spread over Jerrol's face as the sheltered cove came into view. Yes, he saw precisely what he needed to do. The deep horseshoe-shaped bay bracketed by tall headlands would be ideal for the harbour. He could build up into the cliffs and raise the beach. The *Scout* drifted up to the shelving golden sands and beached herself. Jerrol and Gael jumped down into the soft sand and pulled the *Scout* a little higher to make sure she didn't float off without them, and then Jerrol led Gael up the beach.

"This will be the harbour. We'll have a stone quay

shoring up the beach, warehouses for storage, plenty of mooring. Off the east and west headland, we'll build staggered storm walls, defending us against the storm surges, and provide safe and protected mooring for our fleet. Over there will be the boatyard; plenty of space to expand as we need, and we'll build our own home up there; the best view and high enough to be safe from flooding. Come take a look at the view." Jerrol eagerly led the way up the track to the headland. At the top, they paused, breathing in the clear, balmy air as they gazed down at the cove.

"You really think we need that much defence from the sea? Look at it, the tide doesn't come halfway up the beach."

"It will, though," Jerrol murmured. "It will."

Gael rolled his eyes and began picking his way back down the trail.

Jerrol cast his thoughts out to the Lady. "*Bless me with a sign,*" he pleaded. "*I'm stumbling around in the dark. What do you need me to do?*"

His chest tightened as a piercing pain shot through him. Groaning, he hugged his body against the jagged spikes, gasping for breath as he collapsed to the lush, springy grass. A sense of new life, of verdant green, overwhelmed him. Inhaling the aroma of fresh green life, his shudders faded, and Jerrol opened his eyes. Clenched in his fist was a seed pod; a seed for a sentinal tree.

He dug a hole in the middle of the headland with his belt knife and planted the seed. The pain eased to a dull ache as the seed sprouted and grew into a small sapling before his eyes. A hesitant and surprised murmur began in the back of his mind. He soothed the new sentinal and smiled as the tree sprouted another foot in enthusiasm as it connected with Jerrol; its pointy leaves unfurling in the balmy air. The comforting hum strengthened, and a deep tension eased; a tension he hadn't realised he had been carrying.

"Watch over us, my friend. I fear we are heading into stormy waters," Jerrol murmured. "We will be home soon to keep you company. Welcome to Senti in the Empire of Birtoli." Reluctantly, he stood, easing his shoulders against the weight that was there, yet not; a load carried, unseen. He turned away from the new sentinal tree and followed Gael back down to the boat.

They followed the coastline through the Plini straits before running parallel with the mainland after they rounded Plini point. Gael watched the familiar cliffs of home recede behind them and absently wiped the spray from his face before turning back to coiling the ropes. They sailed into the wide-mouthed harbour of Molinti late that evening, hauling in the sails to reduce their speed.

The sun had set in a resplendent ball of fire, turning the ocean a molten orange that mesmerised Jerrol as he steered. Black spots danced before his eyes until it finally sank behind the growing mass of land ahead of them, and darkness suddenly descended as if a lamp had been blown out.

They carefully threaded their way through the moorings towards the sentry light at the head of the jetty, which marked the unloading dock. Gael hung out over the bow with a small lamp, casting a yellow glow onto the still waters, shouting directions. Jerrol worked the steering oar behind the tiller.

When the *Scout* gently bumped against the dock, Gael leapt out to pull the mooring rope tight before they could drift back out into the channel. Tying it off, he raised the lamp, casting a soft golden glow over the *Scout's* deck. "Who's taking the fish?" he asked a little breathlessly, tension edging his voice.

"The palace. Run on up and bespeak the cook. He'll

send down some help to carry it up. And don't worry, we'll sleep here tonight and leave in the morning."

Gael heaved a big sigh of relief before running down the dock, his lantern bobbing merrily in his hand.

Jerrol began heaving his shallow crates onto the deck, checking the fish were still covered in salt and topping up those that needed it. He fervently wished for stocks of Elothian ice, which would preserve the fish much better, but in this heat, the ice would have melted before he had even left the harbour. His rhythm was broken as the harbour-master peered at him over the railings. "Cutting it a bit fine, weren't you?"

"Yes, sorry about that. The sun set a bit too early for us!"

"Well, I'm glad you're here. The palace cook wants to talk to you personally, so I suggest you go up with your catch. I'll keep an eye on the *Scout* for you."

"Do you know why?" Jerrol asked as he nodded in agreement. He continued stacking the crates on the dock.

The port master hovered his lamp over the crates, revealing the red-scaled fish which bled through the salt, and he cocked an eye at Jerrol. "You've been fishing deep? You didn't get them in the straits, I can tell."

"Yeah, out towards Duyli. Be glad to get home though; this has been a long trip." Jerrol eased his shoulders as the last crate landed on the dock. "What does the palace want?" he prompted.

"Oh," the port master raised his lantern so he could see Jerrol's face. "The empress is after samphire; driving everyone mad apparently. You could probably name your price."

"Good to know," Jerrol murmured as the clatter of feet on the boards heralded the return of Gael and his helpers.

The crates were soon loaded, and Jerrol followed the lads up the steep incline, through the town market to the palace, and into a small courtyard around the back of the palace. The emperor's cook erupted from the kitchen door, casting his eye over the crates. He swiftly counted and smiled in relief.

"You must have known exactly what I needed. If you bring the same catch in three weeks I'll buy it all, and the emperor wants a formal dinner so I'll need more. I also need samphire. The empress is desperate for it. I'll pay you a molin a net, with an extra molin if you can bring some samphire with the fish."

Jerrol pursed his lips. "Three weeks is stretching it as I am due to run up to Vespiri. I only have the one boat, and to find Samphire I'll have to go down to the Duyli islands. Rough waters down there; it would be a special trip."

"Two molins a net, plus I'll double the first order if you get it in two weeks."

"I'll see what I can do. Which is the priority?"

The cook struggled with his conscience and finally said: "Mullet."

Jerrol grinned. "Three weeks, then."

"Earlier if possible," the cook beseeched him.

13

___

PRESENT DAY

FEBU 6TH, 4128, MOLINTI, BIRTOLI

The inner courtyard of the emperor's palace was imposing. High ceilings and white marble columns towered above them, accentuating the emperor's diminutive height; he was not much taller than Melahney. His brown hair was receding, and he had a bald patch that he tried to hide with a variety of hats. Today, it was a navy-blue sailor's cap.

King Benedict noted the hat with concern. "Are we going sailing, Geraine?"

Emperor Geraine grinned. "We are an island state. There is so much water that boats and sailing have to come into it at some point. When I was a boy, I spent more time on the water than I did on dry land. I wanted to know every island there was in the archipelago so I would know who my people were. I thought I'd show you Senti, the main island south of here.

"There is a complex harbour system, famous for its slip-ways and boatyards. Birtoli was lucky that a fisherman with vision built a second harbour down there. Otherwise we would have lost so many more people in the great floods.

Even now, in the bad storms that harbour is a safe haven and most boats caught out in it will head there."

"A safe haven?" King Benedict exclaimed in surprise.

Geraine smiled. "You'll see, it's ingenious."

Geraine led Benedict out of the palace to the carriage that waited to take them down to the harbour. Fonorion paced behind the king's shoulder, and once Benedict had climbed in the carriage, Fonorion joined the driver on top.

Once they were settled, Geraine began explaining. "They built storm walls to defend the harbour. No matter how bad the storm, the harbour is protected, and the infrastructure is all built a good three or four feet above today's water level. It's almost as if they knew," he murmured to himself.

"Knew what?" Benedict asked.

Geraine looked around the carriage carefully as if checking for listeners; he leant forward as if about to share a secret. "I heard there was a plot to flood us. Men meet to plan our downfall. I need to find the Fisherman."

"The fisherman?"

"Yes, he knows things; he can help us. He's in Senti, only these busybodies won't let me out of their sight, but if we go together, they can't protest, can they?" Geraine finished happily.

"Geraine, you're the emperor. Who is trying to stop you from doing what you want?"

"Them, those tall men in black; they say things and confuse me."

Benedict peered out of the carriage window. "Which tall men?"

"They've gone now as you're with me. They seem afraid of you. Just as they are afraid of the Fisherman."

Benedict observed Geraine with concern. He seemed rational, but he could see why Melahney was worried. Some people could construe his words as irrational if they wanted to.

They soon pulled up at the harbour, and Geraine jumped out. Benedict climbed down more slowly. "Which vessel are we going out on?" Benedict asked as he searched the harbour for a reasonably sized ship, hopefully along the lines of Roberion's frigate.

"My yacht; here it is," Geraine gestured proudly at what was, to Benedict, a tiny boat with a single mast and an open cabin housing the wheel. He looked at Fonorion. "Is it safe?" he asked under his breath.

Fonorion shrugged. "That would be a question for Roberion, I'm afraid, but I don't think we have much choice unless you intend to offend the emperor."

Benedict watched Geraine busily preparing his boat for sea. "How many crew do you have?" he called down.

"Just the two; they man the sails for us. I can do the rest."

"But what about your guards?"

"They are useless on boats, no point bringing them; they are just ballast."

"What about pirates?" Benedict asked a little desperately.

Geraine laughed. "No pirates here. Anyway, my naval fleet will be shadowing us. Don't worry, it will be safe, give'em something to do for a change. Come on down."

Benedict cursed under his breath and began climbing down the ladder to the boat. Fonorion followed, trying not to laugh.

Geraine rambled on about the history of Molinti until they cleared the harbour and then he suddenly relaxed. All the pent-up tension he had been displaying drained away, and he inhaled the salty air. "The sea, the beautiful waters around our islands teeming with unseen life, sustaining my people. It is a treasure beyond counting, and it soothes my nerves. I love being on the sea," he murmured.

Benedict gripped the rail tightly and glared at Fonorion, who was still trying to stifle his chuckles. "When did you first start sailing?"

"Oh, I must have been about three or four. All children here are taught to swim and sail almost before they can walk. There isn't much land, you see, so you have to learn about the next best thing."

"I never learnt to swim," Benedict admitted, watching the deep blue waves with caution.

"Oh, in that case, you'd better wear one of these. I should have checked, my apologies; they help you float if you fall in."

"Fall in?" Benedict repeated. His grip tightened on the railing as Fonorion tied the float around his waist.

"Don't worry, we'll hug the coastline; it's not far. Isn't it amazing to think that below us is the original Birtolian mainland that once connected us to Vespiri? Towns and villages drowned without notice. Well, it won't happen again on my watch," he said firmly, gripping the wheel.

"Are you concerned that it will?"

"They try, but I'm watching them."

"Who are you watching, Geraine?"

"Them, I told you. They search, but they won't find it."

"Find what?"

"What they are looking for. It is well hidden; they won't find it. They tried before, you know, but the Fisherman tied them up right and proper. He'll know what to do this time."

"Who is the fisherman?" Benedict asked carefully.

Geraine tapped the side of his nose. "Least said, soonest mended, as my mother used to say. She was a great old girl, hated boats though, always got seasick. Refused to come out on anything smaller than the royal barge; used to drive my father crazy. Trouble was, it took a hundred oarsmen to shift the damn thing, it was so heavy. We retired it when my mother died, not much use for it anymore."

Benedict watched him in bewilderment, trying to keep hold of the thread of the conversation. "Have you met the fisherman before?"

"Oh, yes, so have you. We might see him today if we're lucky; depends on the tides."

"What is here on Senti?" Benedict asked, trying to make sense of it all.

"Well, there's the harbour and the town of Senti, which has grown up behind it. The original harbour at Plini was completely lost, you know, submerged under the waves when the headlands crumbled into the sea. There are a few hinterland villages, a lot of pastures, and sheep, and to the west, pine trees, good for boat building.

"A prosperous island: the people are descendants of many island clans lost in the floods. They all came together and decided to become the Senti clan; that's when the island was named Senti." The emperor shrugged. "Sorry, lots of history, but these islands team with it. The clans still live and breathe it. Coming out here makes it all real."

"That is a sentinal," King Benedict said, staring in shock as they rounded the point and turned towards the harbour. A huge tree, silver-trunked with long, pointed leaves arched over the thick defensive walls of the harbour.

"Yes, that's the Senti sentinal. It's always watched over Senti; been there as long as the town has. I need one in Molinti. I must tell the Fisherman," Geraine said. "It was planted by the Fisherman, so legend says, when he first built the harbour. From a seed, so the tale goes. He prayed to the Lady, and it appeared in his hand. There are ballads about it; they'll be sung at the state dinner next week, should be good. I like the old ones."

"He's awake," Fonorion murmured in the king's ear.

"You mean there is a Sentinal in there waiting for us to wake him?"

"No, he's the Captain's sentinal tree."

"Is Jerrol in the tree?" King Benedict looked up, hopefully.

"Not now, but he must have been at some point. I think he may be the 'fisherman' that the emperor is referring to. The Captain must have been here for a sentinal tree to be planted, and that sentinal is taller than mine and yet he is young as well." Fonorion frowned. "He is welcoming us. He's asking where we've been."

"Then it looks like we've found the trail. He couldn't have left a clearer sign than that," Benedict said, shielding his eyes as he stared up at the tree as they entered the harbour.

"We should have known, really. He named the island Senti, after all." Fonorion grinned as he also gazed up at the sentinal. "When he said he would leave clues that would stand the test of time, he didn't do it by halves, did he?" He smiled up at the branches arching over them as they passed through the thick walls and into the sheltered cove. Boats of all shapes and sizes were moored along multiple stone jetties, each with stone stairs leading up to the quayside high above the waterline.

Geraine deftly spun the wheel, and they drifted to a gentle stop next to the central jetty. The sailors tied off the ropes, and Geraine smiled at Benedict. "I wanted to thank you for coming to stay with us. Melahney really appreciates it, you know, as do I. I know I'm not making a lot of sense right now, and Melahney is worried. Still, you understand the responsibilities of guardianship; these are my people, and I have to protect them to the best of my ability."

"You don't have to do it alone, Geraine," Benedict said.

Geraine's smile widened. "That's what the Fisherman said!"

"Then let me help you. Let *us* help you. My Sentinals are experienced at dealing with things that are difficult to explain."

The little emperor nodded. "Come and meet the Jerven family; they run the Jerven Fishing line, amongst other things." He led the way up the stone stairs onto the quay. Benedict followed cautiously. He wouldn't dream of arriving anywhere unannounced and unprotected.

They had barely reached the quay when a thin young man, dark-haired and dark-eyed, typical of the region, came rushing up to greet them. "Your Majesty," he bowed briefly, "what a pleasure, we weren't expecting you so soon."

The emperor brushed off the greeting. "I needed to bring King Benedict of Vespiri and Terolia to see you. He needs to know more about your family, and I wanted to speak to the Fisherman."

The man looked at Benedict in shock. "Y-Your Majesty, it is an honour to welcome you to Senti. I am Gael Jerven, the current harbour master."

Benedict smiled in sympathy. "It's a pleasure to meet you, Harbour Master Jerven. Myself and Sentinal Fonorion here are extremely interested in meeting your sentinal tree."

Gael gaped at Fonorion. "Sentinal?"

Fonorion smiled. "I am one of many Sentinals awoken by the Captain in this age. We have yet to discover any Sentinals in Birtoli."

Gael nodded slowly. "I believe we have the only one. He is rather excited about meeting you."

"You can speak to him?" Fonorion asked.

Gael smiled. "I have the privilege of being his companion until the Captain returns or my child takes on the responsibility."

"The Captain?"

"It's our family history. We guard the sentinal until the

Captain returns. It's passed down each generation. Each child of the harbour master's line is introduced to the sentinal to continue the companionship in the absence of the first Captain. We do not expect the Captain to return, of course. After all, it has been over three thousand years. But the sentinal needs companionship in his absence, and our family swore to fulfil that need, and we have never failed," Gael explained.

"It's an honour to meet you and your family," Fonorion said, bowing low. "Can you tell us what happened to the Captain?"

Gael grimaced. "If you would like to come inside, I would be happy to tell you of our founder and Captain. Please let us get out of the heat; it is much cooler inside."

Fonorion raised his eyes to the sentinal spread above them. "If you would excuse me a moment. I need to greet the sentinal first, and I fear he is impatient."

"He has become a little testy recently." Gael paused. "It's almost as if he knew something was going to happen," he said, his eyes widening as he assimilated the implication of his visitors.

"Your Majesties," Fonorion said, bowing to Benedict and Geraine. "If I could take a moment to speak with the sentinal. He stands vigilant for our safety," he said, forestalling Benedict's protest.

The king nodded. "Very well, tell him I will be up later." He followed Gael and Geraine inside the stone building set back from the quay. Inside the temperature dropped significantly, the thick stone walls protection from the heat, as well as the elements.

"Tell me about your Captain," Benedict invited as they sat in the offered chairs.

"He was just a fisherman, running the circuit of the islands, carrying messages, fishing. He went to sea at a young age, when his parents died of the pestilence, and he had to support his brother. He ran his own boat, a single master; managed it with his brother, Gael, until he had enough money to invest in this land here. Developed trading routes, added more vessels, and expanded his fishing fleet. This harbour was built as their home base. I guess the money he saved on overnight berthing fees enabled him to expand into the boatyard, and as more people came to work for him, so the village grew as families relocated. He gave favourable rates to all who came, and during the storms, many survivors came here for shelter and never left as their islands and homes were lost. After the Great waves, the clans united under the name of Senti in memory of the Captain."

"In memory?" Benedict asked.

"Yes, he was lost in the great upheaval of 1124, along with the *Island Scout*; he was lost helping to find survivors."

"Where did he take the survivors?"

"Molinti. He made two trips to Molinti, where there was higher ground, and they had access to healers there, but he never made a third. There are many ballads sung about the Captain and the *Island Scout's* final journey."

"*The Lost Traveller* being one of them?"

"You've heard that one already? Captain Jerven wrote that about a lost love; it's said he never gave up hope that he would see her one day, though he would never speak of her. His brother Gael added the final verse, we believe."

"The final verse?"

"Yes, after he was lost."

"Do you have the complete song? I am not convinced we've heard all the verses."

"We have the popular verses. Some were a little confusing and aren't often sung. I believe the full song is in his logbook; he kept meticulous accounts most of the time."

"His logbook?"

"Yes, it is in the emperor's archives."

"Geraine, you have the fisherman's logbook?" Benedict asked, his voice sharp. Geraine was no longer paying attention; he had drifted over to the door.

"Yes, yes," he said absently, heading out of the door.

Benedict turned back to Gael. "Does the emperor come here often, unattended?"

"Yes, when he can. He likes to speak to the Captain."

"But you said the Captain is dead."

"Not according to the emperor. He speaks to him here. He says it's safe here. The emperor says the Captain spent a lot of time here, so who am I to say he doesn't speak to the Captain? The sentinal doesn't believe the Captain is dead; only legend and common sense say he is. I keep an open mind; he was a remarkable man."

"That he is," King Benedict agreed fervently.

Gael gave the king a tentative smile. "You speak as if you know him." He rubbed his temple as he glanced out the door after the emperor. "Much as the emperor seems to. I wish it had been possible to meet him. I would have liked to have spoken to him, as would many Sentians. What you see here today is solely due to his vision and foresight. What he created he made to withstand the great waves. How he knew they would come no one knows, but our family would not have survived without him. The least we can do is continue his legacy."

"And what is his legacy?" Benedict asked.

"The continuation of the Island service, carrying word between clans and the emperor, managing our fleet and the trading business. The people of Senti rely on it."

"A legacy indeed," Benedict murmured. "I thank you for your hospitality. I think I ought to find the emperor and take our leave of the sentinal before we depart."

"Let me introduce you."

When Benedict emerged from the Harbourmaster's offices, Geraine was staring out across the harbour, a slight frown on his face.

"Is something the matter?" Benedict asked as he stood beside him.

"The Fisherman isn't here; it's odd, he usually is."

"Let's speak to the sentinal; he might know," Benedict suggested, staring up at the steps leading up to the tall sentinal.

King Benedict mopped his face and tried to catch his breath as they reached the top of the headland and the sentinal, which dwarfed them. Fonorion stood with one hand on the trunk, facing the breeze and gazing out to sea.

"Well?" the king asked softly, plucking at his clothes, trying to catch the cooling air.

"It's definitely the Captain's sentinal. According to the sentinal, he's not long left, headed south around the horn."

"You mean we've just missed him?" Benedict caught his breath. "Or do you mean he's in 1123?"

Fonorion grimaced. "I think the sentinal means 1123. It seems the sentinal is crossing time, both here and there."

"Is there any way we can set up a messaging system through him? Get a message to Jerrol next time he returns here so he knows that we are searching for him?"

"I'm not sure. We can try. He's confused and worried. He remembers something happening, but he also says it hasn't happened yet."

"What?"

"A great storm."

"The upheaval of the stone being broken, do you think?"

"No," Fonorion replied slowly. "I'm not sure if he means an actual storm or whether something terrible is about to happen, or both."

"We need Jerrol's logs. Geraine, we need to return to Molinti; I need to see the fisherman's logbooks."

"Yes, of course, I believe they are in the archive. I'll have to get the librarian to search for them."

"You mean you've never read them?"

Fonorion winced at the exasperation in the king's voice.

"No, no, they are quite faded, you know, difficult to read."

"But you speak to him all the time. Surely you want to know more about him, what he did?"

"But he hasn't done it yet," Geraine said, staring at the king in surprise.

Benedict clenched his teeth against the retort he wanted to make. "Very well, let's return and find out." He nodded to the sentinal. "We will send a Sentinal to keep you company as you wait for the Captain to return."

The sentinal's leaves shivered in response. Fonorion patted his trunk in farewell and followed the king and the emperor back down to the harbour to the emperor's boat and the return journey.

When the king wearily followed the emperor up the steps of the palace, he found Taelia and Birlerion hovering in the hallways, waiting impatiently to see him. He held up his hand. "It will have to wait. I need a bath first. Come back in an chime, and we'll compare notes."

"But, sire." Taelia was almost hopping up and down with impatience.

"One chime," the king said firmly, turning to Geraine. "Geraine, thank you for an enlightening day."

The emperor beamed. "My pleasure, anytime."

Fonorion grinned as the king muttered under his breath, "Once was enough," as he entered his chamber.

A chime later, Benedict relaxed on the sofa and sipped a cold drink. His bath had refreshed him greatly, but his face and neck were turning a bright shade of pink. He was glad the rest of him had been covered, else he would have been boiled like a lobster. He glared morosely across the room at Fonorion. "How come you didn't catch the sun?"

Fonorion smiled. "Lucky, I guess, sire."

"I'll bet it was nothing to do with luck," Benedict grumbled. Fortunately for Fonorion his complaint was interrupted by the arrival of Taelia and Birlerion. King Benedict indicated the chairs across from him.

"Don't ever ask me to go on a boat," he began as Fonorion muffled a snort, and he glared at his Sentinal before continuing, "that is smaller than Roberion's, because I will refuse."

Taelia stared at him. "I wouldn't dream of it, sire."

"Good. I have just spent most of the day risking my life by being tossed around in a tiny skiff, and I don't intend to repeat the experience. The good thing is that we found Commander Haven's sentinal on the island of Senti. And the sentinal is, shall I say, *aware* of the commander rather than in contact with him, though it is a little confusing as to how that works." Benedict frowned. "We couldn't figure out how to get him to pass a message."

"You mean our sentinal tree from Old Vespers has relocated here?" Taelia asked in surprise.

"No. Our understanding is that Jerrol planted it, and as we know, he is the only one who can produce sentinal seeds, that we are aware of, anyway. It confirms that Jerrol is now Jerven, back in 1123. We have the song. He constructed the harbour at Senti and built it high enough above the new water levels to protect them against storm surges. A sentinal stands tall over Senti. Even the name of the island points to Jerrol."

"I found the history of the Jerven family in the archives," Taelia said. "It all starts in 1123; there is little before then. He named his boats after us. The fleet always has active vessels named *Moonlight Kiss*, *Mikke's Ride*, and *Island Scout*. It is a large business, important to the Birtoli economy, according to the transport minister, trading with Vespiri, Terolia, and within the islands."

"And that confirms that Jerrol is Jerven. The *Island Scout* is mentioned in the song," Birlerion interrupted.

Taelia frowned. "No, it isn't."

"Ah, I haven't had a chance to show you, but one of Roberion's crew knew another verse."

"Oh?" Taelia's face lit up.

"Umm, it mentions the *Island Scout*, but Taelia, it doesn't mean it's true." He silently handed her the paper.

Taelia's face drained of colour as she read the words. "No," she whispered.

The king leaned forward and plucked the paper out of her hand and read slowly. He looked at Birlerion. "You know he's fine though, don't you?"

Birlerion shrugged. "We know he's alive at the moment." He winced at the expression on Taelia's face. "That last verse obviously wasn't written as part of the original song. It was added after by someone else; it even sounded different."

"It mentions a storm," Taelia said.

"It also says the captain of the *Island Scout* was lost in that storm," the king said slowly as he looked across at her. "The Senti sentinal was concerned about an approaching storm, wasn't it, Fonorion?"

"Yes," Fonorion agreed slowly, "but he seemed confused. It wasn't clear if he meant an actual storm or a metaphorical one."

"It could be the sundering of the stone; it is the right time," Taelia suggested.

Benedict watched the horror spread over her face. The thought of Jerrol having to survive those terrible events was one more thing for her to worry about.

"The logbook," he said, snapping his fingers. "The fisherman's logs. Geraine said they would be in the archives; the librarian will get them for you. Captain Jerven's logs. Taelia, you need to find them and see what he's written. Bring them here so we can all read them."

Taelia nodded. "I'll search for them tomorrow. Have you heard anything from Roberion yet? Didn't he go to Senti first? You'd have thought he would have sent word about the sentinal."

Benedict shook his head. "Nothing as yet, though you make a good point. And where is Tagerill? Surely he should be here by now. We need him to go to Senti and keep an eye on the place. Geraine said the fisherman returned there regularly. I need to spend some more time with Geraine; he is obviously connected to whatever is going on."

"Oh, Your Majesty," Taelia's eyes brightened, "the Elder of the Jerven clan will be at the state dinner. I asked the Transport Minister for an introduction. I think we need to get to know that family a lot better."

"Indeed," the king said thoughtfully.

14

FEBU 2ND, 1124

BIRTOLI

The *Island Scout* and the *Mari Rose* left harbour with the sunrise and sailed south, Gael and Dion shouting taunts at each other across the water as they worked, each trying to outdo the other. Jerrol planned on showing Marin the fishing waters off Duyli.

The mainland was a smudge off their starboard bow as Jerrol led the *Mari Rose* into deeper waters. The waves deepened as they skirted the submerged reefs off the coast of Geteril, Jerrol shouting warnings across the water. Marin gaped at the white foam that bubbled around the rocks hiding below the surface. He bent over his map, marking the position.

They spent the day fishing around the island of Duyli, and holds full, Jerrol and Marin discussed whether they should head for Vespers and offload there. A four-day trip, but Marin needed the experience. When night fell, they camped on the beach at Duyli. Roasting fish over the open fire, Marin quizzed Jerrol about Vespers while Gael and Dion went off to explore the beach.

"What made you think to open a trade route with Vespiri? Surely Birtoli is business enough?"

"There are more than enough fishermen to cater for Birtoli. We'll get more money for our haul in Vespers, you wait and see," Jerrol promised.

"But why the drive to make more money? Life is simple down here," Marin asked quietly, watching the flames.

Jerrol sighed. "Things change. Birtoli is too insular; we need outside links to support our people. Trading relationships will enable us to bring in other supplies, not just money. We can trade for things we can't get easily. Medicines, for example, or tools."

Marin shook his head. "I don't know where you get the ideas from. Me, I'm just a simple fisherman."

Jerrol smiled and turned the conversation to navigating. "The Guardian star is always in the north. Even in the north it is still north." He grinned, remembering a time when he had ignored the star and relied on his compass, ending up completely lost as the mountains of Elothia confused the readings. *A compass would be handy now*, he thought ruefully, but he hadn't seen any evidence of one in use. "But we're lucky around here that we can sail within sight of the mainland. The islands are not far offshore, so we can sight the landmarks easily. If the star is over land then you know you are going west. If it's out to sea, then you're going east. Simple, really," Jerrol shrugged.

"But what if the stars are obscured?" Marin asked.

"How often does that happen?" Jerrol asked with a grin. "If you have no sightings and you don't know where you are, then don't sail. You know when a storm is brewing; all you can do is hove to the nearest port and ride it out." He knew Roberion would be cringing at his explanation; he had sextants and logs and all kinds of instruments to keep him right.

The boys returned in time to help eat the fish, eager to describe the creatures they had found in the rock pools.

Jerrol pointed out the key constellations: The Lady's belt, three bright blue stars in a straight line, the crown a zigzag of stars, and the Guardians, a small group of four stars low on the horizon and only visible from midnight to third chime. He explained how to read the position of the moon as it traversed the sky, recording its position against the stars. Marin insisted he draw them out on a sheet of grubby paper and noted when to use them. Marin caught on quick, frowning in annoyance. "Why am I only learning this now? It makes it so much easier. How come you know this and I don't?" he complained.

Jerrol shrugged. "If you never sail at night, you'd never notice how to use the stars, though obviously I'd recommend you don't draw near to the coast until dawn. Some of the approaches are narrow, and you don't want to be scraping the hull out of your boat. I tend to only sail at night on the long haul back from Duyli or Astille or back from Terolia; I know I have open seas and no shoals to catch me out. Using the stars keeps me far enough off the coast to be safe but near enough to check my position at dawn."

"We can try it out on the way back from Vespiri," Marin said, eager to try out his newfound knowledge.

Jerrol nodded and eased back on his blanket, staring up at the velvety night sky. The inky darkness sparkled with millions of pinpoints of light, too small to recognise, though he could hear Marin rustling his piece of paper as he strained to find the constellations again. A gentle breeze caressed his skin, cool in the evening air. He closed his eyes, listening to the soft swish of the calm seas on the white sands. The gentle rustling of the broad-leafed trees above him soothed him to sleep.

They were woken early the next morning by the raucous squawking of a group of brilliant green parrots arguing over some scrap or other. The screeches pierced the calm, and the noise caused by their flapping wings was shockingly loud in the pre-dawn air. They took it as a sign, and chewing on dried strips of fish for breakfast, they cast off, continuing their journey north. They rounded the southern most point of the mainland and pulled into Amrilti, an island off the western seaboard, later that evening, trading some fish for a bath and a night in the harbour tavern.

Jerrol had forgotten how much cooler it was up north. After a further two days of constant bright blue skies, the grey cloudy skies over Vespers harbour was a shock to Marin, Dion and Gael. Jerrol grinned as they met on the dock. "I forgot to say that it is winter here. The further north you go, the colder it gets. In Elothia, it's snowing; the rain freezes in the air and coats everything in icy white powder. It's quite an experience. It's likely to be wet and windy here, so we'll have to see about getting some coats."

"How do you know all this?" Marin stuttered, shivering as a blast of cold air whipped across the harbour, his lips tinged blue.

"Stay here, wrap yourselves in the blankets, and I'll go see what I can find," Jerrol instructed as he headed towards the harbour office.

He brandished his trading papers to the administrator in the office. "I have mullet, brannock, and samphire to trade," he said briskly as he spread his papers on the administrator's desk.

"Two obols per day berthing per boat, one obol offloading fee, and you'll need to speak with the trading post regarding trade," the administrator said in a bored tone of voice, barely looking at the papers.

Jerrol dropped six obols on the desk. "I'd like a receipt please, for the *Island Scout* and the *Mari Rose*, out of Plini in Birtoli. One day's berthing, and two offloading fees."

Jerrol took the receipt and left the office. He returned to

the boats. "You can either stay here or come with me into Vespers; it's about half a mile inland. We need to hire the porters to get the goods into town, but I think I'll stop at the Chapterhouse first and see if they are interested. If we could get a regular shipment in there, we'll be made."

"Chapterhouse?" Marin asked.

"Scholars; they do research and experiments. A place of learning; they usually eat well."

"We'll come with you; it's too cold to stay here," Marin said as he sneezed.

"Come on then, we'll get some warmer clothes in town." Jerrol looked at him ruefully. "We'd better get some menthol while we're at it if you are going to catch a chill. I should have thought." Jerrol berated himself for his thoughtlessness as they walked down the track towards Vespers.

His companions stopped in shock as the city opened up before them, the graceful domes and the Captain's bridge sparkling above it all in the grey sky.

After a short pause for them to gaze at the city, Jerrol led them down to the golden buildings of the Chapterhouse, eager to get them out of the chill wind. He soon found his way to the kitchens, where Marin, Gael, and Dion hovered near the open fire in relief, listening in amazement as Jerrol negotiated the sale of their fish.

The cook was eager to take an order of fresh fish, and he agreed to a delivery every two weeks. His eyes brightened at the mention of brannock and samphire, and he agreed the price with barely a flinch, inclusive of porters to come and collect the delivery from the dock. Marin's eyes widened at the price that just one hold would net them. Jerrol wrote out the agreement and the cook signed it with a flourish, then they shook hands and arranged the collection of the first load.

"I wonder if you could advise the best place to get some

warm clothes? We didn't come prepared for the cold weather, and my friends are suffering."

The cook looked over at fishermen huddled by the fire. "Best place is Thurrocks over on the square. Your friends can stay here if you like whilst you go. They'll catch their death of cold dressed like that. Here," the cook reached for a cloak hanging on the hook behind him. "You can borrow this. Return it when you get back."

"Thank you, I appreciate it. The weather is much milder down south," Jerrol said as he wrapped the cloak around him. He looked across at Marin. "Stay here; I'll be back in a bit." Marin nodded uncertainly but stayed by the fire.

Jerrol hurried out, looking up at the palace with some longing. He walked around the Chapterhouse and across the square that opened behind it. The sign proclaiming that the building was Thurrocks swung in the wind, and Jerrol pushed open the door, shutting it behind him with relief. He glanced around the dim interior and selected thick jumpers, trousers, and cloaks. He paid and donned his new attire over the top of his light clothes, the comfort warmth easing his tight muscles.

As he left the clothes shop, he eyed the tavern next door. It looked quite presentable, upmarket even, and he ventured in on a hunch, searching out the kitchens and the head cook. A little later, he hurried back to the chapterhouse loaded with parcels and his fish all sold. The tavern cook had been as eager as the Chapterhouse and willing to place a regular order if he liked the fish that Jerrol delivered.

Arriving back at the Chapterhouse, he grinned at the sight of his crew sitting around the large table, warming their hands around mugs of soup. Gael's eyes were wide with wonder at the discussions going on around him. The art of cooking fish bemused him.

"Jerven," Marin called as he caught sight of him. "Saul

here wants phrist too if we can get it; it's quite a delicacy here."

"They stuff the fish with vegetables," Gael said, his face flushed with excitement, "and tie it up with string to hold it together. We'll have to try that."

Jerrol laughed as he handed out the clothes. "I think you could gain a student if you want one," he said to the cook as he hung the cloak back on the hook.

"He is welcome to join us. That's what the chapterhouse is about; teaching those who want to learn," Saul replied with a grin.

"Gael, you have a choice if you want it," Jerrol said with a smile at the boy's excited face. Gael's face fell. "But you need me on the boats, and we can't afford it anyway."

"We can talk about it. If it's something you really want to do, we could find a way, you know," Jerrol suggested.

"Maybe," Gael said, hesitantly.

Jerrol smiled at the cook. "Thank you for your hospitality; we really appreciate it."

"I will appreciate your fish even more," Saul grinned as he shook their hands. "I look forward to seeing you in two weeks."

"Two weeks," Marin promised.

On their return to the harbour, the Chapterhouse porters were waiting for them, and they offloaded the *Scout's* catch, stacking the crates on the hand carts, and made arrangements for Marin to collect the empty crates on the next trip. They had just finished when the porters for Marin's catch arrived, and they began unloading his crates.

They stood looking at each other as the porters left. "They would take two boatloads easily every week," Marin said in amazement.

"Let's not over commit." Jerrol grinned. "Let's start with one and see how it goes. We can always add another boat to the route if we need to and deliver weekly if it makes sense. It's your route. If you can grow it, let me know."

Marin nodded and sneezed.

"Here, inhale this, breathe it in; it will help clear your nose. And dissolve this sachet in water if it develops into a heavy cold; it will help clear your head for a while." Jerrol handed him a small blue bottle and a sachet of powder.

"What is it?" Marin peered at it.

"Menthol. It works wonders," Jerrol replied, jumping down into the *Scout*. "Gael, cast off. Let's go find the sun," he said with a shiver. "The sooner we get the samphire, the sooner we can return home."

"Yeah, great, and I can look forward to getting scratched to death in the rocks. You know it's not easy to harvest that stuff."

Jerrol grinned. "It's a special request from Empress Olini. How was I supposed to say no?"

"Easily," Gael grumped.

They spent a night in Amrilti and another in Pauul at the most southernmost tip of the mainland, having survived Marin's first attempt to steer by the stars, and then Marin waved goodbye as he headed for Plini, leaving them to stop off in Duyli to restock on mullet and samphire for the empress. They pulled up onto the beach to wait out the worst heat in the middle of the day. Jerrol napped in the shade whilst Gael explored the island. He awoke as Gael clattered back through the undergrowth, a huge green fruit under each arm. "Look, I found some melon. I'll get a knife." He plonked the fruits beside Jerrol and headed for the *Scout*.

He suddenly turned. "Hey, it looks like there's a squall coming! We'd better batten down the hold before it washes all the salt away."

Jerrol stood and peered up at the sky. It did look a bit menacing; a low swathe of black cloud looking out of place in the brilliant blue sky. They sat out the squall under the broad-leafed trees, munching on the sweet fruit, as Jerrol thoughtfully watched the boiling clouds pass over. Before long the sun came back out, and the rain-washed trees sparkled with glistening raindrops as the sun beat down and dried everything out.

The sea was alive with fish eager to throw themselves in their nets after the storm, and the hold was soon full. They dropped anchor off the white beaches of Duyli earlier than expected and carefully waded into the skin-scraping rock-pools to fill the sacks with samphire. Then finally they set off for Molinti, Gael bemoaning his scratches all the way home. He stopped complaining when Jerrol promised him a day off once their haul was offloaded and delivered to the palace.

Present Day. Febu 18th, 4128, Molinti Harbour

Hannah and Mikke walked down the gentle slope towards the small sandy beach to the west of the harbour in Molinti on what had become a daily visit. She breathed in the luxuriously clean salty air and sighed in pleasure. Mikke pointed excitedly at the fishing boats moored in the bay and pulled up on the sand, the hulls painted in bright colours catching his eye. Young, bronzed men scampered across the decks, coiling nets and ropes.

Hannah spread her rug on the sand and took Mikke down to the water's edge, where, firmly holding his hand, she let him paddle. He shrieked in delight as he splashed in the crystal-clear water.

Setting him up with a clay cup and wooden spoon, Hannah watched Mikke dig in the sand. He happily scattered sand around the cup, some of it hitting the target.

Hannah helped him turn it over, bash it with the spoon, and lift the cup up. He squealed with more delight at the resulting mound.

Febu 14th, 1124, Molinti

Jerrol was sluicing out the hold when he heard a child squeal. His heart clenched at the sound. Mikke would make such a squeal at bath time; he loved water. Jerrol jumped down from the deck of his boat onto the sand and drifted down the beach. He strolled along the water line, the warm water stroking his bare feet.

The child was playing in the sand, and his heart stopped. Mikke? Was Taelia here? He drew closer and carefully knelt in front of his son and struggled to breathe. He wanted to touch him, to hold him, to hug him close and never let go, but he daren't. He didn't want to drag him over to wherever he was. Slowly, he removed the leather cord from around his neck; the smooth green stone with the hole pierced through the middle dangled in his hand. He pushed it towards Mikke. The air resisted, but the stone penetrated the barrier and plopped into the water at Mikke's feet. Mikke pounced on it immediately, the biggest grin spreading over his face.

"Papa," he squealed. "Papa." He reached his arms up towards Jerrol.

Hannah lurched to her feet and rushed towards Mikke. Jerrol backed away, unable to stop the tears streaming down his face, his chest tight. Hannah frantically searched around Mikke, but there was nothing except a wet little boy holding a very familiar green stone pendant, about to burst into tears. She gathered Mikke into her arms, grappling to hold him as he struggled to reach Jerrol.

Hannah's mouth worked as her gaze flittered about her. "Jerrol?" she whispered.

"Hannah," Jerrol replied.

"Jerrol?" she said again, staring straight through him. "Can you hear me?" she glanced around her again and seeing no one, continued. "Taelia and Birlerion are here. They are searching for you. Hold on. Please."

Mikke almost squirmed out of her grasp, and she swept him into her arms. Hugging him close, she stood and walked up the beach.

Jerrol reluctantly backed off, allowing Hannah to calm Mikke before he became hysterical. He gathered up their forgotten cup and spoon, and at a distance, he followed Hannah as she carried his still screaming son back up into the town.

She headed straight for the emperor's palace; he knew Emperor Pierien's guards were vigilant and he had no chance of getting inside. In fact, if Gael had returned on time they would have left by now. Hannah waltzed through the guards without stopping. He waited, hoping, and his breath caught as Taelia and Birlerion dashed out of the entrance a short time later.

Birlerion tried to restrain Taelia, who was crying hysterically, his own face strained as he searched the street.

"Jerrol," Taelia screamed at the top of her lungs, struggling to free herself. Her gaze passed over him without seeing him.

"Taelia," he called in return, but they couldn't hear him. He was not helping as they couldn't see or hear him, and he was only causing them grief.

"Jerrol?" Birlerion said, staring straight at him. "If you can hear me, we've found your song, and the Jerven shipping line, and the Senti sentinal. I remember us meeting in Vespers. Keep recording in your log book. We've found that too."

Jerrol's knees almost gave out as relief coursed through him. They were following his trail; they had found him.

Slipping around them, he placed the cup and spoon on the steps behind them, and reluctantly, his eyes drinking in Taelia's face like a parched sailor, he backed away down the hill and returned to his boat. He climbed back onboard and morosely stared out to sea. He still didn't see how they could help him.

Taelia stilled in Birlerion's arms and she drew a shuddering breath. "I'm alright," she whispered, "he's gone."

"He was here? You really think he was here in this street?"

"Yes, he was here," Taelia replied, her heart heavy. She pushed away from Birlerion and turned towards the entrance, halting with a gasp as she saw her son's toys on the bottom step. She knelt and hugged them close. "Jerrol," she whispered, her heart contracting. A flash caught her eye, and she dipped her hand in the wet sand at the bottom of the cup. Two sandy beads lay on her open palm. She polished them off, collapsing on the step as she looked at the gleaming silver pearl and the turquoise bead. Their brilliance muted as the tears spilt over and she rocked on the step.

Birlerion gently gathered her in his arms and carried her inside.

15

FEBU 14TH, 1124

PLINI, BIRTOLI

Jerrol and Gael reached Plini later that afternoon. The harbour opened before them as they popped out of the channel into the calmer waters and skimmed across the bay to the jetty. An array of small fishing boats and skiffs were already tied up to the jetty, and Jerrol counted back. It must be the Lady's day; tonight the town would be busy. Sailors with some coin in their pockets would be ripe for adventure.

Gael hesitated as they approached the jetty. He watched Jerven carefully and then blurted: "I'm sorry I made us late."

Jerrol looked up in surprise. "What?"

"I know you've been angry with me all the way home, but honestly, I only meant to be a chime. They had a camel in the market square, all the way from Terolia. I've never seen one."

"I'm not angry with you."

"You could'a fooled me. You haven't spoken to me except to bite my nose off," Gael said bitterly.

"I'm sorry, I've got a lot on my mind."

"I knew it was too early to get a second boat. How are we going to pay for it? And another crew."

Jerrol laughed. "I've already saved enough to pay for it. Aiden and his boy are going to work the *Moonlight Kiss*. I have orders coming out of my ears and no way to fill them. I need a second and a third boat. You need to start paying attention as I need you to captain one for me."

Gael gasped. "Me, a captain …" he gasped, starry-eyed.

"Only if you start paying attention; you've got to prove to me that you know these waters."

But it was obvious Gael was already planning how he was going to share this wonderful news with his friends.

Jerrol jumped down to join the waiting Gael, and resting his arm across the boy's shoulders, they slowly walked up the jetty. "I'll meet you at Granfer's. I want to go and speak to the controller about my land. I'll be in soon."

Gael flicked a glance at him. "I can come with you if you like," he offered.

Jerrol laughed. "Now, I know you are just dying to go see your friends. You don't have to wait for me." He ruffled the boy's hair affectionately as Gael laughed. "You've been away long enough, go find your friends."

"I'll be back for dinner," Gael promised, and Jerrol waved his hand as his brother sped off down the track.

Jerrol continued walking around the harbour to a small squat building which housed Plini's administrator, the man who managed all the trading and building developments in Plini.

Administrator Aran was a short, thin man, who meticulously abided by the rules. He ensured the boats were moored in regimented rows, diligently charged the taxes on catches and berthing and just as diligently collected them, he allowed a boat only its allotted time in the unloading bays, and ensured the emperor received his due. He controlled everything, even if it wasn't in his remit, and the fisherman laughingly called him the controller.

Jerven had been patiently following every single process that the controller had managed to lay in his way, and Jerrol hoped the money in his belt should finally close the deal. He entered the small office at the front of the building and smiled at the man seated behind the desk.

"Aran, you're looking well," he said as he sat in the single chair in front of the desk.

Aran liked to intimidate his visitors, making them uncomfortably aware of his position over them. Many men were too scared to approach him and flatly refused to enter his office. Jerrol had never had a problem, being used to working with powerful people back in Vespiri, and the controller seemed to recognise it.

"Ah, Captain Jerven, welcome home. Good trip?"

"Indeed, I hope so. Here's Plini's correspondence." He dropped the wallet on the table.

The controller pounced on it. "Good, I have been waiting for this."

"I wanted to make the final payment on my plot. Is everything ready? I'd like to start building before the heat gets too bad."

"Yes, I have the papers here for you. Final payment forty Molins, making the total paid five hundred and sixty-five molins. Here's the entry in the ledger, proof of your purchase. These are the papers you need to sign. I have a copy ready for you."

Jerrol handed over the forty molins. It left his purse woefully thin, but it was worth it. His own stretch of land further round the coast; a location he knew would survive the onslaught of water. The distance from the port of Plini was why he had gotten so much land for such a reasonable price. No one else wanted to travel out that far, but in a boat, it took minutes to round the point. It gave him room to slowly expand a harbour, boatyard, warehouse; he saw it all in his mind—the future island of Senti.

He smiled as he stared at the piece of paper in his hand. Yes! He looked up to see the controller smiling sympathetically. "Feels good, doesn't it?" the controller said. "You've done well, much faster than even I expected. Congratulations." He held out his hand.

The smile broadened on Jerrol's face as he shook the controller's hand in surprise. "Thank you. Join me tonight in the square to celebrate? It's Lady's night; the Lady will watch over us."

The controller's face flushed with pleasure. "You have a good enough reason to celebrate. Everyone will be in the square. It would be my pleasure."

Jerrol carefully folded the paper into his pouch and left the office, his step light as he made his way back around the bay and up into the town. Colourful bunting was hung across the streets. Torches and lamps were positioned around the square, which was full of tables and chairs ready for the celebration later. Strings of coloured glass hung from the tree's branches, sparkling in the torchlight. They would gleam like fireflies as night descended. A huge spit was set up in the corner of the square opposite the dance floor, and the waft of roasting goat made his mouth water.

Jerven's grandfather's rooms were at the back of the Rosa Taverna on the west side of the village square. He only had two rooms, and when Jerrol and Gael were home it was uncomfortably overcrowded; one of the reasons Jerrol had been so determined to buy the land and build. He usually ended up sleeping on his boat. The rooms were too stuffy for someone used to living in the open air, and his grandfather was oppressively set in his ways.

Gael was more comfortable with his granfer, having lived

with him whilst Jerven was at sea. Their parents had died when a pestilence had swept the town, decimating the population, leaving two young boys on their own. Their granfer had stepped in and reluctantly looked after Gael, and Jerven had been sent to sea. Gael had been with Jerven on the *Scout* for nearly two years now, and he was shaping up well.

Jerrol eased his shoulders, concentrating on relaxing his tense muscles. *His* grandfather. Jerven's grandfather always rubbed him up the wrong way. No matter what Jerven did, the old man berated him. He seriously thought about not going in, but he squared his shoulders and entered the dark, stuffy room.

"Hi, we're back," he said into the gloom.

"About time," a gravelly voice responded. "Took your time, didn't you?"

"Winds and tides dictate, you know that."

"Huh." The old man scowled. "Well, I'm off to the corner. You're lucky you found me here; I was just leaving."

"Gael is about somewhere. I'm sure he'll find you later."

'I'm sure he will," the old man said, shuffling towards the door. Jerrol stepped back outside, giving way. His grandfather had lost weight; his face was thin and gaunt, his eyes sunken, and his clothes hung loose on his spare frame.

"Granfer, what's wrong, have you been ill?" Jerrol asked in concern, extending his hand towards his grandfather.

The old man shrugged it off. "No use worrying about it now, you weren't here. You're never here when it matters."

"I can only be in one place at a time," Jerrol said, his granfer's words cutting deep as the old man stomped off.

He sighed and walked around to the Taverna's entrance. He fixed a smile on his face as he entered the dim interior. The owner rented Jerven the back rooms. His grandfather didn't question who paid for his rooms; he seemed to expect them as his due.

"Josef, here's the rent for the old man," Jerrol said, placing the coins on the bar as the man approached. He was a plump man, though his face was pasty; a result of being stuck inside all day.

"Jerven, good to see you home. How long are you staying this time?" Josef asked with a knowing wink as he collected the coins and placed a mug of ale on the bar.

"Not long; boat's not earning moored in the bay, now, is it?"

"True, true. It's about time you brought some of your catch home. Don't see why the Molintians should get it all."

"I thought your son kept you supplied?" Jerrol said in surprise.

"Phrist and sardines. I need some mullet or brannock, something with a bit of flesh, you know."

"I'll see what I can find you," Jerrol promised, draining the mug. "The old man, when was he ill?" he asked.

"Not long after you left. Old Tess looked after him, not that he cared much for it, kept telling her to leave him alone, but he drank the soup quick enough," Josef laughed.

"If I don't see her, thank her for me."

"Make sure you thank her yourself," Josef said as Jerrol waved an acknowledgement as he left.

Jerrol joined Marin and his friends in the shaded square under the broad-leafed tree and sat down in the chair offered before someone else took it. "Where's Myriam? I'm surprised she let you out on your own."

"She wasn't feeling well. I promised I wouldn't stay late, but I needed to talk to you before you left again," Marin replied. "I wanted to accept that partnership you proposed. I discussed it with Myriam. She wants more stability, especially with the baby on the way. A steady income; you said five molins a trip? That would suit me."

"Great, and you know, at some point if you wanted to

come off the boats, I'll need someone to cover the office and track the loads. Though that would mean moving to my yard at Senti when it's ready."

"You still planning on building way down there?"

"Yeah, it gives access to the islands, as well as Vespers and Terolia. Aiden has agreed to captain the *Moonlight Kiss* when I get back from Terolia, and you running the *Mari Rose* will mean we are in business." Jerrol grinned in delight. "Let's celebrate." He called for a round, and they joined in the general merriment.

Jerrol gave Gael the next day off. They had been at sea almost continuously for the last month or more; it was time to stay on dry land for a day or so. Jerrol spent the day pottering around on the *Scout*, splicing rope and repairing nets. The handwork was soothing, and a peaceful day passed. As dusk fell, he sat on the deck, leaning against the railing as the sky darkened and the sliver of the new moon began to rise. He retrieved his log book from under the tarpaulin in the locker and sat staring at the blank page in the light of his lantern. Sighing, he wrote the date and then stared at it. Febu 15th, 1124. It still didn't seem possible.

The water gently slapping against the stern added to the sudden feeling of displacement. He didn't belong here, no matter how well he had adapted. He wanted to go home to Stoneford, to sit with Jason and discuss the management of the Watch, to wrap his arms around his precious family and never let go.

Carefully, he unscrewed the lid of the ink pot, his fingers gripping it awkwardly. No matter how much he practiced, he couldn't get comfortable using his left hand for daily chores. He opened his hand, and a gentle glow illuminated his page as he started writing, carefully dipping his quill into the inkpot sitting next to him and trying not to blot ink all over the page. Taelia would have enough trouble reading his scrawl as it was.

He finally straightened up and put down the quill, flexing his cramping hand. His remaining fingers still ached if he gripped a pen too long, which is why he had switched his swordplay to his left hand, though he hadn't held a sword in months, let alone sparred. He would be so out of shape by the time he got home.

Putting everything away, he rolled into his blankets and, bracing himself against the stern, stared out across the darkened sea. The Oath, which Elder Tuan had passed to him, pressed down on him like a physical weight. He had never considered where the Oath came from, nor what it really was.

Now, he knew it was a physical thing, not alive, but with a definite will, and he was being influenced to return to his new harbour in Senti. He wondered what the Oath wanted in Senti.

Elder Tuan had called him a builder. Did the Elder want him to hide the Oath in his harbour? Jerrol rubbed his temples against his growing headache. Gael would be annoyed at returning to Senti again, but the Oath wasn't going to allow him to go anywhere else. He would pretend he wanted a progress report, trying to explain the Oath was beyond him.

At least Taelia and Birlerion had arrived in Birtoli and found his trail, so that was a hopeful sign. He needed to find Roberion next, and he fell asleep trying to figure out the best way to search for him, after he had taken the Oath to Senti.

16

FEBU 15TH, 1124

MOLINTI

The next morning, the *Scout* left the harbour as the sun rose. Gael gazed out over the bow with a scowl on his face. He had been complaining ever since Jerrol had dragged him out of bed before dawn. Jerrol laughed at him. "Let's pull into Senti; we can see how it's progressing."

"Another delay!"

Jerrol shook his head and steered the boat around Plini point. The hum from his sentinal strengthened, and he relaxed into his welcome as they sailed into the cove. The ching of hammers on chisel echoed across the waters. The cliff face was already hewn back to provide a narrow ledge, which would form the new quay, well above the current beaches. Work was progressing, and Jerrol acknowledged the greetings from the men on the cliff as he swept up to the beach.

"I won't be long," Jerrol said as he jumped down to the sand. Gael rolled his eyes but bent to pick up some netting that needed repairing. Leaving Gael to his work, Jerrol walked up to the headland and greeted the sentinal.

He relaxed into the sentinal's embrace and shimmered

into the tree. Inhaling the vibrant greenness of the tree, he felt a flush of energy, which invigorated him. He smiled his thanks. "I need to reach the Land, I have a request for Marguerite," he murmured. "Or rather the Oath has a request for Marguerite, and I wondered if I could go down through you?" Jerrol was positive it would be easier to reach the Land through the Lady's Guardian, a sentinal tree.

The sentinal's assent shivered through him, and he extended his thoughts down through the roots and into the rich soil below. He encountered a soft query as an ancient awareness encased him. "Marguerite? The Oath has a request," he murmured.

The Land embraced him, and he gasped as the old one sifted through him; it wasn't Marguerite. The ancient awareness that permeated the Land was so old it must have been in situ since the time the world began. Ancient legends said one of the Mother's sons had been bound into the Land. Was this him? Jerrol couldn't identify a person as such, not as he had when he had first experienced Marguerite within the Land. She had a personality and a physical body, but this presence was just … there. No form, no identity, just an overwhelming presence.

The Land's exhaustion dragged at him as if it was his own. The effort to support the cycle of life had taken its toll, and the presence emanated a sense of timeless effort. A constant guardianship that was thin and worn and about to part under the stresses of the current upheaval being thrown around by the Ascendants. The weight lifted as the Land let him go, and he came too, collapsed on the floor of the sentinal.

Jerrol inhaled sharply and choked on a mouthful of dirt. He spat it out, retching as he tried to draw breath, and his sentinal tried to ease his distress. Wearily, he sat up and realised the Land had not taken the Oath as he had thought.

The Land had repurposed it into a rectangular slab of stone, the size of one of the bricks used in the new houses in Old Vespers. A heavy brick, Jerrol found, as he tried to lift it. Its denseness resonated through his hands and up his arms; the Oath recognised the after-effects of the Bloodstone and Jerrol's blood began to hum, his body vibrating uncomfortably. "I cannot assimilate a brick," Jerrol protested out loud. He may have been able to absorb the Bloodstone shards into his body, but a brick was going too far.

A query settled in his mind, a tentative question, as the Oath tested their lines of communication. Jerrol thought his head might explode. Not only had he met the ancient entity protecting their world, he now had the Oath trying to talk to him.

He attempted to form a memory of the Bloodstone crystals melting into his hand. Amusement flowed through him. No, the Oath offered protection, for the people of Birtoli; he was to build it into the foundations of his harbour. *"But shouldn't it protect the Tu'ani clan? The clan who gave me the Oath,"* he thought and relaxed as the Oath explained. The Oath protected all who asked for it, wherever they were. Jerrol's grip convulsed around the brick in shock as the reality of the situation set in. *"The* Oath?" He held the physical Oath in his hands? How was that possible? He frowned at it; it wasn't at all what he would have expected. He would have expected something a little more exotic than a slab of stone. It glistened gently, a sparkle in the darkness. Where to place it?

As a builder he supposed he needed to use it to build something. He sighed as the obvious hit him. The Oath would be the foundation stone beneath his new harbour. He needed to place it beneath the wall. A place of safety, of obscurity, where no one would find it.

An impossible image formed in his mind. *"How am I supposed to place you there?"* he thought in horror. The image flashed insistently. *"Alright, alright, but I don't know how."* Marguerite's familiar face hung before his eyes, and he knew he had to wait until Marguerite took over the guardianship of the Land. She would help him. She hadn't bonded with the Land, yet. He should have remembered; Birlerion had told him she was still at the palace with Leyandrii. *More sacrifice,* he thought, and then *"What do I do with you in the meantime?"*

The brick shimmered, and a small black pendant lay on top. He placed the brick on the floor and hung the pendant around his neck. The brick sank into the sentinal, and the pendant sank into his skin and out of sight.

Jerrol gulped as he stared at the floor. "Look after each other until I get back. I can't take that brick with me." He realised the lie in his words as a second hum started in his head, and he closed his eyes. He missed Zin'talia's company, her constant presence in his mind, but at this rate he wouldn't have room for her when he got back. Rising, his joints protested, a bone deep ache that told him that time had passed. He hoped he hadn't been too long as he had no way of explaining what he had just experienced to anyone. Slowly, he made his way back down to the beach. Exhaustion rippled through him; a deep ache within that left him feeling unsettled.

The sun was high. His stomach growled in agreement. He had been longer than he had intended. What to say to Gael? In the end he said nothing.

The workmen pushed the *Scout* off the beach and, with cheery waves, returned to their work. "There is some lunch in the locker. Why don't you get it out? You must be hungry. I know I am," Jerrol said.

Gael soon returned with a parcel of food, and he happily handed over freshly baked bread sandwiches, his griping silenced as he took a large bite. Jerrol let Gael steer the *Scout* back out of the bay as he lay in the bow and napped, assimilating the double hum that settled in his mind and took root. Sentinal and Oath, Lady and Land, entwined within him. Gael's eyes bored into him, but he feigned sleep, though his mind was too busy to relax.

So, when did Marguerite bond with the Land? He was sure Birlerion had said it was near the end, just before Leyandrii sundered the Bloodstone. They had held off as long as possible, hoping to come up with an alternative plan. He mused on the idea that Leyandrii's sister could still be abroad in Vespiri, along with the follow-on thought of whether he would get to meet her or, more dauntingly, the Lady Leyandrii herself. He had only ever met them in the in-between spaces when he was either in desperate need or performing the impossible.

His exhausted body finally overruled his busy mind, and he drifted off to sleep on the rocking deck, dreaming of the two women who protected the world of Remargaren; the ultimate guardians who had given everything they had to guard the people and the world they lived in.

He awoke much later, feeling refreshed and with a smile on his face.

"What are you so pleased about?" Gael griped, fed up with managing the *Scout* on his own.

Jerrol stretched. "It's a beautiful day."

"Most of which you've slept through. How come you get to sleep and I have to work?"

"Good practice for when you get your own boat," Jerrol said as he took Gael's place at the tiller. He swiftly quartered the sea. Gael had made good time, he thought, as they approached Astille to starboard. It was time to head east to Duyli and the islands scattered around it. Jerrol stared out at the deep blue seas, inhaling the fresh salty air, and considered yet again what a beautiful world they lived in. A world some people would prefer to destroy than enjoy; it was beyond his understanding.

They spent the next few days visiting a myriad of smaller islands, leaving mail and official notices from the administration in Molinti, collecting onward messages, often dictated. Jerrol spent much of the time jotting them down: requests for hard-to-find supplies and medicines, some of which Jerrol supplied out of the trunk he had restocked before they left Molinti, ointments for cuts and burns, needles, rolls of stringy gut for stitching worse wounds, and a range of tinctures and powders that seemed to be popular.

He had even stocked up on powders for upset tummies or vomiting, which were originally viewed with suspicion until it was seen that they worked. The islanders had begun to rely on their service; the only one of its kind. Jerrol frowned over the sparsity of trade or traffic between the islands. The islanders themselves tended to be self-sufficient, staying in the vicinity of their island and only leaving long enough to catch a supply of fish, but not travelling any further.

They reached the southernmost island of Duyli later that afternoon; a large mountainous island with towering columns of grey rock shrouded in creeping greenery and trailing vines. They set the nets in the hopes of some mullet or even brannock in the deep waters off the reef. Samphire was short-lived, and they would collect it in the morning just before they headed home to keep it as fresh as possible.

They stripped off in the evening heat, working bare-chested as they hauled in the nets, sorting the fish, gutting, salting, and resetting again. Sweat glistened on their bronzed skin as they relaxed into a comfortable rhythm. The hold was soon full, crates of mullet packed in salt stacked on the deck. They finally beached the *Scout* in the sandy bay as the sun began to sink behind the Birtoli mainland. They went for a dip to wash the stench of fish and sweat off their skin. Jerrol eased aching muscles as he let the gentle ripples tug him back and forth. He watched Gael splashing about in the surf before reluctantly leaving the seductively warm waters to dry in the sun. He dressed and built a small fire to cook their supper; fish, yet again. He decided, when he finally went home, he would refuse to eat fish for the rest of his life.

He cut a couple of sticks and threaded the fish on to roast them over the flames. He watched the flickering flames curl around the wood. It was peaceful; the swish of the waves on the sand soothing.

Gael, having found some rock pools to investigate, had drifted off down the beach. Duyli was an uninhabited island, there being no reliable water supply to sustain life. A sudden clatter of wings interrupted the peace as long-tailed birds, vibrant with yellow and red feathers, launched themselves into the air with a shriek of protest at their intrusion. Everything was so bright and vivid here; a new world.

Jerrol leaned over to check the fish.

The next biggest inhabited island was Geteril, where the Tu'ani lived. He mused on the words of Elder Tuan. A task had been bestowed on him, to conceal the Oath in the foundations of his new clan. His harbour.

Elder Tuan had been the Oath's guardian for sure, but why pass it to him? Jerrol grew cold at the thought that the Ascendants must be searching for it; that the Tu'ani were at risk. Maybe he was supposed to help protect the Tu'ani against the Ascendants? He realised that, during all their campaigns against the Ascendants in Vespiri, Terolia, and Elothia, not once had they considered that Birtoli may have been affected by the same Ascendant disease.

They had been so focused on their own overwhelming problems, they hadn't considered what had been happening in the archipelago. Maybe an Ascendant offshoot had sprouted in the islands and was only now taking grip? He would see if he could get an audience with the empress when he took the samphire to Molinti. Maybe he would discover something in the palace that would guide him?

He looked up as Gael flopped down beside him, scattering the white sand. He was all legs; he had visibly grown in the time Jerrol had been with him. Already taller than Jerrol, and not yet at his full height. He wondered if Mikke would be the same, sprouting suddenly, growing taller than his father. He hoped he wouldn't miss too much of Mikke's younger years. Tears blurring his gaze, he reached for the fish. He must write up his log, which he now knew Taelia had found. He knew she would be relentless in her search; he was counting on it.

"Just in time for supper," Jerrol said as he handed Gael a fish skewer.

Early the next morning, they were up collecting the samphire. They filled eight sacks with the slippery strands before finally casting off. It would take them two days to reach Molinti; they were cutting it fine to get back in time for the oration. The fact that the emperor would allow the Ascendants to speak … Jerrol scowled. How could he stop it? Could he use the Oath? He wasn't sure what power he had as the Oath was not completely entwined with the Land yet; that was his job. But how to do it.

The Oath had not been invoked in 1123, so, in theory, he wasn't the Oath Keeper, yet if the Oath had dragged him here to this time, then he must have some connection to it in this time. He slapped his forehead, of course he did! The Oath was humming inside him, along with the Bloodstone and the sentinal. He wished it would give him some advice as his mind started the litany again, getting him no closer to a solution.

They pulled into Eyti for the night, Jerrol taking the opportunity to place an order for a second fishing boat, to Gael's horror. The *Moonlight Kiss* was a half-built frame on the beach, and construction was progressing well. He also planted the suggestion of a new boatyard in Senti for any adventurous young boat builders looking for a new start.

They slept on the *Scout*, Jerrol sleeping restlessly under the stars. He awoke as soon as the grey dawn began to creep across the sky, the words of the Tu'ani elder on his lips. *"You have but to ask and help shall be granted."* He needed help to complete his harbour, to hide the Oath. He couldn't do it alone. The Lady was always listening. She had heard him. She was sending Marguerite to help him.

He stared out across the silvery sea, remembering the stone towers in Elothia which had offered much the same advice. The engraving in the stone walls had said 'Ask and you shall receive'. The Ladies were ever vigilant on their behalf. Leyandrii always helped those who asked; he just had to be patient.

He had been avoiding her, worried that she wouldn't know him. He was a fool. Of course she would know him. She was a goddess. It was Leyandrii, probably in concert with the Oath, who had called him here in the first place.

They pulled into the harbour the following afternoon in the burning heat of the day. The golden sunshine beat down on the calm waters of the harbour and reflected the blinding glare. Even the *Scout's* wooden railings and the deck were scorching hot. Jerrol sculled up to the jetty, perspiring in the heat. Sensible people were napping in the shade, and the harbour was deserted.

They tied up to the jetty to unload. Gael gladly scampered up to the palace to get the helpers to help carry the crates. Jerrol began stacking the crates on the quay, topping up with salt as needed. He ducked under the coaming and grabbed the sacks, scanning the harbour as he unloaded. His neck was prickling; someone was watching him, but there was no one in sight.

Gael soon returned with many willing helpers. The cook was eager to get his hands on the fish. The offloading went swiftly and Jerrol followed his haul up the incline into the town, sweating profusely in the strong sun. He left Gael to set the *Scout* to rights.

The kitchens were overly hot, people scurrying from one side to another with arms full of trays, the cook shouting instructions. He spotted Jerrol and came over, his face flushed in the heat.

"Chaos!" he said comfortably, obviously well in control. "We will serve a superb dinner now we have the fish. And in plenty of time, I thank you."

"My pleasure, and the samphire for the empress, as requested."

The cook rolled his eyes. "Thank the Lady. She was starting to get quite agitated. Though why she needs so much of the stuff, I don't know."

"Well, you've never been with child, now, have you? Who knows what is going on? If samphire is her only craving, count yourself lucky." Jerrol grinned, remembering some of Taelia's more extreme requests.

"Well, I'm sure she'll be pleased. In fact, she wanted to speak to you when you came. Take this and wait in the foyer on the third floor and she'll see you."

Jerrol took the platter the cook was proffering and left the kitchens. He strolled through the cool corridors and up the back staircase, noting the lack of sentries. No one challenged him as he made his way to the third floor. The palace seemed eerily quiet in comparison to the hectic kitchens.

He tapped gently on the wooden panel of a tall double door and waited patiently. It opened hesitantly and a young girl peered out. "The empress is expecting me," he said.

The girl opened the door. "She'll be here soon, if you could wait here. Put the platter on the table, if you please."

Jerrol was staring out of the window over the elegant courtyard below when the door finally opened behind him. The empress tottered in on the arm of a courtier, almost in tears. The courtier carefully helped her settle in a chair, and, with a nod at Jerrol, escaped.

"Is everything alright, Your Grace?" Jerrol asked, noting her distress. Her colour was heightened and her hands were busy working a lacy handkerchief between her fingers.

"Yes, of course it is," the empress gasped. "I was just upset by …" her voice faded. "It doesn't matter." She seemed to get hold of herself and then smiled shakily at Jerrol. "You're the Fisherman, aren't you?"

Jerrol frowned at her phrasing. "Yes, Your Grace."

"I wanted to thank you for bringing the samphire, and also to warn you."

"Warn me, Your Grace?"

"Yes, there are men in Molinti who are looking for you. They were asking my husband to search for you."

Jerrol frowned. "But why, Your Grace?"

The empress shrugged, dabbing her face with her hand-kerchief. She smiled at her maid as she accepted a glass and drank the contents in one go, then absently handed the glass back to the maid. "I need your help. He won't listen to me. They are after the Tu'ani; the clan who live on the island of Geteril, and you have to stop them."

"The Tu'ani?" Jerrol felt like he had been punched in the stomach.

"I can't say any more, but you must warn them."

"Against what, Your Grace?"

"Against those men. I don't trust them."

"Keep the Lady close, Your Grace, she is your best protection. You are right not to trust them."

The empress sighed. "I know, I'll try. They befuddle me. I would stay away from them, but that leaves my husband, Pierien, on his own."

Jerrol watched her with concern. "I'll do my best to see the emperor, but I can't guarantee he'll listen to me."

"That's all I ask. Thank you." The empress relaxed and closed her eyes. She seemed to think he would solve all her problems. Jerrol took it as a tacit dismissal and left her room, frowning thoughtfully as he descended the stairs. Although security was lax in the palace, he wasn't sure how he would get an audience with the emperor. He left via the busy kitchens, waving to the cook as he passed through, the activity as frantic as ever.

Jerrol took a deep breath as he stood on the palace steps. He had no way of speaking to the emperor and certainly not before the dinner. He would drop Gael back in Plini and go and find Roberion. He had left it too long; he should have left by now.

17

PRESENT DAY

FEBU 20TH, 4128, MOLINTI

Taelia sat on the floor and frowned over the lyrics of Jerrol's song. Mikke was playing with a set of wooden blocks, a gift from the king, stacking them up and squealing as he knocked them down. He began stacking them up again. Birlerion was seated at the table, poring over Jerrol's logbooks by the light of a golden lantern, straining to see the faded writing.

"Waters boil and fire threatens. The Miracle's here, a promise filled," Taelia read thoughtfully. "What can it mean? Surely it should say *a* miracle? Not *the* miracle."

"Bib, bob, rob," Mikke squealed happily as he knocked down his bricks. Taelia smiled absently.

"I can see why you gave this book to me," Birlerion muttered. "It's impossible to read. Jerrol really needs to practice his handwriting; it's terrible. I think this says *'Berthed in Molinti, Gael taken goods, going to palace to see Empress Olini to deliver the sand for the ailing.'* No, her craving?"

"The empress was expecting, wasn't she? Maybe it *was* craving. She was craving something that Jerrol got for her. There's a list of deliveries at the back."

Birlerion carefully turned the fragile pages and ran his

fingers down the dates. "*Febu 18th 1123, Delivered eight sacks samphire to the palace, Molinti, sixteen molins.*' He looked across at Taelia, "That's some craving, and some profit." He stilled as he bent his head back over the book. The entries went on for a few more days and then stopped. The last entry was the twentieth day of Febu. "Taelia, did you see this final entry? '*Sailing for Terolia, urgently need to find Roberion. Matter of life or death. Geteril!*'"

"What? No there was nothing like that, where did you see that?"

Birlerion passed her the book.

"I wouldn't have missed that. Why, it's the most legible writing there is," Taelia exclaimed. "Unless it's happening now," she continued slowly, "and he's just written it. Maybe he's holding this book in his hands right now?" She blinked back tears.

"Geteril?" Birlerion frowned, as he pulled the maps over. "I know the name, but there is no such place on these maps called Geteril."

She cleared her throat. "There must have been a Geteril back then. Haven't we got any of the older maps?" She rose to help search.

"Bib, Bob, Rob, Bern, bern, bern," Mikke chanted as he stacked his blocks.

Taelia stared at her son. "Mikke, do you mean Roberion?"

"Rob, bob, bob," he repeated happily.

Taelia froze and then let her breath out slowly. "Birlerion. What if the miracle is Roberion's ship, the *Lady's Miracle*? But how can the *Miracle* be with Jerrol? *When* is the *Lady's Miracle* with Jerrol?"

"Let's find out everything we can about Geteril. Maybe we can match events with these dates. One thing we do know is that it hasn't happened yet; we'd have heard from Roberion if it had," Birlerion said, stacking the maps to one side. "I'll go see what's in the emperor's library. Tomorrow, you search the archives. We'll start again in the morning."

"I suppose so." Taelia gave Birlerion a rueful smile. "You know, you would have made an excellent scholar."

Birlerion laughed as he rose. "Not what the Lady had planned for me, I'm afraid." He paused, his eyes going distant, and then he shook himself. "Though things would have been very different if she had; I probably wouldn't be here."

"Well, I thank Her every day that you are here. I couldn't do this without you."

Birlerion twisted his lips as he left. "Lady bless your sleep, Taelia."

Taelia knelt on the floor and gathered Mikke her into his arms. She kissed his chubby cheek, and he giggled as he tried to squirm out of her arms. "Papa loves you very much," she whispered into his curls.

Mikke stopped struggling and stared up at her. "Papa," he said seriously, stroking the pendant at her throat.

"Yes, that's right. Papa," she agreed, breathing in the scent of his skin.

"'uvs us."

Taelia smiled. "Yes, he loves us very much." She rose with him in her arms. Time for bath and bed. Leyarille stirred in her basket and meeped. She would need feeding soon. Taelia was soothed by the evening rituals, and with her children settled, she stood on the balcony and stared up at the moon. She sent Jerrol her nightly kiss before going to bed.

It was much later when Taelia awoke suddenly; she sat up in bed, listening hard. She heard footsteps hurry down the corridor and rose to investigate. Melahney wasn't due yet, but just in case, she slipped on her dressing gown and slippers and opened her door. A dishevelled maidservant hurriedly bobbed a curtsey before continuing down the corridor.

"Wait, what has happened?" Taelia called after her, but the maid didn't stop. Taelia trailed after her, tying the belt to her gown around her as she went. She headed towards the muted voices. There was quite a crowd outside Melahney's chamber.

"What is it? Is the empress alright?" she asked, her voice sharp with fear.

"We think she had a bad dream, m'lady. She's not making much sense."

Taelia peered into the bedchamber; there were far too many people milling about. Straightening her shoulders, she spoke firmly. "Yes, well, if it's a dream you don't all need to be here. The emperor would not expect you to be in his wife's bedchamber. I suggest you leave before he arrives. Go back to bed, all of you." She gestured out the door and waited, hoping no one would argue or suggest the emperor be woken. She sighed out a breath as the staff began to leave. "You," she pointed to a young lad. "Go get a glass of warm milk," she ordered before passing through the heavy wooden doors. Taelia smiled in appreciation as she passed through the outer chambers. They were feminine and comforting. Cushions littered the floor and curtains swathed the walls.

"Your Grace?" she called hesitantly. "Is everything alright? Do you need anything?"

"Taelia?" There was a quiver in Melahney's voice.

"Yes, Your Grace. May I come in?"

"Yes, please do. Such a fuss, over a bad dream, as well," she said with a touch of embarrassment. "But it seemed so real."

"Some dreams are like that," Taelia soothed. "My dreams got quite vivid towards the end. Maybe if you tell someone, it will get it out of your head."

"W-would you mind?" Melahney asked a little tearfully.

"Of course not, let me prop you up a bit. You look really uncomfortable lying like that." Taelia collected a pillow off the floor and wedged it behind the empress. "Where's your hand maid?" Taelia asked, frowning around the room.

"Asleep, I expect," Melahney sighed.

"Well, let me get you a cool cloth." She came back with a damp cloth and gently wiped the sweat off the empress' face. "You know, my body started to run scorching hot in the final weeks, so I know what you are going through. Unfortunately, during the last few weeks, I think every bit of your body is working twice as hard!" There was a light tap on the door, and Taelia went to retrieve the glass of milk. "Go find the empress' maid," she instructed before closing the door on the protesting face of the boy.

"Here," she said gently. "It will help you relax."

The empress sighed. "Warm milk; I haven't had it in years," she said softly as she sipped and visibly relaxed.

"Do you want to talk about your dream?" Taelia prompted.

"I think I'd better." Melahney peered at Taelia. "I think you need to know." She took another sip of her milk before she started speaking. "I dreamt I was in the receiving chamber with Emperor Pierien, waiting for the delegation from Elothia. I had this terrible craving for a local delicacy called samphire; it was making me irritable, shall I say?" she said with a slight smile. "I received word that the fisherman had arrived with a delivery, so I excused myself to go and speak to him.

"The palace seemed a lot smaller. I reached my rooms in no time, and there was this young fisherman waiting for me.

He was dark-haired, tanned, and he had the lightest silver-grey eyes; they were really striking." She frowned before she continued. "I tried to warn him that their were men looking for him. He was eloquent, courteous, and he told me I was right not to trust them. I brushed him off because he was so vague. He was worried when I, I mean Olini, told him the Tu'ani clan were at risk."

"The Tu'ani?"

"Yes, they were a clan that died centuries ago." Melahney looked at Taelia, tears springing to her eyes. "I asked him to help Pierien. He seemed so competent and understanding. I realised, when I awoke, that it was Commander Haven. I recognised him, only in the dream I had no idea who he was."

"That's often how dreams work," Taelia soothed. "What happened to him?"

"I don't know. He wasn't sure he could meet with Pierien before the dinner, though he promised he would try. I saw him leave, but as he left, the delegation from Elothia arrived. The delegation seemed interested in him. They were watching him until they were escorted into the receiving chamber. I hurried to join them as I hadn't had a chance to speak to Pierien."

"Pierien? You keep calling the Emperor Pierien."

Melahney stared at her. "It wasn't Geraine, it was Pierien. He was much taller and golden-haired, with blue eyes. But he was the emperor, and I was his empress, as heavily pregnant as I am now. I was worried about him."

Taelia nodded. "And then what happened?"

"They made flowery speeches, words of welcome, and offers of friendship of working together for the betterment of all. They wanted to speak to the people. I don't remember what they said."

"Do you remember their names?"

"Umm, Dominant Clary was one I think; not sure of the other one. When I heard the words again, they were asking Pierien to help them find the location of the ..." she halted confused, "uh, the location of something they shouldn't have even known it existed; how could they know?" Melahney was getting agitated again.

"Don't upset yourself. It was just a dream. The emperor didn't tell them, did he?"

"I'm not sure. The words kept fading in and out. But I realised these were the men the Fisherman was warning us against, so I prayed to the Lady for help. I said to Pierien that these were not matters for discussion with strangers, but Pierien said they were friends, that we could trust them. I said we could only trust in the Lady, and he got angry with me.

"He said I was obviously overcome with my condition and I ought to retire. He would speak with the delegation alone. I pleaded with him not to, but I was only making him angrier." She looked at Taelia. "And then I woke up in floods of tears."

"I'm not surprised after a dream like that," Taelia soothed, her mind working frantically. "The Ascendants were obviously after something important. If you still have it today, then they obviously didn't get it, so you can stop worrying."

Melahney absently twisted a curl between her fingers. "I need to speak to Geraine. This is not something I can discuss without his permission." She flicked a nervous glance a Taelia. "It was, after all, only a dream," she finished, concentrating on pleating the material of her covers.

"I think you'll find it was a true dream. But you're right, speak with Emperor Geraine in the morning. You should confide in your father. I'm sure this is connected to what is happening to your husband and mine."

Melahney nodded slowly. "I'll speak to Geraine in the morning. Thank you, Taelia."

Taelia smiled. "All will be well," she said as she helped Melahney settle down. She was closing the door when the empress' maid hurried up. "You're too late. The empress has gone back to sleep. Don't wake her up." Taelia strode back to her room, wide awake, her mind buzzing with questions.

What could the Ascendants have possibly been searching for back then? She wasn't aware of anything momentous happening, except for the sundering of the Bloodstone, and the Lady had that, didn't she?" Taelia froze as the thought percolated through her mind. What if the Lady didn't have the Bloodstone and somehow the Ascendants knew? Her stomach flipped at the idea, and she suddenly felt sick. Surely not? She sat on the balcony, staring up at the moon for the rest of the night, too worried to sleep, and impatiently waiting for sunrise so she could wake the king.

Taelia was up, dressed, and tapping on the door to the king's chamber as the servants began their morning duties. She knew Darris would be awake even if the king slept late after the state dinner the previous evening. Darris opened the door, raising his eyebrows at the sight of her. "You do know what time it is?" he said in a soft undertone.

"Yes, I do, but Darris, can you ask the king to see me as soon as he wakes up? It's imperative."

Darris sighed as a deep voice spoke from behind him, and he opened the door wider. The king stood in the middle of the room, wrapped in his dressing-gown. He gestured to the chairs and padded barefoot over to the table to pour himself a cup of coffee. He raised the pot at Taelia, who blushed. "I couldn't, Your Majesty. Please let me."

Benedict rolled his eyes and poured another mug before

bringing them both over to the low table between the chairs. "I am quite capable of pouring a mug of coffee, you know."

"Yes, sire, but you're the king," Taelia said, shocked.

Benedict chuckled. "I may be the king, but it doesn't stop you from tapping on my door at sunrise."

"I didn't think you'd be up."

"Well, I am, so tell me what's got you up so early."

"The empress had a dream last night; a true dream. She woke up quite distressed."

Benedict sat forward, the amusement wiped from his face. "Is she alright?"

"Yes, sire, she's fine, but she dreamt Jerven came to the palace. She didn't know him in the dream, but she recognised him as Jerrol when she woke up."

Benedict gestured for her to continue and then leaned back in his chair, hands cupping his mug.

"She said she asked him to help Pierien with the Ascendants because he wouldn't listen to her. Jerrol warned her not to trust them. She said that, after he left, a delegation from Elothia arrived to see the emperor. She called the Emperor Pierien, sire. I looked him up. He was the Emperor of Birtoli from 1115 to 1142. His wife, Olini, was pregnant with their first child." Taelia hesitated before adding, "She died in childbirth during the great storm on Maru 7th, 1124."

The king nodded slowly. "Go on."

"When she joined Emperor Pierien in the receiving chamber, she said the emperor was already under their spell. He had agreed to allow them to speak to the people. She said it was like the words faded in and out; she couldn't concentrate on what they were saying. It was Dominant Clary; she thinks that was his name."

"Dominant Clary was the head of the Lady's administration," Fonorion said quietly from his position by the door. "He spoke for the government, and he was supposedly a staunch supporter of the Lady. If he betrayed her, it would explain much."

Taelia flashed him a look of apology, she hadn't seen him there as she had been so focused on what she needed to tell the king. She shrugged. "That was the name she said. They wanted the emperor to tell them the location of something. Melahney, sorry, the empress, clammed up at that point. She said she couldn't talk of it, that she needed permission from Geraine to even speak of it. What she did say was that no one should even know of its existence, let alone know it was in Birtoli. She didn't know if Emperor Pierien told them where it was, and when she pushed him to get rid of them, he got angry with her and dismissed her, and that was when she woke up."

The king exhaled slowly.

"Your Majesty, what if it was the Bloodstone? Or part of the Bloodstone? What if the Lady didn't have it all together?"

Benedict looked at Fonorion. "Is it possible?"

Fonorion shrugged, his face dubious. "No one knew of the Bloodstone's existence until she broke it. We had never heard of it until the Captain awoke us and we heard the histories."

"But you said no one should know of its existence in Birtoli. That means it's something that is still here. It can't be the Bloodstone," Benedict mused.

"I'm not sure if she was talking as Olini or herself, sire, and unless Geraine gives permission, she won't speak of it. She was concerned that she had even mentioned it."

"Then no one in this room mentions it again unless I give you permission," the king said sharply, looking at each of them.

"Yes, Your Majesty," they replied in chorus.

"Taelia, research Pierien and Olini. Find out what they

did from Novu 1123 to the sundering of the Bloodstone. We need to get ahead of this instead of trailing behind. Ask Birlerion to check on this Dominant Clary. I want to know who he really was and what he was doing. Send word to Liliian and get her searching for him as well. We need more researchers; this is getting ridiculous."

"Yes, sire. Also, we think we figured out one of the lines from the song. It seems that Roberion takes the *Lady's Miracle* to help rescue some place called Geteril. Umm, in Febu of 1124."

"*What?*"

"The verse in the song goes:

Troubles rise, storm clouds build, a blinding light, the
Captain shields.
Waters boil and fire threatens, the Miracle's here, a promise
filled.
Far from home trials are suffered, yet honour and strength
prevail,
From icy shrouds to balmy waters, again the scout will sail.

Birlerion and I were talking about the phrasing '*the* Miracle' instead of '*a* miracle'. We think it means Roberion's ship."

"And where does Geteril come into it?"

"The final entry in Jerrol's log is on Febu 20th, 1124," Birlerion's deep voice interrupted them. Darris spread his hands in apology as he closed the door behind him. "Saying that he needed to find Roberion. That it was a matter of life and death, and it concerned Geteril. I've been searching in the library all night. Geteril was the home of the Tu'ani clan, and it's thought that the island was drowned in a huge storm surge around that time. I couldn't find anything else. There is no mention of the island or the clan anywhere, and I've searched all night."

King Benedict glared at Birlerion. "Don't you people ever sleep?" he demanded.

"Now and then," Birlerion grinned, easing the lines of strain and exhaustion from his face.

18

FEBU 19TH, 1124

FERIL, TEROLIA

The brilliant red sky blended into the golden cliffs of Terolia, casting a rich rose-gold hue over everything as Jerrol sailed into the port of Feril in the south of Terolia before darkness suddenly descended as the sun disappeared behind the mainland.

Jerrol blinked at the sudden darkness. Torches flared to life along the quayside and Jerrol allowed the incoming tide to drift him up to the jetty. He tied the *Scout* off before glancing around the harbour. There weren't many boats berthed, mainly small skiffs, possibly used to ferry passengers off the larger boats, though this harbour wouldn't hold a ship the size of Roberion's. He walked up to the hut at the end of the jetty, and the door creaked noisily as he opened it to peer inside.

"I'm just coming," a voice shouted from the end of the quay as another torch flared into life.

"I'll wait," Jerrol called back.

The torches rippled in the sea breeze, a nice cool stream of air blowing away the sun-baked heat of the day. "Sorry," puffed a skinny bow-legged man as he hurried up. "Don't usually get arrivals this late in the day."

"I got stalled by the heights. I misjudged the cross currents round the point; took me longer than I thought it would," Jerrol said, apologetically.

"You're up from Birtoli, then?" the man asked. "Didn't think I'd seen you before."

"Just starting out. I was wondering how I go about trading my fish up here. Do I need an agreement or anything?"

"No, come in and offload. But you will need to arrange a haulier to get your goods to the markets if you want to sell anything. Nearest is Melila or Marmera. Further up, you're looking at offloading near Selir."

"Is there a loading charge?"

"Docking fee of two molins, daily charge another two thereafter, then you pay whomever is doing your work for you. Terolians aren't bothered by the sea; they tend to focus inwards, not outwards. A bit of mining in the Telusions; mainly dirt and sand and not much else." The man grinned, revealing stained teeth.

"I was looking for Sentinal Roberion; do you know where he berths his ship?"

"Roberion?" The man burst out laughing. "Ship? More like a skiff; his bucket is smaller than yours." The man continued to chuckle. "He sails out of Selir, rarely comes here."

"Thank you, here's the two molins for tonight. I'll be moving on tomorrow."

"Make sure you leave before sixth chime; you'll get the tide to take you out. Much easier," the man said.

"I will." Jerrol nodded his thanks and left. The Telusions. He shivered, repressing unwanted memories. They were mining even now. He didn't want to go near them.

The harbour boasted one inn; a disreputable building with a sagging roof and crazed glass windows. The door was propped open with a hessian sack as a doorstop, the contents of which had solidified in the damp, salty air. Jerrol skirted it as he entered. The smoky fug drifting in the interior made his eyes water. After months of clear sea air, the smog was almost overpowering; he had forgotten what dire places these inns could be. Jerrol cleared his throat and nodded at the bartender. "Ale," he choked out.

The barman swiped a dirty cloth across the bar and slammed a mug down. "Five coppers," he said.

Jerrol stared at him. He was sure that was an inflated price. "How much?"

"Five coppers if you want the drink."

"What else does it include?" he asked.

"Nothing, that's the price of an ale." The man shifted his eyes looking over Jerrol's shoulder.

Jerrol sighed gently. No wonder this place looked so down beat; no one with any sense came here. He slowly turned and came face to chest with a bull of a man. He looked all the way up.

"Problem?" the man growled.

"Not at all," Jerrol replied politely.

"Well, I have a problem with you," the man said as he prodded Jerrol painfully in the chest with his tobacco-stained finger.

"Oh?"

"Yeah, you're standing in my spot."

Jerrol glanced around the empty bar and smiled. "Of course I am, but if you really want to do this …" He threw the contents of his mug in the man's face and twisted around behind him, slamming his face down on the counter as hard as he could. The man's eyes glazed as he slid off the bar to the floor.

The barman gaped at Jerrol in shock. "Keep the change," Jerrol said as he left the bar before anyone else could arrive to take a disliking to him. He debated about leaving harbour straight away, only he was not familiar with the waters and he didn't want to rip his hull out on unknown rocks. He wondered where the Families were to allow such disreputable people to be the face of their country. The harbour man had been right. The Terolians looked to their own Family before considering anything else. He would have to take Roberion to task.

Climbing back down onto his boat, he dipped his mug into his water cask; the stale, oakey-tasting water was at least clean. He re-knotted a new piece of string to the handle so it didn't get lost and wrapped a blanket around his shoulders. The air was chill on the water.

He stared up at the night sky, observing the spray of stars twinkling in the darkness like a personal map. To what he wasn't sure. He wondered what Taelia was doing. His chest constricted painfully as he thought of his family; he missed them, and he had no idea how he would get back to them. He was missing Leyarille's early days; babies grew so fast, and Mikke wouldn't stay small and cuddly for long. He breathed in the remembered scent of a precious child and his tension eased. He hugged it close and blessed the Lady for the timely memory. He sent Taelia her nightly kiss before turning on his side.

Jerrol awoke at dawn with the rising sun and was soon up and about, intending to cast off and leave with the tide. He couldn't wait to leave Feril, and he had no intention of coming back, but a tall dark-haired man prevented him from following his plans.

"Captain, I would like to hire your boat," he said looking down his nose at Jerrol.

"To do what?"

"That would be my business," the man said, his expression stiffening into a sneer as if the need to explain his actions were beneath him. "I will pay you a talent a day for the use of your vessel."

"And who might you be?" Jerrol asked, taking an instant dislike to the man.

"For that price it doesn't matter, but I am Dominant Clary and I need the use of your boat."

"Dominant," Jerrol bowed slightly. "Sir, I would need to know where you want to go."

The man unbent a little, mollified by Jerrol's submissive demeanour. "Yes, well, I need to transport a cargo to Daarl in Elothia. Three men and five sacks."

"A return journey?"

"I will pay you for the return, though we do not intend to come back with you."

"If you want to leave today, we will need to be on the tide before sixth chime, else we will need to wait another day."

The man turned and signalled, and two similarly cloaked men came down the jetty lugging sacks that clinked slightly as they were lowered to the deck. Jerrol heaved them below decks and stowed them safely, returning for the next two. Once all were stowed, Jerrol held out his hand. "Half before, half on arrival," he said coolly.

The man sneered, it seemed to be his permanent expression, but he dropped a talent in Jerrol's hand.

Jerrol nodded and cast off the bow line, then he sculled back with the steering oar to gain the currents, which would take him out of the harbour. The current soon picked them up and they were skimming across the water and out into the sea in no time. Jerrol set the rigging and hauled up the mainsail and wrapping the rope around his wrist, he lent on the tiller and steered out to sea.

The men huddled in the bow, talking in low tones. Jerrol

left them to it. The waves were deep, and he was sure they would soon retreat to the more stable stern as the *Scout* dipped into the troughs and rose above the waves. Jerrol anchored himself by the tiller and watched the men discreetly.

So, this was a Dominant, one of Leyandrii's administrators who later became known as Ascendants. Birlerion hadn't done them justice. They were arrogant and sure of their power. This was whom the Lady and the Sentinals had been fighting all those years ago. This was the man who, he had discovered, repeatedly tried to kill Birlerion just because he wasn't of an old family.

The sudden realisation that Clary was startlingly similar in looks to his once friend and mentor, Torsion, had him gasping for breath. His stomach lurched, bile rising as memories pressed down on him. Memories he didn't want to revisit. What was it Birlerion had said? They didn't deserve to be granted the light of day. He was right. As he was about so many things. He should listen to him more often.

Clary was older than Torsion and more assured of his power; a vile threat personified. No wonder Birlerion had reacted so strongly when he first met Torsion, the likeness was startling. Jerrol stiffened as he realised it was Clary they were fighting against now and who would ultimately cause the loss of the Lady and the Sentinals.

Having met some of the Sentinals, each and every one of whom he would call a friend, and even some as his family, he felt the beginnings of a slow burning anger that they should bear the brunt of such treachery. He tried very hard not to let his emotions show. The Lady had tried to minimise the destruction caused by the Dominants, but Jerrol knew she had not been successful; many innocent people had suffered as a result.

What it would mean to the archipelago suddenly hit him.

The number of islands, the number of clans that would be lost by the drowning of Birtoli ... he felt physically sick. Some of them he now knew, some he also classed as friends. Could he warn them? Would they even believe him?

The Dominant and his men worked their way back up to the stern and huddled next to Jerrol. "Is it normally this rough?" Dominant Clary asked, his complexion tinged with green.

"Out on the open sea, yes, especially in boats of this size. Larger vessels may cope better as they are more stable, but we have to swing around the Selir point before we can get shelter from the mainland. It should ease off once we round the headland," he reassured them.

The Dominant grunted and hunched against the railing.

Jerrol smiled and kept his heading. A couple of chimes later, they rounded the Selir point and the sea suddenly smoothed out. The *Scout* picked up speed and returned to her usual skim across the top of the waves. Jerrol breathed an internal sigh of relief; his stomach had almost betrayed him at one point. One of the Dominant's men had retched over the side, though he hadn't paid enough attention to know who. He didn't have to; he could guess from the drawn face and sickly complexion.

His thoughts returned to the sacks stowed in his hold. He'd had a good feel of them as he had stowed them, and he thought they might be crystals. Five sacks of crystals. How much damage could they do? His attention was drawn back to his passengers as Dominant Clary spoke sharply. "Stop complaining, this will save us three days at least, if not more. We'll be in Adeeron before you know it."

There was a muffled reply that Jerrol couldn't hear, then, "You know they don't travel well. I'll deal with him when we get there. You worry about how you'll get Guerlaire to follow the trail. We have to draw him out."

Jerrol cursed as the Elothian coastline came into sight and his passengers stopped talking to peer into the distance.

"How long?" Dominant Clary asked.

"We should arrive by sunset. It's further than it looks," Jerrol replied.

Clary nodded and hugged his cloak around him. The men were silent for the rest of the journey.

They swept into the port of Daarl just before dusk. The sun dipped behind the landmass as if dousing a flame and torches flared to life along the stone jetty that ran out from the dock, skimming the surface of the water. There was little depth to the harbour, making it seem like one continuous grey glass surface.

Jerrol eased the *Scout* up to the jetty and jumped down to wrap the bow rope around the post. He tied the mooring line before grabbing the stern rope and nimbly pulling the boat into position. He tipped his cap to Dominant Clary as the men disembarked and then helped offload their cargo. Jerrol tensed as Dominant Clary turned back, but it was only to hand him the talent due for the return trip. Clary's cold black eyes inspected Jerrol, his face severe.

"Captain, I hope we meet again; your services are worth every copper."

"Thank'ee sir," Jerrol mumbled, tipping his cap as his passengers staggered down the jetty. They were met by a horse and cart and soon disappeared down the road. Jerrol searched for the harbour master but the port was eerily deserted. Giving up, Jerrol reboarded and cast off, leaving before anyone noticed he had been there.

Jerrol wondered how the men with the cart had known to arrive at that exact moment, especially as the place had been completely deserted. Why had his passengers been so secretive? And what did they intend to do to draw out Captain

Guerlaire, the Lady's Captain before him, and from where? He needed to find Roberion.

A clear night aided Jerrol's return journey to Terolia, and although he should have berthed in a cove for the night, he didn't. He observed the starry sky above, relaxing under the constant glow of the silver moon monitoring his progress, amazed once again at the often unseen beauty of the world he lived in. The sea was serene and peaceful, yet the *Scout* cut through the waves unimpeded, her red sails full and her jib jaunty.

19

FEBU 21ST, 1124

SELIR, TEROLIA

Jerrol arrived safely in Selir as the golden sun sank back into the sea, casting the waters in a shimmering plumage of burning flame. He breathed a heartfelt sigh of relief as the red sands of Selir came into view; he had seriously thought the Dominant would throw a squall or something at him.

Selir was nothing more than a beach, extending to the headland at either end. There was no harbour or jetty. Fishing skiffs and small fishing boats were pulled up on the beach like discarded toys. There was no one in sight as he gently beached the *Scout* and jumped down into the shallow waters, the brilliant sunset spangling off the rippling waves. There was nowhere to tie up to, so he tugged the *Scout* a little further up the beach and trusted, considering the lack of tidal waves, that it would be safe.

He scouted up the beach and followed a trail that led into the broad-leaved foliage fronting the sands. Overlapping deep green fronds blocked the sunlight and gave everything a subdued hue. As he brushed against the broad leaves, a heady mix of citrus and spicy aromas were released, and he inhaled deeply, and then the foliage opened onto a small rustic village.

The deserted beach was explained as everyone was gathered in the tiny village square, listening to yet another tall, dark-haired man, who was standing on a box, in full oration. The man pumped his hand in emphasis and the villagers swayed.

Jerrol pushed his way forward and blended in with the people at the back.

"You will be honoured, feted, a member of an elite community. Follow us and share in the glory of being part of a greater good."

"Oh yeah? And what do we get apart from the glory?" a deep, cynical voice spoke from the front. Jerrol rose on tip toes to peer over taller shoulders at the speaker.

"You will be supporting those who should rightfully lead; rewarded for making the right choice."

"We already have a leader," the dissenter said. Jerrol cursed under his breath as he teetered. He couldn't see anything. "Do you want to leave Selir on this man's words alone?" the sardonic voice asked.

The speaker's voice droned on as a scuffle started at the front, and Jerrol pushed his way through the watching crowd. It was, as he had suspected, Roberion, struggling with two men. His chest eased seeing the familiar broad-shouldered, bronze skinned sailor, who he had awoken from beneath the Terolian rock. Like Birlerion and Tagerill, he seemed younger than what he remembered. The three thousand year sleep and abrupt awakening in the future had taken its toll on all the Sentinals. Some had hidden it, and others, like Birlerion had to learn to cope with more traumatic experiences that must have superseded his initial shock, but seeing them in their original habitat made the differences blindingly obvious. Guilt shafted through him at his lack of understanding, his lack of care for these men and women, who had looked to him for guidance.

They had trusted him implicitly when he had no idea what being the Lady's Captain meant. He was humbled by their unquestioning belief, by their acceptance. He wasn't sure he could have accepted such a monumental change. He was awed once again by the calibre of the men and women who had pledged their lives in the name of the Lady, and she had rewarded them by encasing them in trees, to sleep for three thousand years until he had awoken them, and not one of them had complained.

He shook off the reflections. He would think about it later. Glancing around the sandy area, he realised none of the villagers were helping Roberion; their attention was glued on the speaker.

Jerrol raised his voice. "So, you would prefer to listen to people who restrain free speech and will? The Lady doesn't do that. A member of your village is being attacked for exercising his right of free speech and you do nothing?"

The villagers stirred and a low murmur began. Jerrol continued to push his way through the crowd. The speaker's voice rose over the murmurs.

"The Lady would be ashamed of you," Jerrol yelled as he launched himself at one of the men restraining Roberion. Released, Roberion swung around low and hard and connected an uppercut under the other man's rib cage; the man collapsed in a groaning heap on the floor. Roberion spun but Jerrol had the other man tied in an impressive knot and going nowhere. Roberion shifted his attention to the speaker. "Your words don't impress me. I suggest you climb back into whatever hole you came out of. These people are not going anywhere; they are of Selir and so they remain," he said as he advanced.

The speaker swayed away from him. "I have the right to

speak. Your elders gave permission."

"I also have the right to speak, and these people are staying right here in their homes; you don't have permission to lead them astray."

"You'll regret this," the man spat.

Jerrol grimaced. They always said that; they had no imagination. The man beneath him stirred, and Jerrol twisted his arm tighter, forcing the man's face into the dust, his knee digging into the man's back.

"I suggest you leave now before these villagers decide that you tried to deceive them with your soft words and misdirection," Roberion said, his voice cutting.

The villagers stiffened and straightened as if released from a heavy weight as an older grey-haired man stepped out of the crowd, a frown creasing his brow. "Roberion, I thank you for speaking up. I don't know what came over me. He convinced me he was here for the good of the village."

"You'll find they are collecting villagers from all over Terolia and enslaving them in their cause," Jerrol said from behind them. "You need to spread the word that your people shouldn't listen to them, else you will lose all; freedom, home, family, and, ultimately, your life."

"But who are they? What do they want?" the Elder asked, perplexed.

Jerrol released his man, who collapsed into the dust. "They were once scholars, but now they want to rule Remargaren, so they have decided to try and ascend to power, to replace the Lady. They are called Ascendants and they will try to destroy your way of life."

The man on the box glared at Jerrol, his black eyes spitting with anger.

"Just look at him," Jerrol gestured. "You truly think he has your best interests at heart?"

"What should we do with them?" Roberion asked.

"Lock them up and throw away the key. Except that would make us no better than them." Jerrol sighed. "Ban them from speaking, advise the families to refuse them, hound them out of Terolia."

Roberion frowned at him. "Who are you? Where do you come from?"

"I am a messenger from the Lady, here to remind you all of your duty, to protect those less able to protect themselves, especially in the coming months of strife, to watch over each other and believe. Never stop believing that the Lady will protect you."

"I know who you are," the Ascendant spat. "Your days are numbered, Fisherman. We will find you and you will regret interfering."

"I will never regret standing up to the likes of you," Jerrol replied, his eyes gleaming silver.

"Elder," Roberion said hurriedly. "What do you wish to be done?"

"Escort them out of Selir. They are no longer welcome here."

Roberion nodded and kicked the man on the floor. "Get up. Benir, Laurie, help me escort them out. The Elder has spoken." Roberion advanced on the speaker, who, taking one look at his face, held his hands up in submission.

"We'll go, but we will be back," he hissed at Roberion before turning to Jerrol, "and you—we know you now, Fisherman, we will find you," he spat viciously.

Jerrol watched the Ascendants leave with their escort. The villagers looked at each other in bemusement as the Elder shooed them home. The small clearing was finally empty, and the Elder stared at Jerrol. "I thank you on behalf of my people for your intervention."

Jerrol shrugged. "Sentinal Roberion intervened first."

"Wouldn't have meant much if you hadn't barrelled in," Roberion's deep voice interrupted them.

Jerrol turned and got a good look at him. His dark brown hair glinted with streaks of red, burnished by the sun. He was slimmer, not so broad across the chest, and he wore a light shirt and cut off trousers. Only his gleaming silver eyes gave away what he really was. A darkening graze was beginning to mar his bronzed cheek.

"You ought to get something for your face."

Roberion tentatively touched his cheek and winced. He looked at Jerrol. "Come, my place is this way. You can tell us why you are here."

Jerrol grinned. "I came looking for you, Roberion."

Roberion's lips twisted. "Somehow, I thought you had. My first break in years and a strange Sentinal turns up."

"It's good to see you; we have much to discuss."

Roberion stilled, considering Jerrol. Abruptly, he nodded. "Come on then."

He led the way to a small stone-built dwelling on the edge of the village. Boat spars were stacked against the wall, along with a mess of nets and baskets.

Roberion rolled a log out in front and then a second. "Sit," he said as he ducked into his home, soon to return with a jug and two mugs.

He poured out the orange liquid and handed a mug to Jerrol. Folding a cloth he had dipped in a bucket of water, Roberion gently pressed it against his face.

Jerrol took a sip. The juice was tart, refreshing, and cold. "Ah, that's good. How did you keep it so cold?"

"Dug a hole and lined it with stone. Keeps it cooler."

"I'm trying to find a better way to preserve my fish instead of using salt. If I could find a way to preserve ice, I'd bring some down from Elothia!" Jerrol said with a grin. "I'll have to ask Niallerion to come up with a way."

"You know Niallerion?"

Jerrol nodded. "Amongst others. I have a story to tell you. It may be hard to believe, but it's all true, and I need your help."

Roberion grimaced and then winced. He refolded his pad, dipped it in his bucket, and pressed it against his cheek. "Let's hear it, then."

Jerrol stared at his mug before heaving a deep sigh. "I'm not sure where to begin. My name is Jerrol Haven and I'm from the future." He held up his hand as if expecting a protest. "Let me explain," he said, looking across at Roberion, who was watching him with one eyebrow raised. "I am the Lady's Captain in the year 4128." He paused as Roberion exclaimed out loud.

"That's what it is, I thought you seemed familiar. I recognise you, but I know we've never met."

"We meet when I awaken you after you have been encased in rock by Marguerite to preserve you after the Lady sunders the Bloodstone. You sleep for three thousand years before I awaken you. The descendants of the Ascendants tried to take control of Remargaren again, much as the Ascendants are trying to do today.

"The Lady charged me to protect her Guardians. Suffice to say, we meet in the northern wastelands of Terolia with Adilion, Marianille, and Niallerion. You were all preserved in the Land until I could come and wake you. Just remember, don't stop calling; your voices were what led me to you."

Jerrol sighed as he looked at Roberion's face. His expression was dubious to say the least. "I know it's farfetched, but it's true. I was at home in Stoneford with Taelia and the children." Jerrol's face softened. "We've just had a little girl, Leyarille. She has silver eyes, and she was a week old when the Lady pulled me here to this time. I must do something in Birtoli. I am a fisherman called Jerven in this time, sailing a boat called the *Island Scout*, but the Ascendants are creeping in everywhere; they are insidious, casting spells, enslaving people's minds to do their bidding, destroying the Families and, ultimately, the Lady. She will soon sunder the Bloodstone to protect us all. I believe that there is something in Birtoli that they are after, something they need for their plan to work, and I need to stop them." Jerrol paused to marshal his thoughts.

"Where do I come into all this?"

"I need you to bring the *Lady's Miracle* to Geteril."

"The *Lady's Miracle*?"

"Your frigate."

"I have a frigate?" Roberion's face was a picture, surprise combined with avarice.

"Yes, she's a special boat."

"Ship," Roberion corrected.

Jerrol laughed. "By the Lady, it's good to see you again, Roberion; I've missed you."

"I have a frigate?" Roberion repeated in awe.

"Yes, a beautiful frigate. You have taken King Benedict to the island of Molinti in my time. When you wake in my time, you are going to remember meeting me and this conversation. When you wake, you need to sail the *Miracle* to Geteril and help me save the Tu'ani clan. The Ascendants will try to destroy them. No matter what happens, you must take the people off and relocate them to the island of Cherni. When you wake up in my time, you must go straight to Geteril, understand? Nowhere else."

Roberion nodded. "Meet you in Geteril and rescue the Tu'ani, got it." He frowned. "Cherni? Where's that?"

Jerrol twisted his lips. "You'll know," he said. "Oh, and can you get a message to Guerlaire? Dominant Clary just took five sacks of crystals to Adeeron. He's planning some diversion to draw Guerlaire out of wherever he is. Can you warn him? Do you have Arifels here that you can use? It will be all out war soon; make sure you get word to him."

Roberion gaped at him. "How do you know this?"

"I just dropped Clary off in Daarl before I came here."

"*What?*"

"It doesn't matter. I have to return to Birtoli. Remember, when you wake up, meet me in Geteril."

Words failed Roberion as he stared at Jerrol. Grimacing, Jerrol dragged his fingers through his salt encrusted hair. He dreaded to think what Roberion saw. A desperate man, no doubt, for that was what he felt like. The silence drew out and then Roberion slowly nodded. "I'll be there, you can count on me."

"Roberion." Jerrol fought against the rising tears as relief swept through him.

Roberion leaned forward and gripped his arm. "I will be there wherever and whenever you need me," he vowed, trying to reassure him.

"Thank you." Jerrol whispered, struggling not to let the sudden emotion swamp him.

Roberion cleared his throat as he sat back up. "You'd better sleep here tonight. You can't traverse the Bolian straights in the dark. You can tell me about Terolia in your time."

"Before I do that, you need to look to your ports; they are the most disreputable places going. No one will want to trade with you if you don't sort them out. The Ascendants will grab them if you are not in control."

"I know, Feril is a dive; it's only used by the miners."

"Miners?"

"Yeah, they are digging out the rock for building, trading it out to Elothia."

"Is that what they are saying? Roberion, the Ascendants

are mining crystals out of the Telusions, *crystals!* Did no one think to check?"

"There aren't enough of us," Roberion protested. "We are scattered all over Remargaren, sent at the Lady's bidding. Guerlaire has us rooting out arrays and defending the towers, but the Ascendants are numerous."

"Not the true Ascendants. Remember, they only allow the pure of blood to lead. Look to the Dominants themselves; the rest are just followers, causing distractions. Let the guards deal with them."

Roberion stared at Jerrol. "Jerrol, come with me to Vespers, speak to Leyandrii and Guerlaire; they need to hear this themselves."

Jerrol shook his head. "I cannot prevent what will happen; that is not what I'm here for. I need to return to Birtoli. You need to tell them."

They talked long into the night, Jerrol relaxing into the much-missed comfort of spending time with a friend who understood and Roberion trying to question Jerrol on what he knew about the current situation and to get as much information about the future Remargaren and his frigate as he could. Jerrol told him about his plans for Senti. "Build a harbour here, so we can begin trading. That way, we can get you the money so you can build your frigate," Jerrol suggested with a grin.

Roberion's face lit up. "I'll be your first trading partner. Most fishermen around here are self-sufficient, they don't look to trading elsewhere." He was still mumbling about his ship as he offered Jerrol a spot on the floor, and they rolled into their blankets and went to sleep.

The next morning, Roberion admired the *Island Scout* as they pushed it off the beach. "Bit heavy just for one, though, isn't she?"

"I usually have a lad helping me, my brother, Gael, but

when I'm visiting old friends, I prefer to come alone. I met Birlerion and Tagerill in Vespers a few weeks ago, and Serillion. It was good to see them too. I miss you guys. You need to find out how to get me back, because I have no idea! And I need to see Taelia." Jerrol tried to disguise the longing in his voice, but from Roberion's expression, he knew he had failed. "Tell her I love her for me? And that I think of her every day. I saw her and Mikke in Molinti, though she couldn't see me. It was like there was a barrier between us."

"Of course," Roberion said gravely as if he knew what Jerrol was talking about. "I'll meet you soon in Geteril, Jerrol, be careful." They hugged fiercely in farewell, then Jerrol heaved himself onboard. He hauled the mainsail up, and with a final salute, the wind took him off out to sea.

Roberion stood watching the red sail until it was hidden by the headland. Heaving a deep sigh, he decided he would sail to Feril and check out the mines before travelling onto Vespers. He frowned. It would have been useful if there was a waystone here on the east coast; he must remember to suggest it to Guerlaire. He would have to sail north to Lintel on the Vespiri-Terolian border and then use the waystone at Stoneford. Decision made, he returned to his home and changed back into his uniform. Strapping his sword over his shoulder, he reviewed his discussion with Jerrol. Clary, huh? Guerlaire would be furious.

20

PRESENT DAY

FEBU 22ND, 4128, BIRTOLI

Roberion lurched up out of his bunk, breathing heavily. The memory of his conversations with Jerrol reverberated in his head. Immediately rising, he dressed and then stuck his head out of his cabin. "Kender, change course for the last known position of Geteril," he yelled.

"What? Geteril? Where's that? There's no Geteril on the map."

"It used to be off the coast of Eyti. Head for Eyti and I'll map the course when I come up."

"Yes, Captain." Kender shook his head at the vagaries of Sentinals.

Roberion called Ari, and sat at his desk furiously scribbling down all that he could remember from his meeting with Jerrol. He rolled the papers up tightly and slid them into a tube ready for the Arifel to take, along with his message about the harbour at Senti and the sentinal they had seen towering over it.

He pulled his maps forward and began calculating the position of Geteril, the coordinates Jerrol had given him ringing in his head. He rolled up his map and left his cabin.

He looked around, noting the position of the sun and the strength of the wind instinctively. Inhaling the salty air, he climbed the ladder up to the poop deck and tugged his cap down against the sun's glare. "Here, Kender, these are the coordinates. Head due east once we reach Eyti."

"But sir, there's nothing there, just empty seas."

"There was once," Roberion murmured softly. "We're on a mercy mission. Prepare below decks for refugees. Make sure the healer has all he needs, spare blankets, water, this could be a bit dicey, knowing the Captain."

"Yes, sir." Kender passed the orders, glaring at any sailor who murmured a protest. Kender shrugged, He had no idea who they were rescuing or from what.

Roberion looked around the empty seas. A grey smudge off the starboard bow was the island of Senti that they had left earlier that morning. The wind pushed them on to empty seas; the sky was just as empty, a brilliant blue, not a cloud in the sky.

The sun advanced as the day progressed. At last, Eyti came into sight, a tiny group of islands lying low to the sea, the remnants of the Birtoli mainland. They headed due east away from Eyti and towards an empty horizon and no known landfall. Roberion cast an eye around his crew; they were a good crew and they trusted him, but this was testing their confidence in him; he could hear the mutters, and he cleared his throat.

"Men, I know you don't believe there is an island out here, but I am telling you there is. The island of Geteril. Captain Haven is expecting us to come to his rescue, and I don't break my promises to the Captain."

"Why didn't you say it was for the Captain? In that case …" one of the sailors quipped. A laugh rippled around the deck and all was right again. The sailors heaved to with a will, and the *Lady's Miracle* cut through the waves with enthusiasm.

Roberion grinned. Sailors were often superstitious, but mention the Captain and their concerns melted away. The Captain was well-respected and even loved aboard the *Lady's Miracle*. His crew had witnessed Jerrol's joining to Taelia on this very ship and seen the Lady's blessing cascade around them and the ship; anything to do with the Captain would be alright with this crew.

Roberion nodded and returned to his cabin, sending another call out to Ari; where was the darned creature? He spent the time pouring over his maps, studying the remains of Geteril; he didn't want to unexpectedly hit a shoaling reef or something. He knew the original island had been much larger, though today only the higher ground was visible as a curving reef. The island had once been completely submerged in a storm, and he knew in his gut it had to have happened in 1124. This had to be the event that caused the total loss of the Tu'ani clan. But with Jerrol in 1124 expecting him to arrive, he wasn't too sure which island he was going to find. He suppressed his fear, his disbelief. It would do no good for the crew to see him uncertain.

The door to his cabin opened. "Ah, Captain. You need to come and see this." Kender, his first mate, hovered in his doorway, uncertainly.

Roberion nodded, rolled his map up, and stored it away safely before following Kender back onto the deck. Boiling black clouds obscured the horizon when he reached the deck, flashes of lightning making the clouds glow eerily. A low rumble accompanied the flashes.

"That, gentlemen, I am afraid, is Geteril," Roberion said.

"That is some storm," one of the sailors said.

Roberion nodded. "And not natural, I'll bet," he said

under his breath. He stared at the roiling clouds and wondered what could have caused such a violent storm, and whether Jerrol was at the centre of it. Somehow, Roberion thought he might be and if he was, that meant there was the possibility that he might be able to save Jerrol as well. The slightest chance that this was a crossing point in time, galvanised him into action. Out loud he began to snap orders. "Prepare for rough seas. Strap down everything you can, stow away anything loose, check the hawsers; let's be as prepared as we can be."

He turned to Kender. "Come in from the south. There was a sandy bay, which will be our best approach; there were no reefs to the south. Once we're in, it'll be difficult to hear anything. We anchor in the bay and use the skiffs to land and pick up anyone we can find."

"But the skiffs will be overturned in those waters," Chamber protested.

"We'll see," Roberion replied. "Back in 1124, today, Febu 22nd, was the last day this island existed. It is possible we are witnessing the final moments of this island's life. If we don't get every person off then they will die and that will be the end of a clan; we're here to make sure that doesn't happen."

Kender swallowed. "Yes, Cap'n."

The *Lady's Miracle* closed in on the storm, the wind whipping through the sails and making the canvas boom. Roberion looked up. "Reef the Mainsail," he shouted as the wind veered and tugged, causing the ship to heel. They were committed now, the wind driving them on into the storm. The clouds closed in around them, the noise horrendous. "Lookout on point," he yelled, as visibility continued to drop. He did not want to run aground on Geteril. He gripped the rail as the deck canted, and men hung on tight as the waves rose beside them and crashed down over them, the foam swirling around their boots as the *Miracle* straightened up.

Ari popped into view right in front of him, chattering in protest at his location. "Take this to the king now," Roberion shouted, shoving the tube at the little creature. Ari grabbed it and popped out of view.

22nd Feb, 1124, Geteril

Jerrol sailed from Selir straight to Geteril. He had a terrible feeling that the Ascendants had already targeted the island. He had a good idea of what they were after. There wouldn't be a guardian if there wasn't something to protect. His stomach sank as he spotted dark clouds gathered on the horizon in an otherwise brilliantly blue sky.

As he neared, the water grew rougher and lightning lit the clouds from within. He steered around the south of the island and fought the wind to steer into the bay. The wind suddenly changed direction and the *Scout* was driven hard up onto the sands, well and truly beached.

He jumped down and ran into the screening foliage, the wind whipping him furiously, the rain beating down on his head. The broad-leaved trees were being shredded by the ferocious wind, and a cacophony of drumming rain beat all around him. As he ran, he felt the familiar weight of his sword settle on his hip, the sword that he had left leaning against the wall of his bedchamber in the cottage in Stoneford, and he knew he was where the Lady needed him to be.

Silently praying to Leyandrii, he skidded to a halt in the village clearing. It was deserted. There was no point shouting; no one would hear him over the howling winds. He ducked into the Elder's hut, his eyes adjusting to the gloom, his ears adjusting to the diminished din. The Elder was seated with his family around the flickering fire, huddling together against the noise outside. The Elder looked up in surprise at the dripping apparition. Two men rose to their feet, filling the small hut, ready to defend.

"Elder Tuan, we have to leave. Your island will be flooded soon."

The Elder stared at him. "I can't leave."

"Father, please, you have much yet to give, the Lady expects more of you. Please, we must leave. The islands will be drowned, they lie too low. You must save your people and build a new life elsewhere. I know of an island; it has higher ground, you will be safe."

One of the Elder's sons entered the hut and peered at Jerol as he dripped on the reed mats. "Father, it is as Jerven says. The ground is flooding; there is water everywhere, and no sign of the rain stopping. You should take our family and seek higher ground. I will remain here."

"My son, we can't leave our birthplace; this is our home."

"You take your home with you, father," Jerrol said. "Your home is in your heart and you carry it always. No matter where you go, no matter how far or for how long, it will always be with you. You are your home."

The Elder smiled proudly. "You learnt the lesson well, my son"

Jerrol bowed his head. "Yes, I did, and that is why you will come with me. The longer we delay the less I can help the others."

"I have a responsibility here; I cannot leave, my son."

"Father, this storm is not natural. There are terrible men who are coming. They seek what you protect; they believe they can take it from you. If you stay here, they will kill you. You need to choose now, otherwise you will be lost, and then you won't be able to protect anything."

"Your boat will not hold us all," the Elder said, spreading his hands.

"There is another boat. It will be in the bay; it will hold all that you need," Jerrol promised.

Elder Tuan stared at him and then at his family gathered in the hut. After a moment he inclined his head. "As you command, my son." He squared his shoulders. "Do as he says, get everyone to the beaches."

His sons ran towards the other huts, the rain drenching them in seconds, and soon reappeared herding men, women and children before them. Jerrol wrapped an arm around his father's frail shoulders as the wind screamed into the clearing, howling in anger and spite. They staggered against the force of the wind, the furious black clouds roiling overhead. Leaning at an angle that Jerrol was not prepared to measure, they fought their way to the *Scout*.

Jerrol staggered to a halt as a black, shrouded figure stood becalmed on the sands. He pushed his dripping hair out of his eyes. "You," the figure spat as he pushed back his hood. The Ascendant from Selir. He grasped his gold medallion, with a clear crystal in the centre, and gestured with his other hand. The Elder was dragged from Jerrol's grasp.

"No," Jerrol howled as he drew his sword and charged the Ascendant. The Elder staggered to his feet and headed for the water.

"Who are you?" the Ascendant growled.

"A messenger from the Lady, you shall not harm these people."

"She cannot stop me." The Ascendant raised his hand and flames flew past Jerrol's cheek. Jerrol launched himself across the sands, forcing the man to defend himself.

"You will not win," the Ascendant laughed, as his sword appeared in his hand and he parried Jerrol's strike. "You are but one and we are many."

"But never enough," Jerrol ground out as he continued to

strike. The sparks from their swords echoed in the flashes of lightning above them.

Jerrol saw the *Lady's Miracle* being propelled into the bay before the ferocious winds, her sails in tatters but comfortingly real. Relief flooded him. Roberion had done as he asked, and brought his ship to the last known location of Geteril. Risking his ship and his men, he had sailed into the maelstrom that was the home of the Tu'ani clan and crossed through time.

The crew were busy in the rigging, and on the portside, they were lowering boats into the choppy waters. He cursed under his breath. It would take too long to get the boats through the rough water. The islanders were beginning to wade into the surf, parents carrying their children in their arms. He wasted more breath cursing again as more black-garbed men appeared on the beach.

Desperately, he opened his fist, the hand into which he had absorbed the Bloodstone, and a brilliant silver light erupted from his palm, blinding the men on the beach and shooting up into the sky like a beacon slicing through the clouds. The light spread through the roiling clouds and pacified the worst of the storm and the waters calmed. Jerrol advanced and, raising his sword high, he forced the Ascendants back, weaving his way forward.

He heard Roberion shouting behind him, but not the words. What was he doing on the beach? He should have stayed on the *Miracle*. Jerrol defended the islanders, blocking the Ascendants advance.

Cursing, the Ascendant before him raised his hands, and then swirling his cloak around him, he dragged Jerrol within, fouling his sword in the material. Jerrol's sword was tugged out of his grip as they suddenly disappeared.

The beach was empty, the rising waters creeping up over the sands, erasing the marks of their struggle. The storm surge built as the winds died and the clouds melted away, leaving a brilliant blue sky and a glaring sun that watched over the swelling waters as it drowned the land.

"Get everyone into the boats, now! Get a line on the *Island Scout*, we'll tow it out," Roberion shouted, spotting Jerrol's boat lifting off the beach in the rising swell. He herded the islanders towards the boats, his men frantically pulling the people out of the sea as they tried to swim in the rising waters. He cast one last glance at the empty beach. There was nothing he could do to help Jerrol now; he had no idea where the Ascendants had taken him. Squeezing his eyes shut, he scrubbed his face. So close! If only he could have rescued Jerrol off the island as well. He could only keep his promise to help the islanders.

Roberion heaved the old man into the boat before him. Kicking hard to keep afloat, he reached for the boat, but a wave smacked him in the face, making him flail and choke on salty water, and he sank below the surface.

Strong hands grabbed him and dragged him into the boat, where he lay gasping out water. A young woman stared at him with frightened eyes and offered him her blanket. "Thanks," he choked as he watched his men man the oars and pull away from the roiling waters around them.

Once they reached the *Miracle* and some semblance of order had been achieved, Roberion climbed down into the *Island Scout* and checked for damage; It seemed sound enough. The hold was empty, the decks cleared; it seemed Jerrol had been prepared. Searching through the lockers, he came across an oilskin-wrapped bundle. His eyes widened as he realised it was Jerrol's log book, and he tucked it in his waistband. He checked that the towing line was secure and then climbed back up to the *Miracle*. He ordered a sailor to take his place, to watch the towing line and bail if needed.

A chime later, all their boats retrieved, the *Lady's Miracle* finally upped anchor and, catching the wind in their reduced sails, they slowly sailed away from the boiling waters, which was all that remained of the island of Geteril. Roberion issued orders to repair the damage where they could; helping the islanders, treating injuries. There were a few broken bones and many minor contusions, but they had survived.

Finally, he made his way to the stern and stood next to the Elder as he watched the roiling water. "I am sorry for your loss," he said.

The Elder shrugged. "It was but sand and rock. As my son said, you carry your home within and you can rebuild it elsewhere. He said he knew of an island with higher ground."

"The Captain said take you to Cherni, but I don't know where it is."

"Cherni," mused the Elder. "Yes, I suppose that will do." He looked at Roberion. "Head north. I think the Lady will make sure we find it. Captain, I thank you for your assistance, but you need to find my son."

"Your son?"

"The captain of that vessel," the elder pointed to the *Island Scout* trailing forlornly behind the *Miracle*. "He will need your help before he can go home, and he has much to do before then."

"You know what he has to do here? In this time?" Roberion asked urgently. "How do we help him?"

"He has already started. He was right, there are terrible people in our world." The Elder looked up at the clear blue sky, his eyes a pale reflection. "This was only the beginning. The storm clouds build. I thank you for your help. My son said you would come."

"I promised I would."

"A promise," the Elder grunted. "Promises can get you into all sorts of trouble. But it is good that you keep your promises. They are what will save us; those with the honour and the strength will see us through."

"I hope so," Roberion said bleakly, seeing the sandy beach in his mind's eye and Jerrol fighting alone against the Ascendants, defending the islanders. That was what had galvanised him to get to shore as quick as he could. Jerrol may be fast but he had been tiring, the sand sucking at his feet and his energy. He had no idea how Jerrol had created the blinding light, but it had calmed the waters enough for them to make shore, but not in time to help him. Roberion's face was grave as he considered where the Ascendants could have taken him. Nowhere good, that was for sure.

Present Day, Febu 22nd, 4128, Molinti

The king sat at his breakfast table and scowled at the piece of paper he was reading. "It seems Tagerill was not so inclined to rush down here at the whim of a peculiar dream. He seems a little disbelieving and asks if we have news of Jerrol." The king looked up with a brief smile and caught Fonorion's eye as he stood guard by the door. "We'll have to roll the kitty over to Roberion," he said as he leaned back in his chair and observed Taelia and Birlerion who had joined him.

Birlerion grunted as he ran his finger down the page of the log book he had brought with him to the table. Benedict had come to realise that Birlerion was as bad as Taelia when it came to single-minded research.

He thumped his hand on the table and Birlerion jerked his eyes up and flushed. "My apologies, Your Majesty."

"I think it's time you got your nose out of those books and went to visit Senti. You haven't been there yet, and you should visit the sentinal, see if you can discover anything."

"Of course, Your Majesty," Birlerion replied, closing the log book.

Benedict scowled at him. "Where is Roberion, anyway? We should have heard from him by now."

As if on cue, the little Arifel erupted into the air in front of the king, cheeping in distress and dripping all over him.

"By the Lady," Benedict exclaimed in surprise as the Arifel dropped the message tube in his lap. Ari chittered in disapproval before descending on Birlerion and rubbing himself against his shirt.

"Ari, " Birlerion said sharply, "where have you been?" Gasping, he flinched back in his chair as visions of the Lady's Miracle riding a ferocious storm appeared before him.

"What? What is it?" Taelia asked worriedly.

"It's Roberion. He's in the middle of a terrible storm, according to Ari."

"This doesn't make any sense," exclaimed Benedict.

Taelia turned to the king. "What?" she asked sharply, then caught herself. "My apologies, sire, I meant no disrespect."

"None taken," the king responded automatically. "Roberion has dreamt that he met Jerrol in Terolia in 1124, and Jerrol told him to go directly to Geteril when he awoke. He says he has gone to help him. But there is no such place as Geteril. I know because he showed me the maps of Birtoli before we left Old Vespers."

"There was once. It was an island off the east coast of Birtoli; it was lost in the upheaval. So it would still exist in 1124," Birlerion said, still staring into space.

"But Roberion isn't in 1124 now," the king exclaimed.

"But he would know where it was," Fonorion said, in his quiet voice. "The storm; it could be a result of time meshing. It would be bound to be turbulent where time overlaps, wouldn't you think?"

"Or it is unnatural? Are the Ascendants causing it?"

Taelia said worriedly. "You said he's gone to help Jerrol, but with what?"

"A mercy mission, he says. Which clan lived on Geteril?" Benedict asked.

Taelia and Birlerion exchanged glances. "The Tu'ani," they said in unison.

21

PRESENT DAY

FEBU 22ND, 4128, CHERNI

The *Lady's Miracle* reached the island of Cherni later that afternoon. The golden cliffs rose before them, a central mountain range towering above, forming the spine of the island as it curved protectively around the bay, dark green vegetation softening the sharp edges of the glistening rock. They angled past the cliffs and into the crescent-shaped bay, with white sands and crystal-clear waters. The air was perfumed with the scent of ripe fruit and flowers; a gentle welcome.

Roberion anchored out in the bay, eyeing the sands shelved up to the island. "How come no one lives here already?"

"I think she has been waiting for us," the Elder murmured, his eyes drinking in the beautiful island. "Come, let us go home. Please stay, Captain, your men need the rest, your ship needs repairs. This sheltered bay will be your respite."

"We couldn't impose; you have nothing."

"We have our lives because of you, and the island will provide. Come," the Elder insisted.

Roberion passed the order and the skiffs were lowered and loaded with whatever spare blankets and clothes the *Miracle* could provide, for the Tu'ani only had what they stood up in.

As they stood on the soft white sands, staring up into the mountains, one of Roberion's crew spotted a faint trail leading into the forest. They followed the trail into the dim interior, through tall trees that blocked the light, the ground soft and moist underfoot with springy moss, the air fresh and humid.

The trail wended its way upwards, and deep steps cut into the rock led to a clearing at the base of a cliff pock-marked with openings and crevices. Further on, a small waterfall fell gracefully into a deep rock pool, which then trickled down between the trees. Feathery ferns arched over the clear waters, and vibrant lime-green moss covered the rocks.

A shout led the Elder and Roberion into a larger cave opening. Stacked against the wall were casks and sacks, crates of food and firewood. The Elder smiled. "I said the island would provide."

Venturing deeper, they found piles of cotton, bedding, and reeds, enough to start them off in their new home. Roberion left the islanders exploring and returned to his ship to oversee his repairs, promising to return for the evening meal. Splitting his crew into watches, he gave them time to rest and relax how they wished, though he warned them they would be leaving with the dawn.

Roberion was amazed when he returned to clearing, a central gathering place had been created around a large fire pit and racks of skewers of meat and fish were already roasting, the aromas making him realise how hungry he was, as his stomach grumbled. Logs had been positioned around the pit, chunks cut out to make seats, the scent of fresh cut wood blending with the roasting meats.

A beautiful young woman handed Roberion a gourd filled with a viscous liquid and indicated a log padded with a blanket for him to sit on. Her large brown eyes flicked up to his face and caught his eyes in an unexpectedly intense stare before she stared demurely back down at the ground. Her black hair was twisted in a plait that reached down to her waist.

"Please, you don't have to wait on me," Roberion protested, embarrassed by the attention.

"You are an honoured guest," the Elder said from beside him, "you saved my people, my clan, you kept your promise. You will always be welcome at the hearth of the Tu'ani. Your name and your ship, the *Lady's Miracle*, will be remembered by my people. When next you visit, we will know you."

"I thank you for the honour, but you have lost everything. I can't take more from you."

The Elder laughed. "My son provisioned us well; he also picked well. This island is fruitful and will support us for many years. I hear plans for making use of fermenting fruits are already afoot. One day, maybe our produce will be famous?"

Roberion smiled. "Well, my crew will be first in line; they'll keep you in business."

"Then that is good. We already have customers."

The young woman presented Roberion with a broad leaf, wrapped around a skewer of meat. Roberion smiled his thanks and she blushed rosily, her sensuous lips curving in a small smile.

Roberion dragged his gaze away from her mouth and concentrated on the meat. Moments later, he realised he was staring at her again as she raised her head and boldly met his stare. Embarrassed, he dropped his gaze, though he was still aware of the young woman watching him.

"You have an admirer," the Elder whispered loudly.

Roberion flushed. "We have to leave in the morning."

"Which gives you one night," the Elder grinned.

"She deserves more than one night," Roberion said.

"Then she will be waiting for you when you return." The Elder chuckled softly. "I should tell you that to accept a gourd from the hands of a single woman is sometimes seen as a signal of intent in the eyes of the Lady."

"What?" Roberion gasped.

"I could speak to her for you. I'm sure she doesn't realise your ignorance of our customs. Though I will tell you, my daughter is very stubborn and I'm not sure she will listen."

"Y-your daughter?" Roberion swallowed, but he couldn't help his gaze returning to where the Elder's daughter sat. "I can't stay here; I have to return to my own time."

"What makes you think we aren't in your time?" the Elder asked, popping a piece of meat in his mouth.

Roberion gaped at him. "There is no island called Cherni in the year 4128."

"There is now," the Elder said with a small smile. "My daughter's name is Lilith," the Elder said, and then he began to laugh at the expression on Roberion's face. "My son, you would be welcome in my family," he said, "but I understand if you need to go."

"I don't know what my future holds. You saw today how precarious life can be."

The Elder shrugged. "Then you should grasp the opportunity to live all the tighter, my son."

"She doesn't even know me," Roberion protested weakly.

"She has been waiting for you to arrive. Your name is in the stars, my son, and my daughter knows how to read them."

Roberion stared at the Elder. "My name?" he repeated, struggling to make sense of the Elder's words. Lilith. Her name echoed deep inside him and was followed by a flush of heat.

"She has been waiting a long time. Are you going to make her wait even longer?" The Elder signalled and Lilith stood. "My daughter, is it truly your wish to have this man?"

Lilith raised her head and stared straight at Roberion. "Yes, Father," her voice was low and warm, and Roberion's innards melted as he drowned in her gaze.

The Elder glanced at Roberion and smiled at what he saw. "So be it."

Lilith picked up an ornately carved gourd and, kneeling before Roberion, ceremoniously offered it to him and gestured for him to drink. Roberion took it, sliding to his knees beside her, his eyes locked on hers. He lifted the gourd and choked a little on the pungent liqueur before passing it to Lilith, who drank and passed it to one of her brother's standing beside her. Elder Tuan placed Lilith's hand in Roberion's, and as she rose, Roberion meekly followed her out of the gathering area.

Lilith led him to a small glade lit by many small dishes of burning oil. The gentle flames caressed her face with a golden glow. Blankets were laid out on the mossy ground and she turned to face him. Her hand reached for his face, her fingers tracing his cheek bones and across his lips. She felt him shiver and smiled. "I've been waiting for you to arrive, I thought you were never coming," she said, her voice a soft vibration that shivered through his body.

"Why are you so sure that I am the one?" Roberion asked, captivated by her sparkling eyes.

"Can't you feel it?" she asked, melding her body to his. His body caught fire at her touch. She arched her neck to look up into his face. "I knew as soon as I saw you on the beach."

Roberion smiled apologetically. "I didn't even see you."

"You were rather busy," Lilith allowed. "But tonight, we belong together, under the Lady's moon, tonight and forever."

"Lilith, I don't even know where I'll be tomorrow night or the night thereafter, I have a duty to Lady, King, and Captain."

"You shall keep your duty, and I will be here, waiting for your return."

"It's not much of a life waiting for me. I can't guarantee when I'll be back. I don't even have a home to give you."

Lilith smiled secretively. "Our home is here. But you'll be back. You won't be able to stay away now that we've found each other, and until you do, you will be here." She placed his hand on her chest. "And I will be there." She placed her hand on his chest. The heat of her hand burned through his shirt, just as the heat of her skin scorched his hand.

His head dipped of its own accord and their lips met. She tasted so sweet, and moulded perfectly to his. The kiss deepened and his hands slid down her body, and he was lost once more.

They lay entwined on the blankets, breathing heavily. He kissed her shoulder, tasting salt, and kissed her again, breathing the satisfying scent of her moist skin. "Lilith," he whispered in concern, "are you sure?"

She raised her head and looked down at him. She smiled at the glint in his silver eyes and gently kissed him. "It was ordained in the stars my love, you never had a chance."

Roberion reached up and drew her back down to him.

A little later, Roberion lazily kissed her neck. He couldn't stop touching her. "Tell me something about you. I don't even know your full name or how old you are."

Lilith laughed. "Of course you do, Lilith, daughter of the Tu'ani, my age no longer matters, much like yours, I think, for I believe we are much of an age."

"You believe we are back in my future?" Roberion considered his words. "That doesn't make much sense. But you know what I mean."

"My father believes we are, and he watches the stars. He said we would travel far, but our home would be waiting for us. And he was right, as usual. We will build you a harbour so your ship will have a home."

"And you watch the stars as well? You saw a harbour?" Roberion teased.

Lilith laughed. "Oh yes, I have to make sure you can come back to me, after all."

"Of that you can be sure," Roberion whispered, kissing her again.

Lilith's face grew grave. "Roberion, my love, I am afraid you just joined with the daughter of the clan chief. We will have duties to the Tu'ani in our time when my father passes to the great beyond, but he says he hasn't seen it yet, so we have time. The Lady still has work for him to do."

Roberion sighed. "Between us, you have turned my life upside down."

"Yes, and for that, I'm sorry, but not for anything else." She grinned at him.

His answering smile faded as he levered himself up on his elbow, looking down at her he asked the question that had been bothering him ever since they had arrived on the island. "Lilith, do you know why the Ascendants attacked your island? Why your people, specifically?"

"We will speak with my father in the morning, before you leave. There is much you need to know, but not tonight.

Tonight is ours," she said as she kissed him firmly on the mouth, preventing further speech.

Present Day. Febu 23rd 4124, Molinti

The Lady's Miracle limped into the port of Molinti late the following morning. Roberion dropped anchor with relief as they drew up beside the quay. The *Island Scout* trailed behind them, a somber reminder of their loss. People gathered along the harbour wall to stare at his battered ship, so he knew word would reach the king before he did.

Roberion reviewed all that Lilith's father had told him about his suspicions and what the Ascendants were after. The Elder had shrugged and said there was no longer any such thing. Roberion had been sworn to secrecy, and the secret weighed heavy on his mind. But he was a Tu'ani now and sworn to protect the clan.

He smiled gently at the thought of his wife waiting for him on Cherni. For it was Cherni that they had awoken to that morning, the island marked on his maps as if it had always been there.

Kender had looked at him rather queerly when he had boarded the *Miracle* at dawn, the islanders rather vocal in their farewell and Lilith rather enthusiastic in hers. A warm glow had settled in his chest and he felt inordinately happy. He remembered the look on Jerrol's face the morning after he had joined with Taelia, and he recognised the same smug look on his own face when he looked in the mirror. How he would explain this he didn't know, and then he thought he had no need to explain anything; his friends would be happy for him and that was all that mattered.

He instructed his men to berth the *Scout* next to the *Miracle* and thought about the log book he had read on their journey to Molinti. His heart ached for Jerrol. His loss and loneliness had come through in his words as he recorded his search of the islands, his initial contact with the Dominants, and his final entry about Geteril. He felt closer to him now than ever before, truly understanding the bond that Jerrol had with Taelia now that he was experiencing something similar with Lilith. Not being with her even after only one day made his chest ache.

22

———

FEBU 23RD, 1124

ADEERON, ELOTHIA

The squat building on the plains near Adeeron shimmered behind its protective barrier, a mere ripple in the fabric that deceived the less observant. Rumours were rife as to the terrible rituals that the strange dark men performed out of sight, and the locals stayed away. They didn't want to know, and if the Grand Duke allowed the men building rights, then it was no concern of theirs. Rumour said that there was quite a complex of tunnels built underground, but no one had seen it, so they laughed and shrugged their shoulders.

Clary preferred it that way. At least in Elothia the Grand Duke wasn't interested in what they were up to. In Vespers, the Lady Leyandrii watched their every move. She seemed to have eyes in the back of her head, demanding explanations for every twitch they made. As if the Dominant family of Clary should have to explain their actions. After all, they had been ruling Vespiri for the better part of a hundred years. Why should they explain themselves to her?

Clary's smile was cold and sharp at the thought of bringing her down, alongside that sycophant of hers, Guerlaire. His smile faded. That man had caused him so many problems, unnecessary delays, and even now, he occupied resources that he needed here, not tied up in Vespers. But not for much longer.

He strode down the narrow passage hewn into the frozen tundra of Elothia. It was far too cold to build above ground; outside, the snows had arrived early this year, the permafrost creeping down passed Adeeron towards Tierne and the Summer Palace. The grand duke would be holed up there, counting his gold no doubt; he was charging them enough of it.

Clary debated about returning to Terolia; at least it was warmer down there. But Car'onel had things well in hand. He needed the power grid set so that Ter'ander could link to it. Once they were connected, they would be invincible. The last chamber was being finalised, and then they could start laying out the crystals. It was important to get the pattern right. One falsely placed crystal could halve the amount of power generated, and he was determined to get it all.

Clary entered his office and sat at his desk. Lis'ienne was due to report soon. He should have the Birtolian emperor in his pocket by now, and then they would have the Tu'ani relic in their hands. With that, their success was certain. His men were too thinly spread to affect enough people quickly enough; the crystals were the key.

Staring at the communication crystal intently, as if by thought alone he could make Lis'ienne report, he scowled as it remained dull and silent. He looked up as his aide entered his office, and taking the proffered piece of paper, he glanced down, frowning at the interruption. The next moment he was on his feet, his chair flying back against the wall.

"What? When did this happen?" he demanded, glaring at his aide.

"The report just came through, sir. Apparently, they have

the Fisherman captive. They took him to the mines, but the Tu'ani are gone. Geteril was completely destroyed."

"The fools. Don't they realise how critical it is that we get the relic? And now the island is lost, too?" He screwed the paper up in his hands. "Prepare the transport, I will go there myself."

"But sir, the crystals; you have to lay the final chamber."

"You can call me when the chamber is finished. I can't do anything right now. Until then, I will be at the mines, speaking with this Fisherman."

"Umm, they gave him to Crute."

Clary paled. "If they let Crute kill him, they will regret it." He swore viciously. "I need the Tu'ani."

He grabbed the crystal and stormed out of his office, a burning rage building. After all his plans, they had come down to this last, final piece. Lis'ienne had better find out where the Tu'ani were.

"Sir." His aide was hurrying after him. "Sir, you need the wrap. The crystal won't transition." He held out a soft leather pouch which would protect the crystal. Transitioning from one place to another caused unprotected crystals to shatter.

Clary snatched the pouch and slid the crystal inside. He nodded before entering the large cavern on his left. It was empty except for an array of crystals hanging from the ceiling, radiating out in a circular pattern. The walls were smooth and decorated by a rainbow of colours refracted from the light of the crystals. "Coordinates for the Telusion mine," he snapped, ignoring the beauty of the array. He extended a tendril of thought, picked up the coordinates, linked to the array, and disappeared.

His aide breathed a sigh of relief. He did not want to be present when the Dominant was informed that the Terrolian array had been immobilised by the backlash from

Geteril. He checked the array above him. With their power drained, the crystals faded to a dull glow. He left the chamber. At least the Dominant couldn't return until the array recharged; that would give him at least two chimes of peace. He shivered; it was getting colder. His breath misted in the air, and he wished someone would figure out how to use the power of the crystals to provide something useful like heat.

~

Jerrol staggered as the Ascendant dragged him forward. His head was full of roaring wind, and he felt disoriented as his feet sank into the hot, red sands of Terolia. The heat burning through his canvas shoes percolated into his mind. He looked up and registered the mountain range, which rose up before them, the jagged peaks of ancient rock piercing the sky. Jerrol's heart sank as he saw the narrow pass that led to the Telusion mines.

The Ascendant tied Jerrol's hands behind his back, and tightening his grip, forced Jerrol in front of him. He was muttering under his breath. "Try it, just try and I'll cut you down. You shouldn't have got in the way, you bastard."

A sharp blow between his shoulder blades overbalanced him, and he sprawled face down in the hot sands, twisting away as he heard the swish of air behind him. The sword narrowly missed him as it cleaved the sands. The Ascendant cursed.

Jerrol wriggled backwards out of reach of the next blow, keeping the mouth of the cave entrance behind him.

"Lis'ienne, what do you think you're doing?"

"He was trying to escape," Lis'ienne growled.

"To where?"

"He's that Fisherman, the one that blocked us in Selir

and now at Geteril." The young Ascendant was so furious, he was physically shaking.

Jerrol closed his eyes against the full glare of the sun as a man walked around in front of him, blocking the light. Jerrol squinted up at him; he didn't recognise him. He was an imposing man, broad chested, with hard blue eyes in a pale face, his blond hair tied in a queue, reminding him of the men of Elothia. Was he an Elothian? He didn't look like a typical Ascendant.

"Really, the Fisherman? And what did he do in Geteril?"

"He prevented us from getting the Tu'ani. He conjured up a strange vessel, the likes of which we've never seen before. It took the Tu'ani away."

"He prevented you from getting the Tu'ani?" The man's voice was cold. "You failed?"

"He must be a great sorcerer," Lis'ienne replied.

"A great sorceror? He doesn't look like one."

"I'm telling you what I saw," Lis'ienne said, his mouth tightening.

"You know how important your mission was, Lis'ienne. Failure was not an option. You said you had it under control. Making excuses is not acceptable. Where are the Tu'ani now?"

"I don't know."

"You don't know?" The man's voice grew colder.

"But he does," Lis'ienne said, desperately nodding at Jerrol.

"He had better, because if he doesn't, you will be taking his place," the man threatened. "Take him to Crute and hope he tells us what we want to know. We are running out of time, and now we need ..." he stopped short and glared at Jerrol.

Jerrol flinched back from the threat clearly visible in the man's eyes. This man would enjoy tearing him apart, and he was obviously getting impatient. The ground shuddered beneath them, and Jerrol dug his hands into the sand behind him.

"Make sure you get what we need," the man hissed before turning away. He turned back. "And tell Ter'ander to stop his barrage; we need more time!"

Lis'ienne dragged Jerrol up on his feet and forced him to walk into the passage. The stench of captivity and lost hope filled his nose, and his stomach turned at the memories they evoked. "If you know what's good for you, you will tell us what we need. I'm telling you now, you do not want him interrogating you; you won't be the same after."

Jerrol shivered as they entered the dim interior of the cavern. A crudely hewn passage led deeper into the darkness. A torch flickering on the wall cast a soft glow, accentuating the shadows in the rough walls. The passage opened into a small cavern with three passageways, much smaller than the cavern Jerrol remembered. It must have taken hundreds of years and thousands of lives to carve out the complex network that existed in his future. Jerrol's stomach cramped and he faltered. Lis'ienne shoved him in the back, pushing him forward. Even though the Ascendants themselves had been banished, their followers must have continued their practices without them.

Lis'ienne shoved him again towards the left-hand passage. Jerrol bounced off the wall, sharp edges slicing his skin as he staggered onwards. The passage sloped downwards, and Jerrol could smell the tang of water in the air. The sound of muted voices reached them as they entered a chamber that was empty but for a crude wooden stool in the middle and two men deep in discussion by the far wall. The sound of running water filled the air. Water, such a precious commodity in the desert. What could they possibly be using it for? He wasn't sure he wanted to find out.

The men looked up as Lis'ienne pushed Jerrol forward. "Crute, this is the Fisherman who stole away the Tu'ani tribe from under us. Car'onel wants to know where he took them. And fast. Find out how he got the vessel and where he took the clan. I'll be back shortly." Lis'ienne nodded and abruptly left.

Crute circled Jerrol slowly, coming to a stop in front of him. His eyes were lifeless pits of cruelty that drilled into Jerrol's, his face hard and relentless. "A fisherman," he said, his voice a grate across Jerrol's nerves. "Let's see who he is." He ran a thin finger down Jerrol's face, leaving a trail of burning acid, and Jerrol's breath caught in his throat as he inhaled sharply, but the cry never left his throat as a vice gripped his neck and forced him into the centre of the room. He writhed in the grip, but a kick to his legs brought him to his knees, and the man wrenched his head back, exposing his throat.

"Tell me," the man murmured, running his finger down Jerrol's throat and onto his chest. Jerrol's chest heaved as he tried to cope with the pain, but the insidious voice crept into his head. "What is your name?"

"Jer-Jerven," Jerrol gasped, sparkling dots before his eyes. He tried to draw breath, but the vice tightened.

"And where are you from, Jerven?" The finger continued down his chest and Jerrol cringed away from the stinging agony, breathless against the sensation of a knife splitting his skin.

He struggled against the man's grip, overwhelmed with burning pain. The vice loosened. "Plini," he whispered raggedly.

"And what do you do in Plini?" The voice spoke softly, curling around his ears. Jerrol focused on the pain, trying to breathe. He grunted as the pain seemed to coil in his stomach and explode outwards, taking him with it. "I said, what do you do in Plini?" The voice stabbed through the pain.

"Fish," Jerrol gasped. "I fish."

"Just fish?" The voice purred.

Jerrol's mind flew out in all directions, the pain overwhelming him, smashing through all thought. He dragged himself back together and tried to concentrate. His body heaved under a fresh onslaught, the vice holding him still. Jerrol tried to remember the question but couldn't. The vice suddenly released him, and he flopped limply to the ground, gasping for breath. He inhaled the scent of wet stone beneath him and he focused on it, something solid and real. The pain had gone as quick as it had started, but his body remembered it and still shuddered as a result.

He stiffened as the voice penetrated his mind, cutting like steel. "Where are the Tu'ani?"

"I don't know," Jerrol whispered to the stone floor, bracing for a new onslaught.

"Yes, you do," the voice insisted. "There, I can see them. You're on the beach with them. What did you do?"

"Nothing."

A white hot slash cut through his memories, dragging out a picture of Gael. A young boy with black eyes. Jerrol moaned.

"Who is he? A friend? A brother? Ah, a brother. If you want to keep him, tell me what you did."

Jerrol's eyes rolled as he tried to grab the memory back. "Ah-ah, tell me what you did on the beach."

"P-protect," he gasped, clawing at the memory.

"What did you protect? I'll kill him before your very eyes and he will be gone, lost, no longer a memory; you'll lose him and wonder what is missing but never know what."

"No," Jerrol moaned. He cried out as the boy was cut down, blood spurting from his stomach, his black eyes accusing, boring into Jerrol. Jerrol lay panting on the floor, the scent of blood in his nostrils, the memory roiling around his head and fading away, leaving an aching wound that jabbed at him.

"Who's next?" The voice bored its way into his mind. "What did you do on the beach?"

"S-saved people from drowning," Jerrol stuttered.

"How?"

"Sh-ship."

"What ship?"

"Lady help me," Jerrol moaned, his body shuddering against the violation in his head.

"Ah, who is this? A friend, someone close?" Serillion's face drifted past Jerrol's eyes and swirled before him. "Ah, he is a soldier. How do you know a soldier? Who is he?"

"No, leave him be." Jerrol tried to block the voice, to protect his memories.

"No, you don't." A sharp slap disintegrated his control and he sagged on the floor.

"Ah, Serillion? A Sentinal? You know a Sentinal? Where is he now?" The voice slashed through his mind.

Jerrol clamped down, throwing up a barrier. The voice shattered it. In desperation, he burrowed deep inside and closed the door.

"You think you can hide? No one can hide from me," the voice laughed, "but you can make it much more fun."

The man looked down at Jerrol trembling on the floor and frowned in thought. "Interesting," he murmured. "Let's bring him out into the open. Put him in the tank. He's a fisherman he says. He should like the water."

Jerrol was dragged across the floor, a chain wrapped around his ankles, biting his skin as they winched him up into the air and swung him over a clear pool of water. They lowered him down. Jerrol twisted desperately but the icy cold water crept inexorably up over his face and halfway up his chest. He struggled, searching desperately for an escape, but with his hands still tied behind his back, there was nothing he could do. He strained all the same.

The pool was made of molten rock, light and dark strata lining the walls. A long time ago this land had warped and folded. He tried to reach for a crevice, get some leverage, but he choked with the effort. Precious air escaped and he took in a mouthful of water. He began to panic. His chest tightened as his body jerked, trying to reject the water drowning his lungs. It was getting darker, and his ears hissed. He gulped in water and his struggles weakened. He finally gave in as he sent his love across time and his body stilled.

Jerrol spasmed as the blow hit his chest and water erupted out of his mouth. He choked, struggling to breathe through the outpouring of water. Chest heaving, he groaned as painful awareness returned. He frantically gasped for air, his defences in disarray.

"Where did you take the Tu'ani?" the insistent voice sliced through his confusion.

Jerrol heaved out liquid and dragged in painful air. His chest hurt; his throat was raw. Crute yanked his head back, and a burning finger stroked Jerrol's throat. "Where did you take the Tu'ani?" The voice was insistent, battering his weakened defences. Jerrol gasped as his head exploded, blinding him, shattering his protections. The words vibrated through his body, the ache absolute.

"Across land and time and seas," he whispered blindly, no longer understanding who or where he was.

"What?"

"She waits for me."

"Who does?"

"I promised."

"What did you promise?" the man shook him. "What … did … you … promise?" he asked, slowly spacing out his words.

"To come back."

"Where did you promise to go? Where did you take them?"

"'Cross land and time and seas."

"What?" The man shook him in exasperation. "Put him back in," he said angrily.

Jerrol was winched back up. The agony of the chain biting his ankles brought back awareness in time for him to realise he was being lowered back into the water. He flinched as the water submerged him, but he was too exhausted to struggle; his limbs were like lead. He choked, panic encompassing him. His chest heaved all the same until the darkness took him away. They pulled him out of the water, and it took them a lot longer to bring him back round this time. He retched as awareness returned, the pain in his chest consuming him. He struggled for breath as the water poured out of his mouth, and he curled into himself, defeated.

Lis'ienne entered the cavern. "Has he told you where they are yet?" He stopped short at the sight of the wheezing man curled up on the floor. "How many times?" he asked.

"Twice so far, but he's not making any sense. I have broken his defences; they were quite sophisticated for a fisherman. He has interesting friends, but he is still not saying anything that will help us, just rubbish about land and sea."

"Let me hear him."

Crute twisted his hand.

Jerrol jerked. "No," the cry was guttural and deep, a drawn out protest.

"Yes, you will tell me where you took the Tu'ani or I will destroy you."

Jerrol stared at them, unseeing. "I promised," he whimpered.

"Promised what?"

"To come back," he wheezed, squeezing his eyes shut. Oh, his chest. It hurt to breathe; it hurt to talk.

"Where did the ship come from?" Lis'ienne demanded.

"Roberion?" Jerrol murmured, confused.

"Wait a minute, let me get a hook into his memory of this Roberion," Crute said.

Jerrol shuddered as the man probed. "I can't get past this promise. Ah, what's this?" He slashed indiscriminately and Jerrol screamed.

23

FEBU 23RD, PRESENT AND PAST MESH

Taelia let out a wail of despair. "No, don't leave me! You promised, you promised you'd come back."

Birlerion burst through Taelia's chamber door. "Taelia? What happened? Is it Jerrol?" Birlerion gathered her in his arms, trying to console her hysterical weeping. "Taelia?"

"Something terrible is happening; he's giving up."

"The Captain never gives up," Birlerion said firmly. "Come, Roberion has returned. I came to tell you."

"But it's too late," she said, distraught. "He needs help *there*."

"We can't give up on him. Come on, Taelia, it's not that easy to kill the Captain. I can still feel him."

Taelia looked up in hope. "You do? He said goodbye." Her face twisted in distress.

"Come," Birlerion said gently. "Let's hear what Roberion has to say."

They entered the king's receiving room as Fonorion was lowering Roberion into a chair. King Benedict was glaring at Fonorion. "What's the matter with him?"

"He started to give me a quick summary of what

happened when he suddenly froze. It seems the Ascendants snatched the Captain off the beach at Geteril. Roberion brought the *Island Scout* back with him here; it's berthed in the harbour next to the *Miracle*. Amazingly, he managed to get all the people off the island. The Ascendants destroyed it. It seems he dropped the Tu'ani people off at another island and came straight here. I'm not sure, but I think he is with the Captain."

"Is that even possible?"

"It seems so; he doesn't seem to be quite here."

The king frowned at Roberion's strained face. "He doesn't look well. Roberion? Can you hear me?"

Roberion lifted his head. The king's chamber wavered, to be replaced by red stone. His feet sank into the hot sands and the king's voice was replaced by a scream that curdled his blood, but he recognised the Captain's voice, and he stiffened.

"Roberion? What's the matter? What do you hear?" the king asked, his voice sharp.

Roberion stared through the king, unseeing and unhearing. All he saw was red rock, surrounding him, and he spun and began running down a dim corridor. "I'm coming," Roberion shouted. He charged through the sandy passageway, cutting down anyone who blocked his way. He heard another cry that twisted his gut, and he veered off to the left, pounding down the passage, the smell of water and vomit in the air.

He paused on the threshold of a dimly lit cavern, taking in the tableau before him. Two men were standing over a third, curled up on the floor and tied up in rope and chains. Another stood to the side, holding the end of the chain near what Roberion sickly realised was a pool of water. The chain, Roberion saw with horror, was wrapped around Jerrol's ankles, biting deep. Blood sluggishly leaked into the puddle of water around him, turning it pink.

"Ah, what's this? The friend with a ship. Roberion. Where is Roberion?" The man's voice deepened, vibrating in the air, and Jerrol spasmed weakly.

"That would be me," Roberion said, cutting the tall, dark-haired man down before he could draw his sword. He twisted on the backswing and decapitated the cruel-looking man, who had been gaping at him in shock. The man holding the chain let go of it and backed away, holding his hands up, babbling nonsense. Roberion cut him down in disgust before checking for anyone else lurking in the shadows.

He dropped to his knees beside Jerrol and drew in his breath. The man before him looked more dead than alive; his face was deathly pale, his lips blue, and his breathing shallow and ragged. There was an angry burn, livid against his pale skin, running down his face, throat, and chest, and he was mumbling incoherently.

"Jerrol?" Roberion sliced the rope off his wrists. They left inflamed red burn marks where he had struggled against them. He was soaking wet, a testament to their treatment of him. Roberion struggled to release the chains that were embedded in his skin. He threw them away from him in horror.

"Jerrol?" he said. "We have to leave." As Roberion knelt on the gritty cave floor beside Jerrol, his guts clenched, roiling with fear, before he gentled his voice. "We have to leave, Jerrol, it's not safe here. Do you think you can stand?"

"I made a promise," Jerrol's voice was a rasping whisper, riddled with defeat and exhaustion.

"I know you did," Roberion replied softly as concern rippled through him. "I'm a friend," Roberion soothed, holding his hands apart in front of him. "I'm here to help you get back to Taelia."

"I said goodbye. They took her away, with a boy. I can't remember his name." Jerrol's voice cracked and then he drew in a painful breath that rattled ominously.

"You didn't tell them anything, and if you did, they can no longer tell anyone else now. You are safe, Jerrol. Come, we must leave. Jerrol, get up, we can't stay here," Roberion struggled to rise with Jerrol shuddering in his arms, his limbs trembling uncontrollably as he cringed away from Roberion. Roberion gripped him tighter, murmuring soft reassurances in Jerrol's ear, and he half-carried, half-dragged him out of the cavern.

He hurried back the way he had come, through surprisingly empty passages and out into the shadowed canyon. The sun had long since passed the rising ranges. He ducked aside as a tall dark-haired man entered the tunnel. Hitching Jerrol up higher, he turned towards the sea. Jerrol's bare feet dragged in the sand, more of a hindrance than a help.

Roberion panted as sweat beaded on his brow; Jerrol was heavier than he looked. "The Ascendants, they are right behind us. You were right, they were mining crystals. Jerrol, come on, the boat is down in the bay. It's not much further."

He lurched as Jerrol staggered against him, barely able to stand. His fingers slid down Roberion's arm as he collapsed bonelessly to the ground. Jerrol's breath came out in a weird groan. "You came for me?" he wheezed, his eyes glazed and feverish.

"Of course I came for you." Roberion screwed up his face in anguish, that Jerrol had thought he was all alone. "I promised you I would come."

Roberion grunted with effort as he dragged Jerrol to his feet, propped his shoulder under Jerrol's arm and pulled him down the trail. Weaving like drunkards, they staggered down the steep path towards the sparkling bay below.

"Jerrol, I'm here, hang on," Roberion said, frantically glancing over his shoulder, back towards the red mountains.

"How long can he sustain this without collapsing both here and there?" King Benedict asked, watching in concern as Roberion's brown complexion paled.

"Not much longer, by the looks of him. His pulse is racing," Birlerion replied, wiping the sweat off Roberion's face. As he spoke, Roberion's eyes rolled back and he would have fallen onto the opulent rug in the king's chamber if Birlerion hadn't caught him.

Clary stepped out into the heat of Terolia and shrugged off his cloak. He began to perspire as he walked across the sands to the entrance of the mine. He held a handkerchief up to his nose against the overpowering stench. A scruffy-looking fellow passed him, dragging an unconscious man. Probably dead; they went through a lot of bodies here. They'd had to start a new cavern to pile them in until they could incinerate them, hence the smell.

Striding deeper into the mountain, he halted at the junction, where a guard stood with a clipboard. "I'm Dominant Clary. Take me to Car'onel," he ordered, waiting impatiently as the guard checked his list.

The guard found his name and swallowed. "Yes, sir, right away, sir, please follow me." He led him deeper into the mine, taking a passage that led upwards and away from the suffocating stench. Clary was reminded why he usually stayed away from the mines. In his anger, he had forgotten.

Car'onel lurched to feet as Clary was shown into his

office. "Dominant, what are you doing here? I thought you were finalising the design for the crystals?"

"I was until I heard about the debacle at Geteril. Who ordered the destruction of that island?"

Car'onel spread his hands. "It had not been the intention. There was a power surge from the island; the backlash wiped out the array. It was not us."

Clary's face paled. "What? The array is destroyed?"

"Yes, sir, I was just compiling a message for you. The crystals were shattered. We need some of the crystals we sent returned to replace them."

"That will not be possible. I need them for the final array. You fools. Why did you attack? You know we need every array, and even then, we might not have enough."

"It was a remote island. You said the Tu'ani were a priority. I sent Lis'ienne and his men, they should have been sufficient. There were no Sentinals there. Guerlaire is cornered in Vespers. There should not have been any risk."

"You were obviously mistaken. I suggest you get mining. You have one month to find enough crystals to get this array back online. I expect it online before the beginning of Maru." Clary snapped his mouth shut, biting off the end of his words in his frustration.

Car'onel blanched. Even if they found the crystals, they would have to be cut and polished.

"Where is this Fisherman? I want to see him."

"Yes, sir, Crute was interrogating him. Lis'ienne said the man conjured up a vessel that took the islanders away. The Fisherman has the information we need."

"How long has Crute had him?"

"Not very long. He's down in the tank. This way, sir." Car'onel led the way through the dim, sandy passages. As they descended, the stink of water, vomit, and blood permeated the air. Clary's face grew even sterner, and Car'onel swallowed nervously as he escorted the Dominant into the chamber. He stopped dead at the entrance.

Clary passed a hand over his face as he looked around the carnage in the tank. "This was no fisherman."

"He was bound. It's not possible. Someone else must have helped him. Crute would not have let him loose," Car'onel protested.

"Check the port, quickly, we have to stop them leaving. And Car'onel, I need him alive," Clary said, the growl in his voice as good as a threat.

Roberion lurched to one side as Jerrol stumbled, and an arrow zipped past him. He dived to the dust, shielding Jerrol's limp body, his chest straining as he twisted to see the threat. He peered back up the trail, but it was empty, and he hoped it was just a wild shot. He hitched Jerrol up on his hip and realised he had passed out. He heaved him over his shoulder instead and set off again.

The *Lady's Dream* was moored at the end of the jetty. He zig-zagged down the beach and on to the rickety planks, praying to the Lady to protect them. He dropped Jerrol like a sack of grain on the deck and hurriedly cast off. Pulling up the mainsail, he tacked out of the harbour. The evening tide did its best to push them onto the rocks, but Roberion leaned heavily on the tiller and the sails caught, and the *Dream* skimmed over the waves and around the headland and out of reach.

Roberion heaved a sigh of relief as he tied the tiller in position. He knelt beside Jerrol, whose skin was pallid under his tan. Apart from the vivid red burns and the damage caused by the chains, Roberion couldn't see any other injuries, but from the way Jerrol had collapsed, he knew something wasn't right.

He gently wiped Jerrol's face with a damp cloth and dribbled some freshwater in his mouth. Jerrol spasmed awake in his arms, cowering away from him, his chest wheezing badly. "Jerrol, it's Roberion, I'm here, you're safe now," Roberion soothed. Jerrol was rigid in his arms. "Jerrol, you're safe, it's Roberion."

Jerrol stared at him, his eyes fearful. "I promised."

"I know you did," Roberion replied, holding him close.

"Across land and sea and time, I promised." Jerrol clung by a thread to his promise.

"Jerrol." Roberion hugged him tightly. "You're safe now," he murmured into his hair as he gently rocked the terrified man in his arms. "I won't let them hurt you anymore," he promised.

"I just sail and fish. Please stop," Jerrol moaned. "No more, I know nothing, I don't know where they went."

"Jerrol, it's all over, you're safe now," Roberion repeated, but Jerrol didn't hear him, he shrank in on himself, curling away from Roberion, consumed by his terror, pupils blown wide with fear and darkening his silver eyes.

"I swear, you can kill me if you want. I don't know where they are. Please don't hurt my family, *get out of my head,*" Jerrol pleaded. "Please, just end it, no more," Jerrol's voice trailed off to a whimper. A desperate mumble of nonsense continued.

Roberion watched him in horror, at a loss as to how to help ease his suffering.

Jerrol shuddered violently in his arms. "I-I can't get him out," he gasped. "He's in my head. There's too much in my head. He is destroying them; *it hurts.*" He cringed into Roberion's chest and gasped for breath, his face taut with distress and pain.

"Hold on, Jerrol, Leyandrii will help. We'll be there soon, hold on a little longer." Roberion tightened his grip as Jerrol moaned. "I've got you. I won't let go," he whispered as he rocked back and forth.

It felt like it took days to reach Lintel, though in truth it was only a matter of a few chimes. The little boat ploughed on through the waves as Roberion held Jerrol, who continued to fight the demons in his head. Whatever the Ascendant had planted, it was ravaging through Jerrol, body and soul. His face was drawn and grey, his eyes dull. He spasmed at intervals, a weak shudder that was all his exhausted body could manage.

Roberion offered comfort as best he could, talking to him constantly, trying to keep him warm. Jerrol's body was cold to the touch, his lips an unhealthy grey, all his energy focusing on his internal battle. He had developed a slight tremour by the time they approached the coastal village of Lintel.

Roberion negotiated away his boat for a horse and tack. He persuaded the reluctant fisherman to pass the semi-conscious Jerrol up into his arms, and he immediately set off for Stoneford. He hustled the horse through the narrow Stanton passes as fast as he could and luckily met no one as he thundered through the trails and out the other side. He cut across the country, picking his way through fields and woods, allowing the horse a breather as they forded a brook, and then he picked up speed again as the ancient oak trees at the Lady's grove in Stoneford came into view.

Pulling his trembling horse to a halt, Roberion ruthlessly walked him through the waystone, stepping out below the Lady's palace in Vespers and straight into a ferocious storm.

The black sky boiled above them, the wind shrieking through the delicate structure of the bridge and making it shudder. Roberion twisted away from the cutting wind, trying to protect Jerrol's face.

A surprised voice hailed him during a sudden lull in the

racket. "Roberion, what are you doing here?" and suddenly sharpened. "What has happened?"

Roberion slid to the ground, pulling Jerrol into his arms and collapsing to his knees. "I need Leyandrii, now!" he gasped as he curled over Jerrol, protecting him as best he could.

Niallerion acted. He signalled to the two guards gaping at them. "Get a stretcher, quick. Don't gawk, move! You take his horse." His voice cracked, and the men jerked into action. He knelt beside Roberion. "Who is it?" he asked, trying to get Roberion to release the man in his arms.

"The Captain," Roberion gasped between sobs of relief; he was almost there.

Niallerion frowned but asked no further questions. Loading the shuddering man onto the stretcher, they left the horse in the care of the guards and battled their way up the steps and into the palace. The wind tugged and moaned, spitting debris and icy pebbles at them. A deep rumble began to build overhead.

24

FEBU 25TH, 1124

VESPERS, VESPIRI

Niallerion hurried on ahead to clear the way and request the presence of the Lady. The commotion drew inquiring eyes, and quite a crowd had gathered in the entrance as Roberion escorted the stretcher in.

The crowd dispersed as a soft, clear voice spoke. "What has happened? Why is everyone blocking the hall?" The crowd melted away as Leyandrii approached. She was dressed in green, flowing silk, which rippled around her as she walked. Her blonde hair was plaited up in an intricate design on her head. Emerald green eyes in an ethereal face assessed the tableau before her. A slight frown creased her delicate brow. "Niallerion, what are you doing here? You are supposed to be on duty, aren't you?"

"I'm needed here, my Lady," Niallerion said, meeting her eyes.

The Lady observed him for a moment. "I see. Roberion, who have you brought in such disarray and what have you done to him?"

"My Lady, the Ascendants have planted some foul attack in his head, and he is struggling to defend himself. He is suffering my lady; you need to help him."

"Who is he?" She frowned, looking down at Jerrol, and her green eyes widened at the sight of him. "Oh," she said. Placing her hand on his forehead, she stilled the tremors, and Jerrol's silver eyes flew open and gazed at her, unseeing. "Bring him to my chamber and get Marguerite for me. Now." Her voice hardened as she turned away and hurried down the hall, not waiting to see if they had obeyed her.

She threw her doors open and directed them to her chamber. "Lay him on the bed," she ordered. The wind howled outside the window, and she drew the curtains against the noise. "Roberion, explain to me how you found him."

"He found me," Roberion said. "He sailed into Selir about four days ago, looking for me by name. He came to my aid when some Ascendants were trying to persuade the people in my village to leave with them. He said he was your messenger, here to defend your people from the likes of them. He said his name was Jerrol Haven and he was- or will be -your Captain from the year 4128, and he needed me to take my frigate to Geteril when I awake in his time. He said the Ascendants would attack the Tu'ani and he needed my help to save them." Roberion frowned. "I know I help him because I remember the frigate, the Lady's Miracle, a three master. She is a beauty! When I get there he is on the beach defending the Tu'ani. The Ascendants are after the elder, but somehow, the Captain holds them off. There is a blinding light, and before we can get to him, the Ascendants disappear, taking the Captain with them."

"And the Tu'ani?"

"He told me to take them to Cherni."

The Lady smiled knowingly. "And did you?"

"I don't know," Roberion said, rubbing his chin as he stared at the floor.

"Oh, you'd know if you had," the Lady chuckled.

"You know him, my Lady?" Niallerion asked in surprise.

"As will you, in time," the Lady replied as she sat on the side of the bed and leaned over Jerrol.

"Is he your Captain?"

"Oh yes," the Lady breathed, "and so much more." She smoothed Jerrol's hair off his face and tutted. "Oh, my Captain, I thought I told you to take better care," she murmured. "Wake," she commanded.

Jerrol's lashes fluttered on his pale cheeks, and he opened his eyes. He awoke to see the exquisite face of the Lady hovering over him. He stared up at her, trying to remember where he was. He tried to swallow, but his throat was dry. His body ached, his chest tight. He felt drained but no longer embattled. Echoes of the visions planted in his head simmered painfully, waiting to rise again.

"My Lady," he croaked, then tried to clear his throat. He shuddered as he tried to control the fear that flashed through him and tensed expecting another strike.

"Hush," she soothed, placing her hands on his temples. She scowled as she stared into his eyes. "That they dare," she whispered.

"My Lady?" Jerrol licked his cracked lips. "I tried, my Lady, I swear."

"They will pay for the suffering they have caused. I am sorry, my Captain."

Jerrol's visions faded, the tension in his head easing. "Drink." The Lady raised his head and held the cup to his mouth; the liquid soothed his raw throat. "How many times do I have to tell you to take more care?"

Jerrol grimaced. "I would if you gave me the chance," he replied, wincing as he heard a gasp behind her.

The Lady chuckled. "You have a point, but my Captain, you are not supposed to be here."

Jerrol rubbed his eyes and hissed his breath out as he

tried to sit up. A new barrage of aches awoke. He relaxed back on what he realised was a comfortable bed. "My Lady?" he asked querulously, still not sure if she was real. He had pleaded with her so often. Confused, he stared up at her. She was even more beautiful than he remembered.

"Yes, my Captain, you are in Vespers. Roberion brought you here."

Jerrol looked away from the Lady and stared at the gilt-framed painting covering the wall; he couldn't tell what the picture was as tears blurred his vision. "The Ascendants found the Tu'ani. They destroyed Geteril." He blinked away the tears and focused on a glowing golden orb suspended above him.

"So I hear. Don't move, your body needs to recover. Why didn't you use the Oath?"

"I tried," Jerrol sighed, mesmerised by the orb. How did it stay in the air? He couldn't see any chains. "I tried to cause a distraction so Roberion could save the Tu'ani." His lips quirked. "I think Birlerion is much better at distractions. I could use his help." He dragged his eyes away from the impossible light to Roberion. He looked as exhausted and wrung out as Jerrol felt. "Roberion, but for you, I would probably be dead. I'm sorry, I couldn't tell who was friend or foe. He was eating me alive."

"What did they do?" Niallerion asked, gazing at him in horror.

Jerrol looked at the young Sentinal standing next to Roberion. "Niallerion?" he asked with a smile creeping across his exhausted face as he recognised the ingenious young artificer. "It's so good to see you. I need you in Senti."

"Captain, you can't come in here and co-opt my Sentinals. We are about to be dragged into a war that no one will win. I need all the Sentinals I have," Leyandrii complained.

"You sent me here to do a job. I am trying to figure out

what it is. A few more instructions would help," Jerrol said, exhaustion threading through his voice.

The Lady smiled. "You're doing fine," she said, patting his cheek gently.

"Dominant Clary is mining crystals out of the Telusions and hoarding them somewhere in Elothia. He is trying to draw Guerlaire out so he can neutralise him. I don't know what else he can use them for apart from communications, but he has sacks of them."

Niallerion's face blanched. "My Lady, that would mean ..."

The Lady held up a hand, forestalling his words. "We are committed. I can't call them back now."

"But you can protect some of them," Jerrol wheezed, catching his breath painfully.

The Lady nodded thoughtfully and looked up as her sister Marguerite entered her rooms, closely followed by her companion, Taurillion. A tall, intense-looking Sentinal, who hovered beside her protectively.

"Leyandrii, what's this I hear? You have men in your rooms?" she asked, gaily inspecting the Sentinals standing before her. She came up beside Leyandrii. "Oh," she said, her laughter fading as she saw Jerrol lying on the bed. She twirled an auburn curl around her fingers. "It's you."

Jerrol stared up at her. She was so similar to her sister in looks and build, yet her sparkling blue eyes and vibrant auburn hair gave an indication of her more vivacious nature.

The room suddenly shook, making them all stagger. The sound of tinkling glass and faint shrieks filtered into the chamber. The tremor died away, and Marguerite's face tightened.

"My Lady, the Land grows weary; he can't take much more," Jerrol whispered, his voice cracking. He tried to clear his throat, but he winced instead at the stinging pain. His chest wheezed, and the Lady frowned.

Marguerite sighed. "I know."

Leyandrii glanced at her. "It's not time yet," she said, reaching for her sister's hand.

"The Oath gave me this for you." Jerrol reached around his neck for the pendant the Oath had conjured for him in Senti. He knew it was meant for Marguerite and suddenly there was a sparkling black stone in his hands. Marguerite leaned forward and hesitantly took the faceted jewel in slender fingers that trembled. She stared at the glistening stone, the animation in her face draining away to be replaced with silent awe.

"How did you keep it from them?" she whispered, staring at him intently.

"I'm not sure, my Lady," Jerrol replied. "They were more interested in where the Tu'ani went, instead of asking about the Oath. If they had asked …" he faltered. "I would have told them."

"But you didn't so there is no point beating yourself up about something that didn't happen," the Lady interjected.

Marguerite caught Leyandii's eye. "Do you realise what they could have done if they had got hold of the Oath?"

Leyandrii rose and gripped her sister's hands. "But they didn't, Marguerite, and you will ensure they never do."

Jerrol watched as the sisters stared at each other. They seemed to reach an understanding and Marguerite nodded. "I see what is needed," she murmured, her gaze drawn back to the stone. Jerrol knew he was witnessing the moment Marguerite agreed to bond with the Land, to take over the protection of the world of Remargaren from the ancient awareness encased at the heart of their world. How she would do that was beyond him, and he winced at the fraught expression on Taurillion's face as he glanced between Leyandrii and Marguerite.

"What?" Taurillion demanded. "Marguerite? What is happening."

Leyandrii released her sister's hands and Marguerite's shoulders drooped for a moment before she straightened and plastered a smile across her pale face. "Nothing you need to worry about, my dear," she replied.

The anxious glance she cast towards him belied her words and Leyandrii spoke, her calm voice drawing the Sentinals' attention back to her and away from Marguerite and her distraught lover. "It's not over yet, far from it. You have to go back to Birtoli. It has to be played out, and, my Captain, I fear your part is not yet finished." Her gaze encompassed Niallerion, and he took a step forward. "Niallerion, You must go with him; his need is greater. And someone needs to keep an eye on him," she finished wryly. "You will take Marianille with you, she can't stay here." She leaned forward to grip Roberion's arm. "You must return to Terolia and resume your duties. You shouldn't be here either. You twist your history and your future suffers."

Roberion stared at her in confusion.

"Suffice to say, Roberion, your part is played. Your reward awaits you when you wake up." She faltered as her gaze rested on Marguerite. "We need to talk. We'll leave the Captain to rest before we send him back." She looked at Jerrol, her face grave. "Know, my Captain, that I am most pleased. What you will put in place ..." She hesitated. "You have surpassed my wildest dreams. The people of Birtoli are fortunate in their Fisherman, and I thank you with all my heart. I will bring Guerlaire to speak to you before you leave." She bent and kissed his forehead before cupping his cheek and whispering softly, and Jerrol slept the sleep of deep exhaustion.

She looked at Marguerite. "It's a sign," she said as the building began to shake again. A crack started in the corner of the ceiling and began to zig-zag down the wall. She sighed. "There were reports of the land ripping apart in Elothia, just opening up and swallowing everything."

"I know," Marguerite whispered. "Do you think it will stop them, though? If we do it, it will be irreversible."

"Do what?" Taurillion asked, his voice sharp with fear.

Marguerite smiled at her Sentinal. "What we must, dear one. Come, we must prepare. There is much to do."

Leyandrii looked down at Jerrol and then turned to Niallerion. "Watch him for me; make sure he comes to no further harm. I will come back soon with Guerlaire." She reached up to hug Roberion. "Roberion, thank you for your care. It's time you returned home."

"Yes, my Lady," Roberion said reluctantly as she released him and left. He stood over Jerrol and gripped his shoulder. "Whenever and wherever you need me," he vowed softly, before nodding to Niallerion and leaving the room.

Niallerion watched him go, a slight frown on his face. He scrutinised the man sleeping on Leyandrii's bed. Who was he to garner such devotion? He watched him intently, waiting for him to wake up.

25

PRESENT DAY

FEBU 25TH, 4128, MOLINTI

Opening his eyes, Roberion groaned. He felt like he had spent the day climbing up and down the rigging; his body ached all over.

"Finally, you're awake." Fonorion's voice, edged with tension, spoke from beside him.

Roberion rolled his head on the pillow and stared at him for a moment, trying to readjust to the fact he was no longer in the middle of storm torn Vespers. Fonorion wrinkled his brow in concern as he searched Roberion's face. Roberion cleared his throat. He was parched, "What happened?"

"Don't you remember? You stagger in to Molinti, trailing Jerrol's boat, begin telling us about your dream and Geteril, and then you keel over, shouting at Jerrol to get up. You looked horrified."

"Oh," Roberion said, closing his eyes again.

"Oh? Is that all you have to say?" Fonorion asked, launching to his feet.

"Don't shout. My head hurts," Roberion mumbled, trying to marshal his thoughts.

"What happened to Jerrol? Is he alright?" Fonorion's voice was dangerously quiet.

"It wasn't a dream and yes, I got him out of the mines and took him to Leyandrii in Vespers; she sorted him out and sent him back to Birtoli." He looked at Fonorion. "With Niallerion and Marianille."

"What?" Fonorion rocked back, stunned.

"Yeah, my thoughts exactly. We thought they had been lost in Vespers, but the Lady made them go with Jerrol. It was nearing the end, Fonorion." Roberion's vision blurred. "The ground tremours had begun. The palace was crumbling; reports of the land shattering were beginning to come in. The winds were terrible."

Fonorion's face tightened. "We cannot change what happened," he said, gripping Roberion's arm.

"I know, but I saw the Lady, and she was worried. They still weren't sure if they were doing the right thing."

"They did the only thing they could in the end. It was the only way to protect her people, and that was her duty," Fonorion replied, his silver eyes flashing.

"Yeah," Roberion breathed, closing his eyes. He opened them again. "Did I tell you I got joined?" he said, the joy of his joining replacing his exhaustion.

"Roberion! When? To whom?"

Roberion couldn't help the smug expression spreading over his face and he was warmed by his friend's effuse response. "To the Tu'ani chief's daughter."

"Congratulations, my friend," Fonorion said warmly as he clasped his arm. "But the king wants to know what is going on; you've a lot of questions to answer.

"And I have so much to tell." Roberion sat up and swung his legs over the side of the bed. His head thumped, a pulsing pain at his temples.

Roberion stood as Fonorion added, "Taelia is about to climb the walls."

"Then we had better go see her. Can you get me something for my head? It feels like it will explode." He wobbled slightly as he stood, and Fonorion gripped his arm until he was sure he was stable.

"You sure you're alright?"

"I will be," sighed Roberion, "I need Lilith."

"Lilith?"

"My wife."

"Ah, where is she?"

"On Cherni."

"Cherni?"

"Yes, that's where I took the Tu'ani."

"Let's go see the king. It will be simpler if you say this once."

"How long was I out of it?"

"A whole day. We could tell you were trying to help Jerrol, but it wasn't clear what was happening. It didn't help that Taelia was in the room."

Roberion closed his eyes, then nodded slowly.

"The king had to order Birlerion to leave. He's gone to Senti to see if he can talk to the sentinal. He didn't want to go after what happened to you and Jerrol, but the king promised to send Ari with news if there was any." Fonorion led the way down the corridor. The king's steward, Darris, opened the door to the king's chamber and gestured for them to come in.

Benedict looked up in relief as they entered.

"Roberion, how are you feeling?"

"I'm fine, Your Majesty, thank you."

The king looked at him cynically. "If you say so," he said. "You still look washed out, so don't lie to me. Sit down. Before you start making excuses, tell Taelia that Jerrol is fine."

Roberion swallowed and looked across the room at Taelia; her face was pale but determined. "He was with the

Lady when I last saw him. She was looking after him, though she was sending him back to Birtoli."

"But he was hurt. You were with him; you saved him."

Roberion inhaled deeply, steadying himself. "I went to the Telusion mines after I first met with Jerrol in Selir. He said that the Ascendants were mining crystals. That wasn't what was reported, so I went to check. Taelia," he spread his hands, "there is no easy way to say this." He took a breath. "They were torturing him. They must have taken him to the mines from Geteril. He did something I can't explain; a blinding light erupted from his left hand. It forced the Ascendants back and calmed the storm enough for us to get to the beach. He had Guerlaire's sword in his other hand when the Ascendant vanished with him."

"He couldn't have, it's in my room. I brought it with me; I didn't like to leave it lying around unprotected," Taelia said.

"Go and get it," the king instructed.

Taelia nodded and left the room.

"How come you went to the Telusion mines? How did you know where to find him?" the king asked.

"I didn't know where they took him. When we first met he had said we should investigate the mines, that we were wrong to allow the Ascendants to mine crystals unchecked." He paused as Taelia returned with the sword. The leather sheath was damp and encrusted in salt. Mutely, she held it out to the king, her eyes large in her face.

"So I detoured to the mines on my way to Vespers," Roberion continued, watching the king unsheathe the sword. "I found him in a cavern under the Telusion mountains. We escaped in my boat. I took him to Vespers to the Lady; she healed him."

"What did they do to him?" Taelia asked, her eyes wide with fear.

"Taelia, don't do this to yourself. Just know that the Lady healed him. He is fine and back in Birtoli with Niallerion and Marianille."

She jerked back in surprise. "What?"

"The Lady sent Niallerion with him to look after him." Roberion smiled. "I'm not sure why Marianille went too; probably something to do with the fact that he is a magnet for trouble. Oh, I found his logbook in his boat; you might find this easier to read than that faded copy in the archives." He held the book out to her.

"Roberion …" she began as tears welled in her eyes.

"Don't. He said to tell you he loved you," he whispered.

Her tears spilt over, and she reached up and hugged him. "Thank you," she breathed. She looked at the king as she released him.

"Go." Benedict smiled. "You can tell me what it says at breakfast."

She gave him a faint smile in return and left.

The king's smile faded as he glared at Roberion. "He obviously used his sword. The sheath is still damp." Benedict pondered for a moment. "I suppose the Lady returned it here when the Ascendants took him. Roberion, tell us what actually happened."

Roberion sighed and started talking. "I was telling Fonorion what had happened when I realised he could no longer hear me. It was peculiar, I could see and hear him, but he was staring at me as if I was crazy, and then I was no longer in this room; the Terolian mountains were all around me and I remembered arriving at the entrance to the mines. Jerrol had said the Ascendants were mining crystals and I wanted to confirm it was true before I sent a message to Guerlaire.

"I heard him scream." He shuddered. "Such an awful sound. But I ran towards it, and when I arrived he was surrounded by men, and he was huddled in on himself in a puddle of water. They wanted to know where he'd taken the Tu'ani, where my frigate had come from, and they tried to drown him so he'd tell them."

Roberion's eyes were haunted as he continued. "He was a mess. A shivering bundle on the floor, and they were trying to rip his memories out of his head. I was so furious, I didn't stop and think, I just waded in and cut them all down, they wouldn't be telling anyone anything Jerrol *did* say. I cut off the ropes, removed the chains, and carried him out, down to my boat. I took him to Leyandrii in Vespers via the waystone in Stoneford." Roberion twisted his lips. "Leyandrii said I'd played my part and I should return here. The next thing I knew I woke up here in Molinti."

The king stared at him aghast as Roberion faltered to a stop. They didn't need to know how terrified Jerrol had been, nor the way he had clung to him, and Roberion avoided everyone's eyes as the silence extended.

Eventually the king spoke. "You're sure he is alright?"

Roberion grimaced and then shrugged. "The Lady healed him. What he still remembers only he knows. I remember she was angry—not at the Captain," he hastened to say, "but at what they tried to do. I know he did something on the beach that I can't explain. He also gave Lady Marguerite something. It was as if there was a second conversation going on at the same time that only he and the Lady Marguerite understood; it was peculiar."

"To do with the Tu'ani?" the king asked.

Roberion frowned. "What makes you say that?"

"Because Jerrol risked his life to save them. Because there is something you're not saying," the king said gently.

Roberion hesitated and then exhaled. "The reason why the Ascendants couldn't find the Tu'ani is because I brought them here; they live on the island of Cherni in our time."

The king gaped at him.

"You need to meet Elder Tuan." Roberion laughed wryly. "My father. I am joined to his daughter, Lilith."

"And when did you manage that?" the king asked, raising an eyebrow.

"I'm not sure. I got a little confused. But I do know that I am joined to Lilith. Leyandrii said I had played my part and to return to Terolia, but that was back then. I'm not sure what still needs to happen now." His eyes fell as he scrunched his fists into his trousers. "He's approaching the day when the Lady sundered the Bloodstone."

The king nodded, his face grim. "What about the logbook you gave to Taelia?"

"There is nothing new in there. It's full of messages for Taelia, for her and no-one else. I think we should place it back in the *Island Scout*. I believe Jerrol will come back for it."

"Did the Lady say what we were supposed to be doing?" the king asked in exasperation.

Roberion shook his head.

"Didn't you ask?"

"The Captain did, sort of, but she said he was doing fine."

"Doing fine?" The king launched to his feet, unable to stay still. "He almost died! Lady knows what they did to his head, and he still has a part to play? What does she expect of him?" The king took a deep breath and stopped pacing.

Roberion glanced at Fonorion and then shrugged. "She expects what each of us can give," he replied.

The king huffed. "Sometimes, she expects too much."

Fonorion looked at the king. "Sometimes, sire, you have to work with the tools you have," he said, his voice sad.

The king's face tightened, but he clamped his lips shut, as they were all reminded of a certain desperate battlefield.

Island of Senti, 4124

Birlerion sat under the Senti sentinal. Leaning back against the trunk, he stared out to sea, smiling as the bark warmed his back. The air was balmy and warm, and a gentle breeze cooled his skin. He was feeling overheated in his uniform, and he shrugged out of his jacket, folding it neatly beside him. He needed to sweet-talk the harbour master into finding him some of the local linen shirts and cut off trousers.

The sea gleamed silver in the sun, extending out to the never-ending horizon until the sky merged with the sea, and he couldn't tell where one ended and the other began.

Shuffling around, he observed Senti Harbour. It was peaceful and lazy. Small skiffs bobbed at anchor on the calm, clear waters. Children played on the small, sandy beach to the east, their laughter drifting across the water. The harbour buildings themselves were built into the headland below him, with the quays jutting out of it made of the same smooth, golden stone, glittering in the morning sunshine. He frowned as he followed the foundations into the harbour waters. The storm walls rose out of the bay, tall and solid. It was some feat of engineering.

He wondered how they had built it with the tools they had back then. The blocks of stone were smooth and perfectly joined, flush against each other as they curved away. They must be crystalline to glitter so much. They would have needed someone like Niallerion, who understood these things. How to achieve such a large area of water that was so calm and unaffected by tidal surges was beyond him.

The small boat he had arrived on earlier that morning, the *Mari Rose*, sculled its way out of the harbour. The harbour may be well protected, but it also meant there was no wind to fill your sails. Oars were needed until you passed the storm walls. His thoughts moved onto Jerrol, and his face tightened in concern. By the Lady, he hoped he was alright. He couldn't believe the king had ordered him away without finding out what had happened.

He shifted to get more comfortable and closed his eyes, then he reached for the sentinal. *"What can you tell me about the building of the harbour?"*

The sentinal planted a vision in Birlerion's mind of the harbour he remembered from when he was first planted, pleased that Birlerion had asked. There was no harbour, just a stretch of golden sandy beach sweeping between the head-lands. The memory showed the Captain arriving in the *Island Scout*, beaching his boat and strolling along the beach towards him, with a young boy beside him.

They came up to the sentinal, and Birlerion could have reached out and touched them. Jerrol was explaining his plans enthusiastically. "A safe haven," he said, his lips quirking at the pun, which the boy missed completely. The boy had black eyes and hair and the olive skin of the islanders. He was obviously bored. Jerrol laughed. He looked well and carefree, bronzed by the sun, his eyes a startling silver in his tanned face. He would be hard to miss. Birlerion was amazed that Jerrol had adapted so well to life on such a small boat, in such a vast sea, and so successfully.

The next memory was the arrival of the workmen. Tools at the ready, they began hewing out the rock, exactly where Jerrol had said, even though they thought he was mad. It was a good twenty feet above sea level. Birlerion knew the quay only cleared the water by a few feet. If he had built any lower, it would have been submerged with the original beach. He gasped and opened his eyes; that meant the storm walls were twenty feet high or more. How deep had the harbour been back then? How had Jerrol managed to get so much *stone?*

Birlerion blinked as he realised how advanced the day had become. The sun was setting behind the mainland and the light was failing fast. He murmured his thanks to the sentinal and stood. The air was cooling with the setting sun. The aroma of roasting meat rose on the evening air, and he headed back down to join the harbour master and his family for supper. They were insistent that he stayed with them, an honoured guest, eager to hear about the Lady and the Remargaren he remembered. In return, they offered to tell him what they knew of Senti and the surrounding area.

He was welcomed into the Sentian home without reservation, offered food and drink and friendship. As he relaxed and bantered with Gael's family, he wondered where Jerrol was at that moment and how he had managed to create such an incredible culture of welcome and inclusion in such a time of destruction and fear. A true legacy of an amazing man. His gut tightened with a thrill of fear. They had to find a way to get him home.

26

FEBU 26TH, 1124

VESPERS, VESPIRI

Sensation slowly returned as Jerrol woke. His fingers spasmed and snagged on the silky material beneath his hands, and he stilled, unsure where he was. Memories flickered, hazy and distant, his heart sped for a moment and then calmed as he remembered meeting the Lady and Niallerion. He was with the Lady in Vespers, he was safe. Roberion had come for him.

A nervous flutter in his stomach made him think he should be concerned about something, but as he carefully tensed his body, he wasn't sure why. Apart from an ache deep in his chest and sore ankles, he couldn't find any injuries, though a flash of anxiety made him check again. His head felt clear, and his memories were his own. He sifted through them, checking; Taelia and the children, Birlerion, Tagerill and Serillion, Hannah and Gael. He stopped and wondered briefly when the Sentinals had become more like family to him. They had slowly inveigled their way into his heart, and he missed them terribly.

Scrunching up his face, he tried to remember what had happened. He knew he had been taken to the mines; the smell was something he would never ever forget. Even now, the thought of that red stone made his stomach turn. The soft sands of the beach in Geteril replaced the image. An Ascendant had dragged him off the beach and taken him to the Telusions. Shivering, he chased after the slippery memory and tensed as the name Crute arose, but he couldn't place the face nor why he knew the name. Just a fleeting sense of fear, which made him cringe. Someone to avoid if possible.

Voices entering the room penetrated his concentration. "He doesn't look strong enough." A man's voice, commanding and stern.

"Well, he is," the Lady replied. "Sometimes being underestimated is a powerful weapon; you know that. They underestimated you enough times, my love." Jerrol's lips twitched as the Lady teased … he groped for the name, it must be Guerlaire.

"But he keeps losing my sword."

"And how many times did I have to retrieve it for you?"

"Well," the man's voice sounded embarrassed; it was definitely Guerlaire. Jerrol tried to open his eyes. He was going to meet Guerlaire! The Lady's Captain before him, a legend in his own right.

"Exactly." Amusement laced Leyandrii's voice. "Jerrol is your match, Guerlaire, help him."

"You're sure this is the only way?"

"Yes, I fear it is the only way to be sure." She sighed gently. "Niallerion, has he stirred?"

"No, my Lady, he's shuddered a few times, but that is all." Niallerion's youthful voice was startlingly close.

"Then go get him some food. He'll awake hungry. Be ready to leave with him," Leyandrii requested as she moved closer to the bed.

"Yes, my Lady." Jerrol heard the door close. He tried to open his eyes but they felt glued together and heavy.

"If we send Jerrol on this venture, he might not come back," Guerlaire warned, continuing their conversation.

"When did the threat of danger ever stop you?"

"That's not the point."

"Yes, it is. You were both made to face down impossible situations. He won't refuse."

"Well, I think he should. He hasn't recovered from the last escapade and you want to send him on another."

"We don't have the luxury of time nor a choice." Leyandrii skirts swished as she paced.

"I know. I'm sorry, it's just …" Guerlaire's stricken voice faltered and Leyandrii must have turned back to him, because her voice was a whisper.

"No. Guerlairion, my love, *I'm* sorry. I know you would go, but I need you here."

Guerlaire fell silent at her use of his full name. "I suppose. But we need to make sure. I should go."

"You know you can't; you're more valuable to us here. Help him."

"Yes, my Lady."

Leyandrii's laugh filled the room, and Jerrol opened his eyes.

"Since when have you ever obeyed my requests so meekly?"

"All the time," Guerlaire replied with a touch of mock outrage.

Jerrol's lips twitched.

"No, you don't."

"Of course I do." Guerlaire sounded affronted. "Let me show you."

Jerrol smiled at their bickering and rolled his head on the pillow; his head felt too heavy to lift. The sight of Guerlaire embracing the Lady made him clear his throat, and they broke apart, somewhat abashed.

"You're awake at last," Guerlaire said abruptly, though Jerrol wasn't fooled. The look of utter devotion that Guerlaire cast at the Lady, had softened the hard edges of his face for a moment, and the reciprocal expression on her face was all Jerrol needed to see. His heart eased, and he relaxed into the soothing sense of absolute trust and understanding that the two had between them. "The world's falling apart and you're sleeping," Guerlaire complained.

"Now, now," the Lady chided. "You know what it's like; you've been where he is."

"Still," Guerlaire smirked at her. "I wasn't out that long."

The Lady tutted and patted his cheek. "After all these years, my love, you've had lots of practice."

Guerlaire choked. "Be off with you woman. Do you want me to help him or not?"

Leyandrii laughed at him, her affection obvious, and she looked across at Jerrol as his stomach growled. Jerrol flushed with embarrassment.

"When did you last eat?" she asked. At his blank expression, she shook her head and continued. "Never mind, I sent Niallerion for food. I'll see where he got to."

Guerlaire sighed deeply, concern flitting across his face as he watched her leave before he hid his emotions and turned back to scowl at Jerrol.

Jerrol sat up and swung his legs over the side of the bed, swaying dizzily for a moment before the room steadied. His clothes were wrinkled and salt-stained, and he ran his hand through his crusty hair causing more grains of salt, or maybe sand to shower around him in a gentle patter on the wooden floor. He'd lost his shoes at some point and his ankles were swollen. No wonder they ached; they were angry and red.

Guerlaire shifted and drew Jerrol's gaze away from his inspection of his feet. The Lady's Captain was smartly dressed in the silver-green uniform of the Lady's Guards. In comparison, Jerrol felt grubby and somewhat battered beside him.

Taking a moment to observe Guerlaire, Jerrol thought he might be slightly taller than he was, though not by much. He was broad across the chest and quite stocky. Yet the power of his voice, and the arresting green eyes caught your attention more than his stature. The Sentinals would still dwarf him. His eyes were deep set on a face that was striking rather than handsome, but he had a presence about him that drew the eye, much Jerrol supposed, as he had back in Old Vespers. Guerlaire's eyes gleamed in the candlelight as he watched Jerrol watching him. He wasn't unnerved by the inspection, in fact, he seemed to be quite enjoying it, and his eyebrow arched in question as the silence drew out.

"You can go with her, you know," Jerrol said as he creaked to his feet.

"What?"

"At the end, if you are determined. She'll take you with her."

Guerlaire's face brightened. "Really?"

Jerrol nodded.

Guerlaire exhaled, an expression of naked relief on his face.

"How do I get home?" Jerrol asked, his heart skipping at the thought that maybe, just maybe Leyandrii could send him home.

Guerlaire grimaced. "With difficulty," he admitted. "The Ascendants are messing with things they shouldn't touch. They've lost all sense of caution and are out to destroy the very thing they desire. Yet they can't see what they are doing," he finished with a touch of frustration creeping into his voice.

"They don't seem to be able to learn that lesson," Jerrol agreed. He paused as Niallerion returned with a tray, which he placed on the bed before nodding at Guerlaire and retreating. The smell of food made his stomach growl again, and he sat and reached for a meat-filled bread roll. He glanced at Guerlaire. "What do you need me to do?" he asked as he took a bite.

"Your discovery about Clary and his crystal mining is cause for concern. I wanted to send Birlerion to deal with it, but Leyandrii needs him here, and well, you heard her, I am more use here."

Jerrol nodded. "You do seem to annoy the Ascendants."

Guerlaire's grin lit up his face, and Jerrol suddenly understood how this man was able to capture and hold so much attention. Sheer charisma radiated off the man, and Jerrol wondered how he was ever supposed to compare to him.

"Leyandrii said your task in Birtoli is nearing completion, Oath Keeper." Guerlaire scowled. "One she said I couldn't help her with, but once you complete her work, I need your help to deal with these crystal arrays."

"Why me? Why now?"

Guerlaire blew his breath out and started pacing. "I made a mistake, showed my hand too soon. I should have listened to …" He flicked a glance at Niallerion and cut off his words and swallowed them. "Doesn't matter, it's done. The Ascendants have grown wise to our attacks, and we can no longer surprise them. The only way is for one of us to infiltrate their defences, and it seems you have already caught their eye."

Jerrol watched him pace, concern rippling through him. "I don't understand why it has to be me."

"There are only three of us who can handle my sword," Guerlaire said. "You, me, and …"

"Birlerion," Jerrol said, knowing he was correct. Birlerion was Leyandrii's shield, and he understood why Leyandrii would be reluctant to send him away. His throat tightened and tears pricked his eyes, but he blinked rapidly to clear them. He could have used Birlerion by his side these last few months.

Guerlaire nodded. "And Leyandrii needs him here, so I can't send him. Whoever goes will need to use my sword to destroy the lodestone and its connections. If you just steal the stone, they'll replace it immediately. But if you can damage the connections, it will take them weeks to realign it, and by then …" Guerlaire pumped his fist. "By then we'll be ready." He spun on his heel and Jerrol stared into his determined face, remembering Birlerion saying how stubborn Guerlaire was. Once he had an idea in his head, it was difficult to dissuade him. And Guerlaire's gaze was unrelenting.

"You have to find and destroy the crystals that they took to Elothia," Guerlaire said. "I can't leave Vespers until you do. Leyandrii will be vulnerable when she destroys the Bloodstone; the only thing that can hurt her are the crystals. They enhance the Ascendants' power tenfold. The crystals will enable them to block the Veil as it descends, and then they will be able to attack her. You have to destroy them."

"How do I find them?" Jerrol reached for another roll; he was starving.

Guerlaire smiled grimly. "I think they will find you," he said. "You've had more interaction with Clary than any of us these last months. Leyandrii said there was an area of emptiness where she couldn't feel anything, a dead zone to the north. They will likely have hidden it, which is why she can't sense anything. That's all I can tell you."

Jerrol stilled, bread halfway to his mouth. "To the north?"

"Yes."

"Adeeron? Is Adeeron here in this time?"

Guerlaire studied him for a moment and then exhaled. "Adeeron? What is Adeeron?"

"In my time, it is a concealed army encampment, a training ground. The home of one of the most elite chevrons of the grand duke's army. It has a protection over it."

"A dead zone," Guerlaire whispered. He blinked and then slowly nodded. "You'll need my sword." He unstrapped the belt from around his waist and held the sheathed sword out horizontally in front of him.

Jerrol took the familiar sword and smiled as it vibrated gently in his hand.

"You'll need to disrupt the alignment of the crystals. Niallerion will explain; he designed them, after all." He flashed a grin at the young Sentinal standing by the wall. "He's going with you. Keep him with you if you can. It would be best if you can take him with you wherever you need to go. He's handy to have around." Guerlaire's face grew grave. "Jerrol, it won't be easy, but it is possible. I hate to do this to you, but we're depending on you. This won't work if the Ascendants have the power to block Leyandrii. If she can't freely link to the Sentinals, then her power alone will not be enough.

"I'd go, but they have me cornered here, and I'm occupying at least half of their magicians, which means they can't attack the others. It reduces their effectiveness and releases you to go and blindside them." He grinned, a vicious glint in his eye. "Every time I poke my head up, they send a barrage and exhaust themselves." He looked around sadly. "The palace won't survive the onslaught, and nor will much else.

"You need to take Marianille with you. She refuses to leave Leyandrii, but she can't stay here. She won't be happy, but you brook no arguments. She goes with you," Guerlaire said.

Jerrol nodded.

"Marguerite has already left. I believe you already know what she plans. We've been discreetly evacuating as many people out of Vespers as we can." He stared at Jerrol, his gaze unfocused. "Those we can get to leave, anyway. So much sacrifice," he murmured.

"But it works, doesn't it? In my time, the Veil is in place and the Bloodstone was sundered."

Guerlaire shrugged. "It hasn't happened yet; there is still time for something to change the course of history. We have hope as the possibility exists, and I'll take that any day in the current circumstances." He stopped speaking as a tremendous explosion rocked the building. The sound of falling masonry clattered in the corridor, plaster shedded from the walls, and a large gilt-framed painting crashed to the floor. Dust hung in the air, and Guerlaire looked at Jerrol a little desperately. "Trust Niallerion. He may be young, but he knows his stuff, and don't underestimate Marianille; she wasn't the Lady's protector for nothing. I'd give you Birlerion, but we need him here."

Jerrol looked at him in surprise. "I thought you were her protector?"

"I wish. Come on, we have to leave." He led the way to the door. "Leyandrii doesn't believe I can be impartial enough." He shrugged. "I expect she's right."

Jerrol laughed.

"I can't help being overprotective."

"I know the feeling," Jerrol agreed as they circumvented the fallen masonry.

Guerlaire glanced back at him keenly. "I'm sure you do," he agreed. "Remember, you don't have to do this alone. Our strength is in our Sentinals; use them, use whatever you can. Marguerite will be listening for you. It is paramount that you destroy the crystals by the seventh of Maru. I can cause one diversion. I intend to do it on the morning of the seventh."

"Do what?" Jerrol asked, catching his breath. The seventh. The day the Lady sundered the Bloodstone.

"It doesn't matter what, just know that their attention will be on Vespers on the seventh. It's the best I can do. You can take the waystone to Stoneford and Leyandrii will transfer you to Molinti from there. She is supposed to be conserving her energy so don't let her persuade you otherwise. Roberion said he left your boat in Molinti harbour. It would be better for you to be seen as going about your business as usual until you complete what Leyandrii has you doing down there. We don't want the Ascendants disrupting those plans."

Jerrol's eyebrows rose as he came to a stop at the top of the stairs. So, Guerlaire didn't know what he was doing in Senti. He was surprised Leyandrii hadn't told him. The Ascendants would not be amused by his escape, and it probably wouldn't take them long to track him down. He peered over the bannister at Leyandrii and the tall Sentinals waiting for them below. "Good luck," he said softly as he held out his hand.

"I think you need all the luck," Guerlaire replied, gripping his hand in return. "I wish …" He stopped short.

"So do I," Jerrol agreed.

Guerlaire nodded in acceptance and pulled Jerrol into a heartfelt hug before releasing him and abruptly descending the stairs.

Jerrol stood staring after him. Sacrifice, so much sacrifice for the greater good. It left a bitter taste in his mouth.

After Leyandrii transported them to the outskirts of Molinti, Jerrol led Niallerion and Marianille down the incline to the harbour in Molinti. He breathed a sigh of relief when he saw the *Island Scout* berthed by the jetty. A young lad was sitting on the quay, his legs dangling over the side. Jerrol hesitated as a frisson of fear flashed through him as he looked at the water, and his chest tightened painfully. The boy stood up as Jerrol steeled himself and jumped down into the boat.

"I was told to keep an eye on that boat," the boy chirped, his black eyes observing Jerrol.

"Well, this is my boat so you no longer need to mind it. I'm taking it, along with my companions here, Niallerion and Marianille." Jerrol grinned as he flipped the boy a coin. The boy grinned back and scampered off. Niallerion climbed down and held a hand out to Marianille. She jumped down, nimble and sure, ignoring his hand, and sat on the bench out of the way. She eyed the water cautiously as if she had never been to sea before.

Jerrol's gaze paused on her, considering. Marianille didn't look anything like her younger brother, Tagerill. Where he was larger than life and loud, she was slender and elegant, her hair thick and black, curled around her face, accentuating her high cheekbones and silver eyes. "Can you swim? Can either of you?"

Marianille shook her head. "Why am I even here? I should be with Lady Leyandrii," she complained yet again, a complaint she had made as they entered the waystone in Vespers to travel to Stoneford and before the final transition to Molinti.

"Because the Lady said so," Niallerion repeated yet again. "Maybe she thought you needed some sun."

"Very funny." She eyed Jerrol suspiciously as he held out a leather belt with small inflated bags attached to it. "What is that?"

"It's a float, you wrap it around your waist; it helps you float in the water if you fall in."

"Fall in?" she repeated, her voice rising. The surrounding seagulls rose into the air above them, screeching loudly.

"It's just a precaution," Jerrol soothed, trying hard not to laugh as he tied it around her waist. Niallerion grinned as he tied his own without protest.

Jerrol checked the water barrel and the hold before climbing back up onto the quay and untying the ropes. As he coiled up the rope, he shielded his eyes and looked up to the emperor's palace at the top of the incline. He gave it a salute before climbing back into the *Scout* and began hauling up the red mainsail. He grabbed the tiller, and as the wind caught in the sail, the *Scout* eagerly raced for the open sea, glad to be free again.

Present Day, Febu 26th, 4128

Taelia raised her head and frowned at the raucous noise of the seagulls; she didn't usually notice them. Slowly, she rose and walked out of the archives, into the brilliant sunshine. She shielded her eyes with her hand and looked down to the harbour and saw a man by the *Island Scout* raise his hand in salute before jumping into the boat and hauling up the sail.

She started to run down through the market square. "Jerrol," she screamed. The man looked back over the stern of the boat and raised his hand in farewell. She ran down the quay, raising her hand in return as the *Scout* raced out towards the open sea.

She was distracted by a small boy standing beside her. "He gave me a dud coin," the boy complained.

"What?"

"The man in that boat, the captain; he gave me a dud coin, look." The boy held the coin up. Taelia took the coin as she looked back out to sea, but the *Scout* had rounded the headland and was out of sight. The coin was a Molinti copper, dated 1102, long since replaced by the more durable silver coins.

She looked at the boy. He couldn't have been much older

than eight or nine, his skin an even golden brown, and he wore a light linen shirt over dusty shorts. He scuffed his bare toe in the dust as she scrutinised him.

"If you come with me, I'll exchange it for a proper coin," she promised. "Tell me what the man said."

"He said it was his boat, and he needs it now."

"Anything else?" she asked as they walked back up to the archives.

"He had companions." The boy stuttered slightly over the word.

"Companions? He had people with him? I didn't see them."

"Yeah, a man called Nially and a woman called Mariany."

"Niallerion and Marianille?" Taelia repeated in wonder.

"That's what he called them. Pretty lady," he said.

"Did he say where he was going?"

"Nah, just that he needed his boat."

"Did he look well?" Taelia asked hesitantly.

"Looked alright to me," the boy shrugged.

"Well, wait here a moment and I'll get you your coin." Taelia nipped into the archive and retrieved some coins from the belt she had hung over the chair. "Here," she said, placing two silver coins in the boy's hand. "Thank you."

The boy grinned his thanks and scampered off.

Taelia frowned down at the harbour. Roberion's ship was still berthed at the outer quay and repairs continued feverishly, the sound of hammers and saws drifting on the air. Hadn't Jerrol seen it?

She took a deep breath and turned back to the archives. She had seen him, actually seen him. He was alive. She hugged the thought close. His logbook, which she had carefully copied out and then written in herself, had been wrapped in his oilskin cloth and replaced in the locker. She hoped he would find it soon.

She had heard his loneliness in the words he had written, worse for having a loving family that had been cruelly ripped away. Though she could tell he was desperately trying to create a new one around him as he built Senti. The inherent need to protect others was part of him. She could see why the Lady had picked him. Sitting back down at the desk, she stared at the manuscripts before her. She was glad Niallerion was with him; he'd be able to help with the building of those amazing walls. She wanted to go and see them herself, but she knew her time was better spent searching for Jerrol in the records. Jerrol would take her to see them when he returned.

They knew it was currently between Febu 24th and about the 28th in his time. Roberion hadn't been too clear about how long Jerrol had been at the mines or in Vespers with the Lady, but Taelia had the impression it was only a few days. Maru 7th was the day when the Lady destroyed the stone. His time was also now approaching theirs. Taelia had the awful feeling that they would reach Maru 7th at the same time.

She had finally found a legible version of Emperor Pierien's memoirs, boring for the most part. Still, they gave her a feel for the man who had been in power when the Lady broke the stone and who was courting the Ascendants against his empress' advice.

Melahney had been certain that Pierien had been enthralled. She turned the page and sat back in shock. She stared at the sketch of Jerrol, on his knees, his arms bound behind his back, cowed before the emperor. Jerrol looked battered and bruised, but it was definitely him. What could have happened in such a short time? She smoothed her fingers over the paper and touched them to her lips, and then she bent herself over the pages, reading furiously.

27

FEBU 1124

ELOTHIA

The wind rose around Marguerite, tugging her auburn curls around her face. She wished Taurillion was with her, but he was keeping an eye on Birlerion. Reluctantly, for sure, but she had impressed on him the importance of keeping Birlerion safe. Ready for when Leyandii would need him.

She rotated, peering up at the grey columns rising around her. Her temple in Cerne was as beautiful as she had planned. Taurillion may tease, but this was her special place, and she had wanted to mark it so that it would be remembered long after she was forgotten.

Kneeling on the ground, she dug her hands into the soil, planting the seeds that Leyandrii had given her. Then, after a moment to bless the seeds, she reached down into the land, deeper and deeper, past roots and burrows and layers of strata, down towards a rising warmth and an ancient awareness. The stone around her neck grew hot, scorching her skin as it sank into her body. Burning heat engulfed her as the awareness drew her in.

"At last," the voice said. A wave of overwhelming exhaustion spread through her and then receded like a reluctant tide. The pressure of the land descended upon her shoulders; truly the weight of her world and all that lived in it. She bowed under the burden and then stiffened. Raising her face to the life above, she opened herself to the Land, and they embraced.

"Rest," she said, "for I am here." She would have gasped if she could, as she sensed a flurry of questing sensations; the enormous expanse of land and sea, the rushing waters of the rivers, and the wind through the treetops, the deep, deep ocean and the majesty of the tallest mountains, all reaching to greet her, overwhelming her, subsuming her in their enthusiasm. In return, she felt herself expand, her senses rushing off, questing, searching, exploring, eager to embrace all that she now was.

The woollen rug ruffled in the breeze that swept across the empty valley. The grasses by the stream bent with the wind, and the branches of the tall sentinal trees arched protectively over Marguerite's temple didn't move. They were as immobile as the stone they protected.

28

FEBU 26TH, 1124

SENTI, BIRTOLI

Jerrol sailed around the headland towards Senti, watching Marianille's face for her first sight of the sentinal. He wasn't disappointed. She gasped in amazement as she saw him arching over the headland. "What a beautiful tree; what is it?"

"I called it a sentinal," Jerrol said with a grin.

"But where did it come from?"

"I planted it. He is a gift from the Lady that each of you will receive." Jerrol had tried to explain what had happened to him, but he had given up before he started; it was too complicated. He had said he had orders from the Lady, had been relocated by the Lady, and became Jerven and left it at that.

Jerrol busied himself with bringing the *Scout* up onto the beach. The harbour offices were beginning to take shape on the rock face, and the men were working industriously. Niallerion was staring up at them with interest. "You believe the water levels will rise that much?" he asked, impressed.

"I know they will," Jerrol replied. "This will become an island, just as Molinti will. Most of the mainland is lost. I have tried to warn people but they don't believe me. I intend to make it a safe place for anyone who needs shelter. Niallerion, I need you to help me design the storm walls; they have to protect against a twenty-foot plus surge."

Niallerion whistled. "That is a lot of wall."

"Just the job for you, then," Jerrol said, clapping him on the shoulder as he jumped down to the beach. "Come and meet the sentinal."

They climbed up the steep cliff to the sentinal, pausing to look out at the flat sea; the view was impressive. Niallerion pivoted to look down at the harbour. "You know ..." he started thoughtfully, and then his voice died away.

"That's it, you'll not get any sense out of him now," Marianille said, watching him with a soft smile.

Jerrol followed Niallerion's gaze down to the gentle waves lapping the beach far below them. "We have a little time here. We have to wait for Marguerite."

"Marguerite?" she asked in surprise.

"She will be here soon," Jerrol said. "Then we need to go to Molinti and see the emperor. We need to help bolster him against the Ascendants. And then onto Adeeron." He stared out to sea, his eyes distant.

"How do you expect to get to Adeeron, wherever it is?" she asked.

"I'm sure we'll find a way," he replied. He shook himself. "Anyway, let me introduce you to the sentinal." He placed a hand on the trunk and smiled. "Please enter," he said, and they all shimmered into the tree.

Niallerion looked at Jerrol sharply. "Jerrolion?" he murmured.

Jerrol smiled. "Yes, he's mine."

Marianille laughed at the exuberant welcome. "You say we will all get one?" she asked, her silver eyes sparkling.

"Eventually."

Niallerion glanced at him, a question on the tip of his tongue, but he didn't comment.

Jerrol sat down with a tired sigh. The sentinal cocooned him in vibrant concern, and he felt the tiredness leach away. He straightened up, refreshed.

Marianille stared at him. "Did he just give you a shot of energy or something?"

Jerrol grinned. "I think it's closer to 'or something.'"

"Your burns are fading," she said, reaching for his face.

"My burns?"

"You had a burn down your face and neck."

He felt the skin on his face; it felt smooth. He looked down at his ankles. The swelling had reduced and the bruises were fading. "Thank you," he murmured.

He felt the returning acknowledgement like a kiss on his cheek, and he smiled peacefully.

"You look much better. I hope my sentinal is as comforting," she said, her voice wistful.

"I am sure he will be. Let's go join the men. They will feed us. We'll see what thoughts they have for the harbour. We're lucky the weather is so good as we'll have to sleep under the stars, unless we get a squall; then we can sleep in here with my sentinal; my house isn't finished yet."

"You're building a house?"

"Of course. I didn't know how long I was going to be stuck here. I must go and get my brother, Gael. I want him here. We currently live in Plini, but it will be lost in the floods, so I don't want him staying there.

"I've asked a couple of other families to join me here too, but they are reluctant to move. I need to offer them jobs to get them here, so I've suggested building a boatyard as well as warehouses. This will be a thriving town, providing welcome and shelter to all who need it." He stood and stretched. "Let's see how many of these stonemasons want to become wall builders, shall we?"

He led the way back down to the beach. "I have another boat on order. I need to go and collect it from Eyti. It's called the *Moonlight Kiss*. It should be ready now. I have a friend who will sail it for me, but I need a harbour to berth her in."

The men welcomed them around the firepit, the smell of roasting lamb a pleasant surprise. "I am never going to eat fish again once I get home," Jerrol vowed with a grin.

Niallerion laughed. "But it is such a delicacy in Vespers. Few can afford it."

Jerrol's eyes brightened. "More reason to start trading it up there, then."

"People will buy it if it's more readily available," Niallerion agreed, biting into the flatbread he had filled with lamb and roasted peppers. "But you can't beat a bit of roast lamb," he said as he took another bite.

Jerrol grinned, and the conversation moved onto the plans for the harbour. Jerrol laughingly tried to rein in their enthusiasm.

The next morning, Jerrol set sail for Plini with Marianille. They were going to get some more suitable clothes. Although Niallerion had stripped down to his shirt-sleeves, the thick cotton shirt he wore was still far too hot, and Marianille's long tunic was impractical. They both needed light linen shirts and trousers and some canvas shoes. As did Jerrol. He was also determined to collect Gael and speak to his friend, Aiden, about picking up the boat he would captain, the *Moonlight Kiss*.

Marianille gazed around, her eyes wide as they passed under the large natural stone arch and into the echoing channel. The steep cliff faces rose up either side of them until they appeared out in the open bay and made their way up to the jetty.

"What an amazing place!" Marianille stood gazing up the valley at the sprawling town before scrambling up onto the jetty. The *Scout* rocked on the swell, and Marianille clutched Jerrol's proffered hand.

"It's the approach that will be its downfall; it's beautiful, yes, but there's nowhere for the water to go, except up into the town." Jerrol's face was grave as they walked up into the village square, acknowledging greetings as they walked.

"You know them all," Marianille said in surprise.

"Jerven had a life before I took it over," Jerrol said quietly. "His life doesn't stop just because I am here. I am living it; they know Jerven, not Jerrol."

Marianille glanced at him in sudden understanding. "It must be very lonely."

"Yes, meeting the sentinal was a great help. I miss my wife, my children, my friends." He sighed. "My life."

He looked up as a shout caught his attention and a young lad came pelting up. "Jerven, where have you been?"

"I told you I was going up to Terolia to arrange some trading agreements. It took longer than I expected."

"You could have sent word. I thought you'd had an accident or something."

"I'm sorry, Gael. I didn't mean to worry you."

Gael nodded. "I'm glad you're alright; I've missed you," he said, dropping his eyes to his feet.

"Well, I've come to collect you. We are moving to Senti. Granfer, too, if he'll come. I'd like to introduce you to my friend, Marian. She is staying with us for a little while before visiting Molinti."

Gael glanced up and smiled at her. "Hi, nice to meet you. I'm Gael, Jerven's brother."

"Nice to meet you, too." Marianille grinned back, and Gael flushed.

"We need to find her some cooler clothes; she's from up north. They have no idea how to dress," Jerrol said.

"You look hot," Gael agreed. "C'mon, I'll bet Mama Eleni has something that would fit."

Marianille followed them across the square which was shaded by a large leafy tree and down a small track behind the Taverna Rosa. Josef stuck his head out the door. "Don't forget my fish! You promised."

Jerrol waved an acknowledgement and kept walking.

"Mama Eleni, you are looking well today," he said as they reached the elderly woman sitting on the corner. She was wrapped in brightly coloured shawls and scarfs, and her hands were busy with clacking needles.

She looked up at him and smiled, her face creasing into more lines and wrinkles. "Jerven, my boy, where have you been? You've been ignoring your Mama."

"Boat needs fishing, Mama. I need some clothes for my friend here; do you have anything suitable?"

"Of course I do," the old woman cackled. Marianille looked at her doubtfully. "Pretty clothes for pretty ladies," she continued, revealing stained brown teeth.

"Good, could you show her them? I need to go down and see Josef."

"Of course." The old woman dropped her needles and wool into the basket next to her. Gael helped her rise and flushed as she patted his face in thanks.

"Just get shirt and trousers; much more comfortable in boats," Jerrol recommended, dropping some Molinti aguins into her hand. "No more than an aguin each, alright?"

Marianille nodded and watched him walk off down the street with his arm around Gael's shoulders, the boy leaning trustingly against him.

"He's a good boy," Mama Eleni said comfortably from behind her. "Nice on the eye, too," she said with a knowing wink.

Marianille blushed to be caught staring. "Oh, I'm just a friend."

"I'm sure," Mama Eleni said as she pushed apart the strands of beads hanging in the doorway. "Come, I have what you need to catch his eye."

"No, no, it's not like that. I just need a shirt and some trousers like his for working in the harbour."

Mama Eleni huffed. "He needs a woman to come home to. It's not right. He works too hard. That granfer of his doesn't appreciate him, never has and probably never will. He's an old fool. If I were younger, I'd show you young'uns how it's done," she muttered under her breath. She led the way into the dim building, raking an expert eye over Marianille as she rummaged through a pile of clothes. "Here, try these on. Tall, you're very tall," she muttered, moving to another pile. "These are the longest I've got, and this," she said, turning to a rail behind. "Every girl should have a pretty dress." She handed Marianille a thin garment in vivid emerald green.

Marianille faltered as she took the material. "Pretty colour," she choked.

"Very nice." Jerrol's voice came from the door, and Marianille looked up, flustered. Jerrol grinned appreciatively. "But not particularly practical on a boat," he finished.

"Oh, you." Mama Eleni slapped him on the arm. "Practical? Who wants practical? She won't always be on a boat."

"True," Jerrol laughed. "I didn't give you enough coin, you need to get shirt and trousers for Niall as well." He dropped some more coins in her palm.

"Go away, we're not finished yet." Mama Eleni pushed him out the door.

"I know." Jerrol called over his shoulder. "I'll meet you in the square."

"Men," Mama Eleni tutted. "Try it. With your complexion and colouring, you will look lovely."

"I have no need for a dress."

"Every girl needs at least one dress," Mama Eleni said wisely. "Try it."

Marianille tried it on. The dress flowed down to her knees, light and airy, sleeveless with a deep v-neck; it clung to her slender body and flowed out as she twirled.

"You look lovely, my dear. Here, try these sandals on with it."

"Really, I just need the shirt and trousers," Marianille said as she took the dress off and tried the trousers and shirt. They made her look much younger, and she found them a lot more comfortable. She folded her tunic and leggings.

"I also need shirts and trousers for a man the same height and build as me, if you have some."

"And the dress," Mama Eleni insisted, tugging out more clothes from a stack at the back of the shop. She stacked them on the counter. "Four Aguins for a friend of Jerven's."

"Oh, are you sure?" Marianille counted out the coins Jerrol had given her. Mama Eleni watched her walk back down the street towards the square, a knowing smile on her face.

Marianille spotted Jerrol sitting in the shade of the tree, a terracotta jug and two mugs on the table before him, his dark head bent over a piece of paper. Jerrol looked up from the paper he was writing on as she slipped into the seat next to him. He looked so relaxed, as if he belonged.

"Feel more comfortable?" he asked with a shadow of a grin, pushing a mug across the table. He poured her some water from the jug. It was filled with chunks of lemon, and she inhaled the lemony scent as she drank. "Gael will be here in a moment, and then we can leave."

"Didn't you want to speak to your grandfather?"

Jerrol lips tightened as he shrugged. "He said no."

Marianille bit her lip, imagining the conversation. It obviously hadn't gone well.

Gael scampered up with a sack over his shoulder. Jerrol smiled at him sadly, and Marianille realised all Gael's worldly possessions were in one small bag. Jerrol drank his water and stooped to pick up a bundle beside him. "Let's go home, then," he said, dropping a coin on the table, and he led the way back to the harbour.

They arrived back in Senti to find Niallerion stripped to the waist, revealing a toned, wiry body, trouser legs rolled up and taking his turn to hammer a pole into the water. His muscles rippled across his back as he swung. A row of poles extended from the quay; proof of their work. His pale skin was tinged pink across his shoulders, and Jerrol frowned in concern. He helped Marianille jump down onto the beach and turned to greet Niallerion as he left the water to join them.

Jerrol pushed a bag at him. "Here, put a shirt on or you'll get sunstroke. The sun is too strong at this time of day; take a break. That's what most sensible Birtolians do at this time of day."

Niallerion grinned and shrugged into a shirt. He left his legs bare to dry.

"This is my brother, Gael. Gael, my friend Niall. He's going to help us build the harbour." Jerrol turned back to take the packages that Gael had ready to hand down. Marianille reached to take a sack.

Gael grinned at Niallerion. "Nice ter meet yer," he parroted.

"Nice to meet you too. They finished carving out the rooms in the headland. We can use those for now," Niallerion said as they walked up the beach.

"What are the poles for?" Jerrol asked.

"Measuring the water depth and any changes. I need to understand the movement of the water so we can position the foundations of the walls in the right place. We need to monitor the water levels for a day. We'll have to take turns. We can split it into three shifts."

"Four," Gael piped up, aggrieved.

Niallerion bowed in acknowledgement. "Four."

"Will we be able to see in the dark?" Gael asked as he followed Jerven up the shallow steps the workmen had carved into the headland, to reach the rooms they had hollowed out from the stone.

"Good point. We'll have to light candles, but it will be enough light for our purposes." Niallerion sighed. "Shame we can't get some onoffs."

"Shame Birlerion isn't here. He could make us some," Jerrol said.

"Birlerion? You mean Leyandrii. She's the only one who can make them," Niallerion replied.

"Ah," Jerrol said, ducking into the first room. He looked around the space; the walls were roughly textured, evidence of the hard work it had taken, but solid, so there would be no natural light. But it was shelter. Another two rooms led off it into deeper darkness. He smiled. The Harbour master's office and the trading office. It was a start.

"At least we have shelter if it rains. We'll sleep outdoors otherwise."

"Does it rain?" Niallerion asked with a grin. "I haven't seen a cloud in the sky since we got here."

"On occasion it does," Jerrol laughed. "We'll store the provisions here, Gael. Niall and Marian will help you unload the rest then find us some lunch. Marian gets the left room, us boys take the right. We've got some blankets; they'll have to do for now. I need to speak to my sentinal."

"I haven't been called Niall since I was a kid. It doesn't sound right."

"What's your name, then?" Gael asked as they walked back to the Scout.

"Niallerion."

"Doesn't he know your real name?" Gael asked.

"Oh, yes, Niall is just easier to say, I expect, like a nickname."

"Niall," Marianille said experimentally, "suits you," she said with a smile.

"Marian," Niallerion said in return, "those clothes suit you." His silver eyes glinted.

Marianille blushed.

Looking between them, Gael shook his head in disgust. He climbed up into the *Scout* and started handing down bundles and casks. They soon had the boat unloaded and their provisions stacked away.

Gael rummaged in the sacks for bread and meat while Niall set up a small campfire on the quay, and they boiled some water Jerrol had had the forethought to supply. Niallerion sniffed the packet of tea that Gael handed him. "Mint," he said in surprise.

"Yeah, we haven't got any milk, so mint is best. We need to get a goat and some chickens, but Jerven said not yet. We need to finish the house and the stalls first. Won't be long, though," he said to himself, looking around his new home. "There's quite a village growing up in the valley. Jerven said anyone who wanted to stay could build their own homes. Most have started. I'm glad they want to stay with us. We won't be on our own."

Marianille smiled at him. "This is a lovely home, with an amazing view. You are fortunate."

Jerrol strolled back down the headland to join them. He paused above the harbour, gazing out across the bay. It would work. He knew it would. Marguerite would lay the foundation for them, and they would finish the rest.

He watched a small boat enter the bay, his friend Aiden right on time. They would go and collect the *Moonlight Kiss*, then Aiden could fish her for him. The second boat of his fleet. Once he had a dwelling built for Marin and his wife, that would be number three, the *Mari Rose*, and number four was on order.

He joined the Sentinals around the fire and accepted a mug of tea. He wished he could find some coffee. He waved Aiden over, pleased to see that he had brought his lad, Tomas, with him, company for Gael, and, sure enough, they soon scampered off on business of their own. He grinned, calling after them. "One chime, Gael, or I'll set sail without you. Aiden, these are my friends from Vespers, Marian and Niall. They've come to help with the harbour."

Aiden leaned across the fire to shake hands. "Welcome to Birtoli, you're far from home. What brings you all the way down here?"

"A chance to earn some money for a change," Niallerion said glibly, "and the challenge, of course; this is not as easy as he makes it sound."

Aiden snorted. His face crinkled as he grinned, hiding the flashes of white lines burned into his skin by the sun. "Everyone thinks he's crazy, too much sun. But I'm all for letting people have their dreams, and if I can benefit from it too, well, here I am. My wife wants a place of our own, a job, and a home. What more can you ask for?"

"It's such a beautiful location, as well. I'm sure you will be happy living here," Marianille agreed.

"I know I will. Once we've collected the *Kiss* from Eyti and we've made a couple of trips to iron out her kinks, I can concentrate on building our place and getting my wife, Teresa, and Tomas settled here."

"Marin is coming as well, with Myriam, so she'll have company," Jerrol said peaceably.

"Even better," Aiden grinned. "If we can find the boys, we ought to get off. It'll be a couple of chimes round trip, and we want to get back before dark."

Jerrol nodded as he rose. "Niall, get a hat; the sun is still strong. It might be cool in the water, but sunstroke is no fun."

"Yes, Captain!" Niallerion grinned, giving him a lazy salute.

Jerrol shook his head as he led the way down to his boat. Aiden gave a piercing whistle and shortly after, his son, Tomas, and Gael came tumbling down the beach. "Pa, we found the best place for our house! We've marked it out in stone. There's even room for Ma's sewing stuff."

"That will please her, then," Aiden grinned as tousled his son's hair. "Come on, we need to get going."

"But you'll come and see when we get back?"

"You can show me everything," his father agreed, boosting Tomas onboard. He leant into the hull and shoved the *Scout* off the sands and then nimbly climbed onboard. Jerrol set a course down the coastline to Eyti. It was a simple run, parallel with the mainland. They would soon be back with the *Kiss*.

29

FEBU 27TH, 1124

SENTI

irlerion jerked awake as someone kicked his boots.

"Birlerion! What are you doing here? When did you arrive? How did you arrive? There have been no boats in today except for Jerrol's."

Birlerion blinked up at a figure. "Marianille?" he gasped. Lurching to his feet, he pulled her into a hug and buried his face in her hair. He inhaled deeply. She was real.

Marianille laughed uncertainly at the ferocity of his hug. "Birlerion? What's the matter? Has something happened to Tagerill?"

"No, he's fine," Birlerion said, looking at his sister closely. "What did you mean there have been no boats except for Jerrol's? Do you know where he is?"

"Well, look, there's only the *Scout* and his new boat the *Moonlight Kiss* on the beach. He brought it in this evening. He's down there with Niallerion discussing walls, of all things; they are so single-minded I got bored, so I came up here to see the sentinal. But what are you doing here? Did Leyandrii send you too?"

"I suppose she must have," Birlerion said slowly, squinting down at the curving beach far below, where the harbour should be. Discreetly pinching himself, he knew he wasn't dreaming; he had awoken in the past. His stomach fluttered at the thought. Would he be able to go home and see Warren and Melis one last time? Would he see Leyandrii?

Marianille interrupted his racing thoughts. "Well, you'll need to get out of that uniform if you're staying. It's far too hot. Jerrol got these for me, much more comfortable." She did a little twirl and laughed. "And according to Jerrol this outfit is more practical on boats." She rolled her eyes. "Come on, he'll be pleased to meet you, I'm sure." Marianille pulled Birlerion down the slope.

"Look who I found up by the sentinal," she called gaily as she dragged Birlerion down to the beach. "Jerrol, let me introduce you to my brother, Birlerion."

Jerrol rose, eyes wide in surprise. "Birlerion?" he said hesitantly.

Birlerion strode forward. He couldn't stop the broad grin from spreading over his face as he inspected his friend. Pulling Jerrol into his embrace, he said, "By the Lady, Jerrol, you had us all so worried. Taelia is climbing the walls." Clearing his throat as his relief threatened to overcome him, he whispered in Jerrol's ear. "We've been searching ever since we heard your song."

Jerrol gripped him tight in return. "Birlerion?" he murmured again, as if not quite believing he was there. Birlerion stepped back, though Jerrol didn't release him.

"Yes, the king sent me to Senti. The emperor said you returned here often. The king thought this would be an important location, and he wanted me to find out anything I could about the building of the harbour. To try to find ways to contact you. Your sentinal was showing me his memories when Marianille came and kicked me awake."

"Taelia and the children?"

"They are all fine, with the king at the emperor's palace.

The king has taken them under his protection. It was the only way to get Taelia out of the archives to eat, by royal command." Birlerion laughed. "She's as bad as you once she gets the bit between her teeth."

"How far has she got?"

Marianille stared at them. "Birlerion, you already know Jerrol? When did you meet him?"

Birlerion grinned at her a little sheepishly. "It's a bit complicated," he said, running a hand through his hair.

"I met him in Vespers with Tagerill when I went up to arrange the trade agreement," Jerrol interrupted smoothly.

"But who is this king you are talking about?"

"Umm," Jerrol looked at Birlerion, and they both burst out laughing.

Gael frowned at Jerrol. "Jerven? Why are they calling you Jerrol?"

"Ascendants balls, I'm not sure I can explain all this. Suffice to say, Jerrol is a translation of Jerven up north; means the same thing," Jerrol said. "I'm still me, it's just a name."

Gael nodded, not particularly reassured.

"Birlerion, we need to talk. Let me tell you what's happened, just in case, umm, just in case you get called away." Jerrol looked at Gael. "We'll be back soon. Niall, we'll continue this discussion tomorrow."

Niallerion nodded. "Of course." He watched them walk down the beach towards the boats, heads together, talking furiously. Niallerion looked back at Marianille. "Birlerion looks like he's been training; he's much bigger than I remember."

Marianille stared after her brother. "He is different, though I'm not sure why."

"I guess you'll have to ask him," Niallerion said with a smile.

. . .

Jerrol halted by the *Scout*. "I met Guerlaire. He asked for my help," he said.

"Roberion said he took you to Vespers, but the Lady sent him back to Terolia before you awoke. They must be nearing the final days. Jerrol, you have to get out before the Lady destroys the stone or you could be trapped here forever."

Jerrol shrugged and stared at Birlerion with haunted eyes. "I can't leave until I've built the harbour here. I need to seat the Oath in the foundations. It's the only chance the Birtolian's have of surviving the floods. The Oath brought me here; it needed my help as the Oath Keeper." Jerrol threaded his fingers in his hair and massaged his temples. "Birlerion, I don't know if I can do what is needed. Guerlaire said they've found another array and he needs me to try and destroy the crystals that the ascendants have collected in Adeeron. Guerlaire believes they will have enough power to stop the Lady bringing down the Veil if I don't."

Birlerion scrunched up his face as he racked his memory. "Another array? I don't remember there being another one. Guerlaire dealt with most of them, and I know I destroyed the one in Vespers." His face tightened in memory of how he had lost control at the end. The Ascendants had killed Celia, the first girl he had ever befriended. He shut down the image of her smoking body and a sudden thought struck him and his stomach dropped. "They may have had time to fix the one in the Telusions, though."

"The Ascendants have been mining crystals for months. There could be even more." Jerrol leaned against the boat. "I'm not sure what Guerlaire expects me to do, or how I'm even supposed to get there. He said he will cause a diversion on the seventh just before the Lady destroys the stone. Niallerion is teaching me about crystals, in case he isn't with me at the end."

Birlerion stared at Jerrol in horror. "Don't even go there. You are not going into some crystal array on your own."

"What? Like you didn't? Who was with you when you went into that Terolian mine?"

Birlerion stilled and when he dropped his eyes, Jerrol gripped his arm, giving it a slight shake. "We do what we have to," he said, keeping his voice low.

Inhaling, Birlerion shook his head. "That is not just a diversion, Jerrol. It is the end of Vespers as we know it. You have to find a way back, for Taelia, for Mikke and Leyarille. They need you," he said, his voice cracking.

"Don't you think I know that? You have two weeks to find a way to get me back, because I have no idea." Jerrol turned away to look out to sea, his body rigid, his hands clenched by his side. "Guerlaire knew it was a one-way trip, and if I don't succeed, nor will our world as we know it. I don't have a choice." He looked back at Birlerion. "I believe everything will culminate on the seventh. You need to warn the king to be prepared; the backlash will reach them in Molinti, I fear."

"I don't know how long I've got here, but I'll stay and help for as long as I can," Birlerion promised. He pursed his lips and struggled with his conscience for a moment, then he exhaled. Twisting his lips, he pushed out the words. "Once you're done here, all you have to do is create a waystone here and in Adeeron. They won't be expecting you. You'll have the element of surprise. If I'm not here, promise me you'll take Niallerion with you." Birlerion gripped Jerrol's arms. "Promise me."

Jerrol slowly smiled and relaxed in his grip. "I promise. Thank goodness you *are* here. You always see things so clearly. Guerlaire gave me his sword, so that will be easy."

"You don't need his sword," Birlerion reminded him and gave him a small shake.

Jerrol huffed out his breath. "You're right! I forgot. Try and act as if you're in 1124; it's less complicated than trying to explain this time thing."

"Marianille is not daft; she's bound to notice. I'm not the same person I used to be. Being nearly killed a couple of times changes your perspective on life."

Jerrol grinned in agreement, relaxing as the comfort of an old friend enveloped him. "Do your best! Tomorrow, we start on the foundations. Niallerion has been busy. You arrived just in time to help." He slapped Birlerion on the back. "I am so glad you're here."

Birlerion gripped his arm. "So am I." He stared into Jerrol's silver eyes. "How are you? Really? I heard what happened to you in the mines." Birlerion's lips tightened. "Is there anything I can do to help?"

Jerrol sighed. "The Lady removed the worst of the memories, wiped away whatever they tried to do, only ..." His voice died away as he stared at the water.

"What?"

Jerrol looked at him, his face tight. "I'm afraid of the water."

"It's not surprising," Birlerion replied gently.

"A fisherman who's afraid of the water? I have to go on it every day, but my gut twists into knots ... and the thought of actually getting in it." Jerrol's face paled.

Birlerion breathed out carefully. "Jerrol, they tried to drown you; any sensible person would be afraid of the water after that, it's only natural. It doesn't mean that the water is bad or a threat. It was the people who were bad, and they paid the ultimate price. They won't be doing it again; Roberion saw to that."

"I couldn't believe my eyes when he turned up. I thought

I was hallucinating," Jerrol said as they began walking back up to the quay.

"Nor could we. He was in the king's chamber at the same time; it was most frustrating. We could see he was elsewhere, but we only got bits of it. The king was not happy and extremely angry with the Lady."

"It's not her fault; she has to protect her people."

"Angry for you, I think. You've already been through so much."

Jerrol grinned. "That's what you get for being a Captain. Wait till it's your turn."

"Lady forbid." Birlerion held his hands up in horror.

"Forbid what?" Marianille asked as she stood in front of him with her hands on his hips.

"I told you," Birlerion said as an aside to Jerrol. Jerrol laughed as he went to sit next to Gael. "I said I never wanted to be a Captain, being a Sentinal is enough for me."

"Birlerion, you have no ambition. You could do so much more if you'd just knuckle down," Marianille said.

Birlerion rolled his eyes, and Niallerion burst into laughter. Marianille glared at him. "And you can talk. Why don't you push Guerlaire to build you a lab? You know you would make much more progress if he did."

"Maybe another time," Niallerion replied. "Right now, he is focussed on other things."

Birlerion and Jerrol exchanged looks. Marianille, ever-observant, caught them. "What? What is it you are not saying?"

"Only that Niall will be spending all his time writing up this project. The first time an artificing feat of this kind has ever been attempted. That should keep you in ale for a few years, hey Niall?" Jerrol said

Niallerion grinned. "It better."

Gael got up and returned with a plate of bread, fruit, and lamb.

"Leftovers?" Birlerion asked with a grin.

"Yes, pretty basic, I'm afraid. We need Kayerille here to cook us a tagine; maybe we should send her a message?" Jerrol suggested.

Birlerion laughed in agreement, and Marianille frowned. "Kayerille?"

"She's good at stretching food out," Jerrol said, kicking himself.

"How come you know Kayerille so well?" she asked, her eyes narrowing.

"I get about. Useful having a boat, you see."

"Still," Marianille was about to ask another question but she caught Birlerion's frown and she glared back, but she took the hint. Birlerion knew he had only delayed her questions and saw the threat of a later inquisition in her eyes.

The conversation became more general and reverted to the plans for the next day. "Hopefully Marguerite will be ready by then and we can get started," Jerrol said finally.

"Marguerite?" Birlerion repeated, and his eyes widened. "Oh, that explains so much," he said softly as he put two and two together. He looked at Jerrol with respect. "How did you know?"

"Know what?" Marianille asked with exasperation. "Honestly, it's like you two are having a totally different conversation to the rest of us."

Birlerion grimaced at Jerrol. "I told you she wasn't daft."

"Just less tactful than Niallerion here."

Gael watched wide-eyed, sensing the undercurrents but lacking the knowledge to understand any of it.

Jerrol sighed. "Very well, I'll explain." He looked around. Aiden and his son were down in the camp with the workers; it was just Gael he needed to worry about. He wrapped an arm around the boy's shoulders and squeezed him tight. "You're not going to understand much of this, and I would have preferred not to tell you, but always remember that you are my brother and I love you," he said, holding Gael's eyes. Gael nodded tentatively.

Jerrol looked at Marianille and began. "I arrived here in Birtoli about three months ago on the *Island Scout* in the middle of the ocean, not a piece of land in sight. I didn't know where I was. I didn't know how I got here. I slowly began to realise that I was now a fisherman called Jerven, with a brother called Gael." He squeezed Gael's shoulders.

"The Lady has sent me here for a reason from our future. In the year of our Lady 4128, I am the Lady's Captain, like Guerlaire. My name is Jerrol Haven, and I have a wife and two children. The Lady has a task for me to complete here in Birtoli. I have been trying to figure it out, and we are now reaching the final phase.

"When the Lady destroys the stone to defeat the Ascendants, and make no mistake she will, the Kingdom of Birtoli will be much affected, submerged under rising waters, leaving a few islands behind; Senti will be one of them. I have been trying to build this harbour as a safe haven for anyone who needs it. I planted the sentinal to watch over us." He glanced up at the sheltering branches and then back at Marianille, whose mouth had fallen open.

"Birlerion here is also from the year 4128. He was communing with the sentinal when you woke him up here in 1124. Birlerion was the first Sentinal I awoke when the Lady made me her Captain."

Marianille gasped as she looked at her brother; he grinned back at her.

Niallerion chuckled. "I told you there was something different about him."

"But what do you mean, 'woke up'?"

"When the Lady sunders the Bloodstone, some of her Sentinals are encased in a sentinal tree, like him." Jerrol nodded up at the sentinal on the headland. "They preserve you for over three thousand years, until I awake you in my time when there is a new Ascendant threat that we have to deal with."

"You said *some* are encased," Niallerion said, his voice soft in the night air.

"It's rather chaotic at the end; the Lady saves as many as she can. Marguerite does her best, but many are lost. Others are preserved elsewhere. I wake all I can find, including both of you. There are none in Birtoli."

"What about me?" Gael's voice interrupted him.

Jerrol looked down into his brother's fearful eyes. "You will build the Jerven fishing line for me. It is what sustains the Birtoli economy after the floods and ensures our people survive."

"But what about you?"

"That story has yet to be played out."

"But what do you have to do? I can help you." Gael offered desperately, his eyes filling with tears.

"I know you will," Jerrol replied, hugging him.

Marianille stared at him. "Why am I not with Leyandrii? This is when she needs me most."

"Because she can't take you with her, and Vespers will be destroyed," Jerrol said sadly. He looked around the serious faces. "You do not talk of this. It does no good to spread fear. We do what we must to help the Lady preserve as many people as she can. This *will* happen; we cannot stop it. Tomorrow we start building the wall. The next day, Gael and I go fishing. After that, we'll see."

Marianille's face crumpled. "Captain, please forgive me," she whispered.

"There is nothing to forgive," Jerrol said as he rose, taking Gael with him.

"You need to learn tact, Marianille; it would have been better for Gael not to have known," Birlerion said softly once Jerrol and Gael had walked out of earshot.

"How was I supposed to know?" she protested.

"I don't remember you being this obtuse, Marianille," Birlerion said, glaring at his sister.

"What can you tell us about what happens?" Niallerion asked, diverting Marianille's biting response.

"You don't want to know. Leave it until you find out for yourselves. It does no good to dwell on it," Birlerion said bleakly.

Niallerion nodded. "Tell us about the Captain, then."

"Well," Birlerion grinned and blew out his breath. "He is not only the Lady's Captain but the Commander of the King's Justice and the Oath Keeper. When he wakes us in 4123, King Benedict is on the throne. The Captain is one of his rangers until the Lady claims him and sets him on a path that still wends its way through history.

"I will tell you this; wherever the Captain is, life is always interesting. Tagerill and I spent most of our time trying to keep him alive until you took over, after ..." he sighed. "There is so much that has happened, I can't possibly summarise it in one night." He looked at Marianille. "He is like my brother. I would die for him," Birlerion said simply as she gaped at him in shock.

Niallerion nodded thoughtfully. "Roberion said something similar. I wondered why."

"He takes on the impossible in the name of the Lady. We are here to help him succeed. He is also a really nice person," Birlerion finished quietly as Jerrol returned alone. He looked up at him in concern. "How is he taking it?" he asked.

"He wanted some time to himself; it's a lot to take in all at once. He wanted to know where Jerven was. All I could say was that I *am* Jerven, but he couldn't accept that I could be Jerven and Jerrol at the same time."

"I'll try and explain tomorrow. You aren't both people at the same time; you are Jerrol in 4128, but here you are Jerven. People from the future know you as Jerrol, but you are still Jerven. If you didn't exist as Jerrol Haven, then there wouldn't be a Jerven," Niallerion said firmly.

"Good luck with that," Jerrol grinned. "I am living it, and I don't understand it."

Niallerion laughed.

Jerrol looked at Marianille, who was still struggling with it all. Niallerion seemed to have grasped it all straight away, his analytical mind sifting through the possibilities and the actualities with no problem. Tomorrow would make it worse as he tried to explain what had happened to Marguerite. He fervently hoped that Marguerite would be able to explain it herself.

30

FEBU 28TH, 1124

SENTI HARBOUR

Staring out across the tranquil waters of the bay, Jerrol listened to Birlerion's quiet voice. How he remained so calm, Jerrol didn't know, for what he was describing would terrify most people. It made sense now, why he would never speak of it before. It was unlikely Jerrol would have believed him.

The notches Niallerion had added to the poles in the water, marking low tide and high tide, gleamed even in the waning moonlight. He idly watched the water part around the obstruction as he concentrated on what Birlerion was saying.

"You have to understand that her people were always Leyandrii's first concern. Everything she did was to provide us a safe place to live. What we did with our lives, for the most part, was the individual's choice. She was there if you needed her; if you asked for her help, she would do her best to respond.

"Most of the time she worked through her Sentinals. She would send us to resolve a disagreement, to ensure safe passage, to speak with her voice where needed." When Birlerion's voice slowed, Jerrol glanced at him. Birlerion was staring up at the moon, his face caressed by the gentle rays, gilding his skin so he glowed.

"I wish I had experienced her care. She always seems so removed. People pay lip service; they still don't believe she is real," Jerrol said into the silence.

Birlerion sighed. "That was her sacrifice. By destroying the Bloodstone, she brought down the veil of protection around our world. That Veil prevented all magic from penetrating it, including Leyandrii's.

"I believe it was her last resort. The only way to stop the Ascendants from destroying us and our world. Of course, we, her Sentinals, were imbued by her magic, so we couldn't stay either. But she couldn't take us with her so she encased us in our trees to sleep until Remargaren needed us again."

"Thank the Lady for her foresight!" Jerrol breathed.

Grimacing, Birlerion gazed back out to sea. "The Ascendants were out of control," Birlerion paused, "or maybe they had lost control," he mused. "They were destroying more than they were protecting. Everything they touched caused a counteraction elsewhere. Those last few months the weather was chaotic; snow even fell in places here in Birtoli."

"I haven't seen any," Jerrol said, his eyebrows raised.

"Someone did, for reports arrived at the palace, along with the most ferocious storm. The winds were terrifying that last week; it was almost impossible to venture outside. It was as if the Ascendants had concentrated on the palace, determined to rip it apart. I think that was Leyandrii's intention. Make them focus on her so they would leave her people alone.

"She made all her staff leave the palace, sent everyone home or to other posts. There were only a few of us left at the end ..." his voice trailed off, and Birlerion audibly swallowed as his gaze rose to stare back at the moon. "Just Lorillion, Taurillion, and I."

Jerrol waited, hesitant to interrupt his thoughts, and he was rewarded for his patience when Birlerion continued.

"The Ascendants were audacious, you had to give them that. They built an array right under Guerlaire's nose, in the Justice building. Leyandrii sent Taurillion and I to nullify it. We met a spot of trouble and Taurillion was injured. By then, Marguerite had bonded with the Land, so she was able to rescue Taurillion when they tossed us in the deepest cell. They didn't realise the floor was compacted dirt, simple for Marguerite to traverse.

"There was a ranger, a lad I went through the academy with. One of Clary's sons. He was the cause of a lot of his father's hatred towards me." Birlerion's jaw hardened as he continued. "Any excuse to attack or belittle me and he would. I never knew why he hated *me* so much. But he did. It culminated that night.

"Clary's son, Tyrler, dragged me into the array for a demonstration, he said. The array was huge, but instead of a black lodestone in the centre, there was a wooden chair, framed with metal. They held me down as a friend of mine, a girl called Celia ... was led to the chair and strapped in. They killed her, and I could do nothing to save her."

Jerrol reached for Birlerion's arm as his voice faltered, and then he continued. Throat tight, Jerrol tightened his grip on Birlerion's arm in support. "They had enspelled her, made her think she was helping them, just so she would go meekly to her death. I tried so desperately to help her, but she didn't hear me, and there were too many of them. When I regained consciousness, I in turn was strapped in the chair."

Birlerion's eyes glistened with tears and he angrily brushed them away. "I, a Lady's Sentinal, failed to protect her people. I was helpless as the Ascendants powered up the array for a second time. They generated an image of Vespers on the ceiling, storm-torn yet beautiful. Guerlaire's bridge still hummed even though they tried to use Celia to destroy it. And then Guerlaire stepped out of the palace and everything clicked into place. I finally understood what Leyandrii intended, and I was so angry. At her, at the Ascendants ..." Birlerion closed his gleaming eyes. "At everyone."

Jerrol held his breath.

"I lost control. I was supposed to use my shield to protect. Instead, I destroyed that array and everyone within it. They didn't realise that all the power from the array only enhanced what I had already had. I staggered out of the building into the storm and looked up towards the palace, and there was Leyandrii, standing beside Guerlaire and ... she raised her hands and I projected my shield over the people of Vespers as she brought down the world around us.

"I couldn't protect her, I couldn't protect her or Guerlaire, and they fell when the palace collapsed. I knew Lorillion had joined us, I felt his presence in the link with Leyandrii. He helped us focus when we trained. Leyandrii drew on all of us. We gave back to her the power she had given us, and in turn she saved our world. There was a moment of calm, of peace, as the Veil descended. It was beautiful, but it didn't last.

"It was as if the world had imploded, and we were all dragged into the maelstrom." Birlerion's voice was soft. "Only for you to find us scattered across Remargaren three thousand years later."

Jerrol dragged his friend into his arms. "You didn't fail anyone," he said, his voice gruff. "You did exactly as Leyandrii asked of you, and you couldn't have done more."

"I know, but it still hurts," Birlerion replied as he hid his face in Jerrol's shoulder and relaxed into his embrace. Jerrol rocked him as his mind spun. The history books had described Vespers as being flattened. Not a building was left standing and yet there had been no fatalities. All because of Birlerion.

What the Sentinals had achieved for Leyandrii was the unwritten history. None of them had survived to tell what they had done. How they had protected in the name of the Lady and still did. Unquestioning and loyal, even though they had paid the price for the Lady's success.

The moon had progressed across the night sky when Birlerion cleared his throat and sat up out of Jerrol's arms. "Old history," he said with a self-conscious smile.

"Important history, Birlerion. Without you and the rest of the Sentinals, the Lady would never have succeeded, and Remargaren would be a very different place."

"Maybe."

"There's no maybe about it and you know it."

"Well, enough of history, I am sure you'd rather talk about your family." Birlerion began describing Mikke's antics on the *Lady's Miracle* and refused to discuss the past any further.

At dawn, Marianille came out onto the quay to relieve Jerrol of his harbour watch. Her keen inspection bored into him as she approached, still grappling with the idea that he was from the future.

Birlerion had kept him company for most of his shift, until he had just disappeared from one moment to the next. It had been unnerving, but he had appreciated the solid comfort of his best friend and Birlerion had only talked about Taelia and the children.

The *Island Scout* and the *Moonlight Kiss* had been tilted at a precarious angle on the beach for most of the night. It had been peaceful watching the waters creep in. The sky was lit by millions of twinkling stars high overhead, a delicate swathe of glittering blue. He knew Taelia would have loved it, especially the gentle passage of the waning moon. The delicate silver glow soothed him. The quiet night eased some of the tension that had been building within him. No doubt it was the calm before the storm, but he embraced it all the same; a moment in time that should be cherished.

He would have to get back out to sea and bag some fish. He needed the boats working and the trade routes active to get them entrenched as quickly as possible whilst he had the time.

There had been no contact from Marguerite overnight, so he planned to go out with Aiden and fish together; an opportunity to make sure all was well with his second boat, the *Moonlight Kiss*, before Aiden took command of it for him. Aiden had seemed well pleased with her so far, so one more trip should be enough. Jerrol looked up as Marianille joined him.

"Anything of note?" she asked quietly as she handed him a steaming mug.

Jerrol shook his head. "Nothing. The tide came in and refloated the boats. It should be high tide by tenth chime if it follows the pattern. Seems pretty regular." He cupped his mug and took a grateful sip of the hot mint tea. The weather had gotten quite cold and damp overnight. Standing, he shrugged off the blanket that he had wrapped around himself, handing it to Marianille.

Marianille swung it around her shoulders as she took his place. "Did Birlerion leave?"

"Yes, just before dawn."

"Go get some sleep then. I imagine you'll need to be out before the tide turns."

"If I can wake Gael up, we'll leave now. I saw Aiden go down to the *Kiss* earlier; fishermen are early risers," he grinned.

Marianille smiled in return and settled in his place gazing out across the calm waters. A faint mist hovered over the bay;

it was a tranquil scene. The sound of gentle lapping waves was soothing. "This is such a peaceful place," she said, her voice hushed in the quiet dawn. "It seems unreal that such horrors are coming."

"Hold on to the fact that places like this exist and we protect as much as we can," Jerrol replied as he left.

Marianille watched him walk around the bay to the *Scout*, his voice clear but muted across the still waters as he greeted Aiden. She was beginning to see what Birlerion saw in him. Her expression grew grave as she considered what he needed to achieve. She vowed that she would do what she could to help. Her expression eased as she saw the sleepy Gael stumble down the beach; he was not an early riser.

They busied themselves in the boats, one hull a grey-blue, the other a bright yellow, typical of the region. Casting off, the creak of the oars blended with the soft swish of the sea as they sculled out of the bay and picked up the off-shore breeze. The sails soon billowed, and they were swiftly out of sight. The sentinal's leaves shivered in farewell high above her.

Marianille still hadn't got over Birlerion's appearance last night. She would never have believed it if she hadn't seen him herself. She stared at the water, wondering how it was possible.

The *Moonlight Kiss* kept position off Jerrol's starboard bow, her rugged lines a mirror of the *Scout*, the yellow hull scything through the water. Jerrol gripped the railing, keeping his gaze on the other boat. He had become quite fond of the *Scout*; he would miss her when all of this was over, even if he would be glad not to be on the water anymore.

Gael was managing her fine. Over the past few months,

he had broadened across the chest, and hauling sails and nets every day had added muscle to his frame. He would be captaining his own boat soon enough.

Jerrol shouted a warning about the reefs off Geteril as they skirted the island's last position, Aiden staring at the rocks that were visible below the clear waters as he marked them on his map before following the *Scout* on to the island of Duyli. They spent the day fishing before drawing up in the bay to finish the messy job of gutting and salting.

Beaching the boats as the sun began to set, they jumped down into the clear waters and rinsed off, the sky full of screeching seagulls and cormorants wheeling and dipping as they plucked the bloody fish entrails out of the water.

They built a small camp high up on the beach and settled to watch the glorious light show, the brilliant orange rays casting the boats into black silhouettes as silence descended —leaving just a gentle susurrus of the trees overhead murmuring in the breeze.

"What a view," Jerrol murmured. "One to remember."

"What's so special about a sunset?" Gael asked suspiciously.

Jerrol laughed and reached over to ruffle his hair. "You haven't got a romantic bone in your body, have you?"

"Gerroff." Gael batted his hand away.

"We see them so often, we forget how amazing the colours are, so rich and warm. Further north, it gets greyer, duller, colder. They miss all this beauty. We should encourage more of them to visit. They would find it rejuvenating."

Aiden laughed. "Another business venture of yours?"

"Why not? Offer a week of relaxation in the sun. I'm sure that would send them home ready to take on the cares of the world again. People would pay good money for that."

Gael squinted against the glare at Jerrol but held his tongue. He was listening carefully.

"The emperor has become too self-contained; we have no interaction with any of the other territories, and we suffer for it. Birtoli will need their help before long. We need something to offer in return. You see, our trade routes are just the beginning, with Marin running the Vespiri route and Aiden here running the Terolian route. Maybe we can even extend on to Elothia? We'll see." Jerrol looked at Gael and grinned. "And young Gael here is getting ready to captain our next boat, *Mikke's Ride*. I think he's about ready. He knows these waters better than I do."

Gael smiled shyly. "You know them better."

"We'll have to find you a crewman before we let you loose!" Jerrol said.

"I thought maybe Micah. He has been working the harbour boat for two years now, and before that, he was on Terry's old boat. He was looking for a new berth."

Jerrol nodded thoughtfully. "It's your boat, you have to work with him; do as you see fit," he said. "I think you should take on the Molinti supply route; that would keep us covered."

"What about the *Scout*?"

"We'll cover the Molinti route until the *Ride* is ready, then I need to finish the harbour and set up the office. I can cover any extras we need."

Gael watched him closely but nodded in agreement. A slow smile spread over his face as he considered what Jerven had said. His own boat. *Mikke's Ride*.

Jerrol smiled to himself. Gael was more than ready; he was a competent seaman, knew the waters as well as any, and could manage the *Scout* on his own if he had to. With Marin and Aiden beside him, he would flourish. He sighed as he checked another action off his mental list. On their return, he needed to get Marianille into the palace to check on the empress and then he needed to speak to the emperor, see what the Ascendants were up to. The Ascendants had failed at Geteril, but he was sure that would not be the end.

Driftwood collapsing in the fire brought his attention back to the present, the flaring flames a reminder that darkness had descended and it was time to sleep. They stoked up the fire and then rolled up in their blankets. They would set off again at first light.

The next morning, Aiden and his son waved farewell as they headed north up towards Selir. Jerrol had told him everything he could about what to expect and who to speak to; he was sure they would be fine.

Jerrol sailed into Senti Harbour, acknowledging his sentinal's welcome as the hum deepened, along with the shivery caress of the Oath. They offloaded their haul into eager hands. More people were arriving, growing the makeshift village and more buildings were being erected as the stonemasons turned carpenters to build more permanent shelters.

Marianille wrinkled her nose as Jerrol and Gael finally jumped down onto the beach. "You need a bath," she said bluntly, "you stink of fish."

"Not surprising," Jerrol said with a grin. "Maybe we need to get a bathhouse built? I'm not scrubbing down in the bay in front of everyone."

Gael nodded in agreement. "Maybe we should charge for the use? It would soon pay for itself; saltwater just isn't the same."

"There you go." Jerrol smiled at Marianille. "A project for you."

Marianille rolled her eyes. "As if I need another one. Niallerion doesn't stop! We've measured every possible angle of this bay and then some. He's got some weird calculation going on about wave strength and pressure and angle of attack or something, it's all beyond me."

"Angle of approach," Niallerion's soft voice behind her made her jump.

Marianille gave Jerrol a swift look of reproach as she turned. "Angle of approach, then. Why is that so important?"

"We need to alleviate the strain on the walls as much as possible; we want them to last for a very long time," Niallerion grinned.

"I'm sure Marguerite will help with that," Marianille argued.

"Maybe, but we can still calculate the best position for the walls in advance, taking into account currents, wind, and tides."

"Enough," Marianille flung up her hand in protest. "Don't start again." Marianille looked at Jerrol. "When will she arrive?"

"Soon," Jerrol promised, leading the way up off the beach.

"This way," Marianille led them up the incline towards the valley, which opened before them. "We got your house started. Everyone pitched in, so it's almost done. We've decided to build one house at a time. It's more efficient, so we can sleep there tonight."

Jerrol looked up at the nearly completed house. It was situated just below the rise of the headland and built into the sandstone ridge, sheltered from westerly and northern winds and facing the harbour, just as he had planned.

"It's pretty much empty now, but the carpenters are knocking up some tables and chairs and some bed frames, so we should soon be off the floor."

"This is amazing and completed so quickly." Jerrol was

speechless. "Gael," he turned towards the boy, but he was already scampering up the steps cut into the rock. Stonemasons up on the roof grinned down at him. "I don't know what to say, except … well, thank you." Jerrol was overwhelmed at the general feeling of goodwill and co-operation that was rife.

"Jerven, come look." Gael was hopping from one foot to another. "Look, there's even a bed."

Jerrol allowed himself to be hauled up the steps, and he slowly went from room to room, admiring the stone slab floor, which would keep it cool, the wide windows allowing the light in, along with the gentle breeze.

"We'll make some shutters in case we do get a storm, but mostly you'll want the breeze, I think," one of the men said shyly.

Jerrol nodded in agreement. He looked out over the veranda, which they had built along the front, giving plenty of space to sit and look out to sea. "What an amazing view," he breathed, a smile creeping over his face as he stared and stared.

The men exchanged glances, well pleased with his response. "It's the least we could do. You giving us work, land to build on, a place we can call home. Least we could do." The man nodded.

"You've earned it," Jerrol protested as he dragged his gaze away from the sea. The soothing hum of the sentinal deepened and he looked up at his tree. He smiled gently and excused himself, walking up the steep slope that led to the sentinal. He placed a hand on the trunk and relaxed into the tree, the soft caress easing tired muscles and coaxing him to sit. Jerrol breathed in the vibrant greenness that permeated the air and smiled as the sentinal cheerily showed him the growing village. The sentinal was pleased.

"I'm glad you're happy," Jerrol said. He hadn't considered

that a sentinal could get lonely. *"Please look after them when I am gone."*

He felt the sentinal's soft query and sighed. *"I serve the Lady in her time of need. I am not sure I will be able to return, but there will always be a Jerven living here with you. You won't be alone."*

"Be careful what you tell a sentinal; they can be very possessive." Marguerite's bright voice interrupted his musing.

Jerrol laughed. *"I am always honest with my Sentinals. Anyway, all they have to do is take a look and they'll know."*

"I hope they are far too polite to do that!"

"How are you? Is all well?" Jerrol asked carefully.

Marguerite sighed, her breath sifting through him, and he shivered. *"It is not what I expected, though the Land was relieved to see me. You were right, he couldn't take much more. He is sleeping now. It took a while to assimilate everything,"* she said, her voice growing colder. *"And to understand what the Ascendants had done. That they could do so much damage and not understand the conse-quences ... everything is out of balance. It will take centuries to put it right."*

"Are you able to help me with the Oath? It wants me to place it in the harbour at the very foundation of the inner walls."

"Of course, that's why I am here. But you will have to lay it."

"But that's under many feet of water," Jerrol protested, an icy cold finger of fear shivering down his spine. He swallowed, his mouth dry. *"Marguerite, I can't go under the water."*

"You don't have a choice. No one can carry the Oath but the Oath Keeper."

Jerrol broke out in a sweat just thinking about it. The sentinal crooned gently, trying to dampen the sudden tension running through him. He closed his eyes and tried to calm himself; the fluttery edges of panic weren't far away.

"Marguerite," he whispered out loud, "there has to be another way."

"There isn't, it has to be you. I'll guide you," she said persua-

sively. *"I won't let anything happen to you, I promise. Leyandrii still expects you to go into Elothia, so she won't let anything happen, either."*

"I think she's a little bit busy right now," Jerrol argued.

Marguerite laughed. *"Not too busy to look out for her Captain, I can assure you. Don't you trust me?"* Marguerite's voice took on a wheedling tone.

"It's not that," Jerrol protested, his voice fading as he realised how fruitless arguing with her was going to be. "You promise you won't leave me?" he asked drearily, an aching pain beginning behind his eyes.

"Never. I promise."

"Well, what do we need to do?"

"Cheer up, for starters. It won't take long, and then I will finish your harbour for you, I promise. I need to speak to young Niallerion; first, he needs some information to complete his calculations, and then we can begin."

"Today?" Jerrol was horrified.

"Yes, today. The sooner we start, the sooner it is finished. I have a lot to do elsewhere, you know."

He almost tripped over Niallerion as he shimmered out of the sentinal.

Niallerion stood up immediately as he saw Jerrol's ashen face. "What happened?" he asked.

"Nothing. Marguerite's here. She wants to speak to you. You can use my sentinal; it's probably better to have the conversation out of sight. I'm not sure how much we want to confuse these folks with!"

Niallerion's face brightened. "I'll be back in a bit."

"Take your time," Jerrol said, walking back down to his new home.

31

MARU 1ST 1124

SENTI

Jerrol found Gael in possession of the veranda. "You can't spend your day sitting there," he said with a faint laugh.

Gael grinned. "I want to see the sunset."

"You won't see much from there. You need to look out west. We'll get to watch the sunrise instead." He turned to look down into the bay. The clear water rippling gently up to the golden sands looked quite harmless, but the thought of getting in it nauseated him. He swallowed against the bile that rose in his throat, the acid leaving a horrible taste in his mouth. "Do we have any tea?" he asked, turning away from the sight of the water.

"Yeah, down in the harbour office. We haven't brought anything up here yet." They had already begun to call the hewn out caves 'offices'. Jerrol smiled. "Well, if you want tea in the morning, I suggest you move it up here. Come on, I'll help you." He led the way down to the caves where they had been sleeping.

They made two trips, loaded with bedrolls and the paraphernalia they had already managed to collect before Niallerion shimmered out of the sentinal. His expression was bemused, and he had a slightly wild look around his eyes as he approached the veranda.

Jerrol stopped beside him, arms full of blankets. "What?" he asked.

Niallerion's silver eyes focussed on him and he exhaled. "She doesn't expect much, does she?"

Jerrol grimaced. "Not in the least. But then it's my fault, I asked her."

"True. Be careful what you ask for, isn't that what they say?"

"Yeah," Jerrol sighed. "Let me dump this lot and we'll go down."

Jerrol stood on the beach and looked at the crystal-clear water, his face pale and tight.

Niallerion was blithely describing the centre point. "I tied a red flag on the middle pole; it's about ten feet deep now the tide is out, so it's not that far down. You can use the pole to guide you."

"Ten feet?" Jerrol repeated. His stomach felt like lead, and he was worried he was going to vomit on the spot. He rubbed his face.

"Yep, it's easy."

"Go down ten feet?"

Niallerion suddenly paid attention as Jerrol stepped back. "What is it?" he asked.

"I'm alright on top of the water, but it's the going under I'm having difficulty with."

"Why? You can swim, can't you? You never wear a life vest on the boat, like you make us do."

"Mmm."

"What's the problem then?"

"I'm afraid of going under the water," Jerrol admitted reluctantly.

"Why? It's nice and warm now, very calm. Nothing to be afraid of." Niallerion eyebrows rose into his hair.

"I'll go," Birlerion's voice spoke from behind them.

Jerrol spun. "Where did you come from?" he choked.

Birlerion shrugged. "I heard you needed assistance."

Niallerion frowned at Jerrol, still confused. "You can't be afraid of the water. You sail on it every day."

"That's on top of it, not under it," Jerrol pointed out.

"But still - a fisherman afraid of the water, that doesn't make sense."

"Jerrol, I'll go. Tell me what you need me to do," Birlerion repeated his offer.

"I can't, Marguerite says I have to do it," Jerrol said, his gaze straying back to the water.

"If anyone should go, it should be me," Niallerion said. "After all, Marguerite's already given me all the instructions."

"Why don't we all go?" Marianille said, suddenly arriving beside them. "We can make it a party."

Jerrol laughed, the tension easing as he looked at his friends. Their palpable concern for him melted away some of the fear that threatened to paralyse him.

"That's better. Take them with you if it helps. I'm sorry you have to do this, but you are the Oath Keeper," Marguerite murmured as she rummaged in his head.

"Marguerite, do you mind? I thought you said you didn't pry."

"Ah, I said sentinals didn't pry. I said nothing about me."

"Marguerite, don't."

"Sorry, but it has to be you, and if I can help remove the problem ... oo'er what's this? You've got to tell Taurillion about this next time you see him," she murmured with delight. *"What have you and Taelia been up to? He needs to know how to do that."*

Jerrol flushed. *"Do you mind? That's private."*

"Spoil sport," Marguerite muttered.

Jerrol choked and turned to face the water. If Maguerite was trying to distract him from his fear, she was doing a poor job. He looked at Birlerion. "I need to go down ten feet to the base of that centre pole. Can you make sure I come back up?"

Birlerion held his eyes. "Of course."

Jerrol shivered. "Let's get this over with then. The longer we leave it, the worse it will get."

Birlerion gripped his arm. "What do you need to do?"

"Lay the Oath," Jerrol said, starting to strip off his clothes. Birlerion followed suit, and they both walked into the water. Marianille, openly admiring their physique, grunted as Niallerion dug her in the ribs.

"Stop staring," he muttered.

Marianille giggled and then tilted her head as she watched Jerrol hesitate and then slowly lower himself into the water and started to swim. "Why is he scared of going under the water? The Captain is usually fearless."

"He said it was a recent affliction. I know he suffered in the mines, but how that could be related to water, I have no idea."

"I'll ask Birlerion. He seems to know a lot more about the Captain than you would think."

"He's also pretty tight-lipped. Let me know if he tells you anything," Niallerion replied as they watched the two men swim out to the centre pole. Birlerion glanced over at Jerrol frequently, obviously encouraging him.

They reached the centre pole, and Jerrol clung to it. He swallowed convulsively, trying to keep the flutter of panic and nausea from overwhelming him. He was freezing and yet overly hot at the same time. There was a hissing noise in his ears, and he thought he might faint.

"Jerrol, you can do this, the Oath needs a new home. It will protect your people. Do it for the people." Birlerion's firm voice penetrated the haze of panic. "I'm right here, I will pull you back up. I won't leave you there, I promise."

Jerrol nodded, gritting his teeth to stop them chattering. *Do it for the people*, he chanted to himself, *do it for the people*. He gripped the pole and shuddered. "I can't do it."

"Yes, you can, you can do anything; you are the Lady's Captain."

"I'm the Lady's Captain," Jerrol repeated. He thought of Birlerion, doing the impossible, and so could he. "Lady, help me," he prayed, clinging to the pole. A warmth suffused him, dispelling the shudders, and before he could think any more, he took a deep breath, and before the panic paralysed him completely, he ducked under the clear water. "Do it for the people," he repeated, swimming strongly down the pole as his ears hissed. Birlerion was a comforting presence beside him. Tiny fish flitted away as he approached, a silver flash gleaming in the clear water as they flicked away. There was a roaring in his ears threatening to overwhelm him.

The Oath humming within him blocked out the roar, and he relaxed. The weight of the Oath suddenly in his arms dragged him down, and he reached the sandy bottom. Drifting to his knees, his hair floated around his face as he wedged the Oath into the Land. Marguerite took it from him and entwined it around her, anchoring herself to the bedrock below. Jerrol felt a tug as he was drawn to the Oath, a tendril snagging him and worming its way within. The hum was diminished, but it coursed through his body, one with him and the Land.

"Build me a beautiful safe haven," he thought, a slight edge of panic creeping in.

Birlerion grabbed him under his arms and pulled, and Jerrol felt the Oath grab him back. *"Marguerite? You have to make the Oath let me go,"* he thought, his chest suddenly tight as he struggled not to breathe in water. Birlerion tugged harder, and he choked, bubbles of air escaping from his mouth. He panicked and began thrashing.

Marguerite's voice murmured persuasively, and the Oath released him enough for Birlerion to rise. The Oath sang through his veins as Birlerion pulled him to the surface. He desperately gasped for breath as they broke the surface, inhaling a mouthful of water that made him choke. Birlerion fought to hold him as he convulsed in the water.

Strong arms pulled him up and into a skiff. A warm blanket was wrapped around him, and the waves rocked him gently as he snorted water out his nose and mouth, tears running down his face as he relived the aftermath of drowning, his lungs wheezing at the effort.

The boat rocked as Birlerion was hauled in. "What made you come out?" Birlerion gasped.

"You were taking too long," Niallerion said, watching Jerrol in concern. "What is the matter with him?"

"Reaction," Birlerion said as he knelt beside Jerrol. "Jerrol, you're safe now."

"Please, not again, please no more, just kill me," Jerrol moaned. "I don't know where they went."

"Jerrol. You're in Senti." He shook Jerrol sharply. "Jerrol, you're not in the mines, you're in Senti. It's Birlerion. You're safe now, I have you." He pulled him out of Marianille's arms and hugged him. "I have you, I promised you'd be safe," he murmured into his hair.

Jerrol shuddered in his arms. "Promise," he whispered. "I made a promise."

"That's right, you promised Taelia you would come home." Birlerion looked up as the skiff beached on the sands. "Let's get him inside and warm him up; he's freezing." Between them they manhandled Jerrol up to his new home. Wrapped in blankets, he lay shuddering on the bed as they made hot tea.

"What happened in the mines?" Marianille asked with concern.

Birlerion sighed and, keeping his voice low, he repeated what he had been told. "They tried to drown him, multiple times."

"What?" she gasped.

"The Ascendants thought he knew something, so they drowned him and then resuscitated him. And then did it again."

"Did he know?" Niallerion asked shrewdly.

"I expect so, but he never told them. Even though they tried to mess with his head. The Lady removed much of it, but I think he's just remembered it all. He panicked as soon as we reached the surface. How he kept it together down there I have no idea."

"I'm amazed he even went down there; no wonder he didn't want to go," Marianille said as she looked over at Jerrol.

"Sometimes you don't have a choice."

"Won't this have made his fear even worse?" Niallerion asked slowly.

"Probably. Let's hope he won't have to go in the water again," Birlerion replied.

Jerrol shivered. His nose and chest hurt, and his throat was raw. Memories of the mines flicked through his head, a confusion of loss and suffering; both his and the poor people trapped in there. Overwhelmed, he struggled to cope with the horror and guilt as tears leaked down his face. He took a deep breath and tried to control his shudders. *"Lady help me. Marguerite? Help me, please."*

"Help will always be given to those who ask," Marguerite soothed, stilling his shaking limbs and easing the tightness in

his chest. *"Hush, you've no need to torture yourself with those thoughts. Let's put them somewhere safe where they will not haunt you,"* she said. *"My dear Oath Keeper, hush now, it's all over, you're safe now, relax, sleep, all will be well, and you will see a fine harbour in the morning. I promise."*

Jerrol sighed out his fear and relaxed. Birlerion's voice was a comfort in the background, and he slept. Birlerion brought over a mug of tea, sat beside Jerrol and watched over him as the tremours stilled; he let him sleep undisturbed.

32

MARU 2ND, 1124

SENTI

he next morning, Gael bounced in with the sunshine. "Isn't he up yet? Have you seen what's outside?" he asked, jigging from one foot to the other.

Birlerion shook Jerrol awake, watching him intently. "Gael has news," he said as Jerrol opened his eyes and stared up at him.

Jerrol blinked, awareness returning as he sat up. He realised he was naked under a bundle of blankets as memory of the previous day returned; he had laid the Oath, it was done. He looked up at Gael. "Has she finished already?"

"I should say! Come see."

"Make the tea whilst I dress and I will."

Jerrol joined the excited Gael out on the veranda and stopped in shock. The reality was even more impressive than in his imagination. Tall, glittering walls towered over the bay. Offset, they extended from both headlands in a slight curve away from each other, the western side curving inwards and the east side curving outwards, leading the offshore current up and away from the harbour. The stone was smooth and golden and the stone blocks joined seamlessly, if they were even blocks; for all he knew, it was one piece of stone that Marguerite had raised in place.

The stone sparkled in the sunlight, adding to its mystery. Multiple jetties extended out from the headland into the bay and a quayside jutted out in front of the offices. Steps were inset into the side, leading down and stopping about ten feet above the current water level. Niallerion was down on the jetty, staring up at the walls in wonder.

The walls looked out of place as if someone had dropped them arbitrarily in the middle of nowhere and expected them to just fit in. Marguerite had outdone herself. He smiled as he felt the contentment oozing out of the air; the Oath was satisfied, and a sense of calm and safety pervaded the air. Yes, this was a safe haven; rather ostentatious at the moment, but it would fit right in once the water levels rose, and unfortunately, he was sure that they would.

Birlerion stood next to him. "I would never have believed it possible," he said, "if it wasn't for Marguerite."

"Well, most people won't believe the truth, will they? They will think *we* built it. Best we leave it like that."

"Let's hope not too many come to visit in the meantime, then." Birlerion grinned. "How else you explain where all that stone came from is beyond me."

"Well, from the Land." Jerrol laughed in relief. So far so good. He strolled down to join Niallerion. "Pleased?" he asked as he reached for the stone wall. It resonated through him; the Oath burbling happily.

"Pleased?" Niallerion grinned. "It's a masterpiece! Look at the curve on those walls; exactly as I planned, down to the last inch!"

"Congratulations on a job well done," Jerrol held out his hand, and Niallerion grabbed it, still riding high.

He suddenly paused. "How much of this can I explain?"

"Whatever your audience can understand, but no mention of the Oath."

"Of course not, I'm not stupid."

Jerrol smiled, hesitant. "Thank you for looking out for me yesterday. I'm sorry I panicked."

"Thank Birlerion. He was the one who dragged you out."

"Still, if you hadn't brought the skiff over, it would have been more difficult. I'm afraid I lost it completely."

"Captain, don't beat yourself up. It happens to us all at some point. We don't do what we do without it affecting us in some way, at some time."

"I know, but still, I bet Guerlaire doesn't freak out underwater." Jerrol grimaced.

"Guerlaire wasn't half-drowned, so that is not a valid comparison."

"I just …" Jerrol sighed, his thoughts all muddled up. The Oath's happiness in the air was uplifting, but he felt raw and exposed; he felt like he had let them down. "I don't want to disappoint anyone."

Niallerion gripped his arm. "You won't. Ever. I fear we're more likely to disappoint you." He looked up as Birlerion approached and gave Jerrol a slight shake. "Are we taking Birlerion with us to Molinti?"

"Molinti?" Birlerion repeated as he reached them.

"We need to get Marianille into the palace, and then I need to speak to the emperor and find out what the Ascendants are up to," Jerrol said.

"Nothing good," Birlerion said, morosely. He looked up at the walls, and his face eased. "This is good, though; this is so good." His face softened in wonder.

"I know," Jerrol agreed. "I just wish we were able to extend the protections further."

"I think it extends further than you think. Marguerite would do all she could to help as many people as possible."

"Help shall be given to all who ask," Jerrol murmured, suddenly understanding.

"But will they ask?" Niallerion asked just as softly.

Birlerion exhaled. "Let's hope so." He shivered. "Anyway, what's the plan for getting into the palace?" he asked, changing the subject.

Jerrol eyed Birlerion. "Are you able to come with us? I would appreciate your company."

"I wouldn't miss this for anything," Birlerion replied as he watched Marin and Dion sail into the harbour, the sails dropping almost immediately as the walls blocked the breeze.

"We'll have lots of sculling practice." Jerrol grinned at their shocked expressions, as they unshipped the oar and sculled passed them.

Marin beached the *Mari Rose* and jumped down onto the golden sands followed by a wide-eyed Dion to greet Jerrol. "How did you do it? When did you do it?" he asked, not taking his eyes off the towering walls. "Do you really believe the waters will rise so high?" he whispered.

"Yes, they will, and if they rise this high here, then think how it will affect elsewhere."

"I'll bring Myriam here tomorrow," he said.

"Let's offload your samphire and mullet. I'll take it to Molinti, and you can go fetch Myriam and whatever you want to bring here," Jerrol suggested. They transferred the load from the *Mari Rose* to the *Scout* and then walked up the incline.

"I still can't believe this will all be underwater," Marin murmured, his shoulders drooping.

"I know, but we are prepared, which means we will be in a better position than many others."

"But still …" Marin's voice trailed off as the small village was revealed, and as they reached the top of the hill, he turned and looked back at the harbour. "This will be the new waterfront?"

"Yes, I believe so."

"It beggar's belief," Marin mumbled as he turned back to the growing array of buildings, "as does this." He gestured at the ever-increasing village.

"Let me show you yours," Jerrol suggested, leading the way to the site that Marin had selected, the boys having tumbled on ahead of them.

"Marin, look, look!" Gael was calling excitedly from the front porch of Marin's new home, grinning with delight.

"Myriam is not going to believe this," Marin gasped.

Jerrol grinned, happy for his friend. Gael and Dion dragged Marin inside, excitedly showing him the rooms. "Look, you've even got a room to eat in!" Jerrol heard the boys' excited voices as they went from room to room. He waited patiently, sitting on the steps outside, gazing down the street at the slowly rising buildings. The workmen were getting quicker. The work gangs were efficiently cladding the latest building with wooden slats, passing the materials effortlessly between them. He was pleased they had decided to stay, some intending to set up businesses, others interested in working in the boatyard or the harbour; the village would soon become a town.

He stood as Marin left the empty building. "Jerven, are you sure? I mean, it will take years for me to pay you back."

"Pay it gradually as you get the money; there's no rush," Jerrol said peaceably. "As long as you take on the Vespiri run for me and build that out. Once you have Myriam installed, you should make a run up there and get your bearings."

Marin nodded. "I can't believe there is a freshwater well right outside our house. Myriam will be thrilled."

"We hit a spring when we were building the wall. It seemed to make sense to harness it for us. I mean, freshwater is usually difficult to find," Jerrol said glibly, inwardly blessing Marguerite for her thoughtfulness. She had thought of so many minor details that would make their lives here so much easier. Things that he hadn't even thought of.

"We need to build a temple in honour of Marguerite; she has blessed our home, and we need to offer our thanks," Jerrol said as he looked at the buildings. They had built along either side of the street, leading to the widening space that would be a square. He called the foreman over. "We need a temple, with a small dome and an oculus to let in the light. At the north of the square, the altar should look down towards the sea. Is this possible? Can we position it so that there is an uninterrupted view? And a building for a healerie off the back."

The man stared back down the street and then back towards the widening square. "I know just the place." He smiled, hesitating. "I also know a healer who would come. My sister. She is currently apprenticed in Aguinti, but she is looking for an opportunity to set up her own healerie."

"Perfect. Ask her to visit. Let her see if this is a place she could live." A shiver of approval rippled through Jerrol as they strolled down to his house and found the Sentinals relaxing on his veranda. Laughing, he joined them, passing Marin an ale as they sat. They looked over the unbelievable harbour and whiled away the afternoon and into the evening, watching the light fade over the ocean as they shared the feast that Marianille had prepared. On the morrow, they would enter the fray again. But today was for them—a much-needed day of rest.

Jerrol smiled up at the brilliant moon rising high above them. He could easily live here he thought; such peace and companionship. It just needed his family to complete the moment. He sighed as he sent Taelia his love, hoping he would see her soon. Maybe she would come here and experience this wonderful way of life with him? He looked forward to showing her the wonders of Birtoli when this was all over.

33

MARU 3RD, 1124
MOLINTI

Jerrol and the Sentinals sailed into Molinti the next morning, a hold full of fish for the palace and some more sacks of samphire he was sure the cook would fall upon with relief. Leaving Niallerion watching the boat, Jerrol led Marianille and Birlerion up the incline and through the empty market place towards the back entrance of the palace. Birlerion looked around him with interest, noting the distance from the harbour as they lugged the sacks of samphire with them.

The plump cook's face lit up as he saw them approach. "Come, come," he said expansively, pulling them into the kitchen. Marianille flicked a glance around the kitchen before her gaze settled back on the cook. He was rummaging through the sacks. "Excellent, this should take her grace up to the end. It's not much longer before the baby will come."

"Is there any chance wc could speak to the empress? Pass on some messages?" Jerrol asked.

The cook looked at him thoughtfully. "I should think so. She was interested in speaking to the fisherman who found her samphire. Wait here and I'll go check." He bustled about, washing a handful of samphire in a bucket of water.

He patted it dry and then laid them on a salver, then he nodded to them as he left the kitchen.

Jerrol went to speak to Birlerion, but he wasn't there. He sighed in resignation and leaned back against the counter. He supposed he had been fortunate Birlerion had remained by his side for as long as he had. Who knew how this was affecting him, being in multiple places at the same time. "I knew it was too good to be true," he murmured. "Change into your dress," he said to Marianille. "We want the empress to hire you. If we can get you into the palace, we might have a chance of finding out what the Ascendants are up to, and I think the empress may be in dire need of some protection."

Marianille nodded and slipped away to a shadowy corner. Shaking out her dress, she changed. Rolling up her shirt and trousers, she stuffed them into an empty sack.

The cook returned, all puffed up with importance. "Come with me, " he instructed, "the empress wants to speak with you now before the emperor returns. He has an important event this evening."

"I heard," Jerrol replied, "there is a big speech tonight, and everyone is supposed to attend. Are they holding it at the palace?"

"Yes, some special guest speaker from Elothia, promising closer relationships or something," the cook said.

"Aren't you attending?" Jerrol asked as they followed him down the narrow passage.

"No, they want a full state dinner afterwards. Who has time to listen to speeches?" The cook grimaced.

"I doubt you'll miss much," Jerrol said.

The cook laughed. "My gain," he agreed, pausing outside a carved wooden door. He tapped gently and opened the door at the sound of a voice inside. He gestured for Jerrol and Marianille to enter as he stepped back.

Jerrol entered a magnificent drawing room, furnished

with comfortable settees and chairs upholstered in dusky pink. Swathes of golden silk dressed the tall windows, softening the edges and golden lamps lit the room, a lady's bower, soft and welcoming. A set of double doors were set into the far wall, leading to another private room. The empress sat at the end of a settee, her pretty face flushed with heat, her brown eyes overbright and her fingers

stretching and refolding a handkerchief. She inclined her head as Jerrol and Marianille entered. "I understand you wish to speak to me," she said, her voice breathless.

Marianille frowned.

"Yes, Your Grace," Jerrol replied as he bowed. "I wanted to ensure that the samphire was what you wanted."

"Oh yes, I don't know why, but I have this terrible craving; it came on all of a sudden, and samphire seems to be the only relief."

"We brought in another supply today, so you should have plenty for your needs, Your Grace, so you can stop worrying about it."

"Oh, you don't know what a relief that is. It was so worrying knowing that we didn't have any. I couldn't think of anything else."

"Who said you didn't have any, Your Grace? It would be simple enough to place an order with any of the fishermen in the harbour."

"Oh no, they said it was challenging to get," the empress disagreed, "that was why I was so frantic."

Marianille spoke under her breath. "Someone has planted a suggestion."

"Yes, a distraction maybe?" Jerrol agreed.

"Your Grace," Marianille smiled. "Where are your ladies? You look most uncomfortable."

"No, no I am fine, they are just over there, see? I asked them to step out for a moment. I didn't want them to hear about the samphire. I wouldn't want anyone else taking it, after all."

Marianille looked over where she pointed, but there was no one there. "Let me help you," she suggested, deftly removing the ruined handkerchief from her hands. "Come, let me help you to the bed. It will be more comfortable for you. You can remove your robe; it will be much cooler."

"No, no, I have to join Pierien; he is expecting me." She flicked a glance at Jerrol. "They seem to think you know something about … it doesn't matter. Dominant Clary thinks you know about something he is trying to find."

"Dominant Clary is here?" Jerrol asked.

The empress' lips tightened. "Yes, he keeps importuning Pierien to let him speak to the staff. I believe he will get his way. Between that and trying to find you, he is becoming most annoying."

"Why are you warning me, Your Grace?"

"You are Birtolian. He has no right to demand that we hand you over, and anyway, I need you to keep bringing my samphire. I can't manage without it."

"Of course, Your Grace. If I may be so bold, you must try and convince the emperor not to let them speak; they do not have Birtoli's best interests at heart. You must be careful what you to agree to."

"I know, I told Pierien that, but he won't listen to me. I don't trust them." She looked beseechingly at Jerrol. "You have to help him."

Jerrol gaped at her. "Me, Your Grace?"

"Yes, you. You know what's going on. I know you do. Help him, please."

Jerrol was aghast. She *must* be anxious to ask him to help the emperor. "You don't even know me, Your Grace."

"You're the Fisherman, and they are after you. If you are

not with them, then you must be with us," she said with simple logic. "You have to help him."

"I'll try, Your Grace, but it's unlikely he'll even see me. I am, after all, just a simple fisherman."

The empress grabbed another handkerchief and dabbed her face as Marianille hovered over her.

"Please, Your Grace, you will be much more comfortable if you have a rest first. Here, let me help you." Marianille helped the exhausted empress over towards the double doors and into the inner room, where she helped make her more comfortable. She poked her head around the doors. "Captain, could you get some iced water?"

Jerrol nodded and left the room. He ventured out into the corridor and finding it empty made his way to the kitchens and returned with a jug beaded with moisture. He poured a glass and cleared his throat. Marianille appeared straight away, a worried look on her face. "She is not well. She is far too overheated for her condition. You were right, they are not looking after her. That the emperor would put her at risk, at such a time …"

Jerrol sighed. "He probably isn't even aware."

"But what do we do?"

"Say you have been assigned by the emperor to take care of her. She is your duty, understood? Her baby is the future of Birtoli. Protect them."

Marianille nodded slowly. "But what of the emperor?"

"I'll try to make him see sense," Jerrol promised as he handed Marianille the jug. "No matter what, you stay with the empress; she is your responsibility."

"Yes, Captain," Marianille responded instinctively to the command in his voice. She turned back at the door, belatedly wondering what else could possibly distract them. But the room was empty. The Captain had already left.

· · ·

Making his way through the empty palace corridors back towards the kitchens, Jerrol tried to think of a way to get into the hall for the speeches. In the end, he didn't have to worry; the palace guards swept everyone before them, forcing all the staff into the large ballroom, which had been set up with a raised platform at one end. A small choral arrangement was singing softly; a prelude to the main event.

Most of the administration and many clan elders were present, seated in gilt chairs to either side of the platform, the staff herded up in front. The sight of an empire about to be overthrown made Jerrol feel physically ill. What could they possibly be after?

He didn't have to wait long to find out. Emperor Pierien led the Elothian delegation out onto the platform. "My people," the emperor began grandly. "It gives me great pleasure to announce that I have concluded a great trade agreement with our neighbours from Elothia, which will secure the future of Birtoli for many years to come. Our partnership will bring wealth and prosperity to all. It gives me great pleasure to introduce Dominant Clary of Elothia, who will provide you with the details."

Jerrol frowned. Clary was from Vespiri. Why would he say was from Elothia?

Clary stood forward and swirled his cloak around him dramatically. "People of Birtoli, hear me." His voice boomed out across the room. "Your emperor commands you to listen and to listen closely." Clary's voice resonated through Jerrol's bones, and Jerrol watched. "Your emperor commands you to listen and obey. We who stand before you will lead you to greatness. Your destiny awaits you. Let us guide you down the path. Look at me and watch carefully." His voice took on a sonorous tone. "Watch me," he repeated, lowering his voice, making his audience strain to hear him. "We are here to lead you, and you will obey. Those who know of the history of the relic of the land will step forward and speak. The emperor commands you to speak. You will tell all that you know without reservation. I know it exists and you will tell me where it is. You will listen to my voice and obey. We expect all men to join us, young and old, as we fight against tyranny and strife. We will rise against the oppressors and free you all. The relic is our talisman, and you will lead us to it."

Jerrol's frown deepened. This was a call to arms, not a trade agreement. Hidden within was a spell to find the Oath. Jerrol felt the men around him sway forward. He swayed with them, trying to blend in, but what to do? How had they found out about the Oath?

He glanced around the room. The emperor's guards lined the walls, stiff in their grey armour, their surcoats of white and gold softening the edges, but not disguising the threat. They would not be gentle; he was sure. He stepped forward. "Your Imperial Majesty, I thought you said this was a trade agreement, not a call to go to war. Who are we supposed to be fighting? And for what? We are already free in the Empire of Birtoli. Under the protection of the Lady, we thrive and flourish." A murmur arose in the room around him and several men frowned in agreement as they looked at him.

The emperor stepped forward. "You do not have permission to speak. Be silent."

Clary stared at Jerrol, frowning as an aide whispered in his ear. "You," he said, "you're that Fisherman, aren't you? Pierien, arrest him."

"Amongst other things," Jerrol replied as the guards grabbed his shoulders and forced him onto his knees. "There are no wars in the waters around Birtoli, except for those that you bring to us." The emperor gestured, and the guards dragged Jerrol out of the hall. "You will bring floods and ruin to us all! Don't listen to him, remember Geteril!" Jerrol shouted as he was hustled away. "Honour the Tu'ani." His voice faded down the corridor and stopped abruptly as a fist found his stomach and a hand clamped over his mouth. He struggled in the iron grip of the guards, but to no avail.

"There is always war. Where there is freedom, there is strife." Clary smiled at his audience who were gaping in horror. "Freedom is worth fighting for, and I command you to join me," he gestured in the air before him, "in the fight of the righteous against those who would restrain and fetter us. To build a better and stronger Birtoli; one that can protect its people. Join me and be proud of your sacrifice. Tell me of the relic. Where did it go?"

A young voice piped up from near the back. "What happened to Geteril?"

Clary frowned. "Who asks?"

A small page boy squirmed forward. "What happened to Geteril?" he asked again.

"Why, nothing has happened to Geteril." Clary smiled down at the boy. "Come, be the first to join me."

The boy shook his head. "The Fisherman said something happened. He said to honour the Tu'ani. Where are they? They are not here, so what happened?" He stared accusingly at the emperor.

"Nothing has happened," the emperor said in a soothing voice. "This is a time for celebration; a great partnership. Listen to Dominant Clary's words. Our partnership is what will protect us, not the Lady. Her time is over. It is down to us to protect ourselves." He glared out across his people as a low murmur spread back through the room.

"The boy's right. Where is the Tu'ani elder? Why isn't he here?" The cook stepped up behind the boy. "What does the Fisherman know that we don't?"

Emperor Pierien glanced at Clary. "Speak to them. I thought you said this would be simple?"

Clary glared at the emperor. "Throw them in the quarries. They will soon realise what is best for them. They'll learn that what they have is not free."

The emperor signalled his guards. "This is not a debate," he said. "We have agreed to work in partnership. You will either go willingly or you can join the Fisherman in the quarries." The guards pulled the boy out of the room, along with the cook.

"Calm, people, calm. Let me speak," Clary continued. "We balance on the edge of momentous times. Do not let it be said that the people of Birtoli did not step forth and be counted when the time came. The people of this empire are proud and strong; they deserve to be at the forefront of history, beside us as we rid our world of those who threaten us and our peace. Listen and be calm; peace is standing before you. Open your arms and welcome it in. Tell me what I need to know." Clary continued to weave his spell, ensnaring the people with his words, soothing the emotions in the room, and firmly laying in his instructions. As he finished, he stood, waiting expectantly before the silent room.

34

PRESENT DAY

MARU 5TH, 4128, MOLINTI

Birlerion's vision focused on the book open before him and he lurched back in his seat as he scanned his surroundings. He was seated in the reading room in what had been the old palace in Molinti and was now the administration building.

The vision of the golden stone walls of Senti harbour gleamed and sparkled in his memory. Leyandrii may be far removed, but Marguerite was just as powerful, if not more so. Jerrol had laid the Oath in the foundations; a last attempt to save some of the people of Birtoli. He stood up, his chair scraping back, and strode out of the room and through the corridors until he exited the old palace. He gazed out over the sparkling sea, grappling to reorganise his memories as the new ones overlaid the old.

Exhaustion swept through him and he leant against the palace wall as his legs trembled. Taking a deep breath, he pushed himself upright and stumbled towards the stables, intent on finding a horse and making his way up to the emperor's palace high on the ridge. He had much to tell the king and Taelia.

"Do you need a horse, Sentinal?" An administrator asked

as Birlerion approached the stables. "Scholar Taelia left about a chime ago."

"I suppose I'm going to need one," Birlerion said, slowly adjusting to the fact that he was back in the present day. He frowned. "What day is it?"

"Maru 5th. The emperor's state dinner is in two days; we've all been invited. It's been a long time since I've attended such a grand event." The man smiled happily.

Birlerion smiled in agreement and followed the man to the stables. The day was much advanced; he had lost all of the morning. He paused at the top of the road and looked down towards the harbour, where there was no jaunty fishing boat tied up to the quay. He sent heartfelt Lady's blessings down upon his absent companions and reluctantly turned away.

When Benedict entered Geraine's study, followed by Fonorion, Geraine was staring across the room and out of the window. His face was strained, and he worried at the tassel on his jacket.

"Geraine, what is the matter?" King Benedict asked as he approached.

The emperor straightened and lifted his chin. Reluctantly, he spoke. "We may have been too hasty in making a decision."

"We?"

"Pierien and I. We let them speak, it seemed like the best thing to do. They were so reasonable, and the administrators all agreed, so we let them speak in the grand hall."

"Let who speak?" the king asked.

"Why didn't he warn me beforehand?"

Benedict frowned, perplexed. "Geraine, I don't understand. What has happened?"

Geraine suddenly sagged in his chair and held his head in his hands. "Where were you? It was Clary and his men. Pierien sentenced the Fisherman to hard labour in the quarries. What has he done?"

"Why did Pierien do that? What did the Fisherman do?"

"That's what I don't understand. Clary was making overtures of friendship and trade, but the Fisherman started accusing him of wanting to start a war or something."

"Are you sure Clary was speaking of trade?" Benedict asked.

"Yes, joining with his people and stuff like that."

"When was this? There has been no gathering today, Geraine."

Geraine stared at him, horror filling his face.

Benedict stilled. "What did you do?"

Geraine looked around him, trying to avoid Benedict's accusing gaze. "We didn't mean it," he said desperately.

"Mean what? Geraine, what did Pierien do?"

Geraine stared at him. "We said that Birtoli didn't need the Lady's protection," he said, his voice anguished.

Benedict looked at him, blankly. "You said what?"

"In front of all the elders, we said the Ascendants would look after us."

"Why?"

"I don't know."

"They must have gained something," Benedict insisted.

"They flushed out the Captain. Maybe that was what they wanted?" Fonorion suggested quietly from behind the king.

Benedict considered the Sentinal's words. "They couldn't have known he would be there, and to have all the elders present? No, the Captain was an added bonus, I think. He tried to stop it. What could they have wanted this close to the end?" He looked back at Geraine. "Think, Geraine, what did Clary say?"

Geraine shrugged, bewildered. "I told you; peace and cooperation, to work together to protect us against those who threaten our way of life. He was asking for cooperation. There was nothing aggressive."

"Then why did the Fisherman speak out against them? They must have wanted something."

"Maybe it was nothing. They wanted the Birtolians to do nothing against them. It was a way of nullifying them," Fonorion spoke again from behind him.

Benedict frowned. "We're missing something," he said scowling at Fonorion. "Jerrol wouldn't have put himself in danger without reason. And an Ascendant would not speak without planting a suggestion; the question is what was the suggestion?"

Geraine's face blanched and King Benedict stiffened. "What?"

"I think we said something we shouldn't have," Geraine admitted.

"What did you say?"

"We told someone about something that we shouldn't have, but he knew about it already." Geraine tried to justify himself.

"What did you tell him?"

"We're not supposed to say."

"Well, if you've already told someone, I'm not sure it'll make much difference now." The king looked around the throne room. Geraine's guards were out of earshot. "Let me make it easy for you," he said wryly. "I am assuming you are referring to the Oath?"

Geraine licked his lips, his fingers busy at the tassle. "W-what? How did you know?" Geraine swallowed.

Benedict twisted his lips. "The Oath has been prevalent throughout everything that is happening. It must be what the Ascendants are after."

"The Ascendants were asking for information about the relic of the land; the Oath. They are searching for it."

"What happened after Clary finished speaking?"

Geraine shrugged. "He stormed off. He was angry because no one stepped forward with information. Of course, they didn't know about the Oath; all who knew had been lost."

"Then the Oath should be safe," the king said in relief.

"They took the Fisherman."

"Are you sure they took the Fisherman? The last message we had from Birlerion was that Jerrol was safe in Senti. Do you know where they took him?"

"To the quarries."

"What is at the quarries?"

Geraine looked at him his face taut. "That's where we send the criminals and miscreants for punishment. It's slave labour."

"Can you order him to be released?"

"Oh no, it's too late. We've passed the sentence; he's already gone."

"But you could rescind the order and tell your guards to release him."

Geraine suddenly straightened. He blinked at the king and looked around his study as if seeing it for the first time. He turned horrified eyes on Benedict. "Pierien sent him to the quarries," he gasped, "and he turned away from the Lady. I knew something terrible was happening."

"What are you afraid of, Geraine?" Benedict asked.

"He turned away from the Lady. Without her protection, Birtoli will be destroyed."

"Not completely. You have the islands. Not all is destroyed."

"But so much more could have been protected; we failed our people." Geraine wrung his hands in distress. "Oh, I understand now. And our only salvation lost," Geraine moaned.

"What do you mean, 'lost'?"

"The quarries were a death trap; accidents happened all the time. Rock faces collapsed, flooding, terrible conditions. I read a book on it once when I was younger, about the building of this palace. I didn't want to live here once I knew what people had suffered to build it, but then, as my father said, if we didn't live in it, their sacrifice would have been all for nothing."

"You said the Ascendants took Jerrol. Why did they want him?"

Geraine shrugged. "I don't know," he admitted, shifting uneasily in his seat.

Benedict considered the emperor. "Geraine, do you still have the book about the palace?"

"I expect it's in the library. There is a whole section on royal buildings; the old palace and this one," the emperor replied, frowning in thought.

"Sire, we should check how Taelia is getting on. Wasn't she checking the census records?" Fonorion asked.

The king nodded. "Yes. I didn't see her at breakfast this morning, so I assumed there were no shattering discoveries."

"Or maybe they weren't what she wanted to read," Fonorion suggested.

The king sighed. "I doubt she'll find much that she wants to read. He's running out of time, and how he gets out of this one, I have no idea." The king caught sight of Birlerion hovering outside the chamber door. "Birlerion, what news?"

"I just accompanied Jerrol, Niallerion, and Marianille to Molinti, to the old palace down at the harbour."

"You did what?" Benedict's jaw dropped.

Birlerion grimaced. "I have much to tell you." He rubbed his hand through his hair and stared at Benedict.

"Sit down, Birlerion, before you fall down. You look far too pale." Fonorion forced him into a chair as the king hovered beside him.

How is Jerrol?" King Benedict asked.

"He is exhausted. Time seems to be running much faster back then. He is catching up with us; I believe we will all reach Maru 7th at the same time. When I left him, he was trying to get Marianille in to see the empress. We just finished building the harbour at Senti; it is quite an amazing sight."

"You saw the harbour walls at Senti built?" the emperor repeated. Birlerion twisted his lips at the disbelief in the emperor's voice. "That's not possible," Geraine said, his gaze still fixed on Birlerion.

"I can assure you, it is. If Jerrol has travelled back in time, why can't I?"

"Birlerion, you are already in 1124; that would make you in three places at once," Fonorion said.

Shrugging, Birlerion leaned forward, his arms on his knees. "That's probably why I feel so exhausted. I sympathise with Roberion; I now know how he felt. It is disorienting as new memories overlay my existing ones. My brain is struggling to match them all up." Birlerion straightened. "Marguerite and Jerrol laid the foundation of the Senti walls. I know because I helped them. Marguerite built the walls overnight out of the land."

"But ... but ..." the emperor stuttered, unable to get his words out.

Benedict glanced at him in sympathy. "Do you think that

is why Jerrol was sent back? To build the harbour? Is his work done now?"

"I believe that was the original purpose. To protect as much of Birtoli as possible." Birlerion smiled. "It was amazing. The golden walls rising out of turquoise seas. They tower above the water line, a warning of how high the seas will rise."

Geraine's eye were wide. "History in the making," he murmured.

"Does that mean Jerrol can come home now? Like you have?" Benedict demanded.

Birlerion's smile faltered. "I don't believe so. There is one more task the Lady requires of him. When I returned here, I left Jerrol at the old palace with Marianille, intending on seeing the empress. I was with him in the palace kitchens one moment, then the next I woke up in the reading room, in the Administration building down at the harbour."

"The empress? According to Geraine, Emperor Pierien sent Jerrol to the quarries as punishment for speaking against him," Benedict said.

Birlerion lurched to his feet. "He what? He can't have. I was just talking to him."

"Apparently he embarrassed the emperor in public."

"I know he was intending on seeing if he could get an audience with the emperor, as the Ascendants are well entrenched. But, Your Majesty, I think he's hanging on by a thread. He can only take so much; the strain he is under, and the demands ..." Birlerion spread his hands. "He is stretched to breaking point," he finished bluntly.

"I don't see what we can do," King Benedict replied. "It has already happened. I don't see how we can affect the outcome. He has Marianille and Niallerion, you say. Maybe they can support him?"

"They don't know him like we do; we need to be there."

Birlerion strode across the room in frustration before turning back to the king. "My apologies, sire, it's just I need to be there, not here. He needs me."

"I wonder if we should call Marianille and Niallerion here? Do you think it would make any difference?"

Birlerion shrugged. "They won't get here in time, Your Majesty."

"What triggers you going back there? Is there anything you've noticed?" Fonorion asked quietly.

The Emperor sat, mouth open, listening in amazement.

"So far, I've always been in Senti. Marianille found me by the sentinal and then Jerrol called me to help him with the harbour. I came back with him to Molinti, and we went to the old palace, and as I entered, I was back in the present. But Jerrol is here in Molinti now, in his time. There's no point me going to Senti. Unless I go to Adeeron," he finished thoughtfully.

"Adeeron?" The emperor asked in confusion.

"What is so important about Adeeron?" the king asked, frowning.

"The Ascendants have a power source there. Apparently, Guerlaire asked Jerrol to destroy it."

Fonorion spoke up. "We need to confirm if Jerrol ever made it to the quarries. If the Ascendants have him, they may have taken him elsewhere, like Adeeron. Birlerion, let's check the records. Maybe you *should* go there. If his need for help is drawing you across time, and he seems to be calling you, then that is the best place you could go."

"Where were the quarries located?" the king asked Geraine.

Geraine wrinkled his forehead in thought. "I believe they were further inland, where the Olini Lake is."

"There's a lake?"

"Yes, the quarry was flooded, centuries ago. They had to

get the stone from elsewhere to finish the palace. It's all in that book I told you about."

"How long ago was it flooded?" the king asked urgently.

"About ten to fifteen years before the palace was finished."

"Possibly before the Bloodstone was shattered, then," King Benedict said. He stared at Birlerion as he ran his hand through his hair. His lips tightened. "Go do the research, Birlerion. There's no point haring off to the wrong place. I'll speak to Taelia, advise her what has happened and see if she has made any progress. Geraine, I'll meet you tomorrow morning at eighth chime. We have a long day."

Geraine nodded.

King Benedict led the way back to his chamber. Taelia's rooms were off his wing, and he tapped on her door before entering. Taelia looked up in surprise, rising as she saw the king in her doorway. Mikke gave a squeal of pleasure and danced up to the king, raising his hands. The king picked him up, absently hugging him. Fonorion took up position by the door after giving Taelia a swift grin. The king gestured for Taelia to sit and joined her at the table, glancing at the piles of books and papers spread out across it.

"What have you found?" he asked as he bounced Mikke on his knee.

Taelia smiled at the sight. Shaking her head, she picked up a manuscript. "There are multiple references to the Fisherman. He was definitely known as Jervcn, su we have confirmation that it was Jerrol. He was well known and respected; people listened to what he had to say when he was in port; he was the carrier of news and messages. It gives the name of his boat even more meaning." She sighed. "There are records of trips up to Terolia and Vespers and quite a bit of coverage about the growth of the port of Senti after 1124, though little about how it was actually built. Which, I suppose, is not surprising as, according to Birlerion, Marguerite was involved in the building of it."

"Ah, yes, Birlerion just returned from Senti. He said Jerrol and Marguerite just built the harbour and laid the Oath at its foundations."

"That explains it!" Taelia said, wrinkling her brow. "I knew the harbour was more than just a harbour." Taelia stilled. "Wait, did you say Birlerion returned? Is Jerrol with him? Is he alright?"

The king shushed her. "Calm down, you'll scare Mikke. Jerrol was fine when Birlerion last saw him but the Lady still needs him for one more task."

"What more can he do? His harbour was what saved the people of Birtoli. The Jerven trade routes brought in much-needed supplies, medicines, tools and food. Many more would have died without it. I have found no mention of Jerrol in the rebuilding of Birtoli after the stone was broken. His fishing line continues, managed by his brother Gael and two other fishermen, but there is no mention of Jerven.

"I also found an entry in Emperor Pierien's diaries dated Maru 3rd, 1124, that Captain Jerven of Senti was sentenced to a year's hard labour for being disrespectful to the throne, along with the palace cook and another servant. The emperor seemed more upset about the cook than Jerven. Apparently, he was an excellent cook." Taelia smiled faintly. She opened a book on a page marked by a scrap of paper and handed it to the king.

The king stared at the sketch of Jerrol on his knees before the emperor, his lips tightened. "Does he say what happened to him?"

"No, I haven't managed to find a record of the labour camps yet. I'm still searching."

"I sent Birlerion to search for any other mention of Jerven. Birlerion left Jerrol at the old palace seeking an audience with the empress. He left Marianille and Niallarion with Jerrol, so he is not alone. Between arriving in Molinti and Birlerion arriving back here, something happened to him. We need to find out what.

"Geraine told me that he once read that people were sent to the quarries for punishment; that would have been when they were quarrying stone for this palace," the king suggested keeping his voice calm.

Taelia's face brightened. "I'll make a note to search for the quarries." Her voice faltered. "I found a legend written about the Fisherman."

"Tell me," the king said, gently hugging Mikke, who had curled up in his lap. Soothed by their voices, his eyelashes drooped.

Taelia sighed as she looked at the king and smiled gently at her sleeping son in his arms, the sweep of his eyelashes so like his fathers. "There is a legend that the Fisherman came out of the sentinal tree on the Senti headland in the middle of the great storm. He had returned to collect the *Island Scout,* which was waiting for him in the newly formed harbour of Senti. He had sworn an oath to protect the people of Birtoli and he had returned to fulfil that oath." She paused, looking at the king expectantly.

"The Oath," he said. "It's all about the Oath, isn't it?"

She nodded. "From what you've said, the harbour is the Oath in action. We know Marguerite helped build it. Birlerion said that Jerrol was adamant that the walls be built just so. He had a plan, and it was supported by the Lady of the Land; the host of the Oath."

"Go on," the king said as she paused.

"The legend says he returned to Molinti, twice loaded with survivors but not a third. It is said that when he departed Molinti harbour, his boat was consumed by a sudden squall and when the squall passed, the *Island Scout* was gone."

"But why would he go to Molinti and not back to Senti?"

"Senti, it is said, was already overwhelmed with survivors brought by the *Mari Rose* and the *Moonlight Kiss* and even the *Mikke's Ride,* which was in commission by then. They took all the people they rescued back to Senti."

"So, we know he survives both the hard labour and the sundering of the Bloodstone. We just have to stop him leaving Molinti on that third trip," the king said, deep in thought.

"It sounds so terrible when you say it like that," Taelia said.

"Don't give up on him, my dear. If he can survive what the Ascendants throw at him, then I am sure the Oath will send him back."

"That's what I was hoping. The fact that there is no record of him in 1124 after Maru 8th must be because he returned to us here. He is not listed in the 1125 census, though so many are listed as missing, I suppose it's not surprising. There is a severe reduction in the population numbers; Birtoli suffered greatly. And yet it was all lost in history. I suppose as the other kingdoms struggled with their own problems."

The king looked down at the sleeping child in his arms. "Such sacrifice," he murmured, kissing Mikke's head gently.

"I should put him to bed," Taelia smiled.

"I'll carry him; he'll not be disturbed," the king said, rising. He carried the child into the bedroom and laid him in his bed and then watched as Taelia tucked him in and kissed him gently. She checked Leyarille, asleep in her cot, before escorting the king back out.

"Sleep well," the king said as he left Taelia stacking her

papers, and he returned to his rooms. He looked at Fonorion. "The Oath," he said.

Fonorion nodded. "That's what they are after."

"And Jerrol knows where it is," the king said.

"How many others know that Jerrol knows where it is?"

"Depends if someone in Emperor Pierien's throne room told them," the king said, his expression grave.

"We have no way of knowing," Fonorion replied just as bleakly.

35

MARU 3RD, 1124

MOLINTI

Niallerion looked up from the Captain's logbook and watched the sun set while literally chewing his nails. It was way past the time he had expected the Captain to return. What had gone wrong? He had spent the heat of the afternoon sheltered under the tarpaulin that he had rigged across the back of the boat, but he was stifling hot, and sweat trickled down his back.

He had spent most of the afternoon figuring out how all the pulley systems worked, though he had arrived at the conclusion that he couldn't improve the design enough to make it worth the effort. Putting that aside, he had spent much of his time reading the logbook he had found tucked in the back of the locker during one of his sporadic investigations of the boat.

The Captain had been busy. His plans for saving Birtoli were clearly laid out, from negotiating new trade routes to the building of the harbour, interspersed with prosaic reports of fishing trips and catches. Yet his desperate need to find a way home to his family came through it all clearly. Niallerion pursed his lips. There had been an entry in a different hand on a dog-eared page, proving it had been much read, sending him everlasting love beneath the Lady's moon and the belief that he would keep his promise.

Niallerion stared blindly across the calm waters of the harbour. There were gaping holes in the logbook; the Captain had not committed to the pages his meeting with the Lady or Guerlaire or what was really at the centre of the harbour, nor his suffering at the hands of the Ascendants. Yet he couldn't read his words without realising that this was a record of a lone man in desperate times acting as he saw fit.

Finally, unable to wait any longer, he climbed out of the boat and made his way up through the busy marketplace and followed the track up to the palace. The golden walls of the palace glowed in the setting sun, reflecting the heat and warmth of the day. Heat radiated off the stone walls as he approached the kitchen entrance but found the way barred by palace guards.

They glared at him. "Kitchen's closed."

"I was looking for a fisherman and his companions. They delivered a load of fish earlier and haven't returned."

"The Fisherman? He's gone to the quarries."

"What? Do you know why?"

"Emperor's word, he won't be coming back. I suggest you move on or you'll be joining him."

"But why?"

The guard stiffened and pointed down the track. "Move on."

Niallerion retreated to the marketplace and threaded through the busy tables in the centre. Contemplating the busy square, he slowly walked towards a small tavern on the eastern side, which was open and serving food.

He found an empty table at the back in the dim shadows, paid for a meal and sat pondering over a glass of wine. Laughter reached him from the square outside, where men gathered around the tables, playing a board game with black and white wooden counters. Much jeering and laughter accompanied it.

The Captain had intended on seeing the emperor. It obviously hadn't gone as planned, but where were Marianille and Birlerion? He looked up sharply as he heard someone mention the quarries. He slid along the bench that ran along the back wall and listened carefully to a group of men huddled around the table at the end.

"Death sentence it is; no one comes out o' there. The emperor ought to be ashamed of hisself." The man looked down into the depths of his mug, wrinkling his brow as he stared. He was dressed in the light linen clothes of the region. "My boy came home tonight and said one of his friends got sent up there today. No one's safe."

"What did they do?" one of his companions asked.

The man shrugged. "My son wasn't too sure. There was a big meeting; some men from someplace in Elothia were given permission to speak. My boy said it was bizarre; all the staff had to attend."

"What did they say?"

"A lot of nonsense about trading partners or something. They were wanting to know where an old treasure was located, though he's only a page boy and he didn't know what they were talking about. He's only been there a couple of months. He said some other folks were arrested too."

Niallerion spoke softly. "I'm sorry to interrupt. I couldn't help but overhear. You said they were trying to find a treasure; what sort of treasure?"

"My boy wasn't sure, they didn't give it a name. He said they called it a ray-lick," the man said, pronouncing the unusual word carefully.

"A relic?"

"Yeah, that's what m'boy said, but no one knew what he was talking about. And then the Fisherman stepped forward and challenged the emperor. Imagine that," the man said, his face horrified. "Imagine telling the emperor he was wrong!"

"A fisherman? Did your boy know him? Did your boy remember what he said?"

The man grinned. "My boy said it was Jerven of Senti, *the* Fisherman. The Fisherman said Birtoli didn't need to go to war, that we were fine as we were under the protection of the Lady."

Niallerion nodded in agreement, as did the listening men. "The Lady blesses us all."

"Yeah, but d'yer know what the emperor said? He said we didn't need her protection!"

"What?" The owner of the tavern paused by their table. "The emperor said what?"

"He said we didn't need the Lady's protection. The Elothians would protect us."

There were shouts of horror. "He never!"

"He did."

"Lady forgive him. What if she takes her eye off us?" The men were horrified, and the word spread through the tavern and out into the marketplace. The man sat back, pleased with the effect of his news.

Niallerion leaned forward. "What happened to the Fisherman?"

"The emperor ordered him to be sent to the quarries, but I heard he won't arrive there."

"Why not?"

"Them Ascendants. They took him. Back to where they came from, I expect."

"And where did they come from?" Niallerion asked.

"Would you believe they came all the way from Elothia? No idea why."

Exhaling slowly, Niallerion nodded his thanks and slid back to his table and his bowl of salad. He looked at the bowl of green leaves blankly. Elothia? Thinking back to Guerlaire's conversation with Jerrol in the palace in Vespers, the only place mentioned in Elothia had been that dead zone in the north. If that was where the Captain had been taken, how could he get there and how would he get him out?

He leaned back against the wall behind him as his mind spun. Had Birlerion and Marianille been taken there too? He pushed his bowl away and stood. He had his weapons in the *Scout* and the Lady on his side; he had to try and help.

Returning to the *Scout*, he strapped on his broadsword and smiled, feeling much better already. He had missed its weight on his back. He made sure everything was stowed back in its rightful place. The Captain's sword and Marianille's were still wrapped in their oilskin cloths, though Birlerion's sword had gone. Niallerion stared at the remaining swords, knowing Birlerion hadn't returned to collect his. Unable to explain the anomaly, he ignored it. He had more important things to worry about.

Leaving the *Scout* ready for departure, he sat and jotted a quick entry in the Captain's logbook, explaining what had happened and his plan to try to rescue the Captain from the Ascendants. Maru 3rd; four days until the Captain had said it was the end of the world as they knew it. He wrapped the logbook up and tucked it away, ignoring the niggling worry growing in the back of his mind. If he could find a horse, he could reach the borders with Vespiri within a couple of days, if he only stopped once to trade it for a new one. He prayed to the Lady, asking her to watch over him, gathered up the swords, and set off for the palace.

Ignoring the guarded entrances, this time, Niallerion climbed through the narrow streets and approached the palace walls from the sheer cliffs of the headland into which it backed. No sentries guarded the cliffs, no one was foolish enough to climb them, and certainly not in the dark.

Niallerion dropped his weighted rope into the sheltered gardens below him and eased over the edge of the cliff. He tested his rope, and although it creaked alarmingly, it held his weight. Slowly, leaning back into the rope that he had wrapped around his hips, he edged his way down the cliff. He stopped as the rattle of loose stones preceded him. Peering over his shoulder, he saw no movement and continued.

It took longer than he would have wished, but eventually he reached the bottom, and he unwrapped the rope with trembling arms. He was not looking forward to the climb back up.

Silently, he traversed the shadowy gardens, tripping over ornamental stones and trailing bushes that tangled his feet. Landing on his hands and knees, he stiffened as a voice spoke above him. He glanced up to see Marianille standing over him.

"You know, you couldn't be quiet if your life depended on it," Marianille said. "Which I would suggest it does if you are breaking into the palace!"

Niallerion exhaled his ragged breath and sat back on his heels. "I was coming to see you," he said.

"Couldn't you come in the front door, like civilised people?"

"They wouldn't let me in."

Marianille's chuckle was low. "I wonder why? What are you doing here Niallerion? You are lucky it's only me, and I only came out for a breath of fresh air."

"I came to bring you this." Niallerion untied the sack across his back and pulled out her sheathed sword. "I thought you might need it."

She took her sword and stared at him. "What's happened? I've been stuck in with the empress. We're trying to keep her quiet."

"Neither Jerrol nor Birlerion returned to the boat. I went to find word and discovered the Ascendants have the Captain. I believe they've taken him to the array in Elothia, just as Guerlaire predicted they would. I promised I'd be there to help him."

"What? I'll come with you." Marianille began strapping on her sword.

"No, you know the Captain wanted you to look after the empress. Your job is here."

"You know you need help!"

"Please, Marianille, you need to stay here. See if you can find word of Birlerion."

"He went back to wherever he keeps coming from. It's the Captain that needs our help."

"Then protect the empress as the Captain ordered you to."

Marianille hissed out her breath and then gave in. "Niall … be careful," Marianille whispered.

"And you," he replied before turning to go back the way he had come.

He jerked to a stop as Marianille grabbed his arm. Cool fingers grasped his chin, and the softest lips in the world kissed him. Niallerion's breath caught. His arms stole around her and she moulded her body to his. Heat flushed through him as he kissed her back, the kiss deepening as they clung to each other.

Reluctantly, Niallerion drew back. "Now?" he whispered. "Now you kiss me?"

Marianille smiled as she smoothed her fingers over his lips and then his cheek. "Make sure you come back to me."

"Always," he replied and melted into the shadows.

36

MARU 6-7TH,1124

EAST MAYER WATCH, VESPIRI

After two days of hard travelling, Niallerion arrived in East Mayer Watch. He had cajoled a farmer into trading his horse at a farmstead on the borders of Vespiri, but the steed stood trembling with fatigue. He slid out of the saddle and leaned against his horse's heaving sides, just as exhausted.

"Niallerion, what are you doing here? How did you get across the border?" A swarthy-faced Sentinal bore down on him.

"Royerion? Thank goodness. I need to get to Vespers, now!"

Royerion grabbed his arm and steered him towards the waystone. "What happened?"

"Can't explain. Need to speak to Leyandrii."

"I'll take you," Royerion said, his face grim. He glanced around and then dragged Niallerion through the waystone and stepped out into a ferocious storm that battered Vespers.

Niallerion groaned. "Can't they give us a break?" he asked as he was buffeted by the gusts, swaying like a sapling before the wind.

"Come on, you don't have time to complain," Royerion said as he dragged him up the steps and into the palace.

The silence inside the palace was sudden and complete. Royerion looked around, uncertain. "Where is everyone?" he asked in a hushed voice.

"I've sent them home, which is where you should be." Leyandrii's stern voice came from the top of the stairs.

"You need to send me to that deadzone in Elothia," Niallerion blurted as he struggled out of Royerion's grip and started up the steps.

"Deadzone?"

"That deadzone in the north Guerlaire told Jerrol about. The Ascendants have taken Jerrol there … I am sure of it."

"There is nothing there. I've been keeping an eye on it, and I think I may have been mistaken."

"I'm sure you're not! They've taken Jerrol there. I need to help him. Just transfer me, Leyandrii. We can argue about it later."

Leyandrii raised a golden eyebrow in surprise, but Niallarion held her gaze without flinching as he looked up at her. She slowly nodded. "As you wish."

Niallerion shimmered for a moment and was gone. Leyandrii observed the empty step. "I wonder how he expects to return?" she mused. "No matter, I suppose I'll have to keep an eye on him." Her gaze focused on Royerion, still standing in awe at the bottom of the stairs. "And you?"

Royerion raised his hands. "I'll use the waystone to return. I didn't think he'd make it here on his own. He was exhausted."

Leyandrii pursed her lips, her gaze distant. "So much sacrifice," she whispered, her expression sad. She sighed out her breath and smiled at Royerion as she descended the stairs. "I'm glad you came," she said as she bent to kiss his forehead. "Go with my blessing. Thank you, Royerion."

Elothia

Jerrol gasped for breath as he was hauled out of the ship's hold. The sack tied over his head was slowly suffocating him, and the sporadic punches and kicks had him shying away from every shadow. The men laughed at his timidity, but he couldn't help it.

The temperature had plummeted as the ship sailed. He knew by the long swells that they had moved into deeper waters and left the islands behind. They were taking him north and not to the quarries as the emperor had commanded. Jerrol wasn't sure if this was any better.

Shivering in the icy air, he knew he was in Elothia. Ice cold water bit his knees through his thin cutoffs as he was forced to the ground while they waited for their transport. He was trussed up like a stuffed fish ready to be roasted. How they expected him to escape was beyond him. He couldn't stop shivering, let alone formulate a plan of escape.

The swish of hooves and wheels through slushy ice preceded him being yanked to his feet and shoved forward. His hip barked against the side of the wagon, another deep ache to add to his growing collection. He was tossed into the back, his breath leaving him with a whosh at the force of his landing, and he dragged in frigid air desperately. Heavy canvas was thrown over him, and what little shadow he had been able to see was cut off as complete darkness engulfed him. At least the heavy material shielded him from the worst of the cold.

The cart set off on its jarring journey, and Jerrol slowly stiffened as a coating of frost covered his clothes. Twisting, he was unable to loosen the ropes; they just burnt his skin instead. When they arrived at their destination, he was frozen solid, unable to help himself.

His breath plumed in the air, the only sign he was alive,

as the men grabbed him by the arms and dragged him across the frozen terrain, scraping his skin raw and shredding his thin clothes. He had already lost his shoes, and his bound feet trailed behind him.

They dropped him in a heap on the stone floor and ripped the sack off his head. He blinked in the sudden light and breathed in the damp air. Something glittered in front of his blurry gaze, and it slowly came into focus as he began to thaw.

A pair of booted feet stopped in front of his face. "You will tell me where the relic is or I will kill you."

Jerrol huffed. "If you k-kill me, I can never t-tell you." His teeth were chattering so hard he could barely speak.

He was jerked to his knees as his head was yanked back. "I didn't say I would kill you straight away," Clary said, striking him across the chest with the baton he held. Heat flushed through Jerrol, quickly followed by a spiking pain that stabbed him repeatedly. His heart thudded as his fingers and toes ached as his blood reached them.

"I heard that you survived the tank and Crute," Clary said conversationally as he inspected Jerrol. "Do you think you will survive me? I am here to disabuse you of that notion." He struck with his baton again, and Jerrol's head whipped back as he collapsed to the floor, warm blood oozing down the side of his face.

Jerrol breathed, gathering his scattered wits. "Why do you hate Birlerion so much?" he asked. He had always wondered why Birlerion caused such a strong reaction in the Ascendants, and his numbed mind asked it before he had thought better of it.

"What?" Clary snapped.

"What was it that made you hate him so much?"

Clary came closer. "What did you say?" His voice was dangerously low.

"Have you not been able to better him?"

"Don't even mention his name. His days are numbered."

"He's just a kid, really," Jerrol mused. "Surely Birlerion is no threat to you?" Jerrol didn't see the stick coming, nor the blow that knocked him out.

Clary stood over him, cursing as he kicked him until one of his companions reined in his anger. "Sir, the array; we must finalise the testing." Clary finally walked away, leaving the bound and unconscious man to be dragged away.

Present Day. Maru 7th, 4128

Emperor Geraine stood waiting for King Benedict in his study. He was horrified at Pierien's behaviour; it was inexcusable. How could he have forgotten his responsibility, his heritage? He felt embarrassed by his ancestor's betrayal of the Lady. No wonder the kingdom had suffered so much. Had he deliberately repressed news of his disgrace? None of this was written in the history books.

Geraine stopped pacing as Benedict paused on the threshold of his study. He stiffened as he met Benedict's sympathetic eyes.

"Geraine," Benedict said as he entered the room. They were both dressed in formal attire, smart uniforms of navy and gold for the king and a silver-trimmed grey for the emperor.

Geraine simmered, trying to control his anger. "I can't believe he betrayed us."

"It wasn't his fault," Benedict said gently. "You know he regretted it immediately."

"Thousands of people died, homes and land lost, because of him."

"The Ascendants had the ability to control minds; he had no choice."

"He should have held to his belief in the Lady, not betrayed us all. I am amazed he managed to keep the throne after that."

"Geraine, you yourself experienced a taste of what they could do. You were fortunate that you have people to help you; he was on his own."

"He had the Fisherman."

"Who helped protect many people who would have otherwise died."

Geraine heaved a deep sigh and sat in a high-winged chair, indicating a similar one opposite him for the king. "I need to tell you something. You know the Oath was lost, don't you? Something else that Pierien failed to protect. The Ascendants destroyed the island home of the Tu'ani clan, the guardians of the Oath. They caused the great storms of 1124."

"How could it have been lost when I invoked it?"

Geraine shrugged. "You must have invoked an Oath with a shadow of its former power. The Tu'ani were lost before the Lady sundered the stone, never to be heard of again. Birtoli lost the protection of the Lady and the Oath in one go. That which they protected was lost with them to be found no more."

"Ah," the king said gently. "I believe you will have the honour of meeting them tonight."

"What?"

"The Tu'ani disappeared in 1124 because they were saved by Sentinals Jerrolion and Roberion. Roberion brought them here to the year 4128."

"He did what?" The emperor looked at him blankly.

"Don't ask me how, but the Guardians of the Oath now live on the island of Cherni off the coast of Senti. I sent Roberion to collect the Tu'ani Clan Elder."

"Senti," the emperor said thoughtfully. "That island has

become the strength of the Birtoli kingdom; they kept the trade routes open, brought in much needed supplies." He looked at the king in sudden wonder but clamped his lips shut on the unspoken thought. A smile slowly crept over his face. "Senti?" he whispered. The emperor stared at Benedict. "But what of the Fisherman? We sent him to the quarries."

"The last we know is that the Fisherman never arrived in the quarries. Birlerion has found no record of him ever arriving. He must have been taken by the Ascendants. The quarry was flooded and became the lake you now know as the Olini Lake."

The emperor nodded. "It was never explained how that happened, but from what I've read, it was a mercy. We owe so much to so many people that history has never mentioned." He looked at the king. "There will be many Elders here tonight from across the empire in honour of your visit." His mouth straightened. "I fear you know more about our history than they will."

"It is still unfolding, and the Oath is at the centre of it." Benedict rose, unable to sit still. "The Fisherman, Sentinal Jerrolion, is caught in a paradox of destruction, yet he has tried to build as many protections for your people as he can. Succeed or fail, we expect that he will be lost tonight as the Lady sunders the stone. Make no mistake, we will be affected. We are traveling at speed towards this event, and Geraine, you need to be careful. Tonight, time will meld. Watch out for the past. Don't make the same mistake twice, understand?"

Geraine flinched back under the king's persistent stare. And then he straightened and nodded firmly. "I will hold the Lady close."

"Melahney will need you, be there for her; it's important."

Geraine nodded. "I will. I promise."

The king nodded, satisfied. He had done what he could.

37

MARU 7TH, 1124

ADEERON, ELOTHIA

Niallerion shivered as he crept through the ice-coated tunnels towards the echoing voices. What were once roughly hewn stone walls were now smoothed with a coating of black ice, absorbing any light trickling in the entrance. He stumbled to a halt as the passageway abruptly finished and an enormous cavern opened before him. He tried to catch his breath, still heaving after his frantic journey and Leyandrii's assistance. His breath misted in the air, and he hurriedly backed away from the entrance. He should have asked for a cloak as well; it was freezing in Elothia.

When he had appeared on the frozen plain of Elothia, he had spun in shock, even though he had told Leyandrii to send him here. He had no doubt she would be having words with him about that. A blanket of snow covered the land, thick and still. The silver moon shone down, making the soft mounds of snow sparkle.

He had found the entrance into a small square building that sat in isolation in the middle of the plain by following the footprints. Lots of them leading into the building and none coming back out, as far as he could tell. There were also signs of someone being dragged, and Niallerion's mouth tightened.

Crouching in the shadows, he rummaged through his pockets and sorted the objects into rough piles. Stuff he had no use for and things that would go bang. He had collected a bag of small quartz stones. Smooth, round pebbles off the beach at Senti. Perfect, hard missiles.

Unravelling his sling, he wished it was Birlerion here and not him. Birlerion's aim was deadly, his not so much. But then, even he couldn't miss that array.

The shimmering crystal array laid out on the rocky floor was huge. A vibration hummed in the air, resonating through his bones. His breath hissed out as he saw Jerrol lying at the side of the array. Jerrol was still alive, if a little battered. His swollen eyes were fixated on the matt black crystal in the centre. It was the size of his fist. But how to reach it?

The array was vast, and he counted at least ten rings of sparkling clear stones. The light flickered off the crystals, reflecting the golden flames of the torches wedged in the walls. His heart sank. They would never be able to destroy them all.

Glancing around the cavern, he couldn't see any guards or Ascendants. The lodestone drew him forward, his eyes fixed on his objective, much as Jerrol's were. Niallerion launched his first stone into the centre of the array. There was a sharp crack, and he released another stone, and another, moving around the array as his stones hit with a loud crack, working his way towards Jerrol.

Jerrol shuddered as his communion with the crystals was shattered. Fissures ran along the clear columns, fracturing the pure alignment, one by one, severing his connection. The discord echoed in the Bloodstone in his veins. The outer crystals began to dim as the fissures spread.

Jerrol inhaled and stirred, groaning against the aches and stabs of pain from too many bruises to count. The Ascendants liked to use their fists and boots much too freely for his liking.

He wasn't sure how long he had been lying there, communing with the crystals, trying to convince them to rebel or something equally stupid. Clary had his men dump him on the floor so he could watch Clary's finest moment.

His breath exhaled in a rush as he saw Niallerion creep around the edge of the cavern towards him.

"Jerrol, I bought Guerlaire's sword," Niallerion whispered as he dropped beside him and sliced the ropes binding him. "Make a waystone so we can get out of here."

"A waystone," Jerrol thought. Why hadn't he thought of that? He must be more shaken up than he realised. He didn't need his sword for that, but he did need it to destroy the lodestone. As he rubbed his wrist, he concentrated for a moment, and then a soft chime resonated through him.

"Our way out," Niallerion whispered, helping him stand. "We go straight to the middle, you smash the settings, and we rush back here and leave."

It sounded so simple. Jerrol eyed the crystal array. It wouldn't be simple walking over all those faceted stones, but he gritted his teeth, and leaned on Niallerion, who half-carried, half-dragged Jerrol's frozen body across the crystals.

Niallerion wrapped his hands around Jerrol's as he tried to grip his sword. The sword vibrated, and a flush of warmth thawed his stiff fingers and loosened his muscles. Jerrol breathed more freely and tightened his grip.

"Now," Niallerion whispered, his cold fingers convulsing around Jerrol's, and they raised the sword.

"I admire your tenacity, but if you don't step out of the

array now, you will be dead," Clary said, his voice strident, his expression unyielding.

Niallerion didn't hesitate. He plunged their joined hands downwards, and the sword cleaved the silver wires, sparks erupting around them. Niallerion tugged the sword back out, ready to force it down again, but an arrow thumped into his shoulder. Niallerion jerked, releasing the sword, and Jerrol stabbed it down into the fine threads, collapsing to one knee as Niallerion staggered and parried away another arrow. He slowly rotated, his breathing ragged as he moved between Jerrol and the Ascendants, and Jerrol stabbed again and again, the crystals detonating as the sword cleaved them, shattering like blocks of ice. He tugged at the lodestone, but the fixings refused to release it.

Men picked their way through the crystals towards him, and he faltered as Niallerion slumped beside him.

"Get them out of the array," Clary shouted as he glared around him. "Check the damage. Replace the crystals, now!"

Jerrol gained his knees, glancing at the arrows trained on him and his shoulders dropped. He was disarmed as he watched Niallerion being carried out of the sparkling crystals and forced to his knees in front of Clary.

Clary's hand shot out and gripped the arrow protruding from Niallerion's right shoulder. "You dare," he spat, glaring at the ashen-faced Sentinal. His gaze speared Jerrol. "Out, now, without any further damage, or your friend suffers." Guards grabbed Jerrol's arms and forced him to follow as men swarmed around the array, hands full of crystal rods and silver wire.

Niallerion moaned, his face paling even further as blood spurted from the wound. Clary pulled Niallerion's head back, exposing his throat.

Distraction, Jerrol thought. He needed to draw attention away from Niallerion. "Why did you bring me all the way here?" Jerrol shouted. "You could have beaten me up just as easily in Birtoli."

Clary jutted his head forward and dragged Niallerion with him as he spun to face Jerrol. "I would kill you here and now, but you know where the relic is. Tell me now and I'll make his death swift and painless," Clary hissed.

"I've already told you, you destroyed it. The island of Geteril is no more," Jerrol replied.

Niallerion gasped for breath, his face glistening with sweat.

"But you saved them, didn't you? The Fisherman hero! Where are they?"

"Nowhere you can reach them," Jerrol said as he reached the edge of the crystals.

"You would be surprised how far I can reach," Clary replied. He twisted the arrow and Niallerion cried out, his face salty white, his lips tinged with grey, and his eyes rolling back into his head. Clary held him up by the arrow, only to kick him in the ribs as he wrenched the arrow out. Niallerion slumped as blood gushed over the stone floor.

Jerrol winced at the agony he knew Niallerion must be in; he was barely conscious. "Even if you could find the Tu'ani, they no longer have it."

"Who does? You?"

"The Land has it," Jerrol replied, desperately trying to think of a way to get back into the array.

"Don't be ridiculous, where did you put it?"

"I gave it to the Land."

"Where? You buried it? Where did you bury it?"

Impossibly, Niallerion tried to inch away, but Clary kicked him in the back, rolling him over with the force.

"You will tell me what I want to know or I will break him bone by bone," Clary threatened as he stomped on Niallerion's ankle.

Niallerion spasmed, and as he curled up, he stabbed at Clary's foot with a piece of broken crystal. Clary howled in pain and Niallerion twisted away, shoving the sharp fragment towards Jerrol.

Jerrol stopped it with his foot and ducked down to grab it before Clary had stopped howling. "Kill him," Clary screeched as he hobbled out of Niallerion's reach.

An Ascendant stumbled into the chamber, his face flushed with excitement. "It's Guerlaire, he's finally made a move; we've got him, come quick!"

Clary glared at the interruption, but he straightened and limped after him. "Power up as much of the array as you can," Clary snapped, his eyes darting over the damage, assessing. "Bring him," he said, nodding at Jerrol. "He'll enjoy watching us destroy Vespers once and for all. Kill the other one."

The guards closed in as Niallerion lurched to his knees. He launched himself towards the crystals again, but he went down as the guards tackled him. When the guards dispersed, Niallerion was a crumpled heap, blood-stained and broken. His slitted eyes gleamed, fixed and unseeing. Jerrol lurched forward, desperate to help him, but was yanked back by the guards. Niallerion twitched and relief flooded through Jerrol, making his knees tremble.

Clary raised his fist and bared his teeth. His voice was loud and confident. "Contact Car'onel and Mur'ata. Get them connected." Clary hissed as a man murmured something. "Then get Lor'enal instead," he snapped, his gaze flicking to Jerrol. "You will regret ever crossing my path," he threatened. "But first you'll see the death of your Lady. Her time is over, and it is time for the Ascendants to rise!"

The hum increased as the array came online. The air sharpened and Jerrol caught a breath of revitalizing energy; the surge of power caressed his skin and tugged him closer.

His damaged hand strayed to his belt, but his sword was gone. An image of the palace at Vespers filled the ceiling, storm clouds roiled overhead, debris flew through the air, and Guerlaire stood on the trembling palace steps, alone and vulnerable.

An image of Birlerion strapped into a chair in the middle of another crystal array filled the ceiling, and Clary laughed as Birlerion struggled. Jerrol shivered at the sound. He knew this was the array in Vespers that Birlerion would destroy in his final moments of anguish and fury, all of which were written plainly on his face.

"Yes! Well done!" Clary shouted, manic glee in his voice, and Jerrol saw the crazed hatred on his face as he watched Birlerion. "Let's start."

Not one ascendant asked what Guerlaire was doing or why, they just blindly seized the moment to strike, and Clary crowed in exhilaration as the arrays connected. The power surged up and away towards Vespers.

The image above them distorted as a blinding flash lit the room. The array whined as it absorbed the backlash, and Jerrol gaped as the damaged crystals fractured, sharp cracking explosions sounding all around him. Above him in the image on the ceiling, Ascendants rushed towards Birlerion in panic. Birlerion rose from the chair, his restraints falling away, raising his clenched fist. He opened his hand and another blinding flash whited out the view, and when it cleared, the Ascendants were sprawled on the floor amongst sparkling shards of crystal and Birlerion staggered out of the chamber, shirtless and bloodied. He was shouting, his body glowing, pulsing in a way Jerrol had seen once before, at Oprimere.

Jerrol realised his guard's attention was riveted on the image in the ceiling, his jaw dropped in horror. He shifted forward. They hadn't damaged the array enough. The only way to disrupt the array was to destroy the lodestone. Before the guard could react, Jerrol threw himself into the crystals, diving towards the centre, much as Niallerion had tried to do. His ropes parted and he reached for the black crystal, tugging it free from the final fixings and disrupting the connections.

He absorbed the sudden influx of power as the Bloodstone sang through his body, until finally, the crystals exploded. Thousands of needles pierced his skin, and he cried out in shock as the power reverberated back through the linked arrays.

Jerrol collapsed, his body consumed by the power, burning away all agony, pain, and compulsions. The Bloodstone and the Oath entwined within him rushed down his limbs, repairing the damage.

Clary's triumphant expression morphed to horror. Above him, the air around Guerlaire pulsed as the Lady joined him on the steps, elegant and poised. Her golden hair rising around her, she clapped her hands above her head. Then the air imploded, and the palace began to collapse around them, but in a *controlled* manner. Birlerion extended a shield of pulsing light, blocking the falling masonry as the walls shook apart. The ground opened, and the palace, the Lady, and Guerlaire disappeared, leaving Birlerion, arms spread wide being battered by the ferocious winds.

The image of Birlerion, swaying on the steps, oblivious to the storm, his expression a mixture of exhilaration and terror, seared Jerrol's mind. As he watched, Birlerion collapsed, swallowed by the heaving land, and the image faded. The Lady had used Birlerion to shield her people from the destruction. It explained why he had been so remote and self-contained when he had first awoken him, from this unbelievable terror to the unexpected quiet awakening of three thousand years in the future. Jerrol was amazed yet again, that he had adjusted as well as he had.

Jerrol was drawn into a maelstrom of chaos and debris. He sensed Guerlaire's wild jubilation as a giant boom reverberated across the ether. Ascendants were pulled passed him into the maelstrom, away into the distance and out of sight. Clary reached for him, howling in rage as he swirled up into the darkness.

Niallerion's body shimmered as he was dragged into the swirling air, drawn back to where he was supposed to be, Jerrol hoped, back where he should have been before Jerrol had borrowed him. He prayed to the Lady that he would be alright. No wonder he had been so weak when he'd found him under the desert of Terolia.

The noise of the swirling maelstrom deafened him. His body no longer felt connected, the pain a distant memory. He felt the Lady's kiss on his brow and saw the fine mist that would become the Veil slowly descend, glittering with the crystal and the Oath, drawing him in. His lips drew back in a travesty of a smile as everything went dark.

38

MARU 7TH, 1124

MOLINTI, BIRTOLI

The Molinti harbour master raised his head and frowned as his desk trembled. His papers slithered across the surface and he slapped his hand down on them to hold them in place. His desk stilled and he rose, hesitant.

Peering out the door across the still waters of the harbour, he saw nothing unusual and turned to inspect the buildings behind him, but all was still and quiet in the early morning air. A faint rumbling made him shiver. It was in the distance but growing louder.

An unexplained fear dogged his heels as he hurried up the incline, following the shallow stream into the market square. He would climb the temple tower, and from there he would be able to see clear across to the Terolian coast.

The soft scent of mint and rosemary drifted on the warm, dawn air, peaceful and soothing. It didn't soothe the harbour master. His guts were tight, his shoulders tense. Something wasn't right, but he didn't know what.

Reaching the top of the tower, he bent over his knees and tried to catch his breath. He was getting out of shape if climbing those few steps made him breathless. Straightening, he peered around the bell, burnished by the rising sun. A red glow on the horizon had him leaning over the barrier—the colour had nothing to do with the sunrise.

The Terolian coastline was ablaze. The sky was lit with shooting fires of gold and red. An orange glow consumed the night sky and he smelt ash and sulphur in the hot air. As he identified the aroma, flurries of ash swirled around him and he gasped. The fire mountains? Had something set them off? He had never seen them erupt, but he had heard stories. None of them good.

More molten fire flared into the air, rising so high he could barely follow its trail, and the temple trembled. Ash fell, coating the roofs of nearby houses. Grumbling voices rose from the streets below as the inhabitants ventured out, wondering what was going on. Children squealed as they tried to catch the flakes falling from the sky.

The harbour master hurried back down the stone steps. Stumbling in his haste, he scraped his palms against the rough stone as he righted himself. "Keep your children indoors!" he shouted as he ran down the street. "The fire mountains have erupted, stay inside!"

The inhabitants ignored him and rushed to the harbour walls, but there was little to see with the headland blocking the view. "Higher ground!" someone shouted, and, en masse the people turned away from the sea and made their way through the city and up to the headland.

Storm clouds built, black and heavy on the horizon, and crept over the turquoise seas, turning the waters grey and angry. Swells deepened as the winds strengthened, and the city folk huddled together. Over the roar of the winds and crashing waves, a keening whine grew louder and louder. The harbour waters grew ruffled as the wind rose, and just as suddenly it dropped and the water stilled.

"Look!" a man shouted. "Where's the water going?"

The harbour drained as if someone had pulled a plug, leaving boats canted over on their side and revealing their barnacle-encrusted hulls.

"Looks like you'll be scraping hulls today," another man joked as they watched the sea recede.

"Get higher!" the harbour master screamed as he ran through the streets. "Move inland, away from the sea! Tell everyone, get to higher ground. When the water comes back it will drown us all! Move higher! Get as high as you can!" The harbour master ran back to the temple and began pulling on the bell, which peeled out over the city in warning. He prayed to the Lady that the people had listened to him as he continued ringing the bell.

All along the coastline, foaming waves consumed the gently curving beaches, dragging away the sand, scouring the rocks. Roiling water swept through open harbours, and the water level rose, tearing away jetties and crashing against the harbour walls. The winds tore through the streets, stripping trees of their leaves and tugging shutters off windows. The clatter of anything loose was drowned out by the winds; chairs, benches, and awnings bounced off the walls and snagged on corners of buildings.

People ran for shelter, pelted by drops of rain that bruised like stones and rattled off the slate tiles.

A lull in the winds, a sudden silence, and the townsfolk breathed a sigh of relief and looked at each other until a growing rumble made the ground tremble and people ran past shrieking, their voices lost as a roar of water swept through buildings as if they were made of paper, collapsing walls, and lifting roofs, leaving only a swirl of muddied water in its path.

In Plini, there was no chance of escape. The narrow entrance forced the water up the gentle valley in an unstoppable tidal wave, washing all before it. Boats tumbled over and over until they smashed against the walls, and still the water rose.

Villagers fled up the valley but the water was faster, swirling round their legs and dragging them under, rushing higher, eager to consume all before it. Cries of fear and terror echoed off the valley walls, and still the water rose. The stone arch collapsed, along with the cliff face, into a boiling cauldron of fury and foam, and the water continued to rise.

Throughout Birtoli, the storm raged and the water rose, scouring all before it. Pillaging, drowning; it was an unstoppable force until it collided with the golden walls of Senti. The walls curved the tidal surge away from the land and back out to sea, where it clashed with the storm and returned to be forced away again. The wind roared, forcing its way through the walls and whipping the water into a frenzy, but although the water rose, it didn't breach the beach.

Elsewhere, the land drowned. Torrents of water carved a new coastline, and the few people who reached higher ground clutched each other in terror as the swirling waters surrounded them. The once calm, turquoise waters were littered with debris; palm fronds, tree trunks, mats of vegetation, and bobbing bodies, people and animals alike, limp and still amongst the devastation.

39

PRESENT DAY

MARU 7TH 4128, MOLINTI

The morning after Geraine's state dinner, Melahney went into labour. Benedict and Geraine waited in the emperor's study, discussing the previous evening.

Geraine still hadn't gotten over the Tu'ani, thrilled to reinstate the long-lost clan. He had spent most of the evening talking with the Elder, learning about the Oath he had believed lost. He had shared with Benedict that the Tu'ani Elder had passed the Oath to Jerrol and he believed Jerrol had given it to the Land. The Elder said it emanated out of the islands of Birtoli, sheltering them under its gentle protection.

The Elder wouldn't say more, but Geraine had been adamant that it was in Senti, and Benedict didn't disagree. Jerrol had built the harbour at Senti; he was quite sure at its foundation was the Oath.

Benedict was still amazed by the news about Roberion and Lilith. How Roberion had managed to meet such a lovely woman and get joined in the middle of a storm and across time he had no idea, but he clearly had. Roberion and Lilith had been inseparable, and the king foresaw the loss of his Sentinal to Birtoli. He had seen the covetous gleam in Geraine's eyes. Roberion had since left to take the Tu'ani Elder and his new wife back to Cherni.

They were interrupted when Birlerion rushed into the room. Benedict was relieved that Birlerion had stayed in Molinti and not gone rushing off to try and save Jerrol once again. He felt guilty at the thought, but Birlerion had been resigned; he knew he wouldn't reach Jerrol in time, even if he knew where he was going.

"Trouble," Birlerion said briefly before hustling the king and the emperor up the stairs to the upper chamber. He had left just as quickly and now Benedict stood guard over his daughter's bed chamber, where she was about to give birth. Benedict scowled. He would be having words with Birlerion after this day was over. He didn't like not being informed about what was going on.

The wind howled around the tower, rattling the windows. Benedict flicked a glance at the building storm, menacing overhead, the once blue sky engulfed in black boiling clouds. Hail suddenly battered against the glass, making him flinch, the constant rattle against the window a counterpoint to the howling wind, both trying to find a way in.

Marianille suddenly stuck her head out of the inner chamber door, and the king stared at her in surprise. "What are you doing here? You should be in Vespers."

Marianille focused on the emperor. "The Lady sent Niallerion and I back with the Captain. He sent me to guard the empress." She shrugged gracefully, the effect of her elegant green dress ruined by the thick sword belt draped across her chest, the hilt of her broadsword peeping over her head. "So here I am."

"Jerrol? Niallerion? Are they alright?" Benedict asked.

"It might be better if you wait within with the empress; she could use your support," she said to the emperor, ignoring the king. "The empress is not well. I am worried for her, and I've sent for a healer. Her ladies wouldn't listen to me."

Geraine gasped. "What is wrong? She was doing fine."

"Those fool women allowed those Ascendants near her. She has been enspelled, I think. That is what is driving the craving. I can't get her to relax. She is not doing herself nor the babe any good."

Geraine hurried into his wife's bedchamber as the noise in the hallway increased, and fear coursed through Benedict. He knew that his Sentinals must be engaged against these strange attackers. "Marianille, do you have any idea who is attacking us? There were no signs of unrest from the clans."

Geraine paused at the door and shook his head. "This is not the clans."

Benedict couldn't help glancing towards the rising commotion outside the door and when he looked back, Marianille had gone. He hurried across the inner chamber and peered through the connecting door. The room was dim and the curtains were drawn around the bed. His daughter groaned in pain. "Taelia? Is Melahney alright? Marianille was saying she is unwell. Has she seen a healer yet?"

Taelia came to the door. "Melahney is fine; she's nearing her time is all. It won't be much longer; the baby is nearly here."

"Marianille said she was getting distressed over a craving or something."

"Marianille? She's not been here."

"I just spoke to her," the king said.

"Melahney hasn't had a craving," Taelia reminded him, distracted by a call from within, which drew her away.

The king shut the door as the outer door flew open under the weight of a falling man, followed by another black clad form with an arrow protruding from his chest. The king watched Fonorion forcing another man back before Birlerion blocked his view by standing in the doorway, whipping arrows over his shoulder and firing in quick succession. Birlerion glanced over his shoulder, his glittering silver eyes connecting with the king's before he focused back on the outer room. The king retreated as Marianille came to stand in front of him, and Birlerion discarded his bow, drew his sword, and charged out the door.

It was definitely Marianille; she *was* wearing a green dress. Benedict hadn't imagined her, though she was flickering slightly as he watched. He rubbed his eyes as she smoothly stepped toward a tall black-robed man who also flickered and seemed blurry around the edges, as if he wasn't quite there. Benedict rubbed his eyes again as he watched her disarm the man with ease and then ran her blade back across his throat. The sword fell from the man's hand as he collapsed to the floor. She kicked the sword across the room and parried the next strike and the next, forcing her opponents back into the hallway.

Benedict frowned as she suddenly appeared out of the inner chamber carrying a bundle, her face distraught. His head snapped to the empty doorway and back to Marianille in confusion. "We couldn't save her, she lost too much blood, but she had a son. He's healthy. We'll need to find a wet-nurse to sustain him." Marianille held up the bundle, her eyes bright with emotion.

Benedict stared at her in shock, the blood draining from his face. Behind him, Fonorion hissed in pain and his hand tensed on his sword. Birlerion shouted, his voice taut with fear, and a body hit the wall. Benedict flinched and hesitantly peered out the door. The sight of his Sentinals being overwhelmed made his blood run cold. When he looked back Marianille had gone. Fonorion was down, weakly parrying an attack, his left arm hanging limply at his side. Birlerion was struggling with two opponents further down the hall, and Benedict couldn't see Marianille.

The king moved quickly, and as Fonorion's opponent raised his blade for the final blow, the king thrust his sword in to block the strike and clumsily twisted the blade away from Fonorion. Fortunately for the king, the man's sword ended up embedded deep in the wood panelled wall from the sheer force of the intended blow, giving him time to stand over Fonorion protectively as the man tried to tug it back out. By then Marianille was between them, and the king stooped to grab Fonorion under his arms and drag him out of the way. He grunted at the weight of the tall Sentinal but dragged him into the outer chamber. Geraine rushed out of Mehlahney's chamber to help him, and between them they tugged Fonorion into the room.

"Taelia, quick, we need pads, bandages, now!" the king called urgently. The king looked down at Fonorion and grabbed a tablecloth to wad as a pad. Fonorion protested but the king overrode him. "I'm not losing any Sentinals today," he said firmly, glaring at Geraine. "I'm so sorry about Melahney," he said, his voice tight with emotion.

"What? Oh, don't worry they keep saying that I'll get in the way. I'll see her after all this is over," Geraine replied.

Taelia came back out of the connecting room, her face triumphant. "A boy!" she grinned, handing the emperor a bundle. "Come and see your wife." Her smile faded as she caught sight of Fonorion lying in a pool of blood on the floor.

She rushed back into the empress' chamber and came out with handfuls of towels and wadding. She knelt beside Fonorion and wrenched open his tunic and the shirt beneath it. Pressing a pad down hard on the ugly wound on his shoulder, she said, "Hold it there," as she searched further down his body. Fonorion groaned, his lashes fluttering on his pale cheeks as the king pressed down hard.

"Melahney is alright?" Benedict asked, bewildered.

Taelia wadded up another towel and looked up at the king, her face pale. "She's fine, as is your grandson. We need a healer. This needs stitching; he's losing too much blood."

"I doubt any healers will venture through all that fighting." The king jerked his head to the noise outside the chamber, still coming to terms with his daughter being alive. He struggled to hold his tears back, unsure whether to grieve or celebrate.

"Hold this one as well; keep the pressure on. I'll be back." Taelia placed the king's hand over a pad against Fonorion's side. Crimson blood immediately started leaking through the white cotton.

Taelia returned with Hannah, who had a cloth sewing kit in her hands.

"We left the emperor with Melahney and the children; he's getting a crash course in parenting. Melahney, bless her, has Leyarille and Mikke on her bed with her." Taelia grinned. "We need to stitch him up until a healer can sort him out. He can't go on losing this much blood. Hannah here will do it."

"Melahney? She's alright?" King Benedict stared at her in confusion.

"I told you, both are fine."

Benedict handed Fonorion into their capable hands with relief. Standing, he went into the empress' room and looked down at his weary daughter and his new grandson in her arms. He gripped the hand that she raised towards him. "Well done," he said gently, smiling at Mikke. "Another baby," he said to the little boy.

Mikke grinned. "A brovver," he said gleefully.

The king laughed. "Indeed, a brother in arms," he

agreed, jerking as a thud hit the outer door. "Stay here with Auntie Mel."

Her hand convulsed under his. "Save my baby," she pleaded desperately. "Leave me, but protect my child."

The king's face stiffened. "Don't be silly, you are quite safe in here," he promised as he kissed her damp forehead. He looked across at the grave face of the emperor and nodded. He was burdened with Leyarille in his arms. Benedict drew the curtain around her bed and left them with the emperor. Closing the door behind him, he faced the hallway and waited. He wasn't sure who was attacking them or why, but they would not reach his daughter or his grandson.

Birlerion braced himself against the palace wall for a moment, frowning at the seemingly never-ending flow of black-robed attackers; where were they all coming from? His opponents flickered, wavering in his view, but they were solid enough when his sword met theirs. Fear flooded through him. Could these be the Ascendants from the past, trying to usurp Pierien? It was the only reason he could think of for Ascendants to still be present in the future when Leyandrii had banished them all, twice!

And where had Marianille come from? He wasn't sure if she had come from Vespers to help. She was wearing a green dress, so was this the Marianille he'd left with Jerrol in the past? Either way, he was relieved to see her and would gladly leave the king in her care.

He parried a strike and flinched as the sword screeched up and scraped his knuckles. He changed hands, shaking the blood off his stinging hand before pushing his opponent back and out into the hall. He heard the clash of swords behind him as Marianille engaged. Exhaling with relief, he observed the King's Guard storm up the stairs.

Birlerion pushed himself off the wall, leaving a smear of blood as he raised his sword again. Parrying another strike, he froze as the Lady claimed him. She pulled his strength away and he staggered, his sword falling from his hand. He flung his hand up and a blue sparkle flickered over his skin. Marianille cried out in horror as Birlerion's opponent thrust his sword into him, but the sword was deflected away, and the man stumbled at the unexpected change in direction.

Birlerion swayed, his eyes distant. "My Lady," he gasped as a huge rumbling boom resonated throughout the palace, blasting the glass out of the windows and allowing the wind to tear through the corridors. The sound of shattering glass was overwhelmed by the shrieking winds.

The winds tore through the palace, sucking up furniture, decorations, and the Ascendants as it passed, swirling them away, up, and out of the windows. It swirled around the Sentinals, searching and questing. The wind suddenly died around Birlerion and he tried to take a steadying breath as his strength failed and he collapsed to the floor, his face grey and drawn.

Marianille stared at him in horror as silence descended. She rushed towards him, her mouth opening to say something, but she was pulled away and her words were turned into a shriek as she was dragged into the maelstrom of wind, Sentinals, and debris. Her sword clattered to the floor and she disappeared.

Birlerion braced himself on the floor, staring in shock at the place where she had been standing. Struggling to his feet, he staggered back into the ante-chamber, leaning heavily against the doorframe. His legs trembled as waves of exhaustion roiled through him.

The king stood in the middle of the ante chamber. He snapped his jaw shut as he saw Birlerion and pointed at him. "Marianille," he said, "she just disappeared, along with our attackers. Do you know who they were?" He inspected the bloody appearance of his normally pristine Sentinal in growing horror and hurried towards him. "Birlerion? You look like you need to sit," he said to the ashen Sentinal.

"Not now," Birlerion whispered. He cleared his throat and tried again. "We're all you've got." Birlerion took a shallow breath, and winced as the king gripped his arm.

Taelia came out of the inner chamber in time to see him wince. "Birlerion, are you alright?" she asked in concern.

He swayed as he nodded. His voice came out as a whisper. "You should all stay here with the empress whilst I secure the palace."

Taelia strode across the room. "Let me see where you're hurt," she said, forcing him into a chair. He slid to the floor in her horrified arms.

"My sentinal will fix it," he said as his eyes glazed over.

"Which would be fine if he was here," Taelia said with a touch of asperity as she tugged at his jacket. She glared at him as he gingerly shrugged out of it, revealing his blood-stained shirt. She scowled at the king. "Your Majesty. Tell him to be sensible, there's no point in him passing out."

"We have to secure the palace," Birlerion protested, raising a shaking hand to stop her unbuttoning his shirt. "We can't trust the palace guards. Those were Ascendants from the past. Did you see how they flickered? They seemed to be crossing over time like I have been, only they came here. There may still be some in the palace."

The king glared at Birlerion. "Listen to her; you can secure it later. If the Lady just sundered the stone in the past, then there won't be any Ascendants left here."

Birlerion sighed. "I suppose not," he said, his face going distant for a moment. "The Captain's last stand," he said, his eyes glistening with molten silver. He drew his breath in sharp, his attention focussing as Taelia prodded.

"I can't see where you were hurt; all the cuts are superficial." She leaned back on her heels and looked at him, her eyes narrowing as she took in his greying face. "Birlerion? What happened to you? Your exhaustion is not a result of a fight."

"The Lady sundered the stone," Birlerion whispered. "I helped her." He shuddered and closed his eyes.

"What's the matter with him?" Benedict asked, hovering over them in concern.

Tapping her lip, Taelia observed the Sentinal. A flicker of blue sparkles danced across his slack face. She suddenly leaned forward and shook his shoulder. "Birlerion? Wake up!"

Birlerion didn't respond.

Taelia grabbed his wrist, searching for a pulse and breathed out a sigh of relief as she found one. "He's still alive, just unconscious. Let's make him comfortable, and keep him warm. Maybe the healers will know what's wrong with him."

Geraine came out of the empress' chamber and stared at them. "The Fisherman." His voice trailed into silence.

"We will not lose him either," Benedict said firmly. "Give him time."

"But …"

"Give him time," Benedict interrupted. "What we need now is a healer, urgently."

Geraine looked at the injured men in front of him and nodded. He turned away and began to issue instructions to the palace guards peering through the door.

40

MARU 8TH, 1124

SENTI

Myriam wrapped an arm around Gael's shoulders as they watched the waters recede below the level of the quay. It had been close. If Jerven hadn't told them to use extra long mooring lines, the boats would have sunk. Instead, they had bobbed securely on the surface.

The storm clouds roiled overhead, whipping across the sky in the strong winds, but within the harbour walls, all was calm and still.

Marin glanced at his boat and back to Gael. "Do you want to come with me? We need to go and help survivors. There will be many people stranded." He looked at his wife. "Get the blankets ready and put something hot on. People will be cold and distressed. Dion can stay and help you."

"I want to wait for Jer-Jerven," Gael said, watching the roiling waters.

"He said not to," Marin reminded him gently.

"Someone has to wait for him; it's not fair," Gael replied, the tears leaking down his cheeks.

"I'll wait," Myriam offered. "You'll feel better if you keep busy, and there are people who need our help now. But

Marin, please be careful," she said to her husband as she watched Gael and her breath caught at the despair in his face. She gathered him in her arms and rocked him gently as he cried.

She looked at her husband's bleak face. He blinked rapidly as he gazed back out over the new harbour. The golden sandy beach had gone, the waters reaching for the scrubby bushes at the top of the rise, all that was left of the rolling dunes. The walls glittered in the sunlight, now only a few feet above the water level and no longer towering over them. They had withstood the onslaught. All who were within had survived. Now they needed to go help those that were still struggling to.

Marin gripped Gael's shoulder. "Come," he said, leading the boy around to the *Mari Rose*. They hauled in the mooring rope and set the sail. Marin worked the steering oar to get them out into the harbour and through the walls. Gael's face firmed with determination as he watched the *Island Scout* bob gently in the swells that they created as they passed. Marin had brought her home from Molinti and moored her in the harbour. He went to help Marin with the sails.

In the maelstrom of wind and chaos, Jerrol had felt Leyandrii's caress and her blessing as she tried to send him home, amongst all the other responsibilities she was trying to honour. He knew his sentinal had tugged him back, snagging him out of the air though he was sure the Lady had tried to fling him back to Vespers.

He wearily sat up, trying to feel happy that he was still alive, that he had succeeded in destroying the crystals, but all he could think of was Guerlaire, Birlerion and Niallerion. The impression of Guerlaire's wild jubilation in the face of overwhelming odds, of Guerlaire's last words to him;

of Birlerion falling, of Niallerion's determination to destroy the crystal array, what a sacrifice indeed, and few people were aware of what they had achieved. Nor the part Birlerion had played. He had always played it down as if he couldn't remember what had happened, all except the fact that the Lady had called him, and he could not help but respond.

The sentinal hummed in concern, and Jerrol stood easing his back. He ached all over. His eyes were sore, and his skin felt sensitised with the glissade of power within him. The touch of his clothes against his skin felt coarse and rough. He shuddered at the thought of the power he now contained, and he seriously hoped he wasn't glowing.

The hum from the Oath in the harbour resonated through him, yet if he thought for a moment, he could see the king's throne room and Parsillion on duty bathed in the pulsing blue light still emanating from the words engraved on the wall. His heart leapt as he looked further, and he saw the king standing in front of the emperor, a sword in his hand. He frowned in concern? A sword in his hand?

He searched further and saw Taelia and Hannah tending a grey-faced Birlerion; it looked like they had already strapped up Fonorion, though he was laying on the floor, far too pale and still. He sent a blessing to Taelia across the ether and she stiffened in surprise. He checked the palace and breathed a sigh of relief as he saw the King's Guards on duty and not an Ascendant in sight.

He thanked his sentinal as he felt an invigorating shot of energy flush through his body and focused on the interior of his sentinal. He was in the Senti sentinal, and it looked exactly as he had left it. His heart dropped. He must be back in old Senti. Why had his sentinal dragged him back here? And then he remembered the harbour and his oath to help protect the island people. Birtoli would be drowned. How many people would lose their lives because the Lady had sundered the stone?

Shimmering out of the sentinal, he looked down at the harbour and smiled. It had worked; not that he had doubted Niallerion's ingenuity or Marguerite's promises, but to see it as he had envisioned, the *Island Scout* bobbing safely at her mooring, along with a few other boats, was a relief. The *Moonlight Kiss, Mikke's Ride,* and the *Mari Rose* were all missing; out searching for survivors, he was sure. He could find them if he searched, but time was of the essence. The water was about three feet below the harbour offices, the steps Marguerite had created running down into the water. The water would settle lower over time.

He watched Marin and Gael arrive with a boat load of washed out survivors. Myriam rushed forward to help wrap them in blankets and steer them to the waiting huts they had prepared. The men had outdone themselves. A veritable wooden village had sprung up behind the harbour; the precursor to the town of the future. Gael jumped back down into the boat, and they sculled back out of the harbour.

Jerrol's gaze drifted to the *Island Scout,* and he found himself walking down the headland and through the crowd of exhausted survivors on the quay. He wondered who had moved it here. He was sure he had left the *Scout* in Molinti. Throwing a few of the blankets into the boat, he detached the mooring rope and jumped down onto the deck. Leaning on the sculling oar, he was out across the calm bay and passed the first wall before anyone noticed the *Scout* had gone.

As he left the harbour, the full force of the wind hit him. He battled the rough seas, trimmed his sail, and, leaning on the Oath humming through his veins, he sent a soothing thought out across the sea. The wind eased, calming the waves. He headed west across what used to be the Birtoli mainland, praying that he wouldn't run aground on unseen rocks or reefs. He tested his reach, and his thoughts sank below the clear waters; the land was still settling down below.

He headed to what used to be the coastal town of Amri, but there was nothing left. He continued west towards the island of Amrilti, his face tight. He hauled in his sails as he encountered debris, palm fronds, and branches, planks of wood and barrels bobbing by. He scrambled to the side as he spotted a man in the water, hanging on to what looked like the remains of a skiff. He leaned over precariously and hauled him in. The man shivered uncontrollably, and Jerrol wrapped him in a blanket. He stared at Jerrol glassily. "Th-the waves," he stuttered, "they were so high, they engulfed everything. Everyone."

"We'll try and find more people," Jerrol promised, steering through the wreckage. He spotted someone else clinging onto what looked like the remains of a reed roof, the reeds acting like a matted raft. He leaned over and pulled in an exhausted woman, who was barely conscious, though her hands gripped a bundle tight, keeping it balanced on the raft. Jerrol lifted the bundle in and a tiny baby stared up at him with wide black eyes. He thanked the Lady and placed the baby in the mother's arms. She convulsed round the bundle, jerking upright. Shudders wracked her body and she began to rock. "Oh, th-thank you! I didn't think there would be anyone left to c-come."

"There are other boats out searching," Jerrol reassured her, wrapping her in a blanket. He heard a weak shout and turned back to the side of the boat. He lent over and pulled in yet another survivor, a young boy who grabbed his hands. And so it went on until the *Island Scout* was running deep in the water and Jerrol headed towards Molinti.

He gaped at the flooded harbour, as did his weary passengers. Wrecked boats lay littered high above the harbour walls, one even lodged in the market square. A testament to the strength of the waves. The waters were receding back towards the walls, but still lapped at the incline that led up to the palace. The market place had been washed bare, a skiff smashed into pieces washed back and forth in the waves, along with a few chairs. Jerrol steered towards a group of men who stood waving at him. He recognised the garb of the local administrators and he offloaded his grateful passengers.

"We have help, come with us." A grey haired administrator reached for the young woman and her child. "Come, we have a place to shelter; a healer if you need one. Let's get you inside," he murmured, gently leading the traumatised woman up the incline.

Another man looked at Jerrol keenly. "Captain, do you need a healer? You look like you've been injured as well."

"Me?" Jerrol exclaimed in surprise. He felt numb, exhausted even, but he hadn't considered the injuries he had received at the hands of the Ascendants, and the exploding crystals. He had just assumed his sentinal had healed him when he awoke. He rubbed his hand over his face and came away with blood. Maybe his sentinal hadn't had time to do more than treat the more serious injuries. "I'm fine," Jerrol said as his face began to sting. "There are others in need of help more than me."

Jerrol cast off before the man could say any more, and he threaded his way back through the channel and out towards the area where the coastal village of Dona had been. He had seen people struggling to stay afloat on various bits of debris, he just hadn't had the room to bring them on board. He stared out across the open, calmer water. The wind had dropped to a gentle breeze that propelled the *Scout* over the surface. There was no evidence Plini had ever existed. The stone archway, the headlands, the gentle valley had all been swept away. A sense of loss and grief overwhelmed him. He was sailing where land had been, where his family and friends had lived. For it to be subsumed beneath the water so quickly and with no warning was frightening. The *Scout* sailed on, the sun beating down out of a clear blue sky, and he soon became consumed with other people's needs.

Marin and Gael returned from their second trip with survivors. They had found many desperate people off the coast of Eyti. There were just a few small islands peeking above the water. The whole coastline had disappeared. Marin was still horrified that Jerven had been right and yet no one had listened to him. Even he had only nodded and smiled to keep him happy; he hadn't really believed him. The job at Senti had been the reason he'd moved, not the threat of flooding. He was followed into the harbour by *Mikke's Ride* and a small flotilla of other boats. At least the Eyti boat builders had cast off with their families when they saw the storm brewing. At least they had heard Jerven's warning and taken heed.

There was chaos on the quay with so many survivors disembarking at once. Myriam was overwhelmed, trying to make sense of everything. "Those who need a healer, please say now. We have shelter for all in the village. Please follow Mathias here, who will show you where there is food and dry clothes if you need them."

"Myriam, where's the *Scout*?" Gael asked, staring at the empty mooring in growing hope.

"What?" Myriam asked, distracted by the demands of the people around her.

"The *Scout*, it's gone. Who took it?" Gael demanded.

"It's still moored where you left it," Myriam said, turning

back to the harbour. "Oh," she said as she saw the empty mooring.

Gael rushed up the quay, repeating his question frantically.

"It was the Captain. He came out of that tree up there," one of the stonemason's who had been helping with the survivors said from behind Myriam. "He grabbed some blankets and he jumped in and cast off. He went off on his own."

"Captain Jerven?" Marin repeated.

"Yeah, the captain. He took the *Scout*."

Gael sobbed in relief. "He's alright!"

Marin cautioned him softly. "Remember what he said; he wasn't sure he would be able to return. The Lady had other expectations of him. Wait until you see him yourself. There is still much that could befall him."

"Jerven was here before; there is no reason why he can't be here after as well," Gael said stubbornly.

Marin watched him with concern. Jerven had been clear he didn't expect to survive. He had left his final requests with Marin and Myriam, along with their agreement to provide Gael a home. "Come on, we need to get back out there; there are many people relying on us."

Gael nodded eagerly and Marin sighed. It was obvious he expected to see the *Scout* out on the sea, but the sea was a large place and it had just got a lot larger. They readied the *Mari Rose* and cast off, sculling their way out between the walls, closely followed by *Mikke's Ride*, manned by some of the Eyti boat men. They headed back towards Eyti. Marin steered for what was now the southern island of Serrol, roughly mapping the changed coastline as they went; a more accurate map would have to wait.

Present Day. Maru 8th, 4128, Molinti

Roberion reached Molinti later that morning having conveyed Elder Tu'an back to his new home on the island of Cherni. Leaving his men to tie the *Miracle* up at the quay, he rushed off to the palace. He had managed to borrow a horse from the Administrators office by the harbour and rode up the road to the glistening building at the top of the headland.

He was appalled at the amount of damage the palace had suffered. Groundsmen were sweeping up glass; it looked like every window in the building had been shattered. The King's Guard were placed around the perimeter and checking anyone entering. They allowed Roberion through without issue, the Sentinals obvious by their appearance. When he entered the palace, worrying trails of blood covered the floor; the result of bodies being dragged away. He hurried up the stairs to the king's chambers, his concern mounting.

He was relieved when Darris opened the doors and he saw King Benedict seated at his table as usual. The king looked tired and strained but appeared to be uninjured. He frowned as he looked around the room. Neither Fonorion nor Birlerion were present.

"Your Majesty, is all well?" he asked hesitantly.

"If you mean 'is everyone we brought with us still alive' then, as far as I know, the answer is yes. We are waiting for Ari to return with news of Marianille and we are still unsure where Jerrol is."

"Marianille was here?"

"Sort of," the king grimaced. "It appears Jerrol sent her to help us and she overlapped into the present day." The king held up his hands. "Don't ask me how, because I don't know, but if it hadn't been for her help, we would all have died." His face pinched.

"What happened, Your Majesty?"

"It's not quite clear at the moment. It seems that there was a-a meshing of time. Some of the events of the past seem to have overlapped here in the present. Jerrol warned that we would get the backlash; it seems he was right."

"Where is Fonorion? And Birlerion?"

"In the healerie. They were both injured, but they will recover. My guards are on duty in the palace."

"But who is guarding you, sire?"

The king grimaced wryly. "Against what? According to Taelia, all Ascendants were banished when the Lady sundered the stone. Which is fortunate because the emperor is floating on air; he has a new son and he couldn't be happier."

"Ah, congratulations, Your Majesty."

King Benedict smiled, his face softening. "Yes, a grandson. He arrived in the middle of the battle; he couldn't have timed it better."

"And the Captain?"

"No word. According to legend, he returns to Molinti twice with survivors. He doesn't come back a third time. He is engulfed in a storm."

"Do you think we should return to Vespiri, now then? He'll return to the Oath, won't he?" Roberion suggested.

"I don't know," the king admitted. "I need to formally acknowledge my grandson at a ceremony, which is supposed to be in two day's time, if they can straighten up the palace in time; then we can go home. Hopefully by then we will have received some sort of word."

Roberion nodded. "Very well, sire. The *Lady's Miracle* will be ready whenever you need her. In the meantime, I will go check on Birlerion and Fonorion." Roberion left to visit the healerie. Searching the beds lined up along the walls, he stopped at the foot of Birlerion's bed. "Birlerion," he said, his voice hushed. Keeping his face neutral, he observed his friend.

Birlerion's face was gaunt, his eyes glittery. His hand trembled as he clasped Roberion's arm. Looking up at him, with over bright eyes, Birlerion asked, "What news?"

"None yet."

"I bet he's sailing around, collecting survivors. Visiting new harbours that used to be fifty leagues inland." Birlerion's tired laugh had an edge of hysteria to it.

"Can I get you anything?" Roberion asked, watching him in concern, not sure if he was serious or delirious.

Birlerion's face fell, the strain in his face standing out in stark relief. "I need my sentinal," he murmured, suddenly exhausted, just the effort of talking had depleted what little strength he had.

"Rest. We'll take you home as soon as the king is ready to leave," Roberion promised.

"Good." Birlerion sighed, and closing his eyes, his face relaxed as he dozed off.

Roberion moved deeper into the healerie. "I'm looking for Sentinal Fonorion," he said to one of the healerie assistants. The assistant gravely pointed to a room off to the left.

The small room was dimly lit, the window shaded. A single bed stood in the middle. The man lying in the bed was motionless, his shoulder and chest heavily bandaged. A tube was strapped into his arm, a bag of dark red blood slowly dripping down the tube. As Roberion approached he realised Taelia was sitting in a chair beside Fonorion, gently stroking his hand.

"How is he?" he asked, shocked at the sight of the normally vigorous man.

"Weak. He lost too much blood. They've got him stabilised, but he's not regained consciousness."

"The king didn't say he was this bad," Roberion said, aghast.

Taelia shrugged wearily. "We haven't told him yet; we thought he'd bounce back. I wondered whether we ought to ask the Senti sentinal to take him in? I think it's too far to take him back to Vespers."

"I'll go ask him. Birlerion should go as well. He is feverish and talking nonsense. He needs a sentinal as well. I'm sure the Captain wouldn't object."

Taelia nodded. "I know he wouldn't. You are all like family to him."

Roberion walked around the bed, lay a hand on her shoulder and gripped it gently. "He will come back. He made you a promise."

"I know," Taelia said, tears glistening in her eyes.

After returning to advise the king about the true condition of his Sentinals, Roberion left the shocked king hurrying to the healerie, and armed with the king's agreement, he set off to go and speak to the Senti sentinal.

Present Day. Old Vespers, Vepiri

Marianille woke up in her sentinal and breathed a cautious breath. She took another breath and sat up. She checked her body, expecting to see blood everywhere, but she was fine, whole, no blood in sight. Hearing her sentinal's concerned hum, she laughed with relief. She was fine; she was home in Old Vespers and then she remembered helping Empress Olini and Jerrol.

Niallerion! He had gone to help Jerrol! What had happened to him? She rushed out of her sentinal and placed her hands on Niallerion's. "Niall?" she called, fear coursing through her body.

After an excruciating moment, Niallerion shimmered out

of his sentinal, looking disoriented but whole. She reached for him and hugged him tightly. "I thought," she breathed, tears springing in her eyes. "I thought I'd lost you," she finished breathlessly. He smiled down at her and, watching her carefully, he kissed her on the lips.

"You have terrible timing," he said and kissed her again.

Marianille leaned into him. "You'll have to help me improve," she said as she kissed him back.

He wrapped his arms around her and smiled into her glinting silver eyes. "I look forward to it."

41

MARU 8TH, 1124
AGUINTI, BIRTOLI

J errol sailed into the new bay at Nikri on the new island of Aguinti and carefully drifted up to a gap in the wall, which, at one time, had held the waters back. Each wave trickled more water over the breach. He climbed out of the *Scout* onto the wall and tied the rope around a large rock. He wearily advised his passengers to stay put for a moment before walking slowly up the incline towards the town. He was met by a shocked group of clan elders demanding to know what had happened.

Jerrol repeated his story of the Lady breaking the Bloodstone and banishing the Ascendants and explained that the waves that had flooded Birtoli had been caused by the backlash of power which had triggered the fire mountains and had flooded Birtoli. By now, it had become quite glib the number of times he had repeated it. "I have survivors from the mainland who need help and shelter. Can you take them in?"

"Of course." An elderly man said. He had thinning grey hair and was garbed in a brown robe, cinched by a rope belt around his thin waist. "The Lady grants shelter to all," he said firmly.

"That she does," Jerrol agreed.

The man peered into Jerrol's pale face. "My son, stop, eat with us. You do her no favours by not looking after yourself."

Jerrol nodded slowly, hearing an echo of the Lady's scolding voice, and anyway, darkness would fall soon. She would tell him to rest as well. He helped the exhausted people off the *Scout* and followed them up the hill to the town. He knew Nikri was a substantial town, benefiting from being near the borders of Vespiri. He wondered how they would get on now being separated by quite a distance of water.

Jerrol struggled to focus on the conversations going around him. Now he had stopped, his exhaustion caught up with him. His eye lids were so heavy he couldn't keep them open. He had no appetite for the food offered to him. He had offloaded countless boatloads of survivors, each load easing the terror in his heart as he thought of the Birtolians who had needlessly perished. When the grey-haired Father had asked who he was, he had numbly replied he was just a fisherman from Senti.

The Father found Jerrol nodding off over his bowl of stew. He took the bowl away from him and helped him to his feet, steering him to a cot in the corner of the room. Jerrol was asleep before the Father had time to cover him with a blanket. "Lady bless you, my son," he whispered and stiffened in shock as he felt the blessing leave his hand. The sleeping man was bathed in a golden glow as he absorbed the blessing. For the rest of the night, the Father sat watching over him.

The next morning, Jerrol awoke to the aroma of coffee. He opened his eyes and sat up, intending to swing his legs over the side of the bed, but he was pulled up short as every muscle in his body protested. He relaxed bonelessly into the bed and groaned.

He sensed the presence of the Father next to him and opened his eyes. He carefully eased his legs over the side of the bed and slowly levered himself upright; he looked up to see a knowing smile on the face of the elderly Father. "Here, make you feel better," he said, handing him a mug.

"I haven't had coffee for months." Jerrol sighed in pleasure as he took a sip.

"Coffee? You mean Kafinee. We get it from Mortelin in Marchwood Watch on the Vespiri Borders. Well, we used to," the Father said bleakly, his thin face dropping.

"I'm sure you still can. I believe it's on the coast now," Jerrol said with a wry smile.

"Much like us, then," the Father said with a grin.

"Yes, a lot of change everywhere. If you need help, send word to the Jerven Shipping company; they are based on the new island of Senti. I'm sure they would help you set up a supply route with Mortelin. I expect one of the sailors out of Aguinti could take word for you."

The Father nodded. "Here, eat. You hardly took a mouthful last night." He handed Jerrol a steaming bowl of porridge.

Jerrol took it with relief. He was suddenly ravenous. After a few mouthfuls, he looked up. "What time is it?"

"Still early; the sun is only just rising. I thought you'd sleep longer."

"There are people out there that still need our help," Jerrol said.

"I know. The Lady watches over them," the Father said, watching Jerrol closely.

"That she does," he agreed, feeling a gentle lassitude

creeping over him. He shook it off. "I've overstayed my welcome. I need to get back out there and help."

"You have done enough, captain. It is time for others to take the burden. Jerrol looked up startled, and the Father smiled at him. "It's time for you to go home," he said. "Your family is waiting."

"Really?" Jerrol asked, tears springing in his eyes. "I can go home now?"

"Yes, my son."

Jerrol exhaled deeply. "How?" he asked.

The Father smiled. "You'll know when the time is right."

Jerrol creakily rose. "Then it's time I left; they've been waiting long enough."

The Father escorted him down to the *Scout*. "Safe journeys, my son."

Jerrol shook his hand. "Thank you, Father, may the Lady bless you always." A frisson of recognition passed between them.

The Father laughed. "I knew it."

Jerrol smiled and jumped down into his boat. He cast off and raised a hand in farewell.

Watching the red sail disappear around the end of the newly formed island, the Father smiled and turned to walk back up the hill. "Who was that, Father?" a young boy leaning against the wall asked.

"That? That was the Fisherman. The captain of the *Island Scout*. If you come to the service of thanksgiving tonight, I'll tell you all about him," the Father said as he began the walk back into town.

Jerrol sailed around the new island of Aguinti, collecting survivors as he went. He steered towards Molinti and a feeling of peace settled within him. The intense need to act was soothed, and he instinctively knew what he had been sent to do was finished. The people of Birtoli were resilient.

With the foundations he had laid, they would survive and become the island kingdom they knew in the future.

He smiled and joked as he offloaded his passengers in the harbour in Molinti. The wreckage had already been cleared, and temporary jetties had been extended into the water, providing safer moorings, the old ones washed away or drowned under the rising waters.

Giving the harbour master a salute, he wished them well and cast off, intending to return to Senti. He thought he heard someone shout his name, but when he looked around, he couldn't see anyone.

The *Island Scout* sailed back out towards the open seas and was never seen again.

Present Day. Molinti

Roberion watched the red sail disappear around the headland and frowned in concern. He wasn't sure if it had been Jerrol or not. The sailor had turned around when he had shouted, but he hadn't heaved to. He hurried up onto the deck of the *Lady's Miracle*, casting instructions around him to ready the ship for departure; they were leaving for Senti. Maybe they could catch up with him; they were much faster, after all. The *Miracle* soon left harbour and rounded the point. Roberion gave the instruction to set full sail and let her leap across the waves.

After about a chime of skimming the waves and sighting no other ships, the lookout, sounding somewhat surprised, reported bad weather ahead; a grey squall was approaching, blanketing the silvery horizon. Roberion reluctantly ordered the men to reef the sails, and they prepared to ride out the weather. The heavy squall soon passed over them, and they were out into the sparkling sunshine and calm seas on the other side. Roberion suspiciously watched the squall recede, fading away to nothing. The cerulean blue sky spread from one side of the horizon to the other, not interrupted by a single wispy cloud.

They arrived in Senti shortly after and manoeuvred through the glittering storm walls. Harbourmaster Gael stood waiting for him once he docked. "You're back sooner than we expected," he said with a brief smile.

Roberion grimaced. "I need to speak to your sentinal. There's been trouble in Molinti. Some of my colleagues have been injured. We need to bring them here if possible, to the sentinal tree."

Gael looked at him quizzically. "To do what?"

"I need to ask him if he can heal them."

"He can do that?"

"Some can, not all," Roberion admitted.

"Well, you can ask, but he seems a bit preoccupied at the moment," Gael said dubiously. "He hasn't been responding to me."

Roberion looked up at the tall tree. It seemed to be glowing in the sunshine, and Roberion felt a sudden shiver pass through him, a premonition that maybe, just maybe, the Captain had returned. He started walking up the hill to the headland, hurrying to get to the sentinal. He paused, hesitating before the smooth, silvery trunk. It was definitely glowing. "Can you see it glowing?" he asked in a hushed voice.

Gael frowned at the tree. "It's just the sunshine."

Roberion lay his palm on the trunk and closed his eyes. The tree was occupied, but the Sentinal within was sleeping. The Sentinal's name resonated through him. Jerrolion. He exhaled in relief. It was the Captain, but he was deeply asleep; the sleep of a dormant Sentinal. Roberion supposed that made sense. He'd had to survive over three thousand years, just like all the other Sentinals he had awoken. But who would awaken the Captain?

Roberion tried a different tack and reached for the sentinal tree. As Gael had said, he was preoccupied, focused on the Captain within. *"I need your help. The Captain needs your help. His friends have been injured. They won't survive without your assistance."*

The sentinal ignored him.

"Captain, your Sentinals need help. Fonorion and Birlerion were injured protecting the king. Please, they won't survive without the sentinal's intervention."

He felt the faintest whisper of a command.

The sentinal snapped to attention, his branches swaying above them. The glow deepened to a burnished gold. Roberion felt the assent in the air.

Roberion sagged against the trunk in relief. *"Thank you,"* he replied. "I need to return to Molinti immediately," he said out loud.

Gael looked at him. "He said yes?"

Roberion nodded and pushed himself off the trunk, hurrying back towards the harbour as Gael trailed after him. "The Captain commanded it so."

Gaels eyes widened. "The Captain?"

"If you are very, very lucky, you'll get your wish and meet the Captain," Roberion said with a faint smile.

"What?"

"I need to get moving. I'll be back soon. We'll need to get two stretchers up here. Can you devise a way whilst we're gone?"

Gael breathed out with a whoosh. "We can try." He looked up at the now visibly glowing sentinal. "The Captain?" he breathed in awe.

"Good, otherwise, we'll have to carry them up there, and I'll tell you now, neither of them are light!" Roberion gave him a nod and he set off back down to the harbour, his step light, a thrill of expectation running through him.

His crew looked at him askance as he ordered them to return to Molinti. He grinned to himself as he thought about how they would feel about returning to Senti for the second time that day. His grin widened at the thought of telling Taelia and the king that he had found Jerrol.

42

PRESENT DAY
MARU 8TH, 4128, MOLINTI

Roberion and the crew of the *Miracle* arrived back to find the town of Molinti in the throes of baby fever. Word had spread of the arrival of the new royal baby, and the banners were being raised around the city; good news like that was not to be ignored after such a terrible storm. Many people were having to manage running repairs as the colourful 'It's a boy!' banners rose around them, but it was all good natured. Everyone was agog to find out his name; the next emperor in waiting.

Roberion made his way up to the palace, now knowing the way without direction due to the amount of times he had made the journey. He would suggest that the Captain made some waystones when he returned; it would be much simpler.

He hurried to the healerie and found the situation unchanged. Taelia looked up from Fonorion as he entered the room. "He said yes. We need to get them prepared for travel, and Taelia," Roberion gripped her shoulder. "Jerrol is in his sentinal, he's asleep. You need to go and wake him up."

Taelia gasped. "I knew it, I knew he would return," and she promptly burst into tears.

Roberion hugged her. "Go get the children ready. I'll tell the king." He paused to observe Fonorion, who looked even paler to his eye. He gently gripped his hand, which was icy cold to the touch, even though the room was warm. "Hold on, Fonorion, just hold on a little longer. The Captain's waiting for you." He tucked Fonorion's hand under the covers.

In the end it took a royal command from the king to make the healer's part with the Sentinals. They threw their hands up in disgust and foretold of dire endings. "In that case," Benedict said, "one of you had better accompany them to make sure they are still alive by the time we reach Senti."

The king got his way, and an infuriated healer reluctantly accompanied the stretchers down to the harbour. The cart seemed to hit every bump, and Birlerion complained loudly as they were jostled, the healer fretting over their bandages and warning of split stitches and worse. Fonorion lay silent and pale. They finally reached the harbour and were gently loaded on board the *Miracle*. Roberion directed them to his cabin; it was the easiest to reach without awkward steps and galleys.

Birlerion groaned with relief as he was deposited next to the bed. "What are you trying to do to me?" he complained fretfully, his face flushed and hot.

Hannah leaned over him and wiped his face with a cool cloth. "Taking you to see the Captain," she said soothingly, offering him a glass of water. "Just sleep, we will be there soon."

"Jerrol? You found Jerrol?" Birlerion frowned. "He's asleep!"

"Yes, as you should be. When you awake he will be with you."

"About time," Birlerion slurred as he closed his eyes.

"How much did you give him?" Taelia asked.

"Enough to get him to Senti." Hannah looked at Taelia. "This had better work. The last thing we should be doing is moving them. The healer was right about that, especially Fonorion." Hannah looked at the unconscious Sentinal with concern.

"I know, but he won't survive if we don't try."

Hannah sighed, nodding in silent agreement. She didn't think there was much hope personally, no matter how much she prayed for a different outcome.

Taelia left to check on her children. She found the king and Mikke deep in a picture book in Roberion's day cabin. The king looked up questioningly. Taelia nodded slightly and the king returned his attention to Mikke, who was tugging his shirt to get his attention. Taelia smiled. Mikke had adopted the king as his personal playmate and he was unlikely to give him up easily.

She hoped seeing his father would help detach him. She sat at the table and worried about Jerrol. Would he be the same after all this? He had been through so much. Even though the king had tried to shield her, she was not stupid; she could read the histories and draw the same conclusions they had.

Taelia had seen their concern as they discussed Jerrol, his life had been in peril so many times; when would they let him live in peace? She sat and stared into the distance, aware of the surreptitious glances the king gave her as he entertained Mikke. He was just as worried about Jerrol as she was and she was comforted by his concern. She only hoped they would be able to wake him up.

· · ·

Later that afternoon, Taelia and the king stood on deck gaping at the glowing sentinal tree and the unusual harbour walls as the *Lady's Miracle* passed between them. The crew eyed the glittering walls a little sourly as they unshipped the oars and pulled up to the quay. They were greeted by the harbour master, who was somewhat overwhelmed by his royal guest.

"Your Majesty, welcome back to Senti. I didn't realise you would be accompanying the Sentinals."

"It's my fault they were hurt," the king said, his face grave. "I want to ensure they are looked after well."

"Of course," Gael muttered distractedly as Mikke came rushing down the gangplank, followed by Taelia shouting at him to take care.

"Children are amazing, aren't they? They have no fear," the king smiled.

"We didn't prepare quarters for so many guests," Gael began hesitantly.

"Please don't worry, we are not staying long, and we can sleep on board the *Miracle* if needed." The king looked up at the tall sentinal above them; the trunk was a burnished gold, which glowed brightly. "How do you propose we get them up there?"

"We set up a pulley system; we can guide the stretchers up the cliff face, then it's a short distance to the tree."

"If you say so," the king said.

Gael cleared his throat. "We have the best engineers working for our boatyards. If they say it will work, then I am sure it will work. Your Majesty, may I suggest you make your way to the tree? We'll meet you up there."

King Benedict nodded as he watched the deathly pale Fonorion carried out and strapped into the cage-like contraption. Two men held the stretcher straight at either end. The men swiftly ascended, guiding the stretcher, and the king gaped as they walked up the wall.

He looked at Taelia and shrugged. "Who would have known," he said with a grin, and, accompanied by Roberion, they turned to climb the steep steps up to the headland, passing a large white house set back into the cliff face and surrounded by a wooden veranda. By the time they reached the top, the men had arrived with Birlerion, who was querulously asking where he was.

"Stop complaining, Birlerion, and pay attention," the king said sternly. "Jerrol is asleep in his sentinal. He has commanded his sentinal to heal you and Fonorion, and we need you to tell us how he is."

Birlerion stared up at him. "I told you he was asleep," he said. "He's slept the transition like we did."

"Yes," the king said. "But how do we wake him up?"

Birlerion gave a weak smile. "Command him, I expect. You hold each other's Oath, don't you?"

The king looked at Taelia. "Do you think it's that simple?"

Taelia shrugged. "It's worth a try," she said and grabbed Mikke as he tried to run up to the tree.

Birlerion inhaled sharply and the king looked at him in concern. "Let's get you both in the sentinal first; the sooner he can help you both the better."

Roberion stooped and lifted Birlerion easily in his arms, then he strode to the tree and shimmered into the trunk. The engineers stood gaping as, after a moment, he came out alone. Roberion looked at the king. "The sentinal is focussed on the Captain. I'm not sure he will be that easy to wake," he said in concern as he stooped to pick up Fonorion. Taelia held up the bag of blood still connected to his arm and followed him. They both shimmered into the tree, along with Mikke, who gripped her skirt.

Taelia gasped as she saw Jerrol lying cocooned in a nest of a light. She saw a similar cocoon being woven around Birlerion, who looked a lot more relaxed. Roberion gently placed Fonorion on a third cot and stood back as the bright swirls of golden light started to flow around him, encasing the bag of blood as Taelia released it.

Approaching Jerrol, Taelia reached through the strands to touch his face, tracing the new scars on his cheek and neck. He looked much thinner and tanned. His hair was bleached a light brown and a lot longer, flopping around his face. He was dressed in faded cut-off trousers and a thin shirt, and his feet were bare.

She leant forward to kiss him on the lips and he stirred. "You made me a promise," she said, and his lips curved into a smile. "You promised me you would come back," she whispered.

His right arm snaked up around her and he pulled her down into his bed. "I made you a promise," he repeated, his voice a soft whisper, and he opened his eyes. "Is it really you or am I still dreaming?"

"It's really me," she said as she snuggled close against his chest. He smelt of the sea and sunshine.

Jerrol inhaled the scent of her hair and relaxed. "It really is you," he murmured and tightened his embrace. She reached a hand up to trace his beloved face, noting the new lines, and stretched up to kiss him.

Ari popped into the air above, chittering, before he landed on Jerrol's chest and stared at him. He meeped and then went to inspect the other Sentinals. Jerrol smiled at the little Arifel and reached an arm to hug Mikke as the small boy climbed up beside him. His son stared at him quizzically as his father closed his eyes again, a tear sliding down his cheek. Jerrol began to shake, and Mikke reached a small hand to touch the tears in wonder.

Roberion grabbed Mikke and shimmered out of the sentinal.

He grinned at the king. "He's awake," he said as he tossed Mikke in the air, making him squeal. "I thought they needed a moment."

The king exhaled in relief. "You were taking so long I was getting worried."

"I didn't think he was going to wake, but he stirred as soon as Taelia got near him."

"Thank the Lady," the king breathed.

"Yes, well, we don't know how he is yet," Roberion said in concern. "In our time, the sentinal has only had him for a day; we don't know what injuries he had."

"Well, let's return to the ship. I'm sure Taelia will come and tell us. I expect Jerrol will want to see his children, if nothing else."

The king and Roberion led Mikke back down to the harbour, swinging him between them. The engineers looked at each other and shrugged before they began to dismantle their equipment.

It was much later when Taelia left the sentinal and returned to the ship. She slowly walked up the gangplank onto the deck and smiled at the sailor on duty. "King Benedict?" she asked.

"In the captain's cabin, ma'am."

"Thank you." Taelia paused outside the cabin and lent her forehead against the wooden door. She heaved a deep sigh and tapped on the door before opening it. The king looked up from the papers in his hand and raised his eyebrows.

Taelia's answering smile wavered, and the king stood in concern. He led her to a chair, and Roberion handed her a glass of amber liquid.

"Drink," the king commanded, not allowing her to speak until she'd emptied the glass.

"He's confused," she said finally. "At times he still thinks he's in 1124; he still thinks he's Jerven. He said he threw himself into the crystal array to disrupt the power, but the Lady and the Oath healed him. I think he was severely injured; it's taken its toll. The sentinal won't let him go. He fell asleep again. I left Ari watching him."

"Give him time," the king said gently. "He lived a different life for months, whereas for us it's been weeks. He is bound to be disoriented. Let the sentinal heal him. He can come home with Fonorion and Birlerion when they are ready. He is in good company."

Taelia nodded as her eyes wandered around the cabin. "He was worrying about Niallerion. Apparently Niallerion tried to rescue him in Adeeron. Jerrol had to leave him there; he's not sure he survived."

"Well, when he wakes again, you can tell him Niallerion is fine. He and Marianille woke up in their sentinals in Old Vespers," the king said carefully.

"He was also worrying about his brother, Gael. He kept speaking as if he was with him. Trying to apologise for not staying with him; something about not being able to be in two places at once."

"He is a protector; he feels his responsibilities keenly," King Benedict said. "We wouldn't be here if he didn't. The Lady chose well."

Taelia sighed, blinking back tears. "He has responsibilities here. He's done enough. His children need him; I need him."

"That he has. Stay here for as long as he needs. As you say, he has done enough," the king agreed. "I have to return to Vespiri. I'll be here for the naming ceremony, then we'll have to leave. I highly doubt any of them will be fit to travel by then. I've rented the house up on the ridge; it should be big enough for you all."

Taelia nodded slowly. "Thank you, Your Majesty."

Taelia, Hannah, and the children moved into the white house with the veranda the morning the *Miracle* left for Molinti. Hannah took Mikke down to explore the beach whilst Taelia fed Leyarille. Rocking gently in the warm breeze, she looked over the harbour and out to sea; the view was amazing. She settled Leyarille in the basket and carried her into the sentinal, placing her beside Jerrol. She checked Birlerion, who was showing signs of consciousness. His complexion looked much better as did Fonorion's, though the nest of light around Fonorion was as bright and intense as the one around Jerrol. The light around Birlerion was fading, and as she watched, his lashes fluttered open and she found herself looking into a pair of bright silver eyes.

She smiled, tentatively. "How are you feeling?"

Birlerion blinked at her and carefully sat up. He looked around the sentinal and his eyes widened at the sight of the two brightly lit cocoons. "Better," he replied. "How are they doing?"

"I was hoping you could tell me," Taelia said.

Birlerion seemed to look inwards for a moment and then smiled in obvious relief. "On the mend, though the sentinal says it will be a few more days before he'll release them."

"Will he let you leave now?"

Birlerion chuckled. "On the condition that I rest and don't undo all his hard work. He's a perfectionist, obviously."

"Well, I know a nice quiet veranda you can sit on while you wait for these two to wake up. The king said we were to stay here until all of you were well enough for the journey home, so take your time and make the most of the rest.

Roberion is with the king so you don't need to worry about him. They are on their way back to Vespers, so he will have plenty of protection."

Birlerion sighed, his shoulders drooping with exhaustion. "Good, I don't think I have the strength to pick up my sword."

"Don't even think of it. Rest now. I'm going to sit with Jerrol for a bit, and then I'll show you where we are staying."

Birlerion lay back down and closed his eyes. Even that short conversation had tired him. She looked worriedly at Fonorion and Jerrol. The sentinal was busy, the light pulsing gently around them.

Taelia leaned over the sleeping Jerrol and kissed him. His lashes fluttered but he didn't wake. She picked up his left hand and held it against her cheek, watching him. She caressed his arm gently. The scars on his face and neck had faded, leaving a silvery sheen to his skin, a subtle glow under his tan, and he didn't look so strained.

She was horrified by the thought of him flinging himself into harm's way; a last desperate act of sacrifice she was sure he hadn't expected to survive. No wonder he was distressed and confused. Facing certain death was enough to distress anyone.

Leyarille stirred and murmured gently. Taelia watched as a tendril of light caressed her baby's face, and Leyarille opened her silver eyes and chuckled as she looked up at her mother. Taelia scooped her up and smiled back. Kissing her gently, she placed her beside Jerrol, pulling his arm around her. Leyarille gripped her father's finger and Jerrol smiled.

Taelia rose to help Birlerion out of the Sentinal.

Later the next day, Birlerion and Taelia were seated on the veranda when Ari popped into view above them. Mikke laughed in delight as Ari dropped onto Birlerion's shoulder and allowed him to remove the message tube. He let Mikke stroke his furry head before he chirped and popped out of view again.

Birlerion unravelled the paper and skimmed down the message. "It's from Niallerion," he said, looking up. "The king has arrived safely in Old Vespers, and he wants to know when we are returning." He scrunched up the paper and lay back in his chair with a groan. "Not anytime soon, I hope," he said as he closed his eyes.

"You are not going anywhere until you are all recovered," Taelia said firmly as she sat beside him. She reached to grasp his arm. "Birlerion. What happened to you? The healers couldn't explain why you collapsed. Nor why you lost so much weight."

Sighing, Birlerion opened his eyes and stared out across the harbour. "When the Lady sundered the stone in 1124, a combination of events happened. She drew on the magic she had given to her Sentinals, drawing it all away with her. At the same time, I projected a shield over the people of Vespers, to protect them. Discharging so much magic takes a toll on your body."

"But that was thousands of years ago, and you were here in Molinti with us."

"I think time overlapped. She called me, I felt her pull my power away. I remember falling … and yet not falling." He rubbed a hand over his face. "It's exhausting just trying to explain it. Being in multiple places at once is not natural; it drains your energy. I have been crossing time for weeks now, I think it all caught up with me at that moment and I couldn't function any more."

"Then don't over do it. You should just sit here and doze or admire the scenery, but I forbid you to anything else."

Birlerion gave her a tired smile. "Yes, ma'am."

. . .

Five days later, Taelia helped Fonorion out of the sentinal. Taelia wormed under his arm and helped support him across the headland to the house. He collapsed weakly into a chair on the veranda and, uncharacteristically meek, allowed Taelia to fuss over him. Birlerion watched Fonorion with concern as he allowed Taelia to prop his legs up and cover him with a light blanket. "Don't exhaust him Birlerion, he needs to rest."

Fonorion grimaced. "I shouldn't worry. I feel as weak as a newborn babe. All I want to do is sleep."

"Sleep then," Taelia said firmly, "your body knows what it needs." She glared at Birlerion until he raised his hands in submission.

"I'm going," he said as he strolled down to the harbour. Unable to sit still for more than a couple of days, he had struck up a friendship with the harbourmaster and visited daily. Birlerion was eager to learn more of the history of the harbour, while Gael was eager to hear more of the Captain.

The warm sun, fresh air, and the daily walk had begun to ease the gauntness in his face, and he was feeling much better. Seeing Fonorion made him realise just how much stronger he was. He silently worried about Jerrol. Fonorion's and his own injuries had been purely physical. Jerrol had been caught between time and life, and the sentinal was concerned, though Birlerion hadn't mentioned it to Taelia.

Jerrol drifted in a sea of light. He wasn't sure where he was or how long he had been there, it just felt like he had been there a long time; too long maybe? He had dreamt he had been talking to Taelia. He had spoken to her so often it had become second nature. The light surrounding him began to diminish and awareness returned. He opened his eyes and recognised his sentinal.

The gentle hum of the sentinal entwined with the resonance of the Oath vibrated through his body, and memories washed through him; Guerlaire's jubilation, Clary's horror, the crystal piercing his skin. He sat up in horror, looking down at his body.

His eyes darkened in memory as despair washed over him along with memories of sailing through a sea of debris and bodies, not being able to save everyone.

Jerrol swung his legs over the cot and stood, surprised that he felt physically fine. He shuddered as he remembered the journey to Adeeron. It had only been adrenalin and the fear of failure that had kept him moving. He wondered what he was supposed to do now; he felt lost and adrift. He shimmered out of the tree and resting a hand on the sentinal's trunk, he stood looking out over the harbour.

The impossible walls no longer looked out of place. They glittered subtly in the early morning sunlight. A sloping beach he didn't remember led down to the waters on the far shore and wooden buildings rose on the banks, the muted sound of hammering a gentle reminder of the boat yards he had planned. The brilliant blue sky arced over him, meeting the silvery sea in a thin dark line on the horizon. It was Senti as he remembered but subtly different. The harbour was full of strange boats, buildings had grown up around the new waterfront, and he was sure the village would have grown.

Fonorion almost tripped over Taelia as she came to an abrupt halt in front of him on the veranda.

"Taelia?" Fonorion's voice died as he followed Taelia's gaze. The Captain stood beside his sentinal, one hand on the trunk, staring out over the harbour. Fonorion wondered what he saw. He looked so forlorn and lost, dwarfed by the tall tree trying to bend protectively over him; the sentinal's concern was obvious.

Taelia gave a small sob and rushed down the steps and along the headland. Fonorion grasped the railing as he watched her, his throat tight with emotion. Jerrol turned and straightened his shoulders. He opened his arms and Taelia ran straight into them.

Jerrol's head dipped and their lips met. Fonorion smiled with relief and carefully sat in the lounge chair. He relaxed as Birlerion joined him, who passed him a mug and looked towards the sentinal.

"Do you think he'll want a kafinee?" Birlerion asked with a grin.

"Sure to," Fonorion replied.

EPILOGUE
SENTI, PRESENT DAY

Jerrol dozed in the sunshine beside Fonorion, both snoring gently in the drowsy warmth of the sunny afternoon. He woke when Mikke climbed into his lap. The little boy was covered in sand and was cheerfully holding out a small blue bucket containing a crab he had caught and dripping cold water over Jerrol's chest. The smell of salt water and seaweed brought Jerrol fully awake, making him think he was on the *Scout*. He blinked as he realised that he was not on a rocking boat. He looked at his son and smiled gently. "Hello, my love, what have you got?"

"C'ab," Mikke said proudly.

"And a fine crab it is too. Are you going to eat him for dinner?"

Mikke looked at him, horrified. "No! Let 'im go."

Jerrol nodded. "Good decision, he's not big enough to eat." They both peered into the bucket as the tiny crab scuttled sideways along the bottom. "Shall we go down and let him go?"

Mikke nodded and Jerrol stood. Hannah smiled at him as she mounted the steps and passed into the house with the towels. Jerrol hugged his son close before putting him down. Although his injuries had healed, his strength was slow in returning. He had been quietly convalescing with Fonorion and Birlerion, swapping stories, embracing their shared history, and easing the displacement he felt as the echoes of the past faded along with the loneliness that had threatened to consume him.

Taelia was determined to keep him still. Though he didn't argue, the sight of the pale and weak Fonorion had brought it home to him how close he had come to losing everything. Even now he couldn't prevent the distressing memories from returning as he sat on the veranda and blindly watched the comings and goings in the harbour.

He was sure the harbourmaster's avid curiosity in the Fisherman hadn't helped. The harbourmaster had been desperate to learn his reasoning behind the building of Senti and what he had planned. Having spent the previous evening being interrogated by him, Jerrol had explained what he could and then fallen silent when he learned about Gael's death forty years after the sundering of the stone. It didn't seem right.

Gael's son, Jerven, had continued the family business, along with Marin's son, Mikke, who was born not long after the great floods. Their descendants drove the recovery of Birtoli. Gael had looked at Mikke and Leyarille in awe as he realised who they were, and then at Jerrol as the realisation that he really had been the Fisherman sank in.

Jerrol had finally stirred himself enough to create a waystone. He'd sworn he would not go on another boat. He missed the *Scout* but Jerven was the sailor not him. Taelia had watched him with concern as he'd stared at a spot on the headland, but even though Birlerion said the waystone was active, none of the Sentinals were inclined to use it.

Mikke held his pa's hand as they slowly made their way down to the harbour, he squinted up at his father.

Jerrol's lips quirked. "What?" he asked gently.

"Pa sad."

Jerrol knelt beside him. "I am very happy to see you. I missed you terribly."

Mikke placed his hand on his pa's pendant; the green stone glistened gently at his throat. "Lady sad," he said clearly.

Jerrol looked at him in surprise. "Yes, Lady sad," he agreed slowly, knowing it as truth. He stood and looked around them, aware of people discretely watching him; he hadn't gotten used to his notoriety. "Let's release your friend, then we can go and try to cheer the Lady up," he suggested.

Mikke smiled in pleasure and tugged his pa down towards the beach. Together, they knelt by the water's edge and carefully tipped the bucket over. The crab scuttled off into the clear waters lapping at their feet. Jerrol stiffened as the water crept closer. "Come," he said, fixing a smile on his face. He lifted his son in his arms and turned away from the water with a slight shudder.

He walked up the beach towards the town, the valley opening before him as they followed the main street up from the harbour. The town sprawled halfway up the sides of the valley where terraces had been cut into the valley, providing space to build. He passed Marin's old house, replaced now by a stone structure where his descendants still lived. They reached the busy market square and Jerrol halted, staring at the temple. The white walls glistened in the sunshine; a small dome rose above them. It was situated opposite the harbour road, and Jerrol knew if he turned around, he would have an unfettered view of the harbour, just as he had requested.

Mikke squirmed in his arms and Jerrol put him down. The little boy scampered ahead and Jerrol followed more slowly. He paused at the bottom of the steps before raising his head. He mounted them and passed into the dim interior.

Birlerion looked up as the waystone chimed and Niallerion and Marianille shimmered out onto the headland. He watched them pause and grip each other as they looked down in awe at the harbour. Gently, he shook the sleeping Fonorion's shoulder. "Visitors," he said.

Fonorion blinked and sat up, looking around him blearily. "Where's Jerrol?"

"He went down to the harbour with Mikke."

Birlerion stood as Niallerion approached, Marianille close behind him. "Niallerion, Marianille, how are you both?"

"We should be asking you that. You are the convalescents!" Niallerion laughed.

"We're fine, enjoying the sunshine and the peace." Birlerion grinned as he hugged Marianille.

She looked at him closely. "You have to stop doing these heroics, brother dear," she murmured. "One day you might take it a step too far."

Birlerion hugged her tight. "Sometimes you just don't have a choice," he replied, his eyes distant.

Marianille shook him. "We need you back here, with us."

Birlerion smiled down at her. "I'm here," he reassured her as he released her.

"It is beautiful, and just look at those walls," Niallerion said with a grin. "They are amazing."

Marianille laughed. "Oh, you. Don't you dare start measuring again. You drove us all mad with your demands." She looked around her. "Where's the Captain?"

"Down at the harbour with Mikke."

"How is he?"

Birlerion shrugged. "Subdued, I think is the word. It's almost as if he is only half here."

Marianille nodded. "He has some goodbyes to say, I think. That's why we came, to give him some support. After all, we knew them too," she said, her face sad.

Fonorion rose. "Let's go meet him, then. I believe there is a temple in the town; I think it's time we all gave our thanks to the Lady."

Birlerion paused to lean through the door. "Taelia, we're going into the town; we will be back soon."

Taelia's acknowledgement echoed back from the depths of the house and Birlerion shrugged. "Come on."

Marianille watched Fonorion's slow progress with concern. She caught up with Birlerion and tucked a hand through his arm as Niallerion fell back to keep Fonorion company. "How are they really? It's been two weeks since you came out of the sentinal. The king was expecting you back by now. Especially since Ari told us about the new waystone."

Birlerion sighed. "It's not so simple, and to be honest, I don't think Fonorion will ever be the same again. He has a long way to go, even though the sentinal healed what he could. I think we were all caught in an extraordinary situation. It's like you can't get free of it; it keeps dragging you back. I know Jerrol is struggling. He keeps reverting, thinking he is back then. He tries to pretend, but it's obvious if you know the signs."

Marianille pursed her lips. "What can we do?"

"It takes time, we can't rush them." Birlerion looked around the marketplace. It was busier than usual and the inhabitants were all watching the temple expectantly. "What's going on here, I wonder?"

They walked up to the temple and entered the arched door. They halted as they saw Jerrol kneeling at the altar,

Mikke beside him. They could hear Jerrol talking but not the words, and hesitant to intrude, they sat in the wooden pews at the back and offered their own prayers.

Marguerite's laugh tinkled in the air and Jerrol looked up. *"It took you long enough! Where have you been? We thought you would have come here before now,"* she scolded.

"I had to find my way back. I got lost."

"A scout who gets lost? Tsk, tsk, you need a better map, my Oath Keeper."

Jerrol smiled. *"I suppose so. How do you like your temple?"*

"Very much! Your friends have arrived. They are worried about you. It's time to let go. You won't ever lose him, you know. Jerven is in your heart, a part of you, but now it's time for Jerrol to return. Let it all go," Marguerite soothed.

Jerrol felt an oppressive weight lift, and he suddenly exhaled as the miasma of sorrow that had been suffocating him shrank and took its proper place, never forgotten, but no longer all encompassing. His clothes shimmered into the colours of the Lady. He looked down at Mikke, a twinkle in his eye. The boy was staring up at the light above in awe. "Did you say your prayers?" he whispered.

"Yes, Lady talk," Mikke said, his eyes rounded with amazement.

"Good. Never forget her and she will keep you safe," Jerrol promised. He glanced behind him and smiled. "Look, Niallerion and Marianille have arrived," he said as he stood, and he picked Mikke up and walked towards them. Gripping Niallerion's arm, he groped for words.

Niallerion grinned. "We survived, leave it at that." He flashed a smile at Birlerion. "I now understand why you always say that. There are just not the words …" he trailed off.

"Thank you," Jerrol said, giving Niallerion's arm one last squeeze, and then he led them to the engraving on the floor. The engraving for him, in memory of the heroic deeds of the Fisherman and the Island Scout who saved so many lives. "It doesn't seem real does it?" he murmured, staring at the words.

Marianille hugged him. "It's real enough to all these people; they wouldn't be here but for you."

"And all of you. We did it together," Jerrol said. He looked at the plaques on the wall. "Along with Gael and Marin." His fingers traced the worn letters engraved in the wall. "They did all the hard work; they saved Birtoli." He sighed, looking around the temple. "I miss them. I keep thinking they are going to sail into the harbour and ask me where I've been."

"It's only natural, it takes time," Fonorion said, his eyes sad. "You have to embrace the life you have in front of you; you can't live in the past. At least you have your family around you; we had to build a new family. A new way of life."

Jerrol looked at him and nodded as he gripped his arm. "You're right, I'm sorry. You know how I feel better than I do. It's time to go home."

"'ome," Mikke repeated happily, hugging his father's neck. "Pip."

"Yes, I am sure they are missing us," Jerrol agreed. He missed Zin'talia's voice. He led the way out of the temple, flanked by his Sentinals, and stopped short on the steps as he saw the gathered people.

The villagers stared at the Sentinals in awe, the tall men and women standing around a slighter figure in the middle, all with the unusual silver eyes of the Fisherman gleaming in the sunlight. There was a sudden silence as Jerrol continued down the steps.

A man stepped forward, barring Jerrol's path. "Is it true?"

"Is what true?" Jerrol asked.

"That you are the Fisherman?"

Jerrol smiled, his silver eyes glinting with mischief. "What do you think?"

"It's not possible. It's a myth; you would be over three thousand years old!"

"Ah, those who believe in the impossible are the ones who make the possible happen, so says the Lady." Jerrol smiled as he continued walking. He could hear the ripple of voices preceding him. He felt renewed. The Oath bubbled up inside him and he laughed out loud, hugging Mikke close.

In the throne room of Old Vespers, the Oath flared bright blue and then settled into its former golden glow. Parsillion, the Sentinal on duty, heaved a sigh of relief as the brilliant glare subsided and then sent word to the king.

When Jerrol, Taelia, and the Sentinals stepped out of the waystone in Old Vespers, a summons from the king was waiting for them. Jerrol gave Taelia a reassuring hug before leading the Sentinals to the king's throne room.

King Benedict watched Jerrol approach with a keen eye. He looked well, calm, and centred. The reports of his distressing confusion were incorrect, it seemed. He was tanned and relaxed, as were two of the accompanying Sentinals, both tall and straight. The Oath flared a brilliant white in greeting before settling back to its more normal golden glow.

Jerrol knelt before the king, followed by the Sentinals.

"Rise," King Benedict said. "The sun in Senti seems to have agreed with you."

Jerrol smiled. "It can be a relaxing place, sire," he agreed.

The king chuckled, a smile of appreciation on his face. "I'm glad to see you well. We were worried about you."

"Thank you, sire."

The king looked at him, pretending to be concerned, but he was enjoying himself. "But now I have a new job for you."

Jerrol bowed, stiffening slightly. "Of course, sire."

The king smiled, aware of the sudden tension in the room. "It has been agreed that it is time to allow Lord Jason to retire; he awaits to hand the keys of Stoneford to its new Lord." Benedict chuckled at Jerrol's surprise. "You are now Lord Jerrol of Stoneford. It will be confirmed at the council meeting next week, but the vote was unanimous.

"Bryce is doing such a good job, and you are never here anyway, so I decided to make his position as Commander of the King's Justice permanent." Benedict grinned at the relieved expression on Jerrol's face. "Your Watch awaits you. Niallerion and Marianille have agreed to step into Fonorion's shoes, allowing Birlerion and Fonorion to accompany you to Stoneford, if they so choose."

He looked expectantly at the Sentinals, who grinned in return and bowed. "As the king commands," they replied in unison.

The king nodded in satisfaction. "Thank you," he said to Jerrol. "Thank you for the Fisherman. For making the impossible possible and saving us all."

The End

Did you enjoy *Sentinals Across Time*? Then please leave a review. Reviews help authors raise awareness of their books and drive visibility to other readers. A bit like book match-making!

Amazon direct review links:
UK: Amazon.co.uk/review/create-review?
&asin=B09PZKHHBV
USA: Amazon.com/review/create-review?&
asin=B09PZKHHBV
CANADA: Amazon.ca/review/create-review?&
asin=B09PZKHHBV

You can find out more about my books, sign up to my newsletter and receive a free ebook of *Sentinals Stirring* at www.helengarraway.com.

ACKNOWLEDGMENTS

It feels quite surreal to be writing that I have completed my fourth book in the Sentinal series. I have had such fun writing these stories and the ideas continue to flow.

If it wasn't for my mother, Margaret, instilling in me a love of books, and reading, I would never be writing these words today. I wish I had started writing earlier so I could have shared this moment with her because I know she would have loved my characters and the world they inhabit.

I am thankful for my darling daughter, Jennifer, who encouraged me to take the step and self-publish, and go social, and build a website, and take to twitter.

Thank you to my wonderful editor, Maddy Glenn, who makes me add in more words than I take out and keeps my books on track. My beta readers Michael Strick and Tom Eklof. Jill Wells for typo hunting, though if you find any lingering it's all my fault! and all my wonderful ARC readers who are gagging at the bit to get this installment!

Thank you to Jeff Brown from Jeff Brown Graphics for designing yet another beautiful cover, and Tom from Fictive-Designs (https:// www.fictive-designs.com/maps) drew the exquisite maps of Birtoli.

I hope you enjoyed reading *Sentinals Across Time* as much as I enjoyed writing it, and I look forward to continuing the adventure with you in my fifth full length novel which will be the prequel to the Sentinal Series, and is planned for 2023.

Other books in the Sentinal Series:

Book 0.5: Sentinals Stirring (Novella)
Book 1: Sentinals Awaken
Book 2: Sentinals Rising
Book 3: Sentinals Justice
Book 3.5: Sentinals Recovery (Novella)
Book 4: Sentinals Across Time

ABOUT THE AUTHOR

Helen Garraway lives in the UK and has been writing about the world of Remargaren, a fantasy world of her creation since 2016.

Sentinals Awaken, which was Helen's debut fantasy novel, won the 2021 Readers' Favorite Finalist Award in the Epic Fantasy category. It was followed by Sentinals Rising which was released on March 17th 2021 and received a 2022 Readers' Favorite Five Star Review; Sentinals Justice, which was published on 7th September 2021 and Sentinals Recovery a novella set in Remargaren on December 2021.

An avid reader of many different fiction genres, a love she inherited from her mother, Helen writes fantasy novels and enjoys paper crafting and scrapbooking as an escape from the pressure of working for a video conferencing company, as a Product Manager.

Having graduated from the University of Southampton with a Degree in Politics and International Relations, she remains an active member of their alumni.

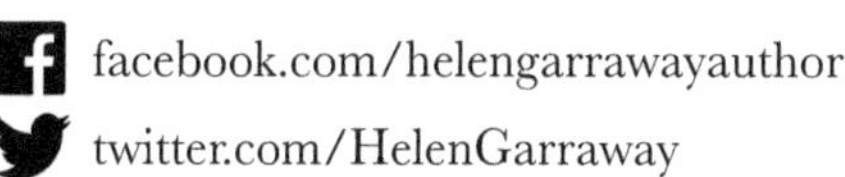

facebook.com/helengarrawayauthor

twitter.com/HelenGarraway

instagram.com/helengarrawayauthor

bookbub.com/authors/helen-garraway

www.ingramcontent.com/pod-product-compliance
Lightning Source LLC
Chambersburg PA
CBHW061051210726

48294CB00001B/95

9 781739 934446